Furors Die

Other Fiction by William Hoffman

Novels

The Trumpet Unblown (1955)
Days in the Yellow Leaf (1958)
A Place for My Head (1960)
The Dark Mountains (1963)
Yancey's War (1966)
A Walk to the River (1970)
A Death of Dreams (1973)
The Land That Drank the Rain (1982)
Godfires (1985)

Collected Stories

Virginia Reels (1978)
By Land, by Sea (1988)

Furors
Die

A Novel by William Hoffman

Louisiana State University Press   Baton Rouge and London   1989

First printing
99 98 97 96 95 94 93 92 91 90   5 4 3 2 1

Designer: Diane Batten Didier
Typeface: Galliard
Typesetter: G&S Typesetters, Inc.
Printer and Binder: Thomson-Shore, Inc.

Library of Congress Cataloging-in-Publication Data

Hoffman, William, 1925 –
    Furors die : a novel / by William Hoffman.
    p. cm.
    ISBN 0-8071-1560-6 (alk. paper)
    I. Title.
    PS3558.O34638F87   1989
    813'.54—dc20   *89-33735*
                                            CIP

For
Kathryn and Steve

Book One

1

Lord, Wylie thought, the dive Amos "Pinky" Cody could do, a slow half gainer off the high board at the Pinnacle Rock Club, the dive a work of art, a sculpturing of flesh over a shimmering turquoise plane. They all practiced it, the competitive girls as well, but Pinky worked it out for himself at the grimy downtown YMCA, he often at the lysolic indoor pool before the lifeguard came on duty.

He rode the smelly city buses to the YMCA because he didn't own a car. He did have a bicycle, yet after everybody was sixteen and could drive, to be seen on a bike was a social disgrace. His mother wouldn't allow him to buy even a jalopy, though he'd sweated at half a dozen jobs to save the money.

Pinky unveiled his half gainer during the July 4 party at the club. Casual he acted. He seemed to have no intention of diving when he climbed the chrome ladder. It was more like a stroll, his lean body loose, his hands negligent, the smirk switched on, and he didn't rise far when he sprang either, yet as he arched off the board and strained his suddenly muscled physique backwards, his arms became crucified, and sunshine illumined his rigid length. Time slowed till the dive was transformed into a ballet of a spiraling body so lingering that he appeared to breaks laws of gravity and motion.

There were gasps. Girls wearing slickly colored bathing suits reared from brilliant beach towels. The white-jacketed waiters lowered their serving trays to goggle.

"What vulgar ostentation!" Airy said, "London" Airy, named that

3

because of the song and the fact he moved often in a fog. London was a pretty, milk-skinned boy whose golden hair shone silkily. He was also a snob about Pinky.

"You wouldn't dive like that if you could?" Wylie asked.

"And have myself ravished by every beautiful girl around the pool?" He covered the crotch of his red lastex swimming trunks with dainty hands. "Frankly I value my cod too highly."

Pinky hadn't been invited to the party. Sis Asters, daughter of West Virginia's lieutenant governor, had asked to bring a date. Damon thought it would be a boy named Ralph who went to The Hill School, but when Sis arrived in her new car, a tan Ford convertible with white sidewalls, Pinky sat behind the wheel.

"I'm teaching him to drive," Sis said while Pinky went to the locker room of the white brick clubhouse to put on his trunks. "He pretended to know, but it was all bluff. He almost hit a Budweiser truck."

In the crowd Sis was the boldest of the girls, always reaching out for more experience. She was a small brunette, slim, quick, with hazel eyes in an impish face topped by bangs. Her little mouth was humorous and wicked.

"But Pinky Cody!" London said. He rolled his blue eyes upward and lifted his palms as if despairing.

"He's whipped cream with a cherry on top," Sis said.

She wasn't swimming that day and wore saddle shoes, a Kelly-green skirt, and a sleeveless orange blouse. As soon as Pinky crossed the grass from the locker room, she hurried to him. He didn't act unsure the way most people would their first time at the Pinnacle Rock Club but walked with his head up and his arms swinging fully.

He was even haughty till Sis reached him, slid a hand around his bare waist, and tickled his rosy belly with a pointed red nail. The loftiness of his expression collapsed, and his body broke as he bent to escape.

"What do you suppose Sis meant by calling him a cherry?" London asked. His thumb and forefinger pinched at golden fuzz of his chin.

"You treat him right," Wylie said.

"Oh, naturally, but that female must be hard up." In his gliding gait, London started toward the pool. "Whatever happened to the standards this club used to have, anyway?"

2

Wylie knew Pinky during summer vacations from White Oak School when Pinky worked for Wylie's father—washed windows at the office, carried out trash, mowed grass, sharpened pencils, waxed floors, and ran crosstown for stamps and mail. He ran more often than he walked.

The office was not a concrete building but a gray-and-white Victorian house three stories high which had a broad porch and brass lighting fixtures converted from gas. The house faced the Kanawha River, whose pale greenness was carried not within its waters but a reflection of the rounded wooded hills on the south side of the hot, hazy valley.

The first time he met Pinky, Wylie intended to enter the office by the back way and ask his father for money to go to Virginia Beach. As he climbed the steep wooden steps, a boy rose from the darkness of the basement entrance. He lugged an oak clothes rack which had antler arms. He wore sneakers, corduroy pants, and a white football jersey. Lettered in red across the jersey, surrounding the picture of the grim, lemon-sucking general himself, were the words Stonewall Jackson High School.

"No you don't," he said.

"No I don't what?" Wylie asked.

"You've swiped your last egg from this henhouse," he said and set the clothes rack on the brick walk beyond the basement steps. He squinted threateningly. He wasn't tall but meanly wiry, strong with that strength of redheaded up-hollow people, the kind who entered coal mines sunless white and trudged out sullen, gritty, and raccoonlike because of bug dust around their eye sockets. He edged toward Wylie.

"You think I'm after eggs?" Wylie asked.

"I think you snuck to the cookie jar once too often."

The boy's blunt chin was outswept and lifted. He had a pug nose. His red hair was short, a crew cut like men who'd returned home from World War II.

"Excuse me please," Wylie said and meant to continue up the steps and into the house, but the boy grabbed his shirt and jerked him back.

5

"Giving you a chance," the boy said. "I believe in giving even a dog a chance."

"Chance of what?"

"Getting right with God."

When Wylie shook his head and again turned to the house, the boy attacked. The punch was so quick the fist struck Wylie's cheek before he understood. He fell sideways off the steps. Bubbles floated up behind his eyes into the dimness of his skull. Too surprised to react, he straightened, touched his cheek, and blinked.

"Bring it back, and we'll see Mr. DuVal," the boy said.

"I don't know what you're talking about," Wylie said. Mr. DuVal was his father.

"It's not too late. It's never too late even in the last second of your life. Mr. DuVal will treat you right."

"I'll go around to the front," Wylie said and tried to slip past.

"Oh no!" the boy said and spread his arms as if guarding Wylie at basketball. Maybe he was suspicious because of Wylie's clothes—the grubby polo shirt, the clay-stained tennis shorts, the leather moccasins broken at the heels.

"You're confusing me with somebody else," Wylie said. "I came to see Mr. DuVal."

The boy still blocked him. Wylie attempted a sprint around him, but the boy tackled him low and hard. Wylie's face slammed down into the dry, bitter grass. Before he could protect himself, the boy dropped onto his back, turned him, and dug sharp knees into Wylie's biceps. Fingers clawed his wrists and pinned them against the ground.

"Bring it back and I'll put in a word for your with Mr. DuVal," the boy said. Sweat beaded reddish down on his face as he glared above Wylie. The sweat stank.

"Get off me!" Wylie shouted.

"Repent and give you life up to Him," the boy said. "Think of the thief on the cross."

Wylie bucked and twisted, but the boy rode him. Wylie writhed and hipped upward. The body on top him became heavy to one side. He rolled left, then right. The grip on his wrists weakened as he wrestled, but the boy scissored him. Wylie hit him about the neck and head. The boy drew in his head till he had no neck. He punched, and Wylie tasted hot blood from his fiery nose.

Groaning, straining against the force of the squeezing legs, Wylie stood. The boy kept the scissors on and tightened till Wylie gagged. Slowly he began to spin. The boy snatched at grass in an attempt to anchor himself and stop it.

Wylie revolved faster. The boy's body angled out, yet he wouldn't release his constricting legs. He threw wads of grass and dirt. Wylie staggered and spun toward the board fence which blocked off the alley. The boy tore loose a moccasin from Wylie's foot and hurled it. Wylie spun into the fence.

The boy's body cracked against it. He protected his head by covering it with his arms, but still he'd banged hard against the planks. His legs opened. Wylie lurched free and gulped air.

Quickly the boy was up, though he too staggered. Both bled and snapped at air. The boy had Wylie's blood on him, and Wylie the boy's on himself. The stained Stonewall Jackson jersey was ripped at the throat.

"You hillbilly trash!" Wylie said.

"You going to be sorry for that," the boy said.

Humpbacked he rushed Wylie, who stood in the boxer's stance taught by Yank Wynne at White Oak School. He jabbed, but the boy ducked, and they closed and fell. As they rolled and hooked at each other, Miss Burdette, Wylie's father's secretary, peered from the back door, opened her mouth wide, and shrieked.

Wylie's father hurried from the house. He buttoned his seersucker jacket while running down the steps and across the grass.

"Stop it!" he ordered. He arched over and pried at them.

"I caught him!" the boy said, proud and panting. "He's the one been stealing stuff off the porch."

"Amos, it's my son Wylie," Wylie's father said as he helped them up and stood between them, a hand rounded to a shoulder of each.

"Huh?!" Pinky asked. The aggression, the fury, seeped from him. He appeared smaller and stupid.

"You didn't explain to him?" Wylie's father asked.

"Try explaining to a cyclone," Wylie said and pinched at his nose to stop the bleeding.

"Let's get inside and clean up," the father said.

That night after dinner, the door chimes at Wylie's parents' house sounded. His family lived on the river, uptown toward the domed capitol. The house was built of stone, blocks of it which had once been tawny but had darkened over the years.

Pinky stood at the front door in the gloom of the cool, fortress-like porch. He'd washed till he shone and wore a white shirt, a brown tie, and a dark woolly suit—his go-to-meeting clothes.

"I apologize," he said.

Wylie shook his hand. Pinky walked down to the dusky boulevard and became a shadow among the sliding lights of traffic. His parents probably sent him. Wylie hadn't invited him into the house.

3

Wylie's father decided Wylie should do summer work and asked him to help Pinky paint the garage behind the office. The garage had once been a stable and carriage house. It still held grain bins as well as two cobwebbed box stalls. The hayloft was empty except for rat droppings, old harness, and dust.

"He's a good worker," Wylie's father said of Pinky, though the father called him Amos. "You'll be hard put to keep up."

"But where did he come from?" Wylie's mother wanted to know.

Wylie's mother and father hadn't turned forty, yet always seemed out of time. Change, revolutions, disasters didn't affect them. The father kept his father's gold pocket watch in a small bell jar on his bureau to protect the Hamilton from the Kanawha Valley's corrosive air. Wylie sometimes thought of his parents as living in a private, immaculate bell jar of their own.

Wylie's father hadn't gone to war because of his periodic asthma attacks. He became the block's air-raid warden. Wearing an English-type helmet and a white slicker, he carried a flashlight and gave the job importance and elegance.

Throughout the war Wylie's mother retained her maid Viola and her man Ed, the latter hired to do heavy work about the house, to care for the lawn, and to help in the flower garden. Viola and Ed were colored. Wylie's mother raised their wages to prevent their being lured into defense jobs at smoking factories along the river.

She also promised that if they were loyal, she would remember them in her will.

Though a lady, she wasn't soft. She wouldn't allow herself to be pampered. She gave steady, dedicated hours to the Red Cross and the Civic Music Association. To receive money for work, however, would've greatly embarrassed her. She never owned a checkbook. In her house finances were not considered table conversation.

Proper people from proper people Wylie's parents were—stately ships untouched by storms. The father never wore spats, yet was easily imagined in them. Wylie's mother stored no floppy hat with a chestnut feather curving from it, but he wouldn't have been surprised to see her descending the balustraded steps dressed in one. They drove modern cars, though he felt they were more attuned to a Stutz or Pierce-Arrow.

"He turned up at the office," Wylie's father said, speaking of Pinky. "Lying in wait he was."

The father was tall and erect. No athlete, he did enjoy his weekly game of golf. He wouldn't bet his game or take his score seriously. His hair was off-blond, and he had a full-lip British mustache. He often seemed to be standing before a fireplace, hands flapping behind him toward the heat. He was gentle of voice, and when he really wanted a person's attention, he didn't lift that voice but lowered it.

"Why'd you hire him?" Wylie's mother asked.

She was a full-bodied woman beautifully postured, yet in no way forbidding. When Wylie pictured her, he thought of her at her Steinway, her fingers dipped delicately to shaded keys. She had brown resplendent hair, which she wore longer than was fashionable. She controlled the velvety hair with brightly colored ribbons. Her face was long and sympathetic. Her hands too were long, regally feminine, though mercilessly quick to seize at any weed foolish enough to rear itself among rows of her flaming poppies.

"I didn't mean to hire him," Wylie's father said. "I told him I had no work for him. He stood stubbornly in front of my desk. He would've stayed there trying to talk me into a job if Miss Burdette hadn't practically pulled him out. I believed we were finished with him. That was on a Friday afternoon."

On Saturday morning Pinky came back. Nobody was at the of-

9

fice. He pushed a lawn mower and carried a rake, sickle, and broom. He cut the lawn and trimmed around the pyracantha. With his stubby pocketknife he edged the grass along the brick walk. He raked clippings and swept up after himself.

Monday when Wylie's father arrived at work, Pinky waited in front of the door.

"Your grass ever look better?" he asked.

"No, I don't think it has," Wylie's father said.

"I sharpened the mower blades before running them over your lawn here. I notice now your windows is dirty. Not good advertisement for your business."

"Are you as good at washing windows as you are mowing?"

"If you don't like how I do windows, you don't have to pull even a dime from your pocket."

Pinky did the windows, and when Wylie's father inspected them, he admitted that never had the quality of sunshine in the office been so radiantly unfiltered. Pinky then asked for a regular job of mowing and keeping those windows washed.

"Stealthily he broadened his duties," Wylie's father said. "Without being asked to, he emptied wastebaskets, beat the rugs, and fixed a latch. He took an inventory of supplies. By the end of the month he'd made himself essential."

When school started in September, Pinky still came to the office after classes. He watered ferns placed at the windows. He sharpened pencils on the father's and Miss Burdette's desks. He dusted and mopped. He laid logs in the iron holding racks on the green tiles of the hearths.

"His pencils are so sharp we have to be careful not to impale ourselves," Wylie's father said.

"But why did he present himself in the first place?" Wylie's mother asked.

"To that question I have no answer," the father said and drew fingers of his right hand along his mustache as if calming it.

4

The job Wylie and Pinky did on the garage turned out to be more than just painting. Steel roof shingles had rusted through. Termites had chewed a sill to shreds. He and Pinky could've painted over lacily rotted boards, but Pinky would have none of it. He acted as if the property were his own.

"The job has to be done right from the first lick of the hammer," he said. "Takes more time in the beginning but makes it easier later on."

He assumed he was boss, Wylie the apprentice. The truth is Wylie hadn't worked much in his life. He'd done a little studying at White Oak School, but he'd never knocked together even a doghouse, though he owned an Irish setter named Tristan. Ed, Wylie's mother's colored man, had built Tristan's shelter.

Pinky became impatient. He couldn't understand why Wylie felt no desire to learn carpentry or work with his hands.

"You can't just pick out a single shingle and replace it," Pinky said. "They go in layers from bottom to top. Each depends on the other."

"Thanks for clearing that up," Wylie said.

"And inspect the planking underneath before driving a nail. Take your knife and punch the boards to see if they've rotted."

"Don't have a knife."

"You don't carry a knife?" Pinky asked and stared. "You telling me you go around without a knife in your pocket?"

"Don't faint."

"How can anybody get through the day without a knife?"

While Wylie measured, sawed, and pounded, the girls came by to watch him work. They rode their pretty bicycles and rang their merry bells. Spotless tennis shoes they wore, white shorts, and red and yellow blouses. Their tan legs, which had grown longer, were now shaved. Earrings flashed, and bracelets jingled.

They leaned those bicycles against an elm whose shade was as large and feelable as a black island. Roots had buckled the brick sidewalk and pavement of the alley. Locusts chirred along the branches. The girls sat on the knobby contorted roots to drink their icy Big Oranges and called teasingly to Wylie.

He'd take breaks from the hot garage roof, but not Pinky. Pinky didn't talk to the girls or even look at them. He drove nails as if killing snakes.

"He can speak, can't he?" Sis Asters whispered when Wylie sat beside her in the shade.

"Truth is he's a redheaded moron," Wylie whispered.

"But cute," Sis said and smiled.

11

Pinky climbed down the wooden ladder from the roof, crossed to a horizontal metal strut supporting a power pole, jumped to it, and began chinning himself. Muscles braided his glistening sweaty back. After his tenth one, Wylie and the girls counted loudly each time he pulled himself up. Their voices rose along the street: ". . . eleven, twelve, thirteen . . . !"

Pinky did twenty-five before turning loose and dropping to rounded bricks of the alley. He knelt to drink from the spigot, the copper-tasting water splashing into his cupped palms. He climbed the ladder and again started hammering.

"He did it for me," Sis said, pleased. "That's his way of talking."

Wylie hated the work, but at least he was improving his tan. He and Pinky hung their shirts inside the garage before climbing the ladder. Rather than tanning, Pinky became rosier. Their sweat dripped to and spotted the reflecting steel shingles. Every time Wylie missed a stroke with his hammer, Pinky eyed the bent nail.

For lunch daily Wylie walked home. His parent's house was only three blocks upriver, and he kept to the thick shade of oaks and elms which grew from mossy yards of the old mansions. The street along the Kanawha was the first in town because the original inhabitants had built beside the water, their only highway through the grudging valley wilderness.

Salt deposits drew them, Indians first, then white settlers, just as salt later attracted chemical plants whose sooty smokestacks Wylie, when a boy eight or nine, imagined were hot cannons aimed at the pale yellow sky.

His mother would be waiting. She'd make him shower and change into freshly washed khakis. She and Wylie ate their decrusted sandwiches and cool salads on the screened porch at the side of the house, a view to her weltering red flowers and the stone wall around the property. The phonograph would be playing Offenbach or Gounod.

Feeling refreshed, Wylie walked back to work always to find Pinky returned to the job. He liked to shame Wylie for taking so much time to eat. Again Wylie would hang his shirt on the nail and climb the ladder. Pinky's fast reddish-brown eyes took in the clean, pressed khakis Wylie wore and his face tightened.

"Oysters on the half shell today for lunch?" he asked.

"Shrimp salad with a lemon sauce and a dish of lime ice," Wylie said. "You ever seen an oyster?"

Pinky ate thick cold meat on brown bread for his lunch. He called the meat mutton. Wylie wasn't certain what mutton was till he looked it up in the unabridged Webster's on a revolving oak stand of his father's library. Mutton was sheep, rank, smelly old sheep. So Pinky's family ate mutton. Wylie assumed there was a family.

When they painted shingles, Pinky was faster with his brush.

"Metal has grain you got to go with," he said. "Who does your nails?"

"What?"

"Your fingernails are like a woman's."

Wylie's mother did his nails. She sat him beside her in the cushioned windowseat of her upstairs bedroom where they could look out at the white paddlewheel tugs breaking the murky fabric of the river. She held his hands in her warm lap, and as she filed and buffed, they chatted, gossiped, and laughed—the moment a tender one each loved.

"Do clean fingernails offend you?" Wylie asked Pinky.

"Why not wear a skirt to work?"

Wylie slapped him with the paintbrush. The bristles had been dipped into red lead roof paint, and they left a broad dripping swath across Pinky's cheek and mouth.

He stood spitting and enraged. They were again about to fight, this time right there on the garage roof, like western movies where saloon brawlers tumble off balconies and smash through tables and chairs. They'd have a shootout using dripping brushes.

But Pinky turned away and climbed down the ladder. He wiped his face with a rag he poured paint remover into. He recorked the glass jug before coming up to the roof. He worked for twenty minutes and said nothing.

"The only reason I don't tear you up good is your father," he blurted out.

"Why are you so respectful of my father?"

Pinky didn't answer. That was mid-afternoon, and they painted till fifteen past five when they closed cans and cleaned brushes. They wiped paint off their arms.

"I saw him help a man," Pinky said. "This man was cross-eyed

13

drunk down on lower River Street, staggering along the sidewalk, bumping into store windows and power poles. People was so disgusted they got out of his way.

"A city policeman arrested him just as your father came along and saw what was happening. Your father could have circled around full of disgust like everybody else, but he felt sorry for the drunk and stopped and talked to the policeman. He waved down a taxi, paid the driver to take the drunk home, and gave a dollar tip. And your father didn't even know the man's name."

"He does enjoy helping people," Wylie said.

"An act of kindness and charity. I was looking for a job. I knew I wanted to work for him."

"How'd you find out who my father is?"

"Asked the policeman. They always know who the people with money are."

Wylie buttoned his shirt and brushed back his hair.

"What say we don't fight anymore?" he asked. "I don't want to be scrapping with anybody who cares for my father as much as you do."

"It's going to be tough you're so dumb," Pinky said.

5

That same summer Pinky talked Wylie's father into allowing them to paint the roof of the office itself. The roof was three stories up, and Wylie didn't like high places. He had no wild fear on swaying ladders but was constantly uneasy. He experienced dizziness. Moreover, to be doing jobs men in the valley needed seemed unintelligent. What he really wanted to work on was his backhand at the Pinnacle Rock Club.

He and Pinky perched and painted. They watched cars speed along the white concrete boulevard above the river. A new bridge was being constructed across the Kanawha, and several times a day rivets fired to white heat would be missed by welders' catchers and drop hissing into the water.

Tugs bullied coal barges around red and black buoys. The tugs' whistles sounded like ocean liners. After a rain the river would clean itself to wanness, but then coal washings upstream again wove dark curls into the flow.

On the other side of the valley the C&O passenger trains slid fast along the hill-shadowed tracks. Slovenly coal drags clanked monotonously, their whistles steaming. Often the valley trembled with the trumpeting of locomotives and tugs.

Toward the west the factory chimneys shot hot black discharges into the summer sky and filled the valley with a twilight haze. People in the city hardly noticed the smoke unless they left and came back, the return like entering an infernal region. Wylie's father had an explanation.

"Where there's no smoke, there's no human endeavor."

Fine new houses were being built on hills across the river. Trees fractured, tipped, and fell, and raw ground spread in the forest like mange. People with money were attempting to elevate themselves above smoke.

"I guess the rich can't stand to breathe the same air the rest of us," Pinky said. He glanced at Wylie. "I take it back."

"How come?"

"I forgot you're rich too."

"Then why am I doing the same work you are?"

"I'm surprised your mother allows you up this high."

"She doesn't and don't you let her find out."

Pinky eyed those houses being constructed across the river, but he wasn't particularly angry or fiercely resentful. His belligerence was automatic, a sort of armor.

He considered it a challenge to walk the roof's crown. The pitch was Victorian steep, and while painting, they always tied themselves with safety ropes knotted to the chimneys. They also laid ladders down across the gleaming steel shingles.

"To do it we have to take off the ropes," Pinky said.

"I don't have to take off mine."

Pinky shrugged, untied his rope, and moved on all fours astride the crown. He stood and leveled his arms. He advanced with feet slewed like a tightrope walker. The toes of his brown, paint-spattered sneakers bent downward. People paused on the boulevard sidewalks to look upward and point.

"Your turn," Pinky said after crossing the eighty feet from chimney to chimney.

"Not me."

15

They painted awhile, with Wylie slowly realizing what was happening: if he didn't walk the roof, he'd lose his physical equality, and Pinky would consider himself superior. It was an affair of honor.

Wylie climbed to the crown of the roof, untied his rope, and steadied himself on rough mortar atop the brick chimney. A western breeze carried the sharp odor of sulphuric chemicals. When he released the chimney and started across, his legs quivered. He had trouble swallowing. He couldn't get enough air in his lungs. He was trembling.

Sweat ran into and stung his eyes. His vision became blurred, yet he saw people on the boulevard talking, looking up, gesturing. He heard his own fast breathing. He swayed.

He tried to keep moving, but halfway across the red expanse he stalled. His feet wouldn't advance. He felt dizzy and tired. The breeze nudged him. I am, he thought, about to fall, tumble, and die. Yet giving up seemed easier than going on. The sulphurous air coaxed him to let go, to surrender to space, to tip outward into the comfort of everlasting darkness.

"Hey, I'm coming," Pinky called. "Just hold what you got."

"I don't want you."

"Then get a move on."

With great effort Wylie slid his left foot forward. Shaking caused his teeth to click. He forced the right foot to follow the left. He felt drunk, and the valley pitched around him. He heard the organ notes of whistles.

Again he was tempted to let go, to give himself up to limpness and fall to the stones. His father's voice drifted up. He stood with people at the front of the house and shouted.

"What are you doing?"

"Just a few more yards," Pinky coached.

"Don't you do a damn thing to help!" Wylie said.

"Boy, are you proud."

Wylie shuffled, knelt, and crept along the roof's crown till he made it to the chimney, whose rasping bricks he grabbed and embraced as if they were salvation. His eyes clenched, and he would've been sick had not people been down there watching. He'd never puke before an audience.

His father was shouting. Wylie gulped air and retied the safety rope around his waist. When Pinky tried to support him as they moved toward a ladder, Wylie shook off his arm.

"You'd die rather than bend," Pinky said.

6

Wylie's father attempted to be severe, the corners of his patrician mouth turned downward, dragging after them the tips of his off-blond mustache.

"No horseplay up there again," he said. "Suppose your mother had seen that foolishness?"

He believed they'd been romping on the roof. Wylie promised he'd never again play around up high. Pinky tried to take the blame, but Wylie wouldn't allow it.

He and Pinky worked steadily and seriously. Heat lifting off the steel shingles bent the valley air and their vision. Tension thickened that air. Wylie felt he'd been tricked into the roof walk, and it shamed him he'd shown fear. Pinky offered him half a mutton sandwich. Wylie suspected it was the gesture of one who felt victorious.

Wylie often kept his back to Pinky. Down the block toward Commerce Street was the old Boone house, a decaying stone mansion. Rank blooming weeds grew from cracked driveway pavement, and dirty white paint flaked to and speckled the unmowed grass. The house was for sale and had rain-washed, droopy Rooms-for-Rent signs tacked to peeling porch columns. At the rear a garage slowly buckled under the weight of grasping honeysuckle.

From a taxi a man and woman hurried onto the porch. The man jangled keys before being able to unlock the door. He was middle-aged and bald, she young, her short hair dark. He wore a tan summer suit, she a blue dress. They entered the house. Moments later they appeared in a back room on the second floor. From the roof Wylie looked down at the couple as they reached for each other and kissed.

Wylie's snicker caused Pinky to turn and watch. The man slid his mouth along the young woman's throat to her breasts. They stepped apart to strip off their clothes. The woman held to the man as she raised one leg, then the other, from her white panties.

"Free show," Wylie said, laughing.

Holding each other, kissing, the man and woman worked down to a mattress on the floor. She still wore hose. His mouth was pecking along her pale body.

"You shouldn't look at that," Pinky said and turned back to painting.

"Why not?"

"Stuff like that gets in your mind, and you can't get it out."

"Who wants to get it out?" Wylie asked, grinning.

"I won't permit myself to think of people doing that," Pinky said.

Stretched out on the roof, Wylie continued to watch. For a while the man was on top the woman, and then she sat on him. The way she rode him was funny, but she was serious about it. The man held to her thighs and bowed up. They were having themselves a canter.

The woman's head lazed backwards. Wylie saw her full face. Her eyes were almost shut, but when she opened them, she spotted Wylie. Her mouth opened, though Wylie heard no sound. Hands covering her breasts, she kneed herself off the man. He reared from the mattress, blinked, and gazed through the window. They crawled into shadows of the room. Clothed again, they left by the back door, the man glancing angrily at the roof where Wylie still watched.

Though Wylie laughed to himself, the rest of the afternoon Pinky was sullen. Wylie couldn't understand what keeping stuff like that out of your mind meant. At White Oak School they had virtually nothing except screwing on their minds. Masturbation was practically a varsity sport.

Pinky hunched to his painting. He didn't even look in the direction of the other house.

"Some people ought to read the Bible," he said before leaving at the end of the day's work.

7

When the girls came by on their bicycles, Wylie lowered a line tied to a galvanized bucket so they could arrange icy Big Oranges, peanut brittle, and foil-wrapped candy kisses for delivery back up to the roof. Sometimes a pop bottle had a bright silk ribbon fastened around its neck.

"You never played with yourself?" Wylie asked Pinky.

"I'm not even talking to you about that subject," Pinky answered.

"You ever date a girl?"

"You ever seen me I wasn't working?"

"What do you have against fun?"

"Fun you can't put in the bank, and the kind of fun you're talking about is dirty."

Wylie was squiring Bebe Stanniker, daughter of a Du Pont chemist, Bebe a honey blonde who seemed mostly made of satiny legs. She and Sis Asters were friends. Sis wasn't old enough to have a driver's license, but she was daring and sneaked her mother's Buick from the garage when her parents were out for the night or away from the city. She let them all wheel it around.

In her mother's car they drove to Blacktown, where Wylie gave a one-legged darky who waited on the corner money to crutch himself into the state liquor store and buy them a bottle of sweet Rosary wine.

Or they crossed the bridge to one of the disreputable drive-ins along the C&O tracks where they could buy beer no questions asked. Neon fired the air, and when trains passed, cinders pinged the Buick, and coal smoke settled to flavor the beer.

Sometimes they'd swipe a pint from a parent's whisky cupboard and park at Buzzards' Roost to look at the river—the Esso and Duquesne signs, the green and red running lights of tugs, and the factory furnaces reflecting across the black water. They were not only experimenting with drinking but also fooling around with each other's bodies.

Friday afternoon at quitting time Bebe and Sis bicycled to the office. With them came Lois May, a cousin of Bebe's from Wheeling. Lois May was a short, plump girl who had auburn curls, and she eyed Wylie as if she knew a secret about him. He guessed Bebe had been talking.

"Lois May needs a date," Bebe told Wylie as they stood in the elm shade. She looked at Pinky, who was hammering lids on paint cans. "How about old red-on-the-head there?"

"You don't want him," Wylie said.

"True, I don't, but this is desperation. Everybody's out of town."

"It won't work anyhow," Wylie said.

"Don't know for sure unless we try," Bebe said. She wore her honey-blond hair dangling over her left eye. When she needed to see clearly, she fingered the hair aside as if drawing a curtain. "You talk to him."

"No."

"Or else," Bebe said.

Wylie helped Pinky carry cans into the garage and take down the ladders. Pinky shook his head.

"It's our duty to be hospitable to out-of-towners," Wylie said.

"I don't belong with you all."

"What are you talking about?"

"I don't eat shrimp salads and go to country clubs." He snatched his blue workshirt off the nail sticking from a garage stud. "Besides, you're all heathens."

"I'll ignore that last remark and ask you as a favor to come along."

"Beg me a little."

"Damn if I will."

"No cussing either." Pinky started away but stopped to look at the girls in the elm shade. They smiled and waved to him. "I don't know how to talk to them."

"I doubt you'll have to do much talking."

He frowned. "What you mean?"

"I expect Lois May'll do enough talking for both of you," Wylie said, which wasn't what he meant at all.

"You hate asking me, don't you?"

"It's not easy. Now if you just tell me how to get where you live, we'll pick you up at your house."

"Naw, I'll come to yours," Pinky said.

He came overdressed—the starched white shirt, the black tie, and the dark woolly suit warm enough for a January blizzard. He'd wet and combed back his red hair, though it was too short to stay flat and appeared hedgehoggy. He kept pressing a hand down against it.

"I'll wait out here on the porch," he said.

Wylie would've left him, but his father called from inside the house.

"Bring Amos in here to meet your mother."

Wylie's mother and father were sitting on the screened porch. Viola had cleared the table and brought lime ice served in silver sherbets. The late afternoon was still hazily bright and hot. Cardinals splashed in the birdbath, and a breeze faintly scented by Union Carbide stirred the red blooms.

"Well, Amos," Wylie's father said and stood. He wore no tie but did have on yellow slacks, a yellow shirt, and a white linen jacket.

Wylie's mother also stood. She held Pinky's hand. He looked trapped and about to flee, but she wouldn't release him.

"You're the young man my husband's always praising," she said. She wore a green silk dress, pearls, and her rings.

"Amos holds our feet to the fire," Wylie's father said.

"Yes'm, I mean no'm, I don't do much," Pinky said.

Wylie's mother was gracious. She wouldn't allow Pinky to feel uneasy in her house. She bound him up in the fine thread of her words.

Wylie hadn't finished dressing, though, unlike Pinky, he was wearing a simple white cotton sport shirt, tan gabardine slacks, and scuffed loafers. He led Pinky to the front hall steps. Not only had Pinky come twenty minutes early, but Sis Asters would be late. She was again swiping a car from her parents and had to be sure nobody saw her slip into the garage.

Pinky gawked at everything in the house. He eyed the chandeliers, the oriental rugs, the books, and the niche in the upstairs hallway where a genuine Greek cylix was illuminated by a small spotlight.

He looked at items on Wylie's mantel: tennis trophies, snapshots of friends from White Oak School, Bebe wearing a white strapless evening gown. He spotted the English riding boots and spurs. He touched the inkwell on an antique cherry desk.

"Whose initials?" Pinky asked, peering at the hinged silver lid's engraved English script.

"My great-grandfather's," Wylie said. "He had the desk in his office."

Pinky examined the framed coat of arms and leaned closer to read the Latin: *Nullus Passus Retrorsum.* If he asks for a translation, Wylie thought, I'll tell him. No step backwards. But Pinky didn't. His eyes kept moving. He reminded Wylie of a cat in strange surroundings.

As they left the second floor to go back downstairs, Pinky glanced into the master bedroom, where an oil portrait of Wylie's mother hung over the fireplace, a painting done during the early years of her marriage. She sat in an ornamental peacock chair, and behind her were green tresses of a weeping willow and a garden of blooming tulips. She wore a gray chiffon dress and a gray hat with a red band. The brim shadowed her long composed face. Her hands were laid in her lap, her ankles crossed.

Hushed, Pinky stood staring at the picture. His mouth sagged, and had he worn a hat, he would've removed it. For him the moment was reverent and mystical. Wylie had the feeling that if he hadn't spoken, Pinky would've been drawn into the rose-colored room.

"Ready to come along?" Wylie asked.

Pinky followed down the stairs and to the basement game room. There was time for a quick rack of eight ball. Wylie switched on the lights and phonograph. He couldn't believe Pinky had never before held a cue. Wylie explained the rules. Pinky tried hard.

At eight o'clock they left the house and walked to the corner, where they sat on a stone retaining wall under a motionless dusty elm. It wouldn't do for Wylie's father to see Sis driving. He knew she wasn't old enough and might ask questions. Wylie had never yet lied to him. Of course his father was always gentleman enough not to press for answers which might be embarrassing.

It was almost nine before Sis, Bebe, and Lois May came not in the Buick, but in the black LaSalle that belonged to Sis's father, the lieutenant governor. The girls were cool and perfumed, their summer dresses crisply fresh. They gazed at Pinky's woolly suit.

Blue Bales, Sis's date, also sat in the car. Blue was unhurried, flowing, easy. Unlike the rest of the males in Wylie's crowd, Blue wore his hair long—bleached brown hair swept back in a ducktail. His name was based not on eye color but the fact his privates had been painted with gentian violet at White Oak.

"I've just survived a horrible trek across the steaming desert," Blue said and rubbed his throat. "My camel died on the trail, and my canteen's filled with sand. I'm in desperate need of life-giving fluid for my dehydrated body."

"I know a place you can be saved, Blue-o," Sis said.

She sped them across the river at the old downtown bridge, followed the C&O tracks, and turned into the King Tut, a white stucco drive-in shaped like a pyramid. Red neon tubes lined its four edges.

A jukebox under a striped awning glowed—a bejeweled shrine. The carhop was a thin aging brunette dressed as an Egyptian dancing girl except she wore tennis shoes.

"You kids old enough to buy beer?" she asked.

"Listen, I'm just in from the China Station" Blue Bales said. "I been at sea more than two years. Three of our ships went to the bottom. You're not going to deny me a little drink of life-giving fluid?"

"You don't look old enough," the carhop said.

"It's the clean life at sea," Blue said, and the girls giggled. "Keeps you young and healthy. Bring us six Falls Cities, and I'll send you a genuine lotus blossom next time I pass through the Suez Canal."

Disbelieving but reluctantly complying, the skinny carhop started toward the buzzing, thumping pyramid. Her tennis shoes squeaked on the dirty asphalt. It was then Pinky spoke.

"I don't drink beer," he said.

The carhop stopped and slapped her order pad against her palm. Blue reached to the rear where Pinky sat to shush him.

"He's joking," Blue called. "Keeps us all in stitches."

"I really don't—" Pinky said.

"Then we'll drink it for you!" Blue whispered furiously. At the same time he motioned the carhop to go on. In ill temper she did. Blue smacked his forehead and faced Pinky. "You could've caused us all to perish in the desert," he said.

Pinky, glazed with sweat, fidgeted.

"I honestly don't—"

"Will you for God's sake just be quiet about it?" Blue asked and glanced toward Wylie as if it were Wylie's fault and he ought to be sent hurtling into the outer darkness for bringing along such a toad.

Sis elbowed Blue to silence him. The jukebox flashed and glittered. Even with six people in the LaSalle, Pinky seemed to sit apart. While five of them drank beer, he kept his hands on his knees and stared straight ahead. Lois May attempted conversation with him. She might as well have been talking down a hole.

"Well at least take off that coat and tie," she said and finally got his tie loose. She draped it around her own neck. "Now let's unbutton your collar. You go to White Oak School with Blue and Wylie?"

"I go to Stonewall Jackson," Pinky said, trying to push away from Lois May.

"I don't believe I'm familiar with Stonewall Jackson," Lois May said.

"You should read your history," Pinky said.

"You're a terrific wit," Lois May said. "I mean the school, not the man."

"It's a very exclusive school," Pinky said. "You have to be alive to get in."

Any effort at humor coming from Pinky seemed terribly funny, and they laughed, even Blue. They were also feeling the beer. They made so much noise laughing that people in other cars looked toward the LaSalle.

"You have to be alive to get in!" Blue and the girls called out the windows.

Pinky seemed surprised he could amuse anybody. He was also nervous about Lois May's crowding against him. She sucked at her moist bottle of Falls City and rolled her eyes upward at him.

"I go to Miss Leach's School for Girls," she said.

"I'm not acquainted with Miss Leach's School for Girls," Pinky said. "What's she got against boys?"

"She doesn't have anything against boys. In fact she's dead."

"Must be pretty tough to run a school when you're dead."

Sis and Bebe giggled, Wylie snickered, and Blue cackled.

"Miss Leach's is the best school in Wheeling," Louis May said. "When I graduate I'm going to Holyoke."

"How do you half a yolk?" Pinky asked, and they thought that also hilarious.

"Where you going?" Lois May asked when they quieted.

"I think maybe to Hell," Pinky said.

That was the funniest of all, and they lolled about laughing. Blue pounded his feet against the floorboards. Bebe's head fell back against the seat, and her throat became ruddy with neon. Sis hooted and clapped her hands. Wylie ached for breath, and his eyes wetted.

"I mean to college, fool," Lois May said, laughing close to Pinky's ear.

"I won't be able to afford college," Pinky said.

That killed the fun. Pinky couldn't have dealt himself out of the crowd more completely if he'd admitted to being a Negro infected with ringworm and siff. Not go to college! Everybody they knew would have money for that.

"Trouble is you have to be alive to get in," Wylie said, wanting to bring back the good feeling. He glanced at Pinky, who sat rumpled, sweaty, and tense.

"Let's allow the gals to buy another round and drive up to The Roost," Blue said. He too was trying to salvage joy.

Buzzards' Roost was an outcropping of rock high above the river. You reached the place by driving illegally along a fire trail through a state forest. The Roost was where kids parked to play around.

"Not me!" Sis said in mock horror.

"You won't go to The Roost with us?" Blue asked.

"I won't buy you another round," she said.

"A girl's reputation can be ruined at The Roost," Bebe said.

"Only if she's lucky," Sis said, and everybody laughed except Pinky. Wylie could've killed him.

Sis drove the lumbering LaSalle along the serpentine trail, causing the limousine's springs and shocks to squeak and groan. Headlights glittered on empty beer bottles and swept shadows among locust trees. Other cars were pulled under dusty drooping boughs.

Sis stopped at the outcropping's edge. The LaSalle tilted slightly downward. She left the car in low gear and jerked on the emergency brake. Below were the C&O tracks and the raven river with its blinking navigation buoys. Red and green lights burned between bridge pilings. The city sparkled under haze. Furnace flames licked over the river, and the capitol's gilded dome seemed unsupported.

On the capitol's north lawn stood an illuminated bronze statue of a Union infantryman forever treading, on the south lawn another of Stonewall Jackson, hands resting over the hilt of his grounded sword, both figures, Wylie's father said, emblematic of the state's schizophrenic birth during the Civil War.

Bebe and Wylie finished their beer before settling into each other. He tangled her legs in his. Sis bent Blue backwards on the broad seat. She'd switched on the radio. All the parked cars were tuned to the same station, and Les Brown's "I've Got My Love to Keep Me Warm" became part of the forest like the crickets, tree toads, and whippoorwills.

Wylie peeked at Pinky through Bebe's sweetly scented hair. Lois May had gotten the spirit and was all over him.

"Ah!" Pinky said and tried to swim away from her.

"What's wrong now?" Blue asked as he and Sis rose from the front seat.

"Let them work it out," Wylie said to Blue.

"I thought maybe they were working it in," Blue said.

"What a depraved pervert you are," Sis said to Blue.

"Takes one to know one," Blue said.

He and Sis again dropped to the front seat. Bebe and Wylie refitted their squirming bodies. Wylie was hoping for at least a nipple.

"Quit!" Pinky said loudly.

"Will you knock it off back there?" Blue called. "I don't mean literally."

"Can't you stick something in his mouth?" Sis asked. "And I do mean that."

"Him's a darling, darling boy," Lois May said.

A third time they all snuggled down in the plush, cavernous LaSalle. Bebe and Wylie were practiced and efficient with each other. Their bloods beat together.

Lois May was struggling. She had a leg across Pinky's lap. When flesh gleamed, Pinky shouted. He thrashed about to free himself from Lois May. He opened the door, fell out, and scrambled up to run among the chirring trees.

"Don't leave me!" Lois May called after him.

"What'd you do?" Blue asked her. She was straightening her clothes and giggling. She still had Pinky's tie.

"Just blew in his ear a little. We do it all the time in Wheeling."

"Tasty," Blue said.

"Dear boy!" Lois May called. She stepped from the LaSalle and stared at the blackness of the woods. Faces appeared at windows of other cars.

"You can blow in my ear," Wylie said to Lois May.

"He was so nervous," she said.

"How will he get home?" Bebe asked.

"He can practically dive home from here," Sis said.

"Or fall," Blue said.

"Which would be a good idea," Wylie said.

26

"Pinky!" Lois May called forlornly one last time.

"Come in and be happy with us," Wylie said, reaching for her.

"What am I supposed to do by myself?" Lois May asked.

Since she was the guest, all five of them gathered in the limousine's back seat. Blue and Wylie took time out from Sis and Bebe to neck Lois May. They developed a routine. The free girl blew into ears.

8

Monday Wylie was late for work. The night before he and Blue had courted Lois May. Wylie limbered a brush, filled a can with gray paint, and climbed a ladder to the side of the office. Pinky didn't speak or look his way.

They painted along the south side of the office, and the day became so hot Wylie wilted on the ladder. His sweat shone on the rungs. He was not well at all. He and Blue had arranged the secret date with Lois May. They sat her between them in Blue's brother's Plymouth, filled her with Falls City, and picked off her clothes. Blue sucked on one nipple, Wylie the other. Cooing, Lois May spread her plump knees. Blue had the Sheiks.

"I believe I'll reward myself with a little break," Wylie said, moving down the ladder. He needed shade and a long, cooling drink of water.

"Dissipation," Pinky said.

"The man can talk after all."

"Carousing."

"Going to preach me a hellfire sermon?"

"You rich kids don't have morals."

Wylie was in no shape to discuss the charge. He crossed from the ladder to the elm shade, where he screwed the top off his thermos of ice water and sprawled among the scaly roots to watch a white cloud with a dark underbelly drift over The Roost. Old Lois May, on her way back to Wheeling, one contented gal.

Wylie's father looked out an office window at him. Wylie again climbed the ladder. Though weak and nauseated, he tried to keep up with Pinky. Under eaves wasps were buzzing about. Wylie closed his eyes and leaned against the ladder.

"You all right?" Pinky called from his ladder.

"Just don't ask me to dance." Wylie groaned. "How'd you get home?"

"My Packard and chauffeur were waiting in the woods."

"Grand."

"How you think I got home? I walked. Where's my tie?"

He would've had to hike to the bottom of the hill, cross the tracks, and dodge traffic along the weedy shoulder of the highway till he reached the downtown bridge.

"Ask Lois May. Maybe she's turned it into a keepsake of her exciting night with you."

"I almost got run over. Don't ever try to get me to go out with your friends again."

"Pinky, I tell you, there's not much danger of that."

He glared and slapped his brush against the side of the house. Wylie continued to rest with his eyes closed. He felt very, very sleepy.

"How do girls get like that?" Pinky asked.

"Like what?"

"Like Lois May."

"What'd she do to you?" Wylie asked, not really caring.

"How can you go out with girls like those when you have such a nice mother?"

"I don't see the connection."

"You never see connections. You think you're not being watched."

"Watched?" Wylie asked and opened his eyes.

"All the time, every second of the day and night."

"By whom?"

"By God."

"Oh God," Wylie said, again closed his eyes, and sighed.

"You have heard of sin, haven't you?" Pinky asked.

"You think we were sinning the other night?"

"Boozing and whoring."

"Wait a second, they weren't whores," Wylie said, for an instant forgetting he was high on the ladder. He grabbed at it and pulled himself back. "They were my friends and wanted to be yours."

"Filthy dirty language. I never heard girls talk like that."

"Maybe the truth is there's lots of stuff you never heard."

"I don't want to hear if that's how people act. You shouldn't either with your nice parents. I ought to go to your father and tell him you're ruining yourself."

He slapped his brush so hard against the house that three smutty pigeons bailed out from under the musty eaves.

"We really weren't doing all that much," Wylie said. Well, that wasn't quite the case with him, Blue, and Lois May.

"The body is the temple of God!"

What was there to say to that except poor God? In spite of Wylie's lightheadedness and tumbling stomach, he worked till noon. Wearily he trudged home for a shower and change of khakis. His mother served him iced tea, chicken salad, and strawberries.

When he returned to the job, Pinky was up his ladder. Wylie wondered what his father would think if Pinky came to him to report on his son's morals. Wylie thought of his father as a decent man, good, upright, but not religious. The father believed in correctness, which was gentleness, concern, and wherever possible the avoidance of pain to others.

Wylie's father had played in his day. There were stories about the college years at Washington and Lee, the riotous fraternity doings. The father had been suspended a semester for some prank involving a horse in Lee Chapel. Now he served on the vestry at St. Stephen's, though Wylie had never seen him kneel to pray at home.

Twice during the afternoon Wylie climbed down the ladder to drink from his thermos and rest behind the garage where his father wouldn't see. His sweat was sticky, and the hour hand on his watch moved with agonizing slowness.

"Guess you'll be out tonight carousing," Pinky said at five when they finally began to clean up.

"No, I plan to spend the evening doing my Sunday-school lesson."

"You think that's funny."

"Right now I don't think much is funny."

"Keep on and ruin your body."

"Thanks for permission." Wylie started away.

"You want to know what she did to me?" Pinky asked.

Wylie stopped and turned. Pinky's face worked as if he couldn't believe his own memory.

"She stuck her tongue in my mouth," he said and blushed.

"Not that!" Wylie exclaimed as if horrified and struggled to keep from laughing.

"Such a clean, nice-smelling girl doing that."

"Hard to believe."

"Worse," Pinky said and looked ashamed.

"What could be worse?"

"She touched me," he said and winced.

"Touched you how?"

"She slid her hand down inside my pants and took hold of me."

"Fingered your pecker, you mean?"

"Don't say it!" He was so bothered he covered his eyes. "That pretty little hand. I almost got sick."

Aflame with guilt of sin, he twisted and suffered. Wylie kept his expression serious but couldn't wait to tell London, Blue, and the girls.

"Take my advice and don't let yourself consort with those kind of females," Pinky said. "Remember, it's never too late to set your foot on the path of righteousness."

Wylie didn't break up till he was around the corner and beside the flaking iron fence surrounding the Pioneers Cemetery with its tilted tombstones. He held to the fence, laughed till teary-eyed, and thought that anyone passing might believe he was weeping.

9

After they finished painting the office, Wylie didn't see Pinky again during the summer of 1949. Wylie played tennis at the Pinnacle Rock Club and went to Virginia Beach where London's parents owned a white, shingled, two-story cottage. The cottage had tinkling wind chimes, a shellacked bamboo bar, and colored umbrellas on a deck above the shimmering sand.

The girls were there too—Sis, Bebe, and Boo Dempster, whose father had discovered gas and oil in his own back yard. The girls were supposed to be staying at The Breakers but every night slipped over to the cottage until the wee hours. They all drank beer and lay like lizards under the sun.

In September it was back to White Oak School for Wylie. His

father drove him down to Virginia, or over to Virginia since it was as much east as south. Wylie's father had also attended White Oak and liked visiting the school. He walked around looking at the dorms, the Georgian buildings, and the green playing fields.

Wylie wasn't a serious student. He was smart enough to pull respectable grades but cared nothing about being a genius.

"You will never labor sufficiently in our classrooms to disturb your sleek brain," Mr. Dabney Lamp, the headmaster, said. Mr. Lamp was a thin, scholarly bachelor whose mouth was so tiny and tight he appeared to be forever sucking on a straw. Because of the mouth, the students when not in his presence called him Mr. Sip.

White Oak was located in rolling horse country, a section of stables, riding rings, and white plank fences. Horns were heard, and fox hunters galloped across the lawn in front of the chapel. Students were required to stay outdoors most of the afternoon, strongly urged to join athletic teams. They were supposed to act like porridge-fed English schoolboys, rough-and-tumble lads learning how to win and to rule.

Few entertainments were provided other than a weekly movie, teas, and insipid dances with prissy seminary girls. Blue Bales was the first in the crowd to seek out Bernice's in Charlottesville, a brick townhouse with boxwoods and a polished brass door knocker. It was at Bernice's that Wylie lost his innocence. He didn't feel any different afterwards except he badly wanted to shower.

"Pretty boy, you got to move it around to do me good," Rosemary, the Cajun girl, had whispered, her doll's face above his. She licked him off as if his cod were a lollipop.

London worried about disease. He was usually in the bathroom inspecting himself.

"How do we know they were clean?" he asked. He was so bothered he lost weight and the pinkness of his cheeks faded.

"Bernice sends them to a doctor," Blue said. "You could eat your meals off their—"

"Enough!" London shouted and fled.

Christmases Wylie traveled home by train, the C&O's crack George Washington. Spruce pines in the front yard of his parents' house Black Ed always strung with colored lights, and the front windows held white electric candles with orange bulbs. Holly wreaths

31

were hung about as well as beribboned mistletoe, and small religious figurines were taken from basement storage and placed on mantels.

Ed kept the fires burning. Every room smelled of bayberry, cedar, and chestnut oak. A short circuit caused lights to falter and blink. During an evening meal the house went dark.

For Wylie's parents it was a disturbed holiday because they talked of moving. A blight was spreading along the river, the old houses, like the elms, becoming mortally sick. Those houses were on the market to be bought for radical transformation into commercial property or to be razed to make way for apartments. The street had lost its coal-baron grandeur.

"The Artoy place has been purchased by a veterans' organization," Wylie's father said as they drank their after-dinner coffee at the table. The Artoys owned mines in Mingo County.

"But to move after all these years," Wylie's mother said. She shook her head and looked around as if for a last view of everything she cherished.

"It's not easy for me," Wylie's father said. "My grandfather built this house. He inspected every stone and timber that went into it. What are we to do? In another few years we'll be part of downtown."

"What's happening to the Spratleys'?" Wylie asked. The Spratleys owned coke ovens, though their place wasn't on the river but a street over and backed to the wall around Wylie's parents' property.

"A Bible Institute bought it," his father answered.

"What does a Bible Institute institute?" Wylie asked.

"Nobody knows," his mother said. "Mysterious people go in and out."

"Mysterious how?" Wylie asked as they carried coffee into the music room with its mahogany Ionic columns and golden-oak wood-work. The top of the Steinway was open. On shelves were hundreds of scores bound in maroon leather.

"Long, dark overcoats, the women drab and wearing heelless shoes," his mother said. "Make you think of spies from some swarthy European country."

"They put cash down for the property," Wylie's father said. He stood in front of the fire, his hands flexing toward it.

"But I hate it!" Wylie's mother said, her fingers twisting in her pearls. Light from electric wall candles laid a sheen on her brown hair. "This was the best neighborhood. Everyone planted flowers and played croquet."

"Can't stand against the sea," Wylie's father said.

"I suppose you want us to go up on that hill," Wylie's mother said. "How can I have a garden or croquet on a slope?"

"It's about the only desirable land left, and not much of it is left," the father said.

"I couldn't endure having some fraternal organization in this house," Wylie's mother said. "They'd throw wild stag parties and do Lord knows what else."

"Better than unions," the father said. "Unions too are buying houses—a curse on our state."

Christmas morning Wylie's present was in the garage—a gray Ford coupe. He'd turned sixteen the first of December. The Ford glinted like new money, and he touched it cautiously as if to make friends. Snow fell, big flakes which wetly patted the ground. As much as he wanted to drive his car, he wouldn't take it out in the snow.

His mother had a Christmas present for Pinky, a habit of giving to all people who served Wylie's father. The gift was monogrammed silver cuff links, which the father had neglected to see that Pinky received. Wylie's mother asked him to deliver them.

He waited till the snow stopped. He was ready to drive out in his new Ford before he realized he didn't know where Pinky lived. Wylie walked back into the house. To his mother's surprise, she didn't have the address either. They looked in the phone book. It listed a number of Codys, but none named Amos.

That Wylie's father didn't know the address embarrassed him. He telephoned Miss Burdette, who made a special trip to the office. After a search she found the address on Pinky's Social Security deductions.

The city was trisected by two rivers, the Elk and the Kanawha, and Pinky lived in a northwest triangle of town unofficially named the Wrong Side. Though Wylie drove through the neighborhood occasionally, he never had reason to stop.

Pinky's number was 1419½ Bethel Road. The ½, Wylie assumed, meant he lived in an upstairs apartment. He drove west on Washington Street, crossed the bridge over the Elk, and questioned a taxi driver about Bethel Road. The driver scowled and admitted he wasn't sure.

Wylie turned into a Pure Oil station where a one-armed attendant led him to a grimy city map tacked to a wall. The attendant drew a blood-blistered thumb across the map's torn top edge. Bethel Road rambled off the paper.

Houses in the section weren't stone or brick, but clapboard and frame. They were workers' homes, rented to laborers who earned their bread in mines or factories. Even under the cleansing snow, the area felt impermanent, gave an impression the wind would one day blow tunes on bones of desolation. Already the snow, the slush, was filthy, and Wylie hated having his car in this part of the city.

The address was not an upstairs apartment, but a duplex, a house which had once been a single unit and was later split down the center in order that two families could rent. The small front porch had been divided by a wooden tongue-and-groove partition. Flower pots were snow covered, and a Christmas wreath had fallen. Each of the two front doors had a milky pane of glass shaped like a diamond. The siding was painted a sort of mustard yellow.

Wylie parked carefully and walked to the porch on the right. He believed that side would be the $\frac{1}{2}$. When he knocked, the glass diamond rattled, and a child answered, a little girl who wore red-and-white-striped pajamas. She chewed on a twist of her own dark hair. Sour heat of an open gas fire surged from the house. Wylie smelled what he believed were hot grease and fried onions.

"Pinky Cody live here?" he asked the girl.

Instead of an answer, she closed the door. When it opened a second time, Wylie faced an unshaven Italian or Greek holding a screwdriver and pliers. He wore bedroom slippers and mechanic's coveralls, both of which were new.

Again Wylie asked for Pinky. The man pointed his screwdriver to the other unit. Wylie thanked him, walked down to the street, and climbed the second set of steps. He pressed the white button of the electric bell but heard no ring. Inside, a radio played. He tapped on the glass diamond with his car keys.

A barefooted woman wearing an unbelted brown dress answered. She was in her forties, her skin as pale as a sun-denied plant, her long black hair unkept, her smoky eyes wildly alight, her expression as taut as a scream.

"Pinky Cody's?" Wylie asked.

The woman shook her head violently and would've closed the door.

"Your neighbor told me Pinky lives here," Wylie said.

"His name is Amos."

"Oh, sure, Amos."

She stared so furiously at Wylie he felt like stepping back. Behind her was a small dim room furnished with a leatherette sofa, two stuffed chairs, and an end table on which the radio played hillbilly gospel music. A spindly cedar tree had been decorated with tinsel and a few ornaments.

Hanging from walls were framed pictures of Jesus—kneeling in the garden of Gethsemane, by the waters feeding the multitude, and stumbling under the cruel, crude burden of the cross. On the bare floor a redheaded man lay snoozing, an unfolded newspaper spread over his chest, his mouth open. He wore purplish rayon socks but no shoes. His long skinny feet were angled apart.

The woman pushed the door to. Wylie stood waiting. Across the street in a vacant lot children were building a fort of soiled snow. One was a Negro whose black hands molded and stacked snowballs.

When Pinky came to the door, he too was barefooted. He wore heavy brown corduroy pants and a plaid wool shirt buttoned at the neck. At sight of Wylie he reddened, lifted a foot, and drew it behind the calf of his other leg as if to hide the foot's nakedness.

"You didn't get this at the office," Wylie said and handed him the brightly wrapped present.

Pinky accepted it but didn't lift his eyes. Behind him in the dimness the woman watched fiercely. The body on the floor moved. It flung off the newspaper and sat up—a tall, disheveled man blinking and bewildered as if risen from some deep, dark place.

"Who?" he asked. "What?"

"It's okay, Dad," Pinky said and closed the door. Wylie didn't know whether to wait or leave. He heard talking in there. The hillbilly gospel music switched off. He backed away and stepped down from the porch.

Across the street children dragged unbought Christmas trees to

35

the fort. They were choosing up sides for a battle. Wylie walked to his new Ford and opened the door. When he glanced back at the duplex, he saw Pinky coming. He wore a sweater and had pulled on arctics but not buckled them.

"Is he saved?" the woman called from the doorway. She stood straight and still, resembling some burning, fanatical diviner whose fiery gaze looked into another world.

"Go back where it's warm," Pinky told her. He returned and gently moved her inside. He closed the door. When he crossed to the Ford, he still wouldn't meet Wylie's eyes.

"My father hasn't been feeling too great," he said. "He got wounded in the war."

Wind smelling of coal smoke blew against them, and snow spumed from rooftops. Children outside the fort were attacking those within. Wylie had to say something.

"Hope you're having a good year at Stonewall Jackson."

"I played football but need to gain weight," Pinky said.

He was thinner, more ruddy, and in Virginia, Wylie thought, among the snotty set, he would be classified as a linthead because of his complexion and red hair. Lintheads were the coarse, nearly albinic breed who operated the spinning machinery in southern textile mills.

He eyed the new Ford, and Wylie opened the door wider.

"Like a ride?"

"I can't get away now."

Wylie fitted himself into the car, started the engine, and looked up at Pinky. For just an instant Pinky gave of his eyes. In them were both appeal and anger, as if apologizing, yet daring anybody to feel superior.

When Wylie drove off, he saw Pinky in the rearview mirror. Pinky's wild, rigid mother had stepped onto the porch. She was speaking, but Pinky's head had turned away from her.

After Wylie reached home, he changed clothes and asked Ed to help wash the car. Cindered slush had crusted the fenders, bumpers, and whitewalls. In chamoising the Ford's chrome, Wylie felt he was cleansing off Pinky's neighborhood, parents, and shame. He hosed the blackened suds down the drain.

10

The following summer it was that Pinky came with Sis Asters to the July 4 party at the Pinnacle Rock Club and did his beautiful, time-stopping half gainer off the glittering three-meter board. During the spring Sis had taken up with Pinky.

She was at the pool every day. She drove to the club in her convertible and spread her Joseph's towel on grass near the pool's shallow end. She began her ritual of toasting herself by stretching out face up to the sun, one knee raised and drooped inward, her sexy pose. For such a small girl her flesh was surprisingly loose. Each time she moved, her thighs quivered.

Liking the sun on his own body, Wylie lay beside her. In the locker room each afternoon he stripped off his trunks to check the contrast between his tan and the whiteness the sun hadn't touched. He felt his heat come from within.

"I guess you heard I had to leave St. Catherine's," Sis said. She'd oiled herself and set pink plastic seashells over her eyes.

"The subject has been mentioned."

"It was practically on the radio. Just because I got nabbed with a bottle of scotch in my hatbox."

"Was it good scotch?"

"Cutty Sark."

"Surely not Cutty Sark. No school could be so uncivilized as to kick you out for Cutty."

"They don't know anything about scotch in Richmond. All those Rebels drink bourbon like it's a patriotic duty. If I'd had a bottle of Virginia Gentleman in my hatbox, the Daughters of the Confederacy would've pinned a medal on me."

She shifted to her side to reach for her silver lighter, which she snapped open under a Lucky Strike. She blew a mouthful of smoke at Wylie.

"I had lots of time on my hands," she said. "Daddy made me go to Charleston High, though I'll be at St. Anne's next fall. There wasn't anything to do except watch basketball. Everybody who's anybody around here goes away to school. It's death, pure death, in this city between Christmas and spring."

"You picked up Pinky."

"I went to this stupid game out of boredom—Charleston High against Stonewall Jackson. I didn't know he was on the team. He came down the floor with the ball, all this razzle-dazzle through his legs, behind his back, and under his arms. He looked small, yet he jumped higher than the goons. After the game I spoke to him, and you know what he did? He shook my hand."

"That's Pinky."

"I gave him a ride."

"To his house?" Wylie asked and opened his eyes.

"He said he had some work at your father's office, tending a furnace I think. He's really kind of interesting when you get to know him. I mean it's funny how things change. I thought he was drippy icky at first, red, dumb, and ugly, till I saw him move. Ever had that happen? You start out thinking a person's one way, and they change right in front of you?"

Wylie said he had. Sis herself had once been a skinny, obnoxious brat.

"In motion he's exciting," she said. "You've seen his half gainer. He's the fastest swimmer around, has a nice physique, kind of wiry, but oh is he ever strong! He can chin himself with one arm."

"Grand."

She laughed, tossed the cigarette over her head into the grass, and unscrewed the cap on her flask of oil. She crossed her legs Buddha style to rub her thighs.

"He's always showing off for me," she said. "And he blushes all the time. I have to watch what I say around him."

"You ever met his parents?"

"He hasn't taken me home to meet Mom yet. I'm careful not to shock him, though I enjoy doing that too. He's a Chosen of God."

"A what?" Wylie asked, raising his head.

"A nutty religious group. The Chosen of God."

Wylie had to think to place it, the offbeat church they called a tabernacle, a windowless cinderblock building under the shadow of the old downtown bridge. Somebody attempted a mural of shepherds and wise men on the outer walls, but the cinderblock bled the paint, and the mural was never finished. Close by along the street was a sporting goods store.

"Pinky doesn't cramp your style?" Wylie asked.

"Wylie-o, nothing cramps Sis's style," she said and slapped a palm against her shiny tightened stomach.

That summer Wylie was at the club almost as much as Sis. His father hadn't insisted he work, and Wylie concentrated on his tennis game by taking lessons from the pro, a lanky, weathered hotshot Alabamian who talked like an Englishman. Wylie intended to make the White Oak team.

Sometimes at night Sis brought Pinky to the club, where, protected by darkness, she didn't have to pay a guest fee for him. The young crowd swam in the pool's warm, lettuce-colored water, and then couples separated to the canvas deck chairs on the lawn.

Wylie and Bebe could really handle a deck chair. They'd developed balance and a reverse curve. On the grass beside them they set bottles of frosty Falls City beer. Fireflies glowed in smoke drifting from their cigarettes, and the lighted clubhouse looked like Mount Vernon. The moon laid a gloss on the grass, and they heard Sis's laughter but couldn't see what was happening under the night shade of a soughing willow oak.

Saturday night Wylie leaned over the deck chair to reach for his beer. He fed some to Bebe, who'd released him, letting her arm trail along his hip. Her head was back, her eyes closed, and moonlight glowed on her throat and childish breasts. She still wore her slick white panties.

When the shape rushed from the blackness beyond the wall, Wylie tumbled onto the grass and spilled his beer.

"What—?" Bebe asked, grabbing for clothes.

The shape was closer, a person swift in the night. Wylie called a warning to the others. As he jerked at his shorts, a flashlight flared on him and Bebe, who, crouched behind the deck chair, was frantically dressing.

"Hey now!" Wylie said and shielded his eyes with one hand and held to his shorts with the other.

The light moved on. Its beam scythed over London and Boo Dempster, who hopped in a circle. Her foot was caught in her skirt.

All over the lawn couples rose from grass and deck chairs. Faces were ghostly and afraid. A girl whimpered. Blue Bales had on his slacks inside out.

39

The light sought Sis and Pinky. They were so hot for each other they hadn't heard Wylie's warning. They lay beside their deck chair. Sis was rocking over Pinky, and her dark hair covered his face.

"Abomination!" the shape screamed, and it beat at Sis and Pinky with the flashlight. As they rolled apart, they covered their heads. Sis was bare to the waist, but Pinky still had most of his clothes on. They crawled away from the attack.

Girls, clutching clothes, escaped toward the clubhouse. London ran into the night. Blue and Wylie tripped over each other.

They heard Sis cry out. The shape was beating at her. Wylie and Blue hesitated but then ran to help. Blue, moving low to tackle, hit the shape first, and it would've toppled had not Wylie hooked an arm around its neck. The flashlight dropped. The body Wylie held felt not hard but puffy and smelled of sweat.

"Kine of Bashan!" it screamed.

Weeping, Sis was up and fleeing toward the clubhouse. She held a hand on her head. The shape spat after her, kicked, and tried to bite.

"Ouch damn it!" Wylie shouted. "Somebody grab the feet."

"I'm trying!" Blue said.

But the shape twisted and heaved, and Blue danced around bent over. Pinky snatched the flashlight. He shone it on them.

"Turn her loose!" he said.

"We're being killed!" Blue said.

"Woe and desolation to Sodom!" the shape screamed and kicked backwards.

"Goddamn!" Wylie said and fell away in pain.

"It's my mother!" Pinky said. He was trying to take hold of her struggling, spitting form. He feinted, ducked in, and curved his arms around her in a bear hug. He pulled her so tightly to himself she couldn't fight. Her tossing head flung her hair about. She raged and howled at the sky.

"He's promised to God!"

Pinky still held the flashlight. Its slashing beam passed over her frenzied face. Her eyes gleamed, and her mouth was a writhing wound as she shrieked. Spotlights switched on around the pool and at the walls. Dogs were barking. Colored help ran from the clubhouse.

"We'll take her home in my car," Wylie said.

"No, you just go on," Pinky said. He was crying.

40

"He belongs to God!" she screamed.

Pinky soothed and talked to her quietly. His arms around her, he coaxed her across the lawn, where both appeared unearthly in beads of misted light. He moved her through the wall's exit and beyond the lights' bounds.

The colored help, Blue, and Wylie looked after them.

"You think he'll walk her all the way down the hill?" Blue asked.

"I know he doesn't want us," Wylie said.

11

Wylie's parents finally committed themselves to leaving the valley. They drove up the hill across the river to look at land for a new house with a popular local architect named Marmon who made use of lots of glass and native stone.

There was only an acre, a wooded lot which sank sheerly on both the east and west sides. The front looked north to the river and hills on the far side of the valley where Pinnacle Rock was and radio towers flashed red day and night. The rear view was down over a slope to a dark creek that snaked among decaying vegetation and trash thrown into it before the area became the fashion. A landscaper would send his men to clean the creek and replant the slope.

"None of the hillbillies live up here any longer," Marmon said. "Land's become too dear."

In the new house, each of Wylie's parents would sleep in a large second-story bedroom on the front. His mother was to have a music room for her Steinway and maroon leather scores. There would be an office, a solarium, a hothouse, and a tiled patio with a splashing fountain. Fill soil was to be trucked in so Wylie's mother could cultivate a tiny garden.

"The roads are so steep, what will we do when it freezes?" she asked.

"We'll stay home by the fire and listen to Wagner," Wylie's father answered. He had little ear for music but accepted his wife's judgment of genius.

There was the question of the stained-glass window on the front landing of the old house. Wylie's mother hated leaving it, a representation of a radiant white Christ surrounded by fleecy sheep against a blue background as He stood gazing upward into golden

41

sunbeams. Wylie's father made an arrangement with the realtors that the window not go with the sale of the house, but Marmon couldn't find a way to work it into the new place. Temporarily, at least, the window would have to be stored.

"Perhaps one day we'll build a small wing for it," Wylie's father said.

Wylie's father had never been forced to struggle to earn his bread. His grandfather rode a bay mare from Philadelphia to frontier West Virginia to invest in timber and coal. He also organized a dry-goods supply house which sold to coal-camp stores. The customers were captive trade because no roads connected the camps, led in and out. Salesmen made their calls by train, riding in smoky, jerking passenger cars between the clanking hoppers.

Even during the Great Depression, Wylie's own grandfather increased the family holdings. He withdrew, however, from the management of coal, timber, and mercantile operations to organize the Elk Land and Lumber Company, which leased its mineral and timber rights. He never parted with land but did sell the dry-goods business to a Jewish family from Cincinnati, it headed by a be-whiskered patriarch named Moses Frankenthal. Wylie had played tennis against a Frankenthal grandson named Sonny—he not a member of the Pinnacle Rock Club. In the city the Jews had their own clubs.

Wylie's father was a popular man. He strolled down Commerce Street or stood on the steps of St. Stephen's and appeared loftily distinguished, more European than American. He could've moved with ease among the silks of Ascot's royal enclosure. Men felt privileged to shake his hand, and ladies were flattered, even flustered, when he tipped his hat to them.

Wylie's mother kept photograph albums in which each picture was titled, identified, and dated. Her own pictures made her appear not to belong to the 1930s, to all the grimness and social ugliness. Rather she seemed to hark back to a more formal, gossamer time. The cameras couldn't properly focus on her, as if she were protected by a misty aura which forbade detail.

Wylie's favorite photograph of her was her sitting in a canoe at Sea Island where she carried a frilly white parasol and wore a white hat and dress. She gazed wistfully at water lilies while dipping a finger into the velvety pond. Beyond, two white swans left ripples, and she seemed akin to them.

Her father too was the grandson of an outlander, a lawyer from Massachusetts. The Beales had all been lawyers. He represented the coal operators in their wars with ferocious John L. Lewis and his fanatical mine workers. Mr. Beale lost ground but always little by little through intricately planned legal withdrawals, a tactic giving the operators time to regroup and deploy their capital. They backed him for a term in the United States Senate.

"We're really all Yankees," Wylie's father told him. "Oh we've taken on a few southern touches, but our roots sink deep into the good Union soil of the North."

Wylie's father had been the first in his family not to attend Yale. He went to Washington and Lee, where he made the track team. He also played tennis, and Wylie's mother clipped a picture of him from the *Daily Mail* taken in 1935, the year after Wylie's birth, when his father was paired in an exhibition match against Don Budge. Both he and Budge wore white slacks, long-sleeved white shirts, and white caps.

After the match they posed with their arms around one another. Each held an egg-shaped racket. Budge was so plain he could've been a local freckled hillbilly while Wylie's father appeared to be a young lord. That he was not champion and had won only three games out of two sets from the awkward-looking redheaded Budge seemed impossible.

"Have you begun thinking what you intend doing with your life?" Wylie's father asked on an August evening before dinner. They hadn't yet moved up the hill, and despite the dog-day heat, the old house was cool and shady. Wylie's mother hadn't come downstairs from her bath. Summers she and Wylie's father drank a gin fizz before eating. Winters it was scotch.

"I haven't given it a lot of thought," Wylie answered. He'd given it no thought at all. What he'd been thinking about was modifying his American-twist serve and working more deeply beneath Bebe's complex lingerie.

"I'm not pressing," his father said. He stood in front of the music room's fireplace. "But now and again you might permit the question to drift through your mind."

43

"Pop, are you being sarcastic with me?"

"I'm never sarcastic. Sarcasm is humor deformed."

Wylie did allow the question to drift through his mind, but the truth was he'd never believed he would have to do much. He'd be like his father—mild, benign, living a decorous, cultivated life. Most important of all, he would be nice.

He was pleased to believe he had niceness in his blood, in the genes, and that he would not only carry the family gentility throughout his own day but also, as a living link, connect it to future generations.

12

On a Tuesday morning in late November, 1951, Wylie's father ate his soft-boiled egg, strip of lean bacon, and slice of buttered whole-wheat toast while reading the *Gazette,* the local morning paper he considered too liberal. The breakfast room was sunny, its air fragrant with freshly cut flowers from the gas-heated greenhouse.

Winters he drove to work. Ed would have the black Chrysler at the side entrance, the engine running, the windshield clean, and the interior of the car warmed by the heater.

The father drove to the alley behind his office and parked in the garage which Wylie and Pinky had roofed and painted. He entered the office by the back door. Miss Burdette, as always, was there first and had left the door unlocked for him.

She'd also switched on lamps and turned up the thermostat. Though sunny, it was a raw, blowing day for November, and she lit the chestnut-oak logs on the brass andirons, a fire laid by Pinky the previous night while doing his chores.

Wylie's father hung his coat and Homburg in the hallway closet. The closet was cedar-lined and aromatic. Rubbing his hands, he crossed to the bay window which fronted the river. To Miss Burdette he commented on the swift high water, the absence of barge traffic, and the river's muddiness. He also looked at the mountain laurel growing by the porch. If the leaves were drawn into tubes, the temperature was below freezing.

"Laurel is my thermometer," he said ritually on cold days. He needed lots of heat.

He walked to his heavy wooden desk, held his hands to the fire before sitting, and put on his glasses to go through the mail prior to driving downtown to a board meeting of Mountain State Bank. The city had seven banks, but Mountain State was the oldest, both its granite building and its money were, the latter taken not in nickels and dimes from the general public but in gross amounts from men of commerce, entrepreneurs who dealt in land, coal, oil, and gas. The bank never advertised, and its architecture resembled the Medici Palace.

Newer members of the board desired Mountain State to become a full-service bank attractive to the ordinary citizen. The subject was discussed politely in the flaxen sheen of the paneled boardroom. Wylie's father sided with the younger men.

"When a person becomes opposed to change, it's a signal his brain has hardened," he said. "That person should retire to Florida and the golf course."

While he sat with his back to the fire, he heard talking in the front hallway, where homely, near-sighted Miss Burdette had her desk. The talk was so loud it drew his concentration from a lawyer's brief involving a coal-royalty dispute.

Again he attempted to work. The clamor in the hallway continued, not only a man's voice, but Miss Burdette's, she who habitually spoke in whispered tones. Wylie's father laid the brief down and pressed a switch on his intercom box.

Miss Burdette didn't respond. Wylie's father stood, crossed to the sliding mahogany doors, and opened them. Beneath the hall chandelier Miss Burdette stood terrified and weeping.

The man confronting her was a Negro, and he held a pistol—a U.S. Army Colt .45 automatic. The gun appeared outsized, though the man himself was large and very black, his head bald except for a curly whitish fuzz. Through the fuzz a sickle-shaped scar gleamed pinkly. He wore heavy army shoes, black chino pants, a white cotton shirt, and an Eisenhower jacket with corporal's stripes on the sleeves. The shoulder patch portrayed lightning striking and breaking a chain.

"He the big dog?" the Negro asked Miss Burdette. He'd already swung the gun around toward Wylie's father.

Miss Burdette could've been praying. Her eyes were clenched, her head bowed, and her hands were clasped under her chin. Her body trembled and seemed about to flow to the floor.

"You the bigass dog around here?" the Negro asked Wylie's father.

"Why yes, this is my office," the father said. He walked forward with his right hand extended. He intended to position himself between the man and Miss Burdette.

"Look out here now!" the Negro said and raised the .45 to aim at Wylie's father's face.

The father stopped, lowered his hand, and made himself smile. "Why don't we go into my office and talk?"

"We going in all right, bigass dog."

He meant Miss Burdette too and wagged the gun at her. Her eyes closed, she stood very still. Wylie's father stepped to her and led her as if she were an invalid into his office. The man followed and slid the doors shut.

Wylie's father seated Miss Burdette in front of his desk. She drew her spinsterish knees together. Her back was curved, her body pulling toward a ball.

"Perhaps you could explain how we can serve you," Wylie's father said.

"You took my goddamn house!" the man said.

"I took your house? That's not likely."

"Just shove it over in the hollow. You think because you're a bigass dog you can do that?"

"I don't know what you mean."

"Down in Mingo Valley. Them yellow dozers come in and shove all the houses in the hollow. You think I fought a fucking war so some bigass dog do that to me?"

"Miss Burdette, will you bring us the file on Mingo Valley?" Wylie's father said.

She didn't move. He touched her shoulder gently. Again he asked for the folder. She heard his voice, the command in it, and opened her eyes but couldn't stand. Her tortoise-shell glasses trembled on her powdered narrow nose.

"She no damn good," the Negro said.

"You and I'll go," Wylie's father said. "The file cabinets are in the hallway."

"Hell no, man. I stay, you go. Do something wrong and I shoot her."

46

He stepped to Miss Burdette and pressed the gun against the back of her dry brown hair, the spit curls of which seemed ironed upon her head.

"I'll do exactly what you want," Wylie's father said.

"That's good, bigass dog."

While the man watched through a gap between the sliding doors, Wylie's father walked to file cabinets that lined an alcove of the hallway. Lacking Miss Burdette's help, he had to open several drawers before finding the folder. He carried it back. The man snatched it from him and closed the doors.

As the man cradled the folder to look through it, he shifted the gun and dropped papers. Miss Burdette's eyes were again clenched. She was a rigid, silent curve of horrified flesh. Wylie's father knelt to pick up the papers.

"What these gonna do for me?" the Negro asked.

"I need to review the situation at Mingo Valley," Wylie's father said.

"My house in the hollow, that's the situation."

"I have to understand the problem."

"Paper ain't gonna help me a damn inch!" the man said and threw the folder on the floor.

Wylie's father hesitated, stooped, and gathered the papers. He walked slowly and softly to his desk, where he spread them. The man watched, sweat from his fingers shiny on the gun's dark metal. Wylie's father glanced at Miss Burdette.

"My secretary's more familiar with this side of the business," he said.

"I'll kill both of you if you be dumb," the man said.

Again the father looked to Miss Burdette, but she wouldn't stir. Eyes closed, she waited for execution.

"Your name?" Wylie's father asked as he turned papers.

"So you tell it to the police, hell no."

"How can I help if you won't give your name?"

"Pedigo, bigass dog. Vernell Pedigo."

"Miss Burdette, will you assist me in finding the sheet on Mr. Vernell Pedigo?"

Wylie's father carried the folder to her. He gripped her shoulder and squeezed. Her eyes snapped open. Her eyes were like a person underwater. Wylie's father held the folder close to her face.

47

She looked at it. With shaking hands, she accepted the folder, set it on her lap, and turned pages. Using a short, unpainted nail, she pointed to a typed list. Wylie's father adjusted his glasses and leaned over to read.

"Mr. Pedigo, I believe you said you own your house."

"I born in the back room."

"But the house was owned by Elk Land and Lumber Company. That house has always been Elk Land and Lumber's unless our records are in error."

Wylie's father looked to Miss Burdette. She was able to find the courage and strength to shake her head—just once.

"I live in that house all my life except the Army," the man said.

"But you see, Mr. Pedigo, it was never yours. Those houses were built more than fifty years ago when coal was being taken from the Mingo seam, in 1901 to be exact. Elk has not relinquished title."

"Where I suppose to live?" the man asked and waved the gun.

"We'll find you a place. Those houses are old and in a dangerous state of disrepair. It's necessary to raze them to keep somebody from being hurt."

"You were behind in your rent," Miss Burdette said, she whose devotion was to ledger perfection. Her first words, they surprised the man, Wylie's father, and herself. Realizing what she'd done, she held to the chair as if expecting it to revolve.

"Why I be crazy enough to pay rent when everything falling down?" the man asked. "You think I should pay for roofs and busted pipes. I done put enough money in that house to own it. Bulah and I has."

"I agree, I don't think you should have to pay," Wylie's father said quickly. "Nobody should have to. That's the reason for razing the houses. We sent notices to all the tenants. We can no longer afford the insurance. We did offer tenants the right to buy. Didn't you receive your letter?"

"What I gonna buy a house with? Look at me and say you think I got enough money in my pocket to buy a house."

"But had you come to us, we could've worked out something. It's never been our intention to cause hardship."

"Work out something right now."

"I promise we'll make you an equitable living arrangement."

"Nah, man, you'll put the police on me."

"I give you my word I won't."

"Soon as I walk out this place, you'll bigass the police on me. You never gave a damn about the people in Mingo."

"I swear the police won't hear of this."

"Like I could believe a man who shoved my house in the ditch. Like anybody could believe a man who done that."

"We have other rental property we can place you in."

"What if I just shoot your ass off, Mr. bigass owner?"

Her eyes closed, Miss Burdette twitched and gripped her fingers.

"How does that help anything?" Wylie's father asked. "You mentioned Bulah. Isn't she depending on you? How's it going to help her for you to die in state prison?"

"I die knowing I see you in Hell. You and me dance with the Devil."

At that moment Pinky, dismissed early from Stonewall Jackson High because of heating-plant trouble, entered the house and knocked on the office's sliding doors. He'd come to set out trash for the city pickup and to carry logs from the basement. The Negro aimed the .45 at the doors.

"Tell them to haul ass!" he said.

Wylie's father cleared his throat and raised his chin. "Haven't I told you a thousand times we don't wish to be interrupted."

He'd never told Pinky that or used such a tone of voice, and Pinky became alerted. He backed off from the doors, tiptoed out the front and along the porch, and peeped in the bay window. He saw the man, the pistol, Wylie's father, the terrified Miss Burdette.

Pinky drew away from the window. He slipped inside, telephoned the police from Miss Burdette's desk, his mouth and the receiver covered by his palm, and hurried down to the basement for logs. Whistling, he carried them up and knocked. Without waiting for an answer, he slid open the doors and walked smiling into the office. He acted brightly dumb.

"Thought you all might like more heat from the fire," he said and crossed right in front of the gun and the startled Negro to the hearth. He lowered the logs, removed the brass fire screen, and chunked glowing coals with the poker. He laid on logs. "I'm telling you this is a day for a fire if there ever was one. Even the birds are wearing overcoats."

He stood from the hearth, turned, and kept smiling. He dusted

49

his hands. "I don't believe I know you, sir," he said to the gaping man holding the gun high.

"This is Mr. Pedigo, one of our tenants," Wylie's father said as if everything were normal.

"How you, Mr. Pedigo?" Pinky asked and crossed with an outstretched hand toward the Negro.

"You crazy?" the man asked and jabbed the gun at Pinky.

"Want to welcome you to Elk Land and Lumber," Pinky said. "Why don't you warm yourself at the fire? I'll set you a chair close up."

"I gonna kill this bigass owner."

"You what?"

"He shove my house in the ditch."

"Mr. DuVal did that? I can't believe it. He's a nice man. He wouldn't shove anybody's house in a ditch."

"He gonna eat bullets," the Negro said and brought the gun around to aim at Wylie's father's face.

"Wait a second now," Pinky said. "You look to me like a good and fair man. You wouldn't shoot a person without allowing them a last word, would you? Everybody gets a last word."

"You got a last word?" the man asked Wylie's father, whose skin was ashen.

"He wants to pray," Pinky said and nodded to Wylie's father to start a prayer which could eat up time till the police reached the office. For once the father's poise failed him. He could say grace and read sonorously from the *Book of Common Prayer*, but a back-against-the-wall entreaty to God was as alien to him as a plea to Allah. He stood helpless and mute.

"I'll speak a few words for him" Pinky said, seeing Wylie's father's helplessness and bowing his own head. "Lord God, at this time we want to remember Your sacrifice for us through the death of Your Son Jesus, who returned only good for evil and offered the water of salvation and everlasting life to those who would but drink from His cup."

"What about him?" the man shouted at Pinky. "How many people he shit on?"

"Brother Pedigo, the Lord God is wise and all-knowing. He takes us when He wants us. He don't need the help of your gun to call a man before His throne."

"I got to stop bigass pushing everybody's house in the ditch!"

"You're a troubled good man," Pinky said, sounding like one of those hillbilly preachers who whined and wept from local radio stations all day Sunday. "I see your misery and pain, and I want you to know I understand trouble and hard times. I understand hunger and having no money and being afraid for tomorrow. But the Lord God sees what I am and what you are too. The Lord God knows everything, and when each man's time comes, the Lord God will set him on His perfect scale of judgment."

"What about this bigass rich fucker having high hog every day while me and Bulah got sore bellies from rubbing against our backbone?" the man asked, his eyes like welling bruises. "How come he get so much when we go in the ditch?"

"When you stand before that golden throne, your troubles will count for you," Pinky said.

"I don't know nothing," the man said. He wiped at his nose with the back of the hand holding the gun. "I just a coal-grubbing nigger."

"You've had so much misery you can't see the road," Pinky said and moved easily toward him. "You got to remember this is the Lord God's creation, not mine or yours. We belong to Him. In time He'll right all wrongs and show us His loving kindness face to face."

As Pinky talked he slowly raised an arm till his fingers touched the Negro's wrist. Pinky worked the other arm softly around behind the man. Suddenly the Negro sagged and wept. The hand holding the gun dropped, the .45 dangled. Creases of the black face filled with tears. Pinky held to and comforted him.

Though the police arrived in force, they weren't needed. Wylie's father wouldn't allow them to handcuff Mr. Pedigo. Pinky walked him down to the curb and the black-and-white patrol car where Wylie's father held open the door.

13

Wylie's father was badly shaken and closed the office for the day. Miss Burdette was unable to collect herself the rest of the week. Dr. Airy prescribed sedatives and bed rest.

Wylie's father didn't show how disturbed he was. His style of life rejected deep emotion openly displayed. He spoke with the same voice and followed his usual habits. Unguarded, however, his face was drawn fine by a look of serious reflection, the expression of a man making final decisions. He called Sis Asters' father's law firm to ask that his will be reviewed.

Wylie's mother was the one who suffered outwardly. They tried to keep the news from her, but the papers ran stories, and friends telephoned. She hugged Wylie's father as if never to release him. She followed him around the house fearful he might disappear.

She wired Wylie to take the C&O home from White Oak School, though his father was against disrupting his education. Wylie rode a coach crowded with noisy soldiers going to Korea, most of them drunk. At the house he and his father sat in the music room, where they had a view eastward across their wall to the upper part of the MacMasters' house on the corner. It was being demolished to prepare the ground for a savings and loan association.

"He had remarkable presence," Wylie's father said of Pinky, his fingers composed on his lap. "He handled himself better than most fully grown men would in such a situation."

"Pinky's always seemed older."

"His coolness was amazing. He seemed to sense just how far he could go with that poor, unfortunate man."

Wylie thought of the sooty, clapboard neighborhood where Pinky lived. He would be familiar with the Pedigos of the world all right.

"Coming up with that prayer to buy time was brilliant, for it happens Mr. Pedigo is a very devout man," Wylie's father said.

"Pinky's pretty devout too."

"He must be or he couldn't have been so convincing. It's quite possible I owe him my life. I'd like to do something for him. Your mother wants to heap gifts on him. I told her that isn't the way. Amos might think we were patronizing him."

Wylie pictured his mother, furred and bejeweled, driving into Pinky's ratty neighborhood and being asked by Pinky's fanatical, askew mother whether she'd been saved.

"I want to do something significant for him," Wylie's father said and touched his mustache. "Did you know Amos came to me once about you? He thought you were abusing yourself."

Wylie felt heat in his face, but his father smiled.

"I questioned him about that abuse. Seems you were drinking

beer and chasing the girls. Frankly I had difficulty controlling my expression. He was very sincere, and I didn't want to hurt his feelings. I promised I'd have a talk with you."

"He thinks we're all sinners."

"I gather, and I couldn't very well have that talk with you without being hypocritical. It's logical to expect a certain progression from youth to maturity that leads through the pursuit of ladies to the learning of how to hold your liquor."

"Thanks, Dad."

"He wasn't carrying tales. He was genuinely worried about your moral condition."

"I didn't think he'd come to you though."

"I suppose you could say that Amos has taken us to raise, both you and me, and we definitely owe him. That's the reason I'm sending him to White Oak School with you next semester."

Wylie heard the words, but for an instant they didn't register. An image formed in his mind, the figure of a blackened coal miner walking among the white-linen guests at a garden party.

"You're not responding," Wylie's father said, watching him from pale gray eyes.

"I'm trying to see Pinky fitting at White Oak."

"I've already spoken to Headmaster Lamp and explained the situation. He's interested even to the extent of shaving a bit off the tuition. The Board of Trustees has been considering a few scholarships to restructure, as he put it, the social mix."

"The what?"

"Academic jargon. The trustees want you privileged kids to meet ordinary people. They seem to think you need to be instructed how to function in their midst."

Wylie looked out the window toward the disintegrating Mac-Master house. Workers wearing helmets and goggles used wrecking bars and toppled stones and red tiles from the third story to the ground, where a yellowish dust swirled.

"You're bothered," the father said.

"You talked to his parents?"

"I talked to his father, who's a clerk in the Assessor's Office. Turns out we'd met some years ago."

"Met where?"

"Just a chance encounter."

"Dad, I'd like to know."

"Well he's a veteran who'd had a little too much to drink. It was downtown, and I saw he got home in good shape. Least I could do."

Wylie remembered Pinky's telling about the man drunk down on lower River Street, staggering along the sidewalk, bumping into store windows and power poles, how Wylie's father kept him from being arrested and sent him home in a taxi—the act of kindness which had caused Pinky to come to work at the office in the first place. That man was Pinky's father.

"He isn't enthusiastic about Amos leaving here but has finally agreed."

"What about Pinky's mother?" Wylie asked.

"The father is going to handle that. You don't appear overjoyed."

"I'll have to sponsor him at White Oak, won't I?"

"To a degree. It won't take Amos long to size up the school and realize his great opportunity."

"Must I room with him?" Wylie asked and wondered whether he was being indirectly criticized for his undistinguished record at White Oak.

His father gazed at him and templed his hands. On a finger he wore a gold ring with the DuVal crest. His voice lowered, his face firmed.

"You do remember that Amos most likely saved my life?" he asked. "I've been assuming that fact means something to you as well as to me."

"I'll help all I can."

"If everything falls into place, he'll be entering the February term."

14

Pinky was invited for dinner that same evening. Wylie's mother asked him to bring his parents, but Pinky told her his father had to work nights preparing the yearly municipal tax notices and that his mother was serving a church supper. Wylie thought of Pinky's ugly cinderblock church bleeding paint in shadows of the old bridge— The Tabernacle of the Chosen of God.

Pinky again wore his dark woolly suit, his white shirt, another somber tie. His black shoes shone like hot asphalt. In the high-back Jacobean chair he sat at attention.

For once Wylie's parents gave up their drinks before dinner. They knew Pinky would disapprove of liquor. Ed, wearing a white jacket and a bowtie, carried in a silver tray on which were small crystal glasses of tomato juice spiced with cayenne pepper and Worcestershire sauce.

Each move by Wylie's mother caused Pinky to stand. He seemed to be sitting on a coiled spring. He sirred Wylie's father in every sentence. He mistakenly sirred Wylie too, and his face became even redder.

They walked to the oak-paneled dining room, where Wylie's mother seated Pinky to her right. Ed had lighted two silver candelabra. Wylie's mother used her good heavy English silver during all meals, and Wylie's father wouldn't put up with paper napkins even at breakfast. In the basement was an ancient hissing mangle heated by gas flames for ironing linen napkins and tablecloths as rich and weighty as bishops' robes.

Wylie's father spoke his quick Episcopal grace, more rhythm than message. As soon as he finished, Wylie's mother took up the burden of conversation.

"We'd also like to give thanks to you," she said to Pinky.

"I didn't do much," Pinky said, the golden brocade of his chair contrasting his ruddiness.

"You're now an honorary member of this family," she said.

Pinky was so pleased his ears were on fire. He lowered his eyes. He loved Wylie's mother, both in reality and in her portrait, the one in the master bedroom where she, against a backdrop of blooming tulips and the weeping willow, wore the gray chiffon dress and the gray hat with the red band.

Wylie's father asked Pinky about Stonewall Jackson's football team. Pinky spoke slowly. He didn't intend to make any mistakes in grammar or pronunciation. He was a boy walking a very slippery slope.

"We would've won the city championship except our back pulled a hamstring," he said.

"Is there a hamstring in one's back?" Wylie's mother asked, feigning confusion.

They laughed, and Pinky explained in detail as she'd intended. She would inflate him to importance.

"Still we're doing all right," Pinky said. "So far it's a six-one season." He turned to Wylie. "What about White Oak?"

"I'm not sure of the count," Wylie said.

"Why aren't you?" his father asked.

"I don't go to all the games."

"Don't you read the scores in the paper?" Pinky asked.

"I mean to but somehow never get around to it."

Wylie's mother and father glanced at each other and at him. They didn't care about football but believed he should be more enthusiastic for Pinky's sake. In their world politeness was more important than honesty.

"We did beat Woodberry Forest," Wylie said.

Ed carried in a juicy steaming roast of beef. Wylie's father carved using a knife which had belonged to his father. It had a stag handle, and the blade was made from German steel. Once a year Wylie's father wrapped the knife in cotton swaddling to carry it downtown to an alley shop of an old Jew whose small foot pedaled a whetstone on which he sharpened scissors and other edges. Wylie's father was able to slice meat so thin it was translucent—a slightly bleeding wafer.

Pinky had never been served so elegantly. For a moment he must've believed they weren't going to give him anything to eat except the three slices of rare beef which the father had laid precisely on the gold-rimmed Meissen plate. Pinky's eyes sped to Wylie as if to ask what should be done next.

Uniformed Viola backed through the swinging door with silver dishes of vegetables, and Ed carried the gravy boat and ladle. Pinky wanted lots of gravy but checked his hand and dipped the same amount as Wylie's mother on his whipped potatoes—a dab. He waited until Wylie picked up a fork before selecting his own.

"So much construction," Wylie's mother said. "In this valley the dust never settles, and even at night I hear jackhammers."

"The city's moving west," Pinky said. "If I had money, I'd buy some of those broken-down houses along Goshen Street."

"What would you do with them?" Wylie's father asked.

"Sell them to the wreckers to tear down and haul off. That way you cut your taxes while waiting for a buyer to come along and make you a big offer for the land."

"I see you've thought it through," Wylie's father said and eyed him as if to say, Why is it my son doesn't discover these things?

"You're young to know so much about the business world," Wylie's mother told Pinky.

"Some opportunities hit you slam bang between the eyes," Pinky said.

He was being careful, acting as if the table were wired with explosives. His caution, however, didn't stop him from wiping his plate with half a beaten biscuit till the plate shone as if it'd just risen from Viola's frothy sink.

"I'd like to tell you I think this food's been very well prepared," Pinky said to Wylie's mother.

She and Wylie's father managed not to smile. The remark was surely one Pinky had rehearsed. Wylie imagined Pinky before a mirror speaking the words, changing his expressions, practicing. He also pictured the frenzied, prophetic mother drifting behind him.

For dessert Viola had prepared a three-tiered baked Alaska. Ed carried it in on a shimmering antique plate with a pedestal bottom. Pinky didn't expect the inside of his hot slice to be cold. For an instant he was as awed as a person struck by a vision.

"I'd like to tell you I consider this a very delicious dessert," he said.

"It's Wylie's favorite," his mother said.

"Though somewhat ostentatious," Wylie said. Ostentatious was a word the crowd was using lots that year.

His parents stared at him.

"I'm only kidding," he said.

After the baked Alaska, Ed cleared the table while Viola brought in finger bowls. Descended from Wylie's mother's side of the family, the bowls were silver with a grape and vine motif. The center was a crater of white porcelain. On blue china plates beneath lay thin slices of lemon.

Pinky should've waited but had become too confident. Throughout the meal, encouraged by Wylie's mother, his certainty had mounted. Maybe he wanted to prove he knew something of the world.

His gamble was a good one. Each place had one teaspoon left for coffee. Pinky must've deduced the spoon should be used on what was in his finger bowl. He squeezed his lemon over the water and dipped his spoon.

Wylie's parents were shocked to helplessness. His mother recovered first. She squeezed her slice of lemon, wiped her fingers on her napkin, and lifted her spoon. Wylie and his father did the same.

"I want to tell you this is another delicious dish," Pinky said.

"We're so happy you like it," Wylie's mother said.

"Indeed," Wylie's father said.

They spooned and swallowed the warm lemony water from their finger bowls.

15

Wylie's father planned to drive him and Pinky to White Oak, though Wylie's mother was nervous about the weather. A February wind blew mercilessly cold off the iced hills. She read in the *Gazette* a Greyhound bus had skidded into a ravine near Paris—the Paris, of course, being in West Virginia, not France.

"The train would be safer," she argued.

"Too much baggage, and you and I can drive on down to Boca Raton for a week," Wylie's father said.

Wylie couldn't believe Pinky's mother would allow him to leave home without a squabble. It might be best, Wylie explained to his father, if just the two of them went to pick up Pinky at his house.

"We'll disturb her you mean?" Wylie's father asked.

"She's kind of sick."

"Well we certainly don't want to upset your mother more than she is already."

Wylie drove the black Chrysler to Bethel Road on the Wrong Side. His father didn't comment on the neighborhood's seediness. Once the father turned to look at a building being wrecked—a brick church which fire had blackened. Laborers attacked the scorched walls with sledges.

Pinky's two suitcases waited on the porch of the duplex, and Pinky himself peeked through the door's glass diamond and hurried to the sidewalk. He wore gloves, a brown overcoat too long for him, and a plaid scarf. Wylie kept his eyes averted from the suitcases' cheapness.

"Amos, you ever been late for anything?" Wylie's father asked.

While Pinky lifted the suitcases into the Chrysler's trunk, his father came from the duplex. He wore a pressed blue suit and a blue tie, but the tips of his white collar curled upward. His red hair needed cutting. His glasses had steel rims, the kind men brought with them out of the service, GI issue. When hands were shaken, his were cold, bony, and fugitive.

"The highways are clear," Wylie's father said. "I checked with the State Police."

"The crews ought to be spreading cinders," Pinky's father said.

Tall, thin, angular, his voice was unhurried and soft, a southern hillbilly way of speaking, like Pinky's, though you could never be certain what Pinky would sound like. He was experimenting with talking.

His father appeared preoccupied. His reddish brown eyes were shaded and seemed not quite focused. Wylie smelled hooch on him, not scotch, but corn liquor strong and cheap. Wylie already had a good nose for scotch.

At parting Pinky and his father didn't hug, shake hands, or even look to one another. They were uncomfortable. When Pinky stepped into the Chrysler, his father did close the door but then stood back with his arms crossed, his breath steaming in the wind, the same abstract expression on his face.

"We'll take good care of him," Wylie's father called as Wylie started the car's engine. He glanced toward the mustard-colored duplex and wondered about Pinky's mother.

Wylie sensed his father too waited for some further sign of farewell between Pinky and his family, if not an embrace or kiss, then at least an affectionate word or laying on of hands. In the rear Pinky stared straight ahead. His father backed toward the duplex, the wind flapping his clothes. Maybe, Wylie thought, they've tied up the mother.

She didn't appear till they were driving away. A short, fat woman with cropped white hair was inside with her. As the mother struggled onto the porch, the old woman tried to hold her. Pinky's mother's mouth opened and closed, but in the Chrysler's warm tightness, no sound of her reached them.

Pinky's father blocked the porch steps so the frantic mother couldn't escape into the street. Neighbors looked from doorways and steamy windows. Wylie slowed the car.

"Go on," Pinky said.

"She all right?" Wylie's father asked. He twisted in his seat to look back at Pinky's father and the old woman holding the mother, whose mouth was still opening and closing.

"Just keep going, and it'll be okay," Pinky said.

He never once glanced behind him.

16

Wylie's father drove the pitted, curving highway south toward White Sulphur. Rock slides from the snow-shrouded mountains blocked sections of Route 60, and misshapen icicles hung from boulders. Bleak, leafless trees stood like the condemned in the shrieking, relentless wind.

Wylie offered to drive, but his father said no. He would stay behind the wheel till they reached Virginia and gentler slopes of the ribbed Appalachians. Wylie's mother watched the murky sky for snow. She remained stiffly erect and kept touching her pearl earrings as if they were loose. When nervous, she talked too much. She couldn't help it and became flighty and shrill.

"We usually make this trip in early fall or late spring when there's no danger of weather," she said, turning to Pinky, who sat beside Wylie on the back seat. "Other times Wylie takes the train. He likes the sleeping cars. Do you like the sleeping cars, Amos?"

"I think I would, yes'm, but I never been on a sleeping car."

"Though the coaches on the C&O are very nice," Wylie's mother said. "They are, I'm told, kept clean and have hostesses, don't they?"

"They do," Wylie said, thinking Pinky had never been on a day coach either. He'd never been out of the Kanawha Valley.

"New management," Wylie's father said. "I doubt the hostesses will last."

"I hope you're wrong," the mother said. "They have such attractive uniforms. Dove gray, I believe, with gold epaulets and buttons, very smart. There's really no reason a person shouldn't take the coach. I've never been able to sleep on a train anyway. All that clicking and clacking and bumping. I can't read. The light's different." She tensed. "Isn't that an icy patch?"

"It's been cindered," Wylie's father said but slowed.

"Anyway we've taken this old Route 60 a hundred times and usually stop at The Greenbrier for the buffet," she said. "I think we're extremely fortunate they built The Greenbrier on Route 60."

"The Greenbrier was built before Route 60 existed," Wylie's father said.

"All right, be technical, but it's still a treat to arrive there when you're over the worst of the mountains. It's something to look forward to, an oasis, though the food's not been much to brag on lately. And they've let their darkies go."

Pinky had been looking at the tumbledown shanties of an abandoned coal camp which straggled along a shadowed hollow rounded and purified by snow. He turned his head to stare at Wylie's mother. He had to be thinking that the slaves were freed nearly a hundred years before.

"Yes," Wylie's mother said, nodding but never withdrawing her eyes from the highway, "the management laid off all those good Virginia darkies and hired foreigners, Greeks I think, who just don't have the knack. They're snippity. One was snippity to us last spring."

"He expected me to tip when the filet of sole was dry as cotton," Wylie's father said. "I don't believe in rewarding incompetence."

"We never ate a bad meal while the darkies were still working," Wylie's mother said. "They definitely make the best servants, don't you think, Amos?"

Pinky wasn't sure how to answer and looked to Wylie for help.

"They're having a bad time at White Oak too," Wylie said. "The kitchen's always short of help."

"My mother trained her own help," Wylie's mother said. "She'd hire a young girl, twelve or thirteen, and instruct her in service. After two years with my mother, the girls were so proficient everybody wanted them. Mother felt a responsibility to teach more than just how to clean and cook. They learned to read and write. Our kitchen was a regular little schoolhouse."

61

Using lateral vision Wylie watched Pinky, who sat listening quietly. Words were going into him and being stored. Like the black girls in the kitchen, he was being educated.

"I'm thinking perhaps we shouldn't stop at The Greenbrier," Wylie's father said.

"But the boys would enjoy the buffet!" the mother protested.

"Wouldn't it be wiser to push on before snow traps us?"

"Oh the awful snow!" Wylie's mother said and glared at the sky.

When they crossed the border into Virginia, Wylie felt the rules changed. He'd often had the sensation that the West Virginia land itself might uprear and hurl boulders or that savage, bearded men would leap from the ice-sheathed forest to rape and pillage.

At Virginia the mountains tamed, the roads straightened and became wider, the law took hold. There were manners as well as order among the people, a breeding even among the hayseeds, a rural gentility. The mountains of West Virginia, like a fortress, blocked amenity and refinement.

When they drove through White Oak's brick entranceway, clouds uncovered a warming sun. Across the broad playing fields, the school's red buildings had the symmetry of English estates, and windows reflected a golden light. The bell in the ivy-covered chapel was ringing.

Mr. Dabney Lamp, the thin bachelor headmaster, oversaw the awarding of room assignments in Lafayette Hall. Mr. Sip's tiny mouth pursed as he studied Pinky through polished lenses. Students couldn't look into the sapphire blades of those eyes without feeling pierced.

"Are you as clever as you're reputed to be?" he asked Pinky.

"I don't know," Pinky answered. He appeared cornered and as if sweat were about to pop out his pores.

"We'll find out for you," Mr. Sip said.

Negro help carried Wylie's and Pinky's bags to the second floor of Lafayette. Their room faced west and was furnished with two narrow beds, two black dressers, and two sturdy desks and straight chairs. The fireplace, used before the old building was refitted for steam heat, had been closed.

The bathroom was in the hall, where a lot of horseplay shook the floor. Boys raced around roughhousing. They called to Wylie, and a wadded wet towel smacked him in the back of the neck. As best he could, he introduced untalkative Pinky around.

He and Pinky went downstairs to say good-by to Wylie's parents, who intended driving on to Charlottesville for the night. Wylie's mother kissed not only him but also Pinky. Wylie saw Pinky love her for it in a blush. Wylie's father shook their hands and put his hands on their shoulders. Wylie thought of the farewell Pinky had received from his parents in front of the duplex.

He and Pinky watched the Chrysler drive off under the arch of the uniformly planted dogwood and Judas trees. They returned to their room to unpack before dinner. Unpacking didn't take Pinky long since he owned so little.

Milky, golden-haired London came in. He and Blue Bales roomed together on the third floor. Wylie had meant to room with Blue but had been forced to change because of Pinky. London was on his way down to the basement shower and wore his red kimono with the black fire-spewing dragon entwining it. His feet were stuffed into huge furry white slippers.

"This school's already such a drag," he complained and touched his forehead as if suffering the vapors. "Shall we have a game of cards after dinner?"

"I don't play cards," Pinky said.

"Well you don't have to act superior about it," London said. He sniffed as if the air were bad and in those enormous slippers shuffled from the room.

Pinky looked out the window to the darkening plain of the playing fields and the lake whose silverish skim of ice reflected a reddish glow.

"Nostrils," he said

"What?" Wylie asked as he set his picture of Bebe on his dresser.

"That's all I'm going to see around here—hairy, aristocratic nostrils."

17

It might've been worse. Since Wylie was fourth form, he could give status and protection to Pinky. Except for Latin, they were in the same classes. Wylie had studied Latin three years. Pinky joined the beginners.

London Airy acted bitchy with Pinky, but Blue Bales was friendly, if not warm. Blue wasn't warm to anybody. Others accepted Pinky as long as he stayed close to Wylie. When Pinky moved alone, space opened around him.

Students knew Wylie's father paid Pinky's tuition. London had learned it from his doctor father, and to expect London to keep a secret was to expect a canary not to sing. By the end of the first week, everybody categorized Pinky as a person of no consequence on the White Oak social scale.

Winter afternoons while Wylie hit tennis balls against the green backboard of York Gymnasium, Pinky swam and did his half gainer. The dive interested Hunk Baste, the water-sports coach. He worked with Pinky on speed swimming.

As Wylie knew would happen, Pinky was unswervable in his studies. After dinner, no matter how tired or discouraged, Pinky curved over his desk and hardly looked up before eleven and lights-out. Wylie would slip up to Blue and London's room for bridge, on which they gambled half a cent a point.

"He's a grub," London, a terrible player, said of Pinky.

"Well you're a snot," Wylie said to London.

"But with class," Blue Bales said. "London's snot is imported."

Four or five times a week Pinky received letters in pencil from his mother, often two or three the same day. The envelopes were the pale, flimsy kind bought in packets at variety stores, the writing large, clumsy, slanting, a penmanship out of control. Included were clippings from a religious publication called *The Chosen,* which Pinky bound with rubber bands and kept in a dresser drawer.

"You ever study?" Pinky asked Wylie, who lay reading a dirty book borrowed from London. The plot involved a young knight who sought shelter in a convent full of lascivious older nuns.

"Only when menaced," Wylie answered.

"You could be a brain."

"But you see, being a brain would cramp my style," Wylie said. He closed the book and went upstairs to play cards.

By the middle of March Pinky seemed to be settling in at White Oak. He was able to get about on his own, no longer having to tag after Wylie, though making no friends. He acted suspicious of any-one who drew too close.

On Thursday Wylie lay on his bed reading another book, Henry Miller's *The Tropic of Cancer,* borrowed from Blue Bales. Pinky was restless. Instead of bending to his desk, he kept standing, crossing to his dresser, and scowling at himself in the mirror.

"I'm going out behind York tonight," he said.

Wylie sat up. "Behind York" was a code phrase meaning two students intended to fight. The oak behind York Gymnasium was the dueling ground. Mr. Sip knew and allowed it to continue by pretending not to see.

"Who with?" Wylie asked.

"Archer."

Archer was from Falls Church, the son of a State Department diplomat and number three on the tennis team, a large blond boy with a flat cannonball serve.

"Why Archer?" Wylie asked.

"He's got a dirty mouth."

Archer did talk filth, but so did most White Oak students. They got common with each other while all the time knowing they came from money and background which would enable them to carry on a polite garden-party conversation if necessary. Students spoke and acted like louts, yet could instantly transform themselves into young gentlemen.

"What did Archer say?" Wylie asked.

"He told me to go and do you-know-what to myself."

"It's an expression he frequently uses."

"Not to me he doesn't. Nobody can use that kind of talk around me."

The cold, moist night smelled of smoke and earth. Earlier a shower had blown rain against the dormitory windows. White fog slid across the dark grass. The only lights at the gym were hazy red bulbs over the fire exits.

Wylie stood with Pinky under the wet spidery arms of the keening white oak behind York. Pinky wore sweat pants, a windbreaker, and a wool cap. Wylie had on his overcoat and pushed his fingers deep into its smartly cut pockets.

"You're certain you feel the need to do this?" he asked Pinky.

65

"I warned him."

Archer and his roommate Gene "Little Shovel" Diggs stepped from the fog. Archer too wore an overcoat but under it were his boxing trunks and a training shirt. Little Shovel, a crumb picker from the table of the great, carried the gloves.

"You want them?" Little Shovel asked Pinky, lifting the boxing gloves.

"Whatever way he likes it," Pinky answered.

"It's my opinion gloves get in the way," Archer said. "Only thing is, Cody, I don't see why you're so pissed."

"Your mouth drops manure."

"You think I need your permission to talk?" Archer asked. "I'm fifth form, and you can blow it out your ass."

"There you go," Pinky said and unzipped his windbreaker.

"He thinks that's cussing," Archer said. "Will somebody tell him 'ass' is in the Bible."

"I know what's in the Bible and don't need you to tell me," Pinky said. He handed Wylie his windbreaker and cap.

"Nobody'll believe this," Archer said. He let his overcoat slide back along his arms. Little Shovel was there to catch it.

As soon as they touched fists, Pinky jumped him. He didn't circle or feint to feel Archer out. He went at him as if he meant to pound Archer into the ground.

Archer had training and wasn't dumb. He crouched, covered his head, and backed off. He retreated around the white oak. He was patient as Pinky swung at him. He meant to allow Pinky to wear himself down.

Pinky at last understood he was doing no damage. He slowed himself, stood straighter, and wiped his arm across his face. His breath came hard. As he again stepped forward, Archer rocked him with a fast left jab.

Maybe Pinky had forgotten Archer could hit. He looked surprised, and the jab tilted him sideways. Archer followed with a short right. He was using textbook boxing as taught by Yank Wynne, the school's coach. Pinky wobbled.

Archer moved in and set him up for another combination. Pinky attempted to guard himself, but Archer clipped him with fists as precise as striking snakes. Archer looked so good, so classic, his left foot advanced, his hands up, his chin protected by his shoulder. He never drew back to hit, thus telegraphing a blow. In the fog-shrouded fire-exit lights his punches were so fast they were easier to hear than to see.

Pinky stumbled over a root. Archer hit him three times. Pinky sank, sat, and toppled to his back. He rolled to his stomach and worked himself up to one knee. Blood flowed from his nose. It dripped from his stubborn, outswept chin.

"This is a stupid fight, and I'm ready to stop if you are," Archer said.

"All the dirt out of your mouth?" Pinky asked, heaving for breath.

"You seem to be confused about the rules. I've whipped your ass and don't have to do a goddamn thing to please you."

"You got to be taught," Pinky said.

He charged upward as if in a race off starting blocks, head low, arms wide. Archer saw it and boloed. His right fist thunked Pinky's head. Pinky shuddered, staggered, but kept coming. His arms closed around Archer's hips. A shoulder thrust into Archer's stomach. Pinky drove him against the white oak.

Archer's back slammed into the tree trunk, he grunted, and his body gave. He tried to take his boxing stance, but Pinky was inside hooking, butting, kneeing. Archer had blows coming at him from all directions, yet couldn't retreat.

"Not fair!" Little Shovel protested.

"Hands off!" Wylie warned him.

Archer sagged against the oak. Pinky used fists, knees, elbows, his head. He kidney punched Archer, who cried out. Archer's bloody face became rapt, like Italian paintings of martyred saints receiving the stigmata.

"We got to stop it!" Little Shovel said to Wylie.

"Okay, that's enough, break it up!" Wylie said.

He and Little Shovel pried them apart. Panting, Pinky backed off. His attack had been holding Archer to the white oak. Archer collapsed like rope. He curled and lay groaning.

Pinky knelt to him. Wylie feared Pinky might hit Archer again and moved to prevent it, but Pinky scratched up moist soil with his fingers and cupped it in his palm. He lifted Archer's head in order to force the dirt into his mouth. Archer choked, coughed, and spat.

"You shouldn't do that!" Little Shovel said.

Pinky stared at him, and Little Shovel faded backwards. Standing, Pinky pinched his bleeding nose. He took his windbreaker and cap from Wylie and walked crookedly into the shifting fog toward Lafayette Hall.

Wylie and Little Shovel lifted Archer. He spat blood and soil. He was like a man who'd drowned in earth, and they had to bend him over and shake him so all the dirt would fall from his throat and mouth.

18

Thanks to Little Shovel, after the fight nobody except Wylie and the masters spoke to Pinky, who in his style of combat had broken the code. Backs were turned on him. In the dining hall he ate alone. No student, however, cursed while near him. His path was always clear.

The social leprosy infected Wylie. People treated him as if he were responsible for Pinky. Sometimes Wylie too found himself alone at a table in the Gothic dining hall, where it was twilight, forever twilight, even at midday.

He no longer slipped up the steps each night for the card game. Blue and London wouldn't cut him, but Wylie felt he embarrassed them with their other friends. He sat at his desk resenting Pinky.

Pinky showed no emotion. He probably thought it was holy to suffer. He'd maintained certain religious practices like reading his Bible nightly and memorizing verses. In addition to Mr. Sip's Episcopalian grace, Pinky shut his eyes and bowed his head to recite his own silent prayer before each meal. Before switching off the lights at night, he knelt by his bed, his elbows on the plain army blanket, his hands clasped before his transported face.

He wrote letters home, but not all the letters went to his mother. Some had Sis Asters' name and address on them.

"Didn't realize you and Sis had kept up your relationship," Wylie said.

"You sure you want to speak to me?"

"Don't have much choice if I want to speak at all," Wylie said, his fingers laced behind his head as he half snoozed and pictured Bebe in throes of passion caused by his manliness.

"It must be terrible for you to have to associate with a low-class fellow like me," Pinky said. "If you want to move, I'll understand."

"Generous of you."

"Sarcasm, always sarcasm."

"Sure, why not?"

"I know why you won't move. For your father you'd stick it out no matter what you think of me."

"More or less correct," Wylie said.

"It's the reason I'm sticking it out too," Pinky said.

Sis Asters not only wrote, she also sent Pinky a photograph—a large black-and-white glossy of herself wearing a tight cashmere sweater. She was turned sideways to the camera to show off her breasts. Her expression was teasing, her wicked little mouth parted, her wet tongue pressed against her perfect teeth.

Pinky wouldn't set the photograph on his dresser but kept it under the few cheap shirts in his drawer. Only when alone did he lift the picture out. If Wylie walked into the room, Pinky closed the folder and buried it back in the drawer.

"You ashamed of her?" Wylie asked.

"I don't want their eyes on her. You know what guys around here would think. You too."

"Torrid and lustful thoughts we'd have."

"I respect her."

Pinky made the baseball team. At shortstop he was a crab with his glove. His quick, lunging plays and fast, accurate throws should've drawn applause, but only Boston Bean, the coach, jumped around happily.

Pinky batted .318 and hit with precision. No slop came off his wood. He allowed his bat to rest on his shoulder till the ball was out of the pitcher's hand. Pinky started his swing with a push from the shoulder. He slashed hits dangerous to the health of infielders, yet could lay down a bunt with the gentleness of a youth picking flowers.

Sometimes he'd come from baseball practice and stop by the tennis courts, where he'd watch Wylie a few minutes before going to the showers. Wylie suspected that once clean, Pinky went to the room, closed the door, and gazed at Sis Asters' picture.

"You don't care for baseball?" Pinky asked, turning from his desk, a finger holding the place in his Latin text.

"Never got into the game," Wylie answered. He stood at his dresser mirror stroking a comb through his hair, which was the same off-blond color as his father's. He considered baseball a coal-camp sport.

"You don't like football either," Pinky said.

"I have this aversion to being pounded."

"You like to look pretty. You try to do everything gracefully. You move just so, never hurry, never sweat. You put food in your mouth as if eating wasn't important. When you play tennis, you never strain."

"You attempting to insult me?" Wylie asked and lowered his comb.

"This afternoon you could've made a lot of shots if you'd hustled, but you wouldn't. You might look bad."

For a moment Wylie felt they faced each other not so much with hostility as with the eyes and ears of aliens—two foreigners speaking from different lands.

"Tennis is only a game," Wylie said.

"You're supposed to win games."

"You're supposed to enjoy them."

There seemed no way they could get across to each other. Pinky turned back to his simplified Caesar while Wylie continued to comb his hair.

The big baseball game was with Woodberry Forest, a traditional classy rival, and it was played on a hot, windless Saturday in April. Dogwood and Judas trees dropped white and wine blooms along the drive and in forest shades. The girls were themselves blooms, perfumed and bright, and they swayed in the green bleachers.

Pinky should've been the hero. He worked shortstop in a fury. He made a diving one-handed catch to his right of a smash so hard and vicious it later raised a blister on his palm. His double in the ninth scored a run from first base and won the game.

Spectators ought to have bounded to their feet to clap and cheer, yet hardly anyone in the stands made a sound except parents who hadn't received the word. The girls remained composed and looked at Pinky with the calm stare of judgment.

Walking toward York Gymnasium, Pinky threw his glove to the ground and kicked it ahead of him.

19

At the athletics awards banquet, the felt-covered table in the twilight dining hall glittered feebly with silver trophies, but Pinky won nothing. Trophy recipients were selected by votes of teammates. He kept his head up, though the normal rosiness of his face faded to paleness. Later in the room he sat back from his desk and hurled his rhetoric book against the wall above his bed.

Wylie waited a minute before speaking. "It's only a little cup, not even sterling," he said.

"I deserved one."

"Maybe next year you'll win."

"I might not be coming back next year."

Though Wylie didn't show it, he was excited by those words. Pinky not coming back! He was a cross to bear. Finally to be rid of him and his hateful ways.

Even for his father's sake, Wylie didn't go through a half-hearted ritual of trying to talk Pinky out of not returning. Wylie was feeling too lonely and left behind by his friends. He wanted his school life to be how it was before Pinky came to White Oak. Most of all, Wylie wanted to be elected to the Laurel Society.

He hoped to recoup his place among his peers by doing well in the Spring Gala, the yearly variety show where anybody, including faculty and staff, could present monologues, skits, and musical acts. Wylie meant to use his Eddy Duchin routine. To please his mother, he'd taken eight years of classical piano, but it was cocktail piano which attracted him and that he performed well.

He'd listened to probably a thousand hours of Eddy Duchin, bought his records, the sheet music, and stayed up to the wee hours many a night to hear radio broadcasts from such places as the Bellevue Stratford, the Waldorf, the Starlight and the Rainbow rooms. Elegance was what Eddy Duchin represented, and if Wylie were not himself, that's who he would've wanted to be.

In the nave of the White Oak chapel, he practiced his imitation. It was the one place he needn't fear being disturbed. Red and blue lights from the stained-glass window tinted his fingers on the piano keys. Like his mother he had fine hands. Christ walked on water, St. Francis preached a sermon to the birds, and Wylie hummed "Love for Sale."

His act followed Mr. Sip's on the stage of Southwick Auditorium. Mr. Sip recited from Dante's *Divina Commedia,* the section where the poet visits the inferno and meets Virgil. The students were bored and booed. Mr. Sip's delicate face never changed. For so slight a man he had a piercing voice. "'Help, pity me,' I cried, 'whate'er you are, A living man, or spectre from the shades.'" Mr. Sip lifted soulful eyes and stretched upward his thin arms.

Wylie wore white tie and tails. He'd borrowed his father's opera hat. He had on white gloves, carried an ivory-tipped cane, and crossed the stage smoking a Chesterfield. Opera hat cocked jauntily, he tried to appear urbanely dissipated.

As the audience whistled, Wylie strolled to the grand piano, a Baldwin, raised its top unhurriedly, and tossed his cigarette into the wings where the stage manager, Henry "Little Dick" Spratlin, waited to catch it. Students snickered and jeered. Wylie removed his hat and set it on the piano. From his hands he unbuttoned and stripped the white gloves. He dropped them into the upturned hat.

He settled on the piano stool, rubbed his palms, and flexed his fingers above the keys. Students hooted and neighed. Wylie adjusted the stool as if the most perfect seating were required for him to play. More catcalls and jeers. He raised his face toward the rear of the auditorium. Stage lights dimmed, and a bluish white spot centered him in its beam.

He began "Easy to Love." Slowly, tenderly, he played, and he sang to himself just above a whisper. He allowed a sad smile to shape his lips, the expression of a worldly man who'd seen everything. He tried to think of himself as a suave European lover caressing music from the piano as if it were a beautiful woman's body.

The audience hushed, and when he finished the piece, the applause was general. He sat like a man alone and didn't look at the audience or in any way acknowledge them. Negligently he dipped into "They Can't Take That Away From Me." One of his best pieces, he milked it, slowing the tempo till the notes drifted off his fingers. His relaxed posture hinted he was misunderstood, wounded, yet ever faithful—the sorrows of a nice, dissolute young man. He allowed the last note to linger and fade.

Applause came like a rush of wind. Still he acted as if no other person were present and he didn't hear. He sat with head bowed, hands limp on his lap till the cheering died.

Like the lover rejected and forlorn, jaded and jilted, he pretended to fight weariness and lift his hands to the keys. Tentatively, very nearly silently, he began "Love for Sale." His eyes closed, and he attempted to appear bravely suffering. He broke off as if unable to finish the piece but then took it up again. At the end he slowly mouthed words of the song and used the index finger of his right hand to tap the notes out on the piano. The last note was left unplayed.

Students clapped and stomped. Their girls, the masters, and the masters' wives were all applauding and yelling for him. Whistles shrilled, a bugle was blown. A St. Catherine's girl unpinned a red rose from her black hair and threw it to him.

Languorously he stood from the piano stool, reached for the rose, and breathed of it. He pulled its stem through his satiny lapel. He drew on and buttoned his white gloves. He lifted his father's opera hat from the piano and again set it jauntily on his head.

He was still within the beam of the single spotlight. From an inner breast pocket of his tails, he brought out a silver cigarette case, selected a Chesterfield, and tapped it on the case. He lit the cigarette with a silver lighter. His eyes narrowed as smoke drifted around them. The Chesterfield dangled from his lips. He allowed the cane to slide through his fingers. One hand in a trouser pocket, the spot on him, he strolled casually offstage.

The audience rose from their seats like a breaking comber, and he felt sure he had the prize. His picture would be on the front page of the White Oak *Scholar*. He'd automatically be invited into the Laurel Society.

He didn't know Pinky had entered the Spring Gala till his name was announced. Baseball, yes, pole vaulting, diving, and speed swimming, granted, but not entertainment, especially before a sophisticated crowd which had no liking for him.

Pinky legged onstage dressed like a hillbilly—no shoes, bib overalls with jagged cuffs, a blue workshirt, a corncob pipe, a yellow straw hat. He carried an earthen jug and a flintlock musket. He stopped, appeared confused, yawned, and scratched.

"He's not even acting!" a student called.

The audience laughed, and Pinky blinked into the light. He pretended he didn't understand where he was. Puzzled, he turned in a full circle. Again he scratched and yawned. He tipped the jug to his mouth. He clutched his throat, staggered, and belched.

Done by anybody the act was pure corn, and performed by Pinky it had even less of a chance. The audience hooted and stomped the floor.

"Use the hook!" students shouted.

Pinky tensed, bent his knees, and lifted his eyes as if something circled in the heavens. He set the jug at his feet in order to aim the musket. He faked recoil, which drove him backwards across the stage. A string of hotdogs fell from the sky.

Boos, moans, whistles. "Take him off!" they shouted. Wylie sank in his seat. He didn't want anyone thinking he was connected with Pinky's miserable presentation.

Pinky acted the drunken lout. He'd swig from his jug and tilt across the stage. Gawking, he balanced on one foot precariously. He grew sleepy and yawned, his mouth enormous.

"We're the ones being put to sleep!" a voice in the audience called. Shouts of agreement.

Pinky collapsed to the stage floor, where he pulled off his hat and scratched his head. More booing. Acting as if he'd just at that instant become aware of the audience, he grinned. The grin revealed a gap in his upper front teeth created by sticking tar over an incisor. The audience groaned and threw wadded programs at him.

Pinky slowly stretched out. He propped himself on an elbow and crossed his ankles. He mimed further swigs from the jug, smacked his lips, and began searching in his overall pockets.

"Looking for talent!" a voice from the audience shouted.

Pinky scratched, blinked, and acted as if he suddenly remembered. He reached down inside the bib to his shirt pocket and withdrew a harmonica.

"No!" students called. "Not that!" They threw more programs. Somebody heaved a shoe.

Pinky raised the harmonica, licked it, and settled his lips to it. Twice he blew sour chords and grinned. A cushion very nearly hit him. Mr. Sip stood and looked stern.

Pinky again fitted the harmonica to his mouth. Out came the long, low steam whistle of a C&O coal drag chugging alongside the river and through the Kanawha Valley late at night. It was a sound Wylie had heard many times lying in his bed at home. The big iron locomotive was straining up the grade, its wheels slipping on the rails. As the engine moved closer, it struck sparks and hissed steam. At last the engine topped the grade and picked up ponderous, lurching speed.

The audience wasn't persuaded but stilled. Pinky's hands flapped around the harmonica. His cheeks puffed. The great engine came on faster. Its whistle shrilled at crossings. Pistons pumped and glistened. Fire flared from the stack.

Pinky brought that locomotive right into the auditorium and sent it hurtling among the audience. The whistle howled and moaned, the steam shot hot around students, and they smelled the fiery, bitter coal smoke. That train was flying right at them, and they wanted to duck. It was highballing, bound for glory to the flatlands of Virginia, to Norfolk and the sea.

When Pinky finished, he knocked spit from the harmonica into a palm. The audience stirred but with no quick applause. Southwick Auditorium felt as if it had a hole in it, the way a fast train will leave a vacuum behind it. Students were breathless, yet would give Pinky nothing. Only Mr. Sip, the masters, their wives, and a few visitors clapped.

Pinky scratched his head and tipped the jug. This time when he played, it was no barreling, clanging, fire-spouting locomotive, no torturing of the harmonica, but a simple mountain ballad known by coal miners as "Jenny Gal." The tune was slow and somber, in a minor key, a plaint, a tale of love and loss, a lament for the good gone bad.

Pinky was no longer the hillbilly caricature, the gap-toothed, outhouse fool. In time to his music, he stood with slow dignity, a man rising out of pleasure into suffering.

He sang without accompaniment, his boyish tenor innocent and sincere:

> First time I saw my Jenny Gal
> She was skipping through the grass.
> Last time I saw my Jenny Gal,
> A black hearse drove her past.

75

The ballad was sentimental, maudlin, a Saturday-night-coal-miner-beer-drinking-roadhouse song, but Pinky was so straight, so believing of it himself, that he caught the audience, even the Anglicized masters, all touched by a youth's sorrow at the loss of his first and only true love.

> Oh Jenny, Jenny, Jenny Gal
> Come back, come back to me.
> Oh Jenny, Jenny, Jenny Gal,
> I have need of thee.

When Pinky stopped singing, he played a last chorus on his harmonica. He did it softly, like a distant train whistle heard by a hobo in the cold dark woods, and the audience leaned to him to listen. The final note of the refrain drifted through the auditorium as if smoke from a dying, lonely fire.

There was silence. Pinky lowered his hands and looked out over the audience. Nobody moved. Breathing had been removed from the earth. Pinky continued to stand. He could've been by himself, alone along some coal camp's cindered tracks.

The St. Catherine's girl who'd thrown Wylie the rose was first to clap. She ignited applause. People rose from their seats. Students cheered, stomped the floor, and whistled. As lights switched on, programs were tossed into the air.

Pinky won the laurel. The fifth-form class president's girl crowned him and kissed his cheek. She kissed Wylie too, though being in second place he was awarded no prize.

After the Gala party in the auditorium's streamer-decorated lobby, Wylie walked through the darkness to Lafayette Hall and his room. Pinky hadn't stayed at the party more than a few minutes, had drunk not even a cup of the watery pineapple punch. Stripped to his shorts, he sat at his desk translating one of Virgil's least difficult eclogues. The laurel wreath lay not on his shelf or dresser but had been dropped into the green metal wastebasket.

"Why?" Wylie asked as he lifted the wreath and smoothed its leaves.

"Vanity," Pinky said.

"Explain please."

"All is vanity."

20

During the summer Wylie, Blue Bales, and London Airy flew to England on TWA, supposedly to further their studies. Mr. Winslow Hefferman, shingled, shaky professor of history at White Oak, was their guide, instructor, and chaperon.

Mr. Hefferman loved cathedrals. He would've lived in a cathedral if it provided bed and board. He marched them through the tinted light of stone cool naves and stood them under the gloomy groin vault of transepts. In his dry, scratchy voice he lectured them on the deaths of saints and the symbology of stained-glass windows.

He was a sickly man easily tired. Nights he went to bed as soon as he'd eaten. Wylie, Blue, and London slipped out of their hotels for beer and the generous English girls.

"It's so easy over here," Blue said. "God, the way we work for it at home."

"Ransom your life is all," Wylie said, which wasn't true. Bebe had required only opportunity and safety.

"Maudie likes it standing up," London said and giggled. Maudie was a shopgirl he'd met in Hyde Park.

"You lie!" Blue said. "She's taller than you. Mechanically and scientifically impossible!"

"Hope to die," London said, still giggling.

"You'd lie in church on Sunday," Blue said, agitated by his picture of vertical screwing.

Twice a week Wylie wrote a letter to his parents. He mailed postcards to his friends, especially the girls. He considered sending Pinky one with a picture of St. Paul's. Pinky, a Chosen of God, would probably think the great cathedral a pagan temple. Wylie imagined the postcard's reception at $1419\frac{1}{2}$ Bethel Road.

Like Blue and London, Wylie wanted to escape Mr. Hefferman for a sneak trip to Paris. They found their chance when their teacher's stomach struck him with the galloping trots. Mr. Hefferman lay shaking in his hotel bed, the sheet pulled to the tip of his gray scraggy chin.

Blue made up the story that he'd promised his father to go to Edinburgh and visit the cemetery where many of his ancestors lay buried. Blue said it was a family duty.

"I don't suppose you can get in any great trouble in Edinburgh," Mr. Hefferman conceded, squirming under the sheet. "I'll make a list of places you should visit, and we'll have a little quiz on your return."

Wylie, Blue, and London rode the Folkestone-Boulogne boat train and were in Paris by eight that night. They taxied straight to the cafés of St. Germain. London spoke the best French, using it with broad gestures. They were soused in no time.

A snotty waiter at the Deux Magots refused them anything more to drink. They took a cab to the red glitter of Pigalle, where Wylie ended up in the perfumed bed of a lacquered, vampirelike brunette named Theresa.

"You do me pretty good, Joe," she said.

"I thought you were doing me."

"We do each other okay."

She and Wylie drank white wine while he dressed in the first light of another day. Though he paid her before they undressed, she tried to get more money. He returned to St. Germain and strolled about till the Flore opened and he could order a healing beer. The July morning was dusty and hot. He tasted a vomit flake and smelled Theresa's greasy perfume on himself. As he drank, he fought nausea.

When Blue appeared among the promenaders, he was so tired he walked with his legs spread. His usually groomed bleached brown hair was ragged. Of the three, only he needed to shave daily. As if the earth heaved, he held to a café chair to steady himself before sitting. His brown eyes were out of line.

"I'm near my end time," he said. "Just ship my body home." He ordered beer and looked dazed. "No, it couldn't have happened. No, no girl would do that. It had to be a dream."

Moving from café to café along the boulevard, they watched for London. By early evening he still hadn't shown. Wylie and Blue were so hungry, weary, and drunk, they swayed in the wicker chairs. Waiters eyed them with Gallic superiority.

"Tell you what, you find us a room, and I'll wait for London," Wylie said.

"Can't. I'm paralyzed by a mysterious malady."

" 'kay, I'll go," Wylie said but didn't move.

"Just ship my body home and tell my parents I gave my life for my country in the trenches of love," Blue said and closed his eyes.

When Wylie stood, he staggered against a table where three American girls sat and knocked over their drinks. He apologized in the French manner with great formality and bowing. They laughed and steadied him as he sank to a chair.

"You going to be sick?" they asked.

Wylie tipped off his chair. The girls, who were Wellesley students, helped him up. They sat him in the chair, Again, slowly, he toppled. They caught him.

"Just send my body home," Blue said, slumping.

The girls waved down a cab and took Wylie and Blue to their hotel, named the Hibou on the Rue de Martyrs. Blue tried to feel up the girls. Being older, they laughed and babied him.

"Imagine him at twenty," they said of Blue as they slapped his hands.

The girls had trouble with their concierge till money passed. In the dusky room they let Wylie and Blue fold to the floor for sleep. Later, after the girls went out to eat dinner and came back, Blue tried to crawl into bed.

"Is there such a thing as reverse statutory rape?" a girl asked, pushing him off. He bumped to the floor and lay face downward.

When Wylie woke with a shaft of sunlight hitting his face, he seemed to be looking through jagged glass. It was nine o'clock, and the girls had gone. His head beat like a heart, his stomach fluttered, and spittle had caked around his mouth. He worked himself from the floor to an unmade bed, which had a musty green coverlet. He tasted the foul white wine he'd drunk with Theresa. He tasted her.

"Just send my remains home," Blue said when Wylie woke him. Blue still lay face down on the bare floor. He held to a brassiere.

Wylie peed in the bidet, washed, and walked gently down the hotel steps to the desk in order not to jar his head. The concierge, a tall, dark man with the carriage of a general, muttered and rattled his keys. He knew nothing of London and did not offer to open the door for Wylie, who took a cab to the Deux Magots, where he questioned American tourists.

"Milk-skinned, golden hair, blue eyes?" a Harvard man holding a Pernod asked. "Sounds as if he belongs on a cathedral ceiling."

Wylie ordered hot tea and drank it like an Englishman. Mr. Sip would've been proud. He watched the promenading across the stripes of shade cast by listless chestnut trees. He listened to street performers sing and play their instruments. He thought about the vicious French underworld, a slit throat, and London floating face down in some stinking sewer. Wylie would wait another hour before going to the police.

A funeral procession approached, the shambling mourners carrying the wooden coffin, flowers, and a colored banner of the Virgin Mary. She looked young and pretty enough to date.

When the procession crossed the boulevard to L'Eglise de St. Germain, there was a stir. People rose from their café chairs to see. Wylie believed among the clamor he heard a certain voice. He stood, left money on the table, and scuttled among traffic to the church.

Frenchmen were aggrieved. They circled London, who giggled and held a rose in his pretty teeth. A soutaned priest railed and shook a finger under London's nose. Wylie gathered from the excited speech that London had been sleeping with arms crossed like a corpse under an altar cloth in the sacristy.

"*Sacrilège!*" the priest cried.

"Ready to die, I've done it all," London said, weaving. His seersuckers were soiled, he had bite marks on his neck. He continued to giggle but kept the rose in his teeth.

Wylie bowed and apologized, at the same time edging London away from the outraged crowd. London tried to bow and apologize. He wanted to present the rose to the aged fuming priest. The priest gaped, veins in his reddened face wiggling. Wylie seized the rose and stuffed it into a pants pocket.

He freed London, yet had to hold him up. Rumpled London was humming a French ditty. He tripped over a curb, sprawled, and Wylie stumbled over him. Wylie got them up. Down the street he saw the priest, mourners, and a gendarme all talking and gesticulating. The banner of the pretty Virgin Mary quaked with anger.

Wylie pulled London into a run. London was still humming the ditty. Wylie heard the gendarme's shrill whistle. He and London ran till they wheezed and staggered. London was sinking. Wylie spied a bistro named Le Philosophe. He steered London inside, where they sat at a rear table. He held London in his chair.

Wylie ordered them each coffee, and they stayed twenty minutes. No police or crowds rushed past. Wylie got a taxi to take him and London back to the Hibou. The concierge wouldn't allow them in the hotel. The *américain terrible,* he meant Blue, had left. The girls too. The concierge was extremely upset and stood in the doorway flapping his arms as if he would fly.

Wylie and London searched for Blue. They stopped strangers on the street to ask. "Où est Blue Bales, l'américain perdu?" London cried. In a graveled park near a dry fountain London wanted to sleep on a green wooden bench. Wylie pulled him on till they reached the wicked, wicked Seine, where they sat on stone steps down to the river. London drew up his knees and dozed like a child.

"Not three Yalies, I can't handle three!" he called out.

"Do what?" Wylie asked.

"Lucky Pierre," London muttered.

On the sleek dark water of the Seine, a barge floated past, its engine *tranquille.* Wylie too was sleepy. They had to find Blue and hurry back to England, but he could close his eyes a minute.

When he roused, twilight like fine gray silk lay over them. A boat with colored lights and accordion music slid past. Wylie and London were leaned together. London still slept. At the top of the steps a bearded street cleaner who wore a long leather apron and held a witch's boom looked down at them.

"Cockadoodledoo!" he called and laughed.

Wylie shook London. London tried to bury his face in Wylie's chest.

"I'll never sin again," London said.

"We'll be kicked out of White Oak."

"I demand last rites."

Wylie stood him, and they tottered up the steps to the street, where they rested against the quai till able to hail a cab. They returned to St. Germain and the Flore. Instead of beer they ordered coffee and aspirin. As Wylie was swallowing tablets, he saw Blue. Blue's khakis were wrinkled and dirty, his tie gone. He limped to the table.

"What's wrong with your leg?" Wylie asked.

"Christ, I don't know. I think somebody beat me up."

"Oh do it again!" London said.

"We can tell Hefferman we missed our train, but we need to clean up," Wylie said. "Think the Wellesley girls will take us back?"

"The hotel threw them out," Blue said. "They brought some sailors home, and the Hibou's very moral. Don't they know they're French?"

Wylie, London, and Blue walked till they found a hotel named Le Romain near the golden statue of Jeanne d'Arc. They had to pay in advance, and London was so tired they led him as if he were blind. The three of them dropped crosswise onto the lumpy Victorian bed.

They slept the whole night, Wylie without even taking off his socks. London rang for the femme de chambre to draw him a bath. She was a miniature brunette Blue winked at and leered after. She scooted laughing away from him. They shaved, sponged their clothes, and counted their money. Blue's was gone.

"I think I was robbed by two girls and a pimp," he said.

When they went out for breakfast, the decided to have a beer apiece to settle their stomachs. Then they drank two, three. Like the day, Wylie began to feel warm and sunny.

"It's barely possible I might live," London said.

"Though we might be diseased," Blue said.

"What?" London asked.

"Did you use protection?" Blue asked. "It is France."

"Mine was clean," Wylie said.

"I suppose you can see a spirochete with your naked eye," Blue said.

"I don't like this conversation," London said.

"Maybe it's not too late to do something," Wylie said.

"By now the old spirochetes are drilling into our epithelial tissue," Blue said.

"I repeat, I do not like this conversation," London said.

"We could have it and not know it," Blue said. "Go along for years, the French spirochetes, the worst kind, eating away in our brains. End up like Al Capone. The brain becomes oatmeal—cooked oatmeal."

Wylie understood Blue was talking to work on London.

"Go blind?" London asked, sitting straight now.

"My parents would disown me for paresis," Blue said.

"Our hair'll fall out," Wylie said and touched his. London raised a hand to his own.

"Won't be able to control our bowels," Blue said.

"God, what do we do?" London asked, his eyes shimmering tearfully.

"I'd never trust a French doctor," Blue said. "Either of you feel a burning sensation?"

"I think I might," London said, squirming.

"One thing could help," Blue said. "Alcohol poured straight down the old tube. Anybody got alcohol?"

"I have shaving lotion," Wylie said.

"Better than nothing in an emergency," Blue said.

"Shaving lotion, you're talking about shaving lotion?" London asked. His face turned from Wylie to Blue and back.

"What sort?" Blue asked.

"Aqua Velva," Wylie said.

"Hey, we're lucky, that's the best," Blue said. "High alcohol content."

They hurried to their room in Le Romain, where Wylie unzipped the leather kit he carried inside his overnight bag.

"Let me doctor myself first," Blue said and took the Aqua Velva down the corridor to the bathroom.

"Oh God, oatmeal," London said. "You think it's likely we caught something?"

"Paris practically invented syphilis," Wylie said.

London moaned and kept washing his hands. Blue came back smelling of Aqua Velva. Wylie took the bottle.

"Does it hurt?" he asked.

"The more it burns, the better," Blue said. "Shows it's working. Pour a whole bunch right down the old tube."

"Save plenty for me!" London called.

In the bathroom Wylie patted Aqua Velva on his face so that London would smell it and believe it'd been used elsewhere. London waited in the corridor just outside the door. He snatched the bottle from Wylie's hand.

As soon as London closed the door, Wylie and Blue smothered laughter and made congratulatory jabs at each other. They eyed the door. They heard thumping around in the bathroom. When London came out, he was dancing. His mouth shaped to a silent howl. He kept his legs spread and skipped about stiffly.

Back in the room he zipped open his fly and fanned his cod.

"I'm on fire!" he wailed.

"Proves it's effective," Blue said. "Think how the old spirochete feels."

When they left the hotel, London carried the bottle of Aqua Velva in his jacket pocket. At each café where they stopped, he rushed to the *toilette*. He'd return to the table, near weeping. He leaped and spun on the sidewalk. People stared and curved away. He walked like a cowboy who'd been all day in the saddle.

"Anything so hot's bound to help," Blue kept telling him.

They took an afternoon train from the Gare de l'Ouest. London was still dousing himself with Aqua Velva. Too ablaze to sit, he paced the aisles as if pursued.

Blue and Wylie worried about Mr. Hefferman and the quiz he'd promised to give them. At Calais, Wylie bought from a station vendor a travel book about Scotland. They studied it on the boat. London, trying to learn, hopped from foot to foot. He was so strongly scented everybody sniffed at him.

Mr. Hefferman was nearly hysterical with worry about them. Wearing a long nightshirt like a character out of Dickens, he perched his scrawny body on the edge of his bed and told them he'd been about to notify the American embassy.

They calmed him, Blue making up a story about a train derailment and the time it took to clear the tracks. Mr. Hefferman was suspicious and asked first about the Picts. An ancient, dark-complexioned people who once inhabited the whole of Great Britain, they told him, an answer from the travel book.

"I confess I was almost out of my mind with anxiety that I allowed you to go unescorted," Mr. Hefferman said, pleased by their answers and at last softening. "Obviously you applied yourselves with the exception of Master Airy, who can't seem to stand still and appears to have his mind on other things."

"Oh he applied himself, sir," Blue said. "He applied himself even more than Wylie and me."

"He really poured it on," Wylie said.

"Did you just shave, all that sweetish odor?" Mr. Hefferman asked London. Mr. Hefferman's nose pulled in as if he would peck.

"Yes, sir, freshened up just minutes ago," London said. "Would you please excuse me a second?"

He made another run to the john with the nearly empty bottle of Aqua Velva.

21

By summer's end Mr. Hefferman lugged around a heavy briefcase full of notes on cathedrals. He acted as if those notes were a treasure which might be stolen. During the flight to New York, he held the strapped briefcase across his lap.

Mr. Hefferman flew from New York to Richmond while Blue, London, and Wylie took the train back to West Virginia. London was sullen because of the Aqua Velva trick. Their parents met them at the river depot and sniffed at London. As Wylie drove with his mother and father into the valley's haze, sunshine thinned, and chemical odors stung his nose. The acidic smell was good—the scent of home.

Home had changed, for instead of going to the old house on Kanawha Boulevard, Wylie and his parents crossed the recently completed downtown bridge and drove up the hill to their new place. Again sunshine expanded. The house, not having had time to season, appeared as ostentatious as new shoes. Shrubs had been planted, grass sown, yet raw red soil lay just beyond slate flagstones.

Wylie's furniture from the old house didn't look the same within the freshly plastered walls. His room lacked the shaded, cavernlike spaciousness. He gazed through a green corridor of trees toward the smoky valley. He saw only one small tip of a smokestack and could hear neither steamboats nor coal drags.

His mother still directed Ed in the moving of furniture. She wore her yellow coolie clothes and hat. Wylie's father had retreated down to his office in the valley.

"We've only just gotten in," Wylie's mother explained. "All the pieces haven't been brought up. We own so much, yet I can't let go."

When Wylie's father drove home at five, he showered and joined her under the red-and-white-striped terrace umbrella for their gin fizzes. They questioned Wylie about England. He had gifts—an antique brass fire shovel for his mother, a silver daggerlike letter opener for his father. His parents were pleased, yet distracted.

The old house worried them, and they were still discussing what to do with it. The realtor had received an offer from four doctors who intended to open an eye-ear-nose clinic.

"They're eager to throw their new money at me," Wylie's father said.

"They'll cut up the rooms," the mother said. "They'll build plywood cubicles which smell of disinfectants."

"The State of West Virginia has also made enquiries," Wylie's father said. "The Bureau of Mines needs space."

"Our house to be filled with plodding, begrimed coal miners," the mother said. "I can't stand the thought!"

She and Wylie's father finally agreed the house should go to the doctors. They were young, only a few years out of medical school, but already earning significant money and playing golf at the Pinnacle Rock Club.

Wylie drove his mother down into the valley for a last look at the old house. Hand in hand they walked through the cool, deep rooms, which stripped of furniture appeared naked and shamed, like the disrobing of a noble matron. The stained-glass window of Jesus the shepherd had been removed and taken up the hill to be stored in the basement of the new house. Wylie's mother wept quietly into her white monogrammed handkerchief.

"So many memories," she said. "So much life has been lived down here."

She wanted to see her flower garden, and they crossed a lawn that needed mowing. She knelt to pull weeds from the blooming verbena. Wylie saw somebody dismantling the birdbath. It was Pinky, who during the summer had been working as usual at Elk Land and Lumber. Wylie excused himself from his mother to walk to Pinky.

He had allowed his red hair to grow and was taller, though still shorter than Wylie. He wore overalls and a White Oak baseball cap. He'd come with a pickup to load the birdbath for its trip to the new house.

Wylie helped lift the birdbath onto the truck, which gave under the weight of stone.

"Have a big summer?" Wylie asked.

"Sure, I sailed my diesel yacht through the Panama Canal and sojourned in Hawaii."

"Pinky, envy is a sin."

Pinky glared, spat, and lifted a metal lawn chair onto the truck. Wylie started to help.

86

"I can do them," Pinky said. "Build up my muscles. Keep me from becoming soft like you."

"I built up my muscle on the mademoiselles."

"I'm not listening."

"How's Sis?"

He blushed, and nobody turned redder than Pinky. Sis must, Wylie thought, be doing something interesting to him.

"Well, you all keep it clean," Wylie said.

"You're a great one to talk about cleanness."

"Look at me, I had a shower just this morning."

"You wash your filthy mind?"

"I see your disposition hasn't changed over the summer."

"Why change perfection?"

Wylie laughed, but Pinky didn't even smile. Wylie set back on the grass the lawn chair he'd been about to load on the truck and walked to the garden, where his mother stood motionless, her head bowed, the curve of her like a religious statue among the shedding blooms.

22

Pinky returned to White Oak and during their senior year became a twinkle-toed scatback on the football team, while Wylie climbed the ladder to the number-three rung on the tennis squad. Wylie's grades were also rising, largely the result of again rooming with the industrious redheaded ridge runner. There wasn't much else to do but hit the books. Wylie slacked off before somebody accused him of being a grub.

He and Pinky lived an armistice till late October when Wylie's watch was stolen—a stainless steel, waterproof, shockproof, self-winding Omega. Wylie returned to Lafayette from York, undressed, and, wearing his towel, loped downstairs to shower. He left his watch on his dresser.

Pinky was stained and weary from football practice. His helmet always twisted his red hair into sweaty spikes. Sore and sighing, he'd flopped on his bed, where he pulled up his undershirt to scratch his stomach.

Wylie didn't discover the watch was gone till time to cross to the Commons for dinner. He thought he must've laid the Omega somewhere other than his dresser and looked on his desk, his bed, and in his tennis shorts.

When Pinky came up from his shower, they both searched. Finally they stood in the center of the room and eyed each other.

"Better report it to Mr. Sip," Pinky said.

First he and Pinky retraced his steps to the gym and looked around the tennis courts. Wylie didn't go to Mr. Sip's study till after vespers. When Wylie knocked and entered, Mr. Sip wore a ratty brown bathrobe but still had on black shoes, gray trousers, and a white shirt. Mr. Sip was reading his Greek New Testament. He finished the chapter before closing the book, his thin, ascetic hand raised to prevent Wylie from speaking. Mr. Sip then placed the New Testament in a desk drawer, leaned back, and pushed his glasses to his forehead, the signal that Wylie was permitted to state his business.

At news of the watch disappearance, Mr. Sip's mouth drew in to a tiny O, and he pulled at his nose as if to detach it. His forehead wiggled so forcefully that his glasses fell into position of their own weight.

"When and where are you absolutely certain you last saw your watch?" he asked. "Please be precise."

As best he could Wylie answered the questions shot at him peevishly. Mr. Sip closed his eyes, peaked his fingers beneath his shiny chin, and mused as if he'd forgotten Wylie.

"We'll go to your quarters," he said.

He took off his bathrobe and put on his tie and jacket. In Wylie's room he searched, muttered, and questioned while Pinky stood at the closed door. Mr. Sip turned to him.

"You've seen the watch?" he asked.

"Plenty of times but not this afternoon."

"Wylie still believes it was on his dresser when he left to shower."

"If it was, I didn't notice," Pinky said.

"'Were' not 'was,'" Mr. Sip corrected him. "Conditional uncertainty requires the subjunctive as you ought to know. You left for your shower before Wylie returned from his?"

"I saw him down there under the water."

"We'll keep this among ourselves," Mr. Sip said.

There'd been stealing around White Oak, mostly money, clothes

88

now and then, and another watch besides Wylie's. He wasn't greatly upset. His father would have insurance to cover the loss.

Mr. Sip set a trap. He arranged for "Cheese" Chapman, the smiling student-body president, to leave small amounts of cash around the dorms. Serial numbers of bills were listed. On the third day the Honor Court tried a thief.

The boy's name was Adam Paxberry. His father owned an Oldsmobile-Cadillac agency in Ohio. Paxberry had other loot hidden in his room: pens, rings, knives. He didn't have Wylie's watch and denied to the Honor Court ever seeing it.

"He could've sold it in Charlottesville," Blue said.

Paxberry was dismissed, and stealing stopped. Wylie's father sent him a new Omega. Paxberry's father made him sign up for the Army.

On a dark November morning Wylie woke with light in his face—the room's unshaded ceiling bulb. He looked at his new watch. It wasn't yet five-thirty. He squinted at the window where rain tapped the panes. Pinky sat in a chair and stared at his feet.

"It was me," he said.

"It was you what?" Wylie asked. As he sat up, he felt the room's coldness and shivered. Heat didn't come into the radiator till six. Yet Pinky wore only his white underwear shorts.

"The watch."

"What about the watch?"

"You got a B in English. You ought to at least be able to understand the language."

He stood and crossed barefooted to the fireplace used before steam heat had been installed in Lafayette. He lowered himself to one knee, worked loose a brick under the closed flue, and stuck two fingers into a dark cache. He drew out the shiny Omega.

"You took my watch," Wylie said, still sitting in bed.

"No kidding, how'd you ever figure it out? You're a real authentic genius."

"But you took my goddamn watch!"

"I'm also giving it back, so shut your dirty mouth."

He tossed the watch to Wylie, sat on the chair, and again stared at his feet.

"Why?" Wylie asked, bewildered.

"I don't know why. You all are doing something to me."

"We all?"

"You, your mother and father, White Oak."

"Let me see if I understand this. You're blaming stealing the watch on us?"

"You're changing me."

"We never made you steal."

"You made me want. You make me covet. I was fixing to shower, and there was that Omega shining like silver on your dresser. I wanted it so bad my stomach knotted up. I took it like I'd been stealing all my life and lied slick as a snake."

Hands dangling between his thighs, he shook his head in disbelief. Wylie examined the watch. It was okay.

"I can't see you doing it," Wylie said.

"You think I can see me doing it? I been wanting to jump out a window ever since."

Wylie looked at the watches, the one tossed to him and the one he wore, identical except the original had less gloss and scratches across the crystal.

"What am I supposed to do with two watches?" he asked.

"I don't care. Wear them through your nose."

"How come you're so mad? I should be the one who's mad."

"Then get mad and I'll play bongo on your head!"

He stood ready to fight, his fuzzy arms swinging, his reddish brown eyes bugged, his outswept chin pushed forward. Wylie wasn't afraid, yet he'd never in his lifetime whip Pinky angry, especially when he wasn't himself. In a way he was even pleased. The great moral Pinky had at last revealed an imperfection.

"What am I supposed to do?" Wylie asked again, looking at the watches.

"Tell Mr. Sip. Have me kicked out of White Oak. I don't care. I been thinking of joining up for the fight in Korea anyhow."

Wylie scratched an ear and considered. "Why not have a watch instead?" he asked and handed Pinky the stolen Omega.

Rather than being relieved, Pinky became angrier. His face darkened with blood. He snatched the watch, raised it above his head, and slammed it down against the black, petrified floorboards of the old dorm. He stomped the watch. The Omega was a tough Swiss timepiece, and his bare heel couldn't penetrate the steel casing. He snatched the watch up and flung it against the wall. Still ticking, it lay on its side. He kicked it under Wylie's bed.

"What you going to do now?" he asked, really berserk—puffing, blowing, his skin aflame, fingers clenching as if committing murder.

The door opened, and it was William "Well" Dunn, the pajamaed hall proctor, whose face was misshapened from sleep.

"You toads trying to tear down the dorm?" he asked.

"Killing bugs," Wylie said.

"What are they, big as elephants?" Well asked, looking about suspiciously. "You guys knock it off or your names go to Mr. Sip."

Well switched out the lights and left. They lay on their beds. Wylie listened to Pinky's hard breathing.

"You probably think it's in my genes or something," Pinky said finally. Was he near crying? Wylie wasn't certain.

At daylight while Pinky went to brush his teeth, Wylie knelt under the bed for the stolen Omega. He buried it that afternoon in the field beside the tennis courts. Pinky never asked about the watch, and Wylie never told him.

23

The last months at White Oak dawned rare and mellow—a languid sunshine time. Virginia springs were voluptuous, the blooming Judas trees spreading through shadowed woods like purple flames. Students' bodies gleamed white, and, stripped to shorts, spread themselves on blankets laid across the sheening grass.

Most talk was of colleges and girls. Wylie didn't have to do any big decision making. His father would be pleased for him to go to Washington and Lee, which is where he wanted to enroll anyhow. He liked the picture of himself strolling in seersucker and white bucks among General Lee's southern colonnades.

"You could send an application to Harvard," Wylie's father said. "Your grades approach the respectable, and we have Boston connections."

The connection was between the Corbin interests and Elk Land and Lumber. During Wylie's grandfather's day, old Mr. Corbin used to come south once a year on his private railway car. To serve him in that plush green interior, he employed two black servants, a white cook, and a white Irish guard. The C&O parked the private car on a siding across the river from Wylie's parents' house.

Mr. Corbin once allowed Wylie to ride as far as White Sulphur Springs. From his pocket he gave Wylie bitter unwrapped lemon hard candies which sometimes had lint clinging to them. He didn't act rich and appeared underfed. He attended St. Stephen's with Wylie's grandfather, yet never dropped more than fifty cents in the brass collection plate. His favorite saying was "You take care of your business, and your business will take care of you."

"I'd hate to leave Virginia," Wylie told his father. "Even if I were the greatest brain in the world."

"I know," his father said and smiled. "It happened to me too after White Oak. In Virginia I always felt I was at the true center of the best life."

It was strange, they were both West Virginians by birth, yet had a greater loyalty to the mother state and her traditions.

"Just more rich snot attitude," Pinky said when he heard Wylie explaining his vision of mansions under ancient oaks beside broad tidal rivers. "Your money comes from West Virginia, you ought to be loyal to her."

Till Pinky spoke the word, Wylie never thought of West Virginia as being a "her." The state was more masculine, more "him." If it were indeed female, Wylie figured, the state had to be a bit of a slattern.

Pinky was talking Navy and interrupted his studies to argue the idea.

"I sign up and learn something useful, maybe electronics," he said.

"Pinky, the Navy doesn't need you, Korea doesn't need you, and you have a scholarship offer."

The scholarship at West Virginia University had been awarded not because of his grades but on account of his unerring glove at shortstop.

"What do you care?" he asked, still sullen about the watch.

"I hate to see anybody, even you, be dumb."

"The money's not that much," he said. "I'll have to find more."

"What about all the greenies you worked for and socked in the bank?" Wylie asked.

92

Pinky shook his head. Maybe the money went to his fanatical mother or alcoholic father, or to the Chosen of God Tabernacle.

"I'd like to travel a couple of years," he said. "I don't know anything about the world and never even seen the Atlantic Ocean. The biggest body of water I've laid eyes on is the upper reaches of the Kanawha River."

During a lazy spring evening when earth scents floated about and time slowed to the beat of the heart, London, Blue, and Wylie lounged smoking illegally in the dusk at the rear of Lafayette.

"Pinky's never been bombed," London remarked. He lay on his back, his hands under his golden head. "Can you imagine an eighteen-year-old of sound mind and body who's never been bombed?"

"I don't think he's ever been laid either," Blue said.

"Don't be too sure," Wylie said, thinking of Sis Asters.

"I'm telling you he hasn't," Blue said. "I can detect it. He's got virgin all over him—like a priest."

"But never to have known the soaring glory of drunkenness!" London said. At fourteen he'd swiped a fifth of his father's Haig & Haig and passed out in the boys' locker room at the Pinnacle Rock Club. First drunkenness had been a ritual—like confirmation.

"Not everybody tries to drink the creek dry," Blue said.

"Listen, you pull your long nose out of the jar only long enough to breathe," London answered.

"True, but I never claimed to be pristine."

"Pristine! Ring the bell, he's learned a two-syllable word!" London said.

They smoked and considered. Leaves of a white oak rustled over them and hooded the sky and stars. London stretched his arms across the grass as if he would embrace the world. Blue blew smoke and humped it.

"Practicing to ring my cod," he said. "It feels so good!"

"Pervert," London said.

Blue suddenly sat up, causing London, who believed he was under attack, to squeal.

"I've seen the light!" Blue said. "Suppose we trick Pinky into drinking and send him spinning."

"He has a nose for sin," London said.

"Buy us some grain alcohol like we used to slip into the punch bowl at Miss Charlene Fossinger's School of Ballroom Dance," Blue said. "After a cup, those prissy little girls would rub it against you like minks."

"What an awful imagine," London said. "Minks bite."

"Maybe slip the shine into Pinky's orange juice," Wylie said.

Pinky kept a quart bottle of juice on his window ledge. He didn't allow himself candy and Cokes like ordinary people. He'd open the window, screw the top from his bottle, and drink in long, deep drafts.

"Takes just a dab," Blue said. "He's a virgin on firewater too, and a mere ounce ought to ignite his rocket."

"Another vulgar mixing of metaphors," London said.

"Who'll do it?" Wylie asked. "If Pinky finds out, he'd kill."

"We flip a coin," Blue said. "The thing is how do we get our hands on the grain alcohol?"

"Infirmary," London said. "I know the darky attendant. I'll bribe him to swipe us a bottle while Nurse Armisted's washing her greasy hair."

"Be sure of its quality," Wylie said. "We don't want anybody poisoned."

"Not even Pinky," London said.

"We ought to get him laid too," Blue said. "Long as he's primed, we should do him that favor."

"Maybe a couple of Bernice's girls would drive out and park in the lane," London said. "Properly induced of course."

"My dick," Blue said.

"They'd get lost trying to find it," London said.

"It'll cost at least seventy-five to a hundred greenies," Wylie said. "Anybody here got that kind of money lying around?"

"We can sacrifice," London said. "It's for Pinky's benefit. We owe it to the poor boy. It'll do him a world of good."

"Make him human," Blue said.

There under the darkening oak they plotted. They sneaked through the woods, climbed the school fence, and London telephoned from a Route 29 Amoco station to Bernice, now a shrinking, creased bejeweled crone. She was fond of London. She petted and told him he was witty and cute. She had, she said, known his father.

While London bargained with her over the pay phone, Wylie and

Blue kept watch in case Mr. Sip or one of the masters drove past the station. The price for the girls on weekday evenings would be twenty dollars a go, with an eighty-dollar minimum guarantee. London insisted they be young and white. The girls could use Bernice's Buick. She wanted to charge mileage, but London sweet-talked her out of that.

Slipping six ounces of grain alcohol into Pinky's orange juice that Thursday became a military operation. When they flipped coins, Blue was odd man out. London strolled to the sunny athletic field where the baseball team practiced for Saturday's game. Pinky stood in the batting cage. London waved to Wylie, who waited at the second-story hall window of Lafayette. Wylie whistled to Blue.

Blue tiptoed into the room, slid up the window screen, and reached for the bottle of orange juice, which was full. He carried the bottle to the john, where he poured out six ounces into the measuring beaker he'd borrowed from the chemistry lab. He emptied the beaker into the commode. Like the mad scientist, he tipped the flask of alcohol to the beaker and the beaker to the juice.

"Will it stay mixed?" Wylie asked.

"Some things in this life you have to gamble on," Blue said, shaking the bottle. He set it back on the ledge, positioned it exactly, and closed the window screen.

That evening Pinky was tired from baseball practice and lay on his bed holding a book above his face. Wylie combed his hair. London and Blue sneaked in carrying two grocery sacks full of cold beer.

"Not in this room" Pinky said, sitting up. He held his Virgil as if steering with it. "I'm not getting kicked out because of you degenerates."

"Doesn't the fact that the year's almost finished mean anything to you?" Blue asked.

"Soon we'll go our separate ways, and our lives will never be the same," London said.

London was particularly convincing, his babyishness, his feigned sincerity and innocence. He appeared much younger than eighteen. He was small, neatly formed, a toy golden male that girls believed they could cuddle like a teddy bear till they suddenly discovered a fiend inside their panties.

"Remember these are the best years of our lives," Wylie said.

"If these are the best, we might as well hang it up," Pinky said.

"Now in case you playboys haven't noticed, I'm trying to study for a test."

"You haven't just adored it here at White Oak?" London asked as if shocked.

"I don't count it really living yet," Pinky said.

"How could it be any more life than being among friends, all of us young and about to graduate here in beautiful old Virginia?" London asked.

Pinky, who wore only his white shorts, rubbed his bare feet together and became serious.

"All of this is just getting ready," he said. "It's not real. I want to reach that part of life where things count."

"I understand what you're telling us," Blue said as he opened a beer using a church key. "We all want to go on with living, but I'll always feel grateful for what I got here at White Oak."

"All the good friends, some we'll never see again," Wylie said.

"Terrible things happen out there in life," London said. "The four of us may never be able to sit around like this."

"People even die," Blue said, his foxy face drooping into exaggerated mourning.

"Dying's not the worst thing," Pinky said. "If you believe, dying's nothing at all."

"Believe what?" Blue asked before thinking.

"Let's not be morbid," London said quickly to keep Pinky from preaching one of his sermons. "This is a celebration, the last of the term, the first of life's hurdles cleared. We ought to drink a little toast."

"Pinky doesn't drink," Wylie said.

"You all shouldn't either," Pinky said.

"You don't have to drink suds like us," London said. "Somebody bring him a glass of water. It's the spirit that counts, the civilized gesture."

"Maybe he could drink orange juice," Blue said.

Whether reluctant or suspicious, Pinky looked hard at Blue, but then closed Virgil and swung his feet from the bed.

"It hasn't been all bad," Pinky said and glanced at Wylie. Wylie guessed Pinky was thinking of the Omega.

"We've been through the fire together," Blue said.

"We've forged a bond," London said.

"Okay," Pinky said and stood to raise the window screen and bring in his bottle of orange juice. "What's the toast?" He shook the bottle.

"To us," Blue said. "We're the future, aren't we?"

"And happy memories of White Oak," Wylie said.

"To the battles we've fought with the masters," London said.

"May we all be saved in the end," Pinky said.

"Definitely in the end," London said and kept his face straight.

They drank their beer, and Pinky lifted his bottle to swallow noisily. The Adam's apple bobbed in his clean, rosy throat. He frowned, lowered the juice, and eyed the bottle.

"Tastes funny," he said.

"You can never tell about orange juice," London said. "It's impossible to judge what sort of juice an orange tree will provide."

"Huh?" Pinky said.

"During the season they use lots of amateur squeezers," Wylie said.

"An economic dictate of the labor force," Blue said.

"What you all talking about?" Pinky asked, looking at each of them.

"The chemistry of the soil," London said.

"The amount of rainfall," Wylie said.

"The variety of sunshine," London said.

"How come you guys know so much about orange juice?" Pinky asked.

"I've been considering a science major," Blue said. "Now I'd like to propose another toast." He raised his beer. "To us as individuals."

"Why?" Pinky asked.

"Each of us are important," Blue said.

"Is important," Pinky said.

"Here's to me," London said.

When they drank four individual toasts, Pinky went along but wanted to get back to his Virgil. Wylie, Blue, and London had to keep thinking of new toasts—to the coaches, their wives, to the masters, their wives, to Mr. Sip.

"Let us not forget the business manager," London said.

"Or the cooks," Blue said.

"Or the yard men," Wylie said.

"And the loyal servants who provide us with water," London said.

"Do what?" Pinky asked after drinking. "The water comes from a well."

"A toast to the well diggers," London said. "Wells don't dig themselves, you know."

They watched Pinky grow easier. Usually when he sat, he acted as if a chair or his bed were an affront to his lean body, but now he was soft, at one with his flesh. He began drinking without waiting for a toast. Wylie, London, and Blue glanced at each other.

"You give us something to raise our glasses to," Blue said to Pinky.

"The good folks in the world," Pinky said. "I mean the really good, the people who do things for humanity."

"Surely you don't mean to imply we don't stand for the humane," London said.

"You don't stand for anything except pleasure," Pinky said.

"Actually I typically lie down for my pleasure," London said and giggled.

"Watch it!" Pinky warned, but the warning was more automatic than threatening.

"I stand for my rights," London said. "I also stand for my lefts."

"I stand after sitting," Wylie said.

"I stand for standards," Blue said and saluted.

"You fellows never done anything except play around and go to dances," Pinky said.

"Not everybody can be as purposeful as you," Blue said and looked at his watch.

"I don't blame you but your parents," Pinky said. "Spoiled you." He burped and blinked. "I feel kind of funny."

"Funny?" London asked.

"You're not laughing," Blue said.

"Maybe I'm catching something," Pinky said.

"Get the Aqua Velva!" Blue said, causing puzzlement to Pinky and London to glare.

"There's a bug going around," Wylie said.

"Trouble is you fellows think everything's funny," Pinky said.

"I can tell you forthrightly that I for one don't," London said. "I don't consider White Oak's eggplant casserole at all funny."

"I watch, and you spend most of your time trying to be wits," Pinky said. "You think life is a joke."

"He's got me there," Blue said and opened another beer.

"We're frivolous," Wylie said, nodding.

"No respect for higher truths," Blue said.

"No respect for lower truths either," London said.

"You think life's a porterhouse steak," Pinky said.

"Only if medium rare," London said and Blue snickered.

"See, it's all funny to you," Pinky said. "I try having a serious conversation, but you act as if life's one big circus."

"I definitely don't consider a porterhouse steak funny," London said. "In my time I've known some very serious porterhouse steaks as well as lamb chops."

Pinky, who'd nearly emptied the quart of juice, set the bottle on his desk and lunged toward London. London shrieked, dodged to the door, and ran into the hall. Flight wasn't necessary. Pinky's judgment was flawed. His body not obeying his intent, he tilted left and bumped his dresser.

"What's wrong with me?" Pinky asked and looked down at his legs as if they'd betrayed him.

"You definitely got the bug," Blue said.

"Drink more juice," Wylie said. "Best thing in the world for the bug."

"Drown the bug out of your system," London said.

Pinky held his palm to his forehead. Confused, he walked slowly and carefully back to his bed, where he sat. As he drank from his bottle, Blue checked his wristwatch, eyed London, and jigged his bleached brows.

"Have to see about something," London said from the doorway. He sidled away toward the steps. Pinky stared after him.

"Anybody here ever eaten robin?" Pinky asked abruptly.

"Who's Robin?" Blue asked.

"You going to watch your dirty mouth or not?" Pinky asked, standing, fist clenched.

"I am," Blue said.

"I'm talking about a bird," Pinky said and sat.

"I don't understand the question," Wylie said.

"What question?" Pinky asked.

"About eating robins."

"My whole family's eaten robins," Pinky said.

Wylie and Blue just looked at him.

"During tight times when we lived in Cinder Hollow," Pinky explained. "We ate anything we could chase down."

"Cinder Hollow?" Blue asked.

"We used to play king of the mountain on slag heaps. You never done that either."

"How'd you catch the robins?" Wylie asked.

"We had Italians. Over in Italy they eat songbirds. The Italians carry nets upwind and run down on the birds. Birds have to turn into the wind to take off. We ate robins in a stew with a few potatoes and pinto beans."

"How do they taste?" Blue asked.

"They taste like royal food when you're hungry enough. My mother and I used to climb the mountain behind our house to dig roots. We boilt the roots and called it soup."

They sat soberly and silently. Blue glanced at Wylie. Things weren't going as intended.

"Gentlemen, I have an announcement," Blue said. "This is not a funeral."

"If you never been hungry, you don't know anything about the world," Pinky said.

London came back out of breath. Wylie stood and walked out into the hall with him.

"They there," London whispered. "Two pretty little kitty cats, but they're nervous. We have to move this party quick or they'll leave."

Wylie and London went to the room. Blue was grinning at Pinky, who sat crookedly and blinked as if he didn't recognize anybody. He'd drunk the last of his juice.

"Air's foul in here," Wylie said. "I'm for a walk by the lake."

"Got to finish studying," Pinky said.

"Can't forsake your buddies," Blue protested. "We're one for all, all for one, or at least two for two."

"We stick together," Wylie said.

"We been through the thick and the thin," London said. "Mostly the thin."

They helped Pinky up and supported him as they moved quietly down the steps and out the fire exit. They jogged him toward the golf course. When they let go of Pinky, he ran listing.

"I don't understand what's happening to me," he said.

"Breathe deeply," Blue told him.

"For a bug it feels kind of good," Pinky said.

As they crossed the golf course, he suddenly hooted and did a dance, a sort of frontier hoedown, his bare feet pounding the fairway grass, his arms pumping, his head wagging. Wylie, London, and Blue looked back toward the school's buildings and Mr. Sip's lighted study.

"Bug feels so good I can't help dancing," Pinky said.

"Don't yell," Wylie whispered.

"Feet won't stay still," Pinky said. He flung himself into the pearly air. Laughing, he ran toward the lake.

Wylie, London, and Blue hurried after him to shush him. Pinky tripped over his own feet, fell, but was up again. He stopped at the dark water's edge. He intended to jump into the moon's reflection. They grabbed him.

"A person with the bug should never get wet," London said.

"All the medical books agree," Wylie said.

"Cause very serious complications," Blue said. "Ass might fall off."

"Sure nuff?" Pinky asked, serious.

"Excuse me," London whispered and started uphill.

"Excuse you for what?" Pinky demanded.

"Answer nature's call."

"Anybody hear nature calling?" Pinky asked and cupped a hand to an ear.

"Sharp sense of humor," London said and jogged away around the water and toward the wood's blackness.

"Beautiful night," Blue said, opening a beer. He'd brought a sack. "Wish I had a girl."

Pinky raised his face to look at the night. Grass, water, trees were luminous under the moon. Arms outspread, Pinky spun. He ran sprints around the motionless flag of the seventh green. He stumbled, collapsed, and rolled. He lay laughing on his back.

"God's dust," he said.

"What?" Blue asked, shielding a match to light a cigarette.

"His dandruff," Pinky said. "When God nods, stars fall out of His hair."

"You make that up?" Wylie asked.

"Sure."

"Maybe God should use Vitalis," Blue said.

"You trying to be smart?" Pinky asked, lifting his head.

"I never learned in Sunday school about God having dandruff," Blue said.

"The constellations are the flash of His eyes," Pinky said.

"That's better, more poetic," Wylie said as he lay beside Pinky on the green.

"The oceans are His finger bowls," Pinky said, turning on his side to face Wylie. "Listen, that was a good thing you and your folks did to keep me from feeling bad."

"What'd they do?" Blue asked and looked toward the woods.

"A little private business between—among—Wylie, his parents, and me. I didn't know there was such things as finger bowls when I ate at his house. The first time I read about them, I thought they were dishes people served fingers in. I pictured rich people sitting around gnawing on fingers. I wondered whose fingers they chopped off, maybe Chinese. When I fully understood what you and your parents did to keep from embarrassing me, I almost wet my pants. At the same time I loved you—really did love you."

"Somebody let me in on what we're talking about," Blue said.

"Real class is what we're talking about," Pinky said and again flopped to his back to gaze heavenward. "And the solar systems are the sheen of His golden tresses. I love God."

From the woods London came running. He almost tripped over them lying on the green looking at God's dandruff. He gave a little yelp. He had a stitch in his side and held a hand over the pain as he puffed.

"Marvelous thing," he said. "You won't believe what I found beyond the trees yonder. Can't believe it myself. Beautiful girls."

"Not real life girls?" Blue asked, sitting up.

"Two gorgeously ripe peaches, and they're crazy for White Oak boys," London said. "They love all the White Oak boys."

"How grand!" Wylie said.

"They're dying to meet some nice White Oak boys," London said. "They sent me back to find White Oak boys for them."

"You're making this up," Blue said.

"I swear 'fore God to die there's two beautiful girls on the other side of those trees who are panting to meet some nice White Oak boys," London said. "They particularly want to meet Pinky."

"Me? How they know anything about me?"

"They saw you at shortstop against Woodberry," London said. "They begged me to bring you."

"They know class when they see it," Wylie said.

"Naw," Pinky said.

"What you mean naw?" Blue asked. "If you won't go, I will."

"They don't want a poor thing like you," London said to Blue. "They asked me to bring the boy with red hair who had the magic glove."

"Not going," Pinky said. "No really nice girls would be out this time of night in the woods. I know a trick when I see it."

"You can stuff me in a sack and toss me in the pond if I'm not speaking the truth," London said.

"I can do that anyway," Pinky said.

"Just go along and see, for God's sake," Blue said.

"Wouldn't be for God's sake, and it don't ring right," Pinky said.

"Let me go and find out for sure how nice they are," Blue said. He was up and moving off the green.

"Think I'll go and check again myself," London said.

He and Blue ran into darkness while Wylie and Pinky lay back on the spongy green. The croaking of frogs, *jug o' rum*, seemed to come not from the lake but above.

"I feel so crazy," Pinky said. "I feel touched by the Spirit. You ever been touched by the Spirit, Wylie?"

"Lots of times," Wylie said, thinking the spirit of Cutty Sark.

"Glad to hear that. I worry about your inner life. Guess we're both full of it tonight."

"True. Really full of it."

"Don't it make you feel good to know the Creator of the Universe cares for you?"

"Grand," Wylie said. Thoughts of Bernice's girls had brought a protrusion of goodness within his pants. "Just grand."

"Can't tell you how happy it makes me to hear you talk like that," Pinky said. "You're bound to be growing spiritually."

"I can swear to you I'm definitely growing."

"I been praying for you. Been asking God to give you the strength to forsake cards and beer."

"White of you," Wylie said and closed his eyes on the stars as he pictured what London and Blue were doing with those girls in Bernice's Buick.

103

Pinky began to sing, a hymn. He had a good choirboy's tenor, yet with a whining quality which was strictly hillbilly:

> I come to the garden alone,
> When the dew is still on the roses . . .

London came back and had one of the girls by the hand. Her dark skirt swished, and her midriff was a slash of white under her black halter. Though she carried her high heels, she stood taller than London.

"Here's the owner of the magic glove!" London said, gesturing as if Pinky were about to be shot from a circus cannon.

"Want to meet him so bad it hurts!" the girl said. She held to London's shoulder as she lifted a foot to fit on a shoe.

"Huh, me?" Pinky asked as he sat up, braced himself before standing, and swayed.

"I think you're just wonderful," the girl said. She had a southern voice, almost Negro. She stroked long dark hair away from her face, which was pale in the night.

"Me she's saying this to?" Pinky asked.

"My name's Pauline," she said and moved to Pinky, where she laid both her hands on his right forearm. "Don't mind taking a little walk with me, do you, honey?"

She tugged at Pinky playfully till he stepped away with her. She had to keep pulling at him. As she led him off, he glanced back. She was whispering to him. She slid an arm around his waist. They became dark flat shapes against the silverish glow from the lake.

"She'll fix him up," London said, giggling. "That little old Georgia gal knows how to peel a banana."

"What about me slipping around to the other girl?" Wylie asked.

"I believe Christina's working old Blue over at this minute."

"I want my turn or no money," Wylie said.

"Now don't be rude. Just go on up the lane and you'll see the car under the willows. I'm not exactly retiring from the field myself, but I do believe I'll rest a spell. Whew! This kind of carrying on wearies a fellow."

Wylie left London sinking to the green and hurried toward the woods, which were a wall of darkness. At the first trees a form hurtled out. For an instant Wylie thought he was being attacked.

The body knocked him sideways. It was Pinky, and as he ran across the golf course, he howled.

Chasing him, Wylie jumped over London, who crouched frightened. Wylie couldn't have caught Pinky except he was zigzagging and stumbling. Wylie drew close enough to grab a slippery shoulder. He and Pinky became entangled and sprawled across the fairway grass. Pinky tried to escape, but Wylie held him.

"What you doing to me?" Pinky asked, sobbing.

"Sh-h-h or we're in trouble!"

"You know what that girl wanted to do with her mouth?"

"I have a general idea. Lower your voice."

Pinky jerked loose and was up, but Wylie caught his ankle, and he fell.

"Am I drunk, is that what you done to me?" Pinky asked.

"You're just feeling good."

"Got me drunk and brought me out here for that girl, you think that's a great idea?"

"I admit it doesn't seem so now."

"I have profaned the temple of God!"

"Sh-h-h, you're exaggerating the situation," Wylie said. He held Pinky's slick ankle with both hands.

"You poured liquid sin into me," Pinky said. He stopped struggling and pushed his face into the grass.

"I wouldn't if I'd known you were going to act this way."

"You don't have any morals," Pinky said into the grass. "You know what I think of when I think of you? Feeding all that hamburger to Tristan."

"Tristan, my Irish setter?"

"That's right. At your house you wouldn't eat anything less than ground-up round steak and fed ordinary hamburger to a dog. At my house hamburger was a big meal. We ate robins."

"Don't talk so loud."

"I almost been trusting you lately, since the watch, but here you got me drunk and put a prostitute on me."

Pinky rolled suddenly, kicked, and slipped the hands. He was up and away. He didn't run toward the lights of the school but along the asphalt drive lined with dogwood and Judas trees. Pinky howled as if agonized. Though Wylie ran hard, he couldn't catch up. Wylie stopped out of breath at the highway. He heard footsteps slapping down the road in darkness.

Part of Wylie wanted to let Pinky go, to be rid of him finally and forever. Then he felt as if his father were watching and the ache of responsibility. He ran back to the campus, entered Burke House, and knocked on the door of Mr. Sip's study.

Without taking off his ratty bathrobe or changing from his bedroom slippers into shoes, Mr. Sip drove after Pinky in the school's wooden station wagon. Mr. Sip found him at the C&O depot in Charlottesville. Still wearing only his shorts, Pinky sat weeping behind a baggage wagon. He had neither clothes nor money for a trip home.

Mr. Sip brought him back to White Oak, stood him under a cold shower, and walked him up to the room. He saw Pinky into his bed.

Mr. Sip indicated by a quick flap of has narrow hand that Wylie was to follow. They went back to Mr. Sip's study. Wylie hadn't had to dress because he'd never taken off his clothes.

Mr. Sip let him wait on his feet in the greenish nimbus from the brass desk lamp. Mr. Sip leaned back and stared. His glasses reflected light, but the light seemed to glint off the sapphire blades of his eyes.

"All right, Wylie, you may tell me what happened," he said at last.

Wylie told him all because there was no withstanding the terrible penetration of the eyes. They went straight to the soul. Wylie also gave him London and Blue.

"Can you think of a good reason you shouldn't be sent home?" Mr. Sip asked.

"Yes, sir, I can," Wylie said, talking desperately. "I love White Oak, my years here, the work, and if you'll let me graduate, I'll become a very loyal alumnus."

"You don't believe you should be punished?"

"I never meant to hurt anybody, sir."

"But you have hurt somebody as well as broken the rules. Your trouble, Wylie, is you don't consider the morality of consequences. You're a handsome boy, charming, well endowed, even bright, but you never ask yourself how is what I do related to the moral order. Your motto should be, 'If it's delightful, it's good.'"

"I do go to church, sir, even at home."

"Oh, Wylie," Mr. Sip said, his tiny mouth twitching into a smile as if he meant to nibble a sweet. "Yes, you go to church and wear your blazer and school tie well. Your form is good, none better, but what about your content?"

"I don't understand, sir."

"Of course you don't, and what's the point of awarding severe punishment to someone who lacks a sense of depravity and guilt. Judgment serves no purpose. It would be pain inflicted to no end. Go, go to your bed and sleep the sleep of the placid conscience. I'll reflect on what is to be done with you and your companions in crime. Oh, Wylie, how I almost envy your sleep!"

Book Two

24

Wylie, London, Blue, and Pinky were restricted to campus for the rest of the term. Instead of sports during the afternoon, they worked beside the black men who swept dorms, mowed grass, and pruned oaks, the pollen of which misted like a fine golden rain. Though not allowed to attend the Tex Beneke commencement dance with its colored streamers and clusters of wafting balloons, they were able to graduate with their class.

Pinky's father came alone to the White Oak graduation. Arriving on a bus, he wore a shiny brown suit, the pants of which drew up over his white socks. He didn't do anything terribly wrong, yet he was drinking. During the afternoon garden party, he moved across the lawn smiling lopsidedly. He held a teacup as if it were a curiosity from a lost civilization. He was careful of his feet, walking like a man wary of collapsing ground.

He refused a ride home with Wylie's parents, which was good because so much baggage had to be carried in the new Chrysler. Pinky lugging his few cheap suitcases left with his father in a taxi. Wylie and Pinky had not congratulated each other on graduating. They had spoken only a few words for weeks.

"We'll miss Amos at the office," Wylie's father said as they drove away from White Oak and headed toward the mountains. "Of course I'm pleased he's ambitious."

By ambitious Wylie's father meant Pinky had joined the union and got himself a puddler's job with West Virginia Steel. He intended after all to go to the university at Morgantown on the baseball scholarship.

"We won't let him get away," Wylie's mother said. "I'll have him to dinner."

"He found out about finger bowls," Wylie said.

"You didn't tell!" both his parents said at the same time, glancing sharply at him.

"I think he read it somewhere," Wylie said.

"He's too intelligent not to have found out," Wylie's father said. "You wouldn't want to come down to the office and help out?"

"Dad, I'd be happy to except I've made some plans, and it's my last shot before college."

Wylie's father nodded, and his face didn't change, yet Wylie had the feeling his own tepid ambition was being weighed against Pinky's.

The summer turned out the best of Wylie's life. Days around London's parents' Virginia Beach cottage were steamy, voluptuous like the tropics, and there always seemed to be sunshine, cold beer, the lazy beat of the sea, and the shaved flesh of satiny girls.

Every week new people came to stay, friends and friends of friends, from North Carolina, New York, Texas. They wore out the diamond stylus of the hi-fi, which had speakers on the porches and in the bedrooms. Was there even a moment without music? Several times the police knocked on the screen door but at the teeming resort were not out to punish fun and laughter.

There was so much sunshine that Wylie felt he carried it around inside himself, even at night, the heat radiating from him. He became a sea creature weltering among the waves and giving himself to the languid roll of the ocean. The throb of the sea and his blood became one. As he slid beneath it and spread his arms, he felt more at home than ever he had on land. He dreamed of being a swift, glistening fish.

The girls had sun in their skin, and he'd lay his face against them to feel that heat. On girls he tasted the saltiness of the sea. The crowd all became bleached, and sand fell from them as from conchs. One night while they swam in the moonlit ocean, a large dark fish broke the surface with its fin, and they all dashed for the beach.

They threw beer bottles at the spot where the fish slid under. Some of the girls screamed.

After Labor Day, the crowd convoyed home in convertibles, cooling out on beer and inland air blowing over them. They were so tan everyone else in the world appeared to have risen from the grave. They drove their cars at ninety miles an hour up into the bluish mountains, tossed out empty bottles, and cut close to the edges of deeping ravines.

Before Wylie went off to Washington and Lee, he glimpsed Pinky in grimy overalls, goggles around his neck, a red safety helmet on his head. Pinky was walking down Commerce Street when Wylie looked out of Waldstein's, a men's store, where he'd been buying clothes. The fires of hearths had blanched Pinky into a gaunt, inglorious toadstool. Luckily Pinky passed not knowing Wylie had seen him.

Wylie's mother helped pack his things for college. On the seventeenth of September, his father drove him over the mountains to Lexington. A freshman wasn't allowed a car, so he left his Ford washed and waxed in the garage. Black Ed would look after it for him, promising to turn the tires once a month so they wouldn't develop flat areas or rot.

Wylie had believed London also would go to W&L, but at the last minute he was accepted at Yale, where his father had graduated. Blue had decided on Duke. There were two boys from White Oak who'd also chosen W&L—Bones Finley and Cautious Carrington—but Wylie's friends they weren't. Solemnly pre-med, they acted as if they'd entered the priesthood.

Wylie's roommate was a tall boy with braces and a stammer, a basketball player named Ripinsky from Pennsylvania. Though Polish, he was rich Polish, his father owning a bakery and a brewery. Rip turned out to like drinking more than basketball and never made varsity. From the freshman squad it was all downhill into the gentle mellowness of the bottle.

"I can't understand why anybody would ever want to be sober," Rip confessed. "I mean, my God, drinking is greater than anything, even sex. I just hope the hooch in the world won't run out 'fore I die."

Rip's father mailed him multi-paged typewritten letters weekly full of advice about how to succeed at college. Rip let them pile up

113

without opening them. On his bureau he set a large photograph of a thin, bloodless girl who looked more spiritual than sexy. Her name was Jessie, and he telephoned her in Sharon three nights a week.

"I thought you'd wear clodhoppers and dip snuff," Rip said. He was talking about Wylie's being from West Virginia. "My mother's worried about me catching a disease."

"She think I'm going to bang you?" Wylie asked.

"She thinks you'll leave something on the commode seat."

"Listen, if it weren't for West Virginia, you Pennsylvania and Philadelphia plunderers wouldn't have bread on your Chippendale tables," Wylie said, borrowing part of Pinky's diatribe against absentee landlords. "You robbers have despoiled half our acres."

"Just wish you wouldn't use the same commode," Rip said.

Wylie was being rushed, and each night for a week he reeled back to the dorm drunk. He intended to pledge SAE but wanted to be romanced. He hoped to pull Rip along into the same fraternity.

"Let them woo you," Wylie said. "Let them cover you with Sweet Briar girls who stroke and feed you beer."

"Don't like to drink and be with girls at the same time," Rip said.

"Why not?"

"Girls get your priorities mixed up. Good beer is worth undivided effort."

Wylie had discussed with his advisor what courses to sign up for. The advisor was a young mutton-chopped professor of English, his office in Washington Hall a mixture of antique pieces and modern art. A complicated hi-fi set in a corner cupboard sounded muted strains of Mozart. He wore a tattersall vest, smoked a bulldog pipe, and spat into a polished brass cuspidor. Being sold in the college bookstore was his just published slender volume titled *Images of Ascent Diffusing Milton's "Paradise Lost."*

"You've no particular field of interest?" he asked.

"Wouldn't go that far," Wylie said and laughed.

"I'm not talking about wine, women, and song but course material."

"I expect I'll eventually go into business."

"Yet first want a cultural smattering. I suggest history. History will put a veneer on you, and you'll never have to overextend your brain."

Out of the blue Wiley received a tightly wrapped package from Morgantown, inside a single white sweat sock and a penciled note from Pinky stating his mother had found the sock among his clothes. He assumed it was Wylie's. Nothing else, no word of greeting, no pleasantries. Wylie dropped the sock into the trash.

Washington and Lee was a good college, but after the thoroughness of Mr. Sip's puritanical, prune-eating faculty, Wylie didn't need to do much studying his freshman year. He was permitted to skip the first-level course in composition and rhetoric. He could coast in French and math. And history, well, who cared?

He intended to go out for the tennis team till he saw more than forty names on the ladder. He considered whether or not the prize was worth the battle. He wasn't that hungry for athletic glory. Much nicer to lounge around the SAE house within easy reach of music and beer.

He drifted into becoming a member of the Sweet Briar team, though he sampled Hollins, Randolph-Macon, and Mary Baldwin. Bebe was at Sweet Briar and came to W&L parties and dances. She knew all the brothers at the SAE house.

He and Bebe had a fine relationship. They looked good together, knew how to get each other hot, and were able to keep from lying about love. Only accidentally did he find out she was dating somebody else, a Kappa Sigma from Richmond who went to Hampden-Sydney. The boy's father owned a newspaper, a silver Jaguar, and a fifty-foot ketch moored at Deltaville on the Chesapeake Bay.

Wylie borrowed a car from a fraternity brother named Shoe and drove to Sweet Briar on a Tuesday evening without telling Bebe he was coming. The switchboard operator in Bebe's dorm buzzed her. Bebe's roommate, Gigi Gatlin from Savannah, said she was out for the evening. Wylie waited in not the gilt and red-carpeted parlor but the borrowed car where he could smoke, listen to music on the radio, and sip beer.

The wind picked up, and snow twisted down from the night. To stay warm in the misty interior of the car, he kept the engine and heater running. Later when he wiped a window, he saw Bebe and her new boy standing at an outer circle of light from the dorm. They were kissing, the kiss more than just a goodnight clutch and smooch. It was a real scorching grapple, with Bebe throwing her pelvis into his loins. As they walked onto the veranda, they held each other so tightly they hobbled.

Wylie drove home listening to Symphony Syd's Birdland show from New York. He never mentioned anything to Bebe. Some weekends he still saw her, and when she made excuses, he never pressed. We are, he thought, growing up.

He kept himself open to opportunity. He dated Rip's overweight, introverted sister, fed her spaghetti, and shook her hand in the lobby of the Robert E. Lee Hotel. He took out a student nurse, a waitress, and a girl from William and Mary whose father was a medical missionary in Africa. She was so hot she cracked the windshield of Shoe's car with her frantic heel.

During the spring he caught a ride to Goshen Pass to float the river's white water. In the golden warmth of the sun, everybody had innertubes and beer. Girls bloomed on the lichen-streaked boulders at sides of the stream, and above the roar of water rose sounds of guitars, bongo drums, and recorders, the latter like pipes of Pan.

As he floated the rocking river, his face to the sun, a gang of tubers converged in a slanting chute of turbulent water which in its convulsion was colored silver instead of cold pale green. There were too many people and too much speed. Girls screamed, guys shouted, and they all thrashed under. The boiling river was unforgiving.

When Wylie tumbled deep and bumped and scraped his face and chest against slick, slimy rocks, a girl's body snaked in front of him, a naked body, the girl's hair strung out after her like seaweed. His face rubbed the length of her. Then she was gone among bubbles and white plunging foam.

He fought upward, sucked air, and swam after her. He swung into rocks and was dashed against her humped back. She couldn't set her feet in the relentless flow. He grabbed a handful of black hair, steadied her, and pulled her toward the bank. Current swept her flat. He dragged her over the hissing water.

The force of the river, the slashing flow, had shucked her out of her bathing suit. She was even skinnier than Rip's girl, yet the curve of her, her breasts, were womanly and rousing. He maneuvered her into an eddy and stood her.

"Damn you, will you stop gawking!" she said, coughing. She turned away from him to retch.

He couldn't help gawking. Her long wet black hair lay in twisted strands over goosebumps on the patterned knobs of her spine. Her hips quivered. Those boobs were bluish with cold. When she glanced angrily at him, he saw she had violet eyes.

She wouldn't allow him to hold her while she barfed, and after she finished, she squatted into the river to cover herself but was unable to stay down because of the water's iciness. Her teeth clacked so hard her eyelids batted at the jarring.

"I'm freezing to death," she said, her voice quaking. She started crying.

"Here," Wylie said. He wore a sweatshirt as well as swimming trunks and tennis shoes. He pulled the sweatshirt off and wrung it out. She stood to permit him to roll it down over her body. The sweatshirt stretched to her knees, and he saw through it. She knew he was seeing through it where her nipples punched the cotton fabric.

"What are you, a sex maniac?" she asked.

Their innertubes were gone. They climbed over boulders to the bank, caught at bushes and saplings to pull themselves up. The white rocks glittered with mica and were slippery from water splashed on them by the speeding current.

They hiked the slope of the gorge. She no longer cried. Now her narrow face was boned in anger. Each time Wylie tried to help her, she glared. She had come to the river with Tiger Boxley, a junior at the University of Virginia. She was furious he'd abandoned her, yet feared he'd drowned. They found Tiger downstream, dead they at first believed, lying on his stomach across a fallen sycamore trunk, hands dangling limply into spray. He was dead drunk.

"One more time, gang!" Tiger called when the girl shook him.

"You sonofabitch!" she said.

"Pussy, pussy, here little pussy, pussy," Tiger said.

She kicked him.

Cars were parked along the road near a one-lane bridge. Wylie swiped a beach towel from a VW so the girl could wrap herself. He stayed with the body while she hitchhiked back along the road for her car, a red MG which she drove to the bridge. She was smoking and swathed in the black-and-yellow towel. She made it seem stylish.

Tiger lay sleeping on gravel. They wrestled him up to the MG and dumped him in without opening the door.

"All the way, gang!" Tiger shouted.

117

"Shut up, you filthy bastard!" the girl said.

She walked around the car, got in, and drove off without a word to Wylie. Tiger flopped about and hung over the MG's side to puke a stream of saffron ribbons.

Wylie realized he didn't know who she was. He ran yelling after the MG. People along the bank turned to look. She was speeding out of his life, and he had to see her again. He slowed at a pink Studebaker. The keys were inside. He jerked open the door, started the engine, and scratched away, the tires throwing up gravel. Voices hollered from the river.

He caught her just short of the state road's intersection with the highway, drove honking after the MG, and gestured her to stop. When she didn't, he gunned the Studebaker alongside. She swerved to the shoulder. He parked in front of her and ran back. Tiger had passed out. He slumped forward, his nose flattened against the red padded dashboard.

"I don't know your name," Wylie said, leaning over her.

"Trish my name, boy."

"Got to see you again, Trish."

"You've seen way too much of me already."

"Where do I find you?"

"Briar patch," Tiger said, stirring. "She's a funny little bunny in the briar patch."

"I'm dumping you in the first trash can I come to," Trish said to Tiger.

"Pretty little kitty," Tiger said. He spoke against the dashboard, eyes closed, nose mashed.

"I'll call you tonight," Wylie said. "You do have a last name?"

"St. George," Tiger said. "Dragon killer."

"I'll call," Wylie said.

"Waste of time," she said, reversed the MG, and cut around the Studebaker. Honking, she raised a hand but never looked back.

Wyle heard a car approaching fast along the state route. He remembered he'd stolen the Studebaker. He ran up the dirt embankment to the woods as a Rockbridge County Sheriff's Department cruiser—two-tone brown, with flashing red gumball on top—slewed across gravel. Behind it was a Jeep full of students, all wind blown.

Wylie wiggled his body deeper into rotted leaf mold. Deputies and students circled the Studebaker. They looked up at the woods, and he thought they'd found his tracks and were preparing to come after him. He pressed his nose into the moist decay of the dark earth. Deputies and students talked, milled, and finally drove away, the Studebaker too.

He waited till dusk before slipping through the woods and dodging across the road. Each time he heard traffic, he hid. When he reached the bridge, he found Shoe and fraternity brothers. They rode back to Lexington. Wylie felt exhilarated, much higher than he'd been on beer, white water, and danger.

25

Trish St. George. Either Wylie was at Sweet Briar or she over to the SAE house. They found a cliff up in the mountains of the George Washington National Forest which overlooked the sinuous Maury River, the glow of Lee Chapel, and the yellow turrets of VMI. A little drunk, they went to sleep holding each other. A uniformed park ranger woke them by rapping his flashlight against the MG's hood.

For the Fancy Dress Ball, she went as Madame Pompadour, he as Louis XV—brocaded gown, knee breeches, powdered wigs. They danced the minuet and the frug. Later, lying on the cold grass behind Jackson Hall, he had a terrible time burrowing beneath perfumed folds of her silken undergarments. He half suffocated, pleasurably, and the rustling fabrics were as loud in his ears as wind rising.

She too was from West Virginia, a coal camp, but she was no miner's daughter. She invited Wylie to her house for a weekend. Driving his Ford along the tortured upheaved roads near the Kentucky line resembled a trip into the feudal era. Her place, built by her great-grandfather MacGlauglin, was a granite mansion topped by an algae-colored copper roof. A high stone wall surrounded it, and the entrance was through a spiked iron gateway.

The mansion commanded a hill above a dismal valley where four rows of Jenny Linds paralleled the shallow flow of a muddy creek. Beyond the houses were railroad tracks, a galvanized tipple, and the dark, frightening entry into the mine.

On closely mowed bluegrass within the wall he spotted croquet wickets. He glanced at stone stables, a fenced tennis court, and a swimming pool. Four Dalmatians ran around barking. Grapevines entwined a white lattice arbor, and goldfish circled below a splashing fountain. From a maple limb hung a child's swing, the chain links garlanded with artificial roses. Behind the mansion a black water tank braced on iron legs jutted higher than the oaks.

Wylie expected Trish's father to be a large man. Instead he was stubby and overweight, yet gave no impression of softness. He held himself erect to the point of rigidity. He had hair black as Trish's, trimmed and combed so perfectly it seemed painted onto his rounded skull. His eyes weren't violet like hers but a murky brown. His skin was also darker, and his left eyelid fluttered when he talked. He wore gray flannel trousers, a tweed jacket, and a white scarf.

He already held a glass. He started his drinking early in the day but showed it only by becoming quieter and more wary. Even while enjoying himself, he appeared on guard against attack. Musing, his lips puckered like a musician blowing into an invisible flute. Wylie decided the man's hair, parted on the right, was much too dark for his age.

Trish's mother had died when she swerved on a mountain road to avoid a bear upreared and bleeding. She arced her Cadillac over the shoulder into a gorge whose boulders were ice glazed from the crashing of a stream against them. For months after the accident, the father had refused to speak. A kinsman hired a Baltimore psychiatrist to make a visit, but Trish's father chased the luckless doctor from the house and fired buckshot after the departing car with a twelve-gauge engraved Purdy. He brought down the birdbath.

Trish was like her father—impetuous, strong-willed, and full of absolutes. His scowl was hers, and both carried a sense of being wronged. Each had a mannerism of glancing behind as if believing he would be taken unfairly.

Trish, her father, and Wylie shot skeet at the range beyond the stables. In the cramped high and low houses, two smudged small boys from the coal camp below released clay pigeons. Lead pellets from shells rattled on tin and tarpaper roofs of the miners' cabins, causing women to look up from hanging wash on their backyard clotheslines.

Trish shot with cool assuredness. She broke more pigeons than Wylie, but her father outscored her. He cursed each time he fired whether he hit or missed. He was quick over his English double, which had been tailored for him like a fine suit. The gun was one of a set of three.

After skeet, Trish, her father, and Wylie walked to the mansion. The smudged boys carried the guns to the front door. They were not allowed inside. A Negro servant received the guns, and Trish's father paid each boy twenty-five cents.

Wylie took a bath because his suite had no shower. The tub was pinkish marble and large enough to float a dinghy. Inside the house's hushed, ponderous walls, he felt removed from life and time. He felt fortressed. He put on his freshly cleaned and pressed tuxedo. Trish had told him her father always dressed.

Wylie walked down the baronial oak staircase past oil portraits of MacGlauglins and St. Georges. They appeared imperial, even the women, though the family wasn't old. The first MacGlauglin had crossed the ocean from Scotland, a poor, savage boy, and the money, like new wine, had seasoned slowly to respectability and a royal dominance.

"They battled the union tooth and claw for years," Wylie's father had told him.

The spring day was warm, but night air of the mountain settled with a damp chill. The Negro servant built coal fires in several down-stairs rooms. Trish, her father, and Wylie had drinks in the den among darkened oak wainscoting, ceiling beams, and hunting tapes-tries. Wylie felt there should've been a suit of armor at the doorway and a mastiff bitch gnawing bones on the hearth.

The father and Wylie had stood for Trish, who wore a black gown, a pearl necklace, and silver slippers. The Negro servant, named Josh, served the drinks. He too had on a tuxedo.

Mr. St. George was outraged at the C&O for converting its loco-motives from coal to diesel fuel. He called the railroad's president an ingrate, deceiver, and traitor. Mr. St. George looked as if he'd bite a chunk from his highball glass.

He spoke of his grandfather's standing up to the United States Army when troops were sent in on boxcars to settle the mine wars: "Point of principle. The American government tried to force this family to acknowledge those dirty bastards the United Mine Work-ers and that sonofabitch John L. Lewis. The military of the land of the free laid this house under siege."

121

Fuming, he described how the soldiers set up a tent camp and built fires around the mansion. Bugles blew, horse cavalry arrived, troops armed with sabers and automatic pistols. The brigadier general in charge of the campaign sent a deputation to the house, each member carrying a white flag attached to a guidon.

"Artillery at our front door!" Mr. St. George said.

He called for a flashlight and led Wylie outside the stone wall where he pressed fingertips into gouges caused by bullets. They then went down dungeonlike steps into a basement which had the dankness of a crypt. Mr. St. George unlocked an iron door. Inside was what remained of an arsenal—nearly empty racks for Springfield rifles along the walls, a few wooden cases, casket-shaped, holding tarnished cartridges, and at the center of the room a rusting tripod which must once have supported a machine gun, probably seized by the government.

"My grandfather believed in taking a stand against radicals!" Mr. St. George said.

"They had an armistice and treaty like a real war," Trish said.

"It was a real war," Mr. St. George said.

"But I mean right here, not in a foreign country," Trish said.

"Socialist trash!" Mr. St. George said. "This family learned a lesson. Buy the government instead of fighting it."

The meal was strange, served on a refectory table set with heavy silver, white candles, goblets, yet the food boarding-house plain—dry beef, boiled potatoes, snap beans, and applesauce. Everything lacked salt. No wine was poured. Through an arched window Wylie saw the gleam of illuminated marble statues in the garden, imperial figures bought by Mr. St. George on a trip to Italy.

After eating, they played three-handed poker before the fire in the gloomy den. Chips represented only a dime, but Mr. St. George bet each hand as if his coal mines were in the pot.

Trish was nearly as bad. She had her father's intensity and will to win. Wylie felt any moment one of them might draw a six-gun for a shootout. Their eyes narrowed, their lips tightened. They glared at the other's pile of chips.

Wylie played half-heartedly. His loss of a few dollars was an investment in pleasing them. When he did win a hand with a pair of kings, Mr. St. George, who held jacks, hurled his cards upward, and they fluttered down to the flying-hawk design of the Persian carpet.

Unsummoned, the servant Josh entered and gathered the cards to return them to Mr. St. George, who acted as if nothing out of the ordinary had happened. Even Trish seemed unconcerned.

"Bump me again, and I'll dump strychnine in your hooch!" she snarled at her father on the next hand.

"Oh lovely, lovely!" Mr. George called out as he pawed in chips.

26

At Easter break during Wylie's junior year of college, he spied Pinky on the other side of Commerce Street. There'd been a thundershower, and dark water ran fast along gutters and dipped into storm drains.

Pinky was leaving Mountain State Bank. He appeared taller, rosier, more determined. In his seersucker jacket, charcoal flannels, and white bucks, he seemed almost stylish, though Wylie felt certain everything Pinky bought came off the rack at one of the bargain stores.

Wylie almost let him go without speaking. Then he thought, What the hell. He called Pinky's name twice. As Wylie jaywalked across the street, Pinky waited and stared.

"You not talking to me?" Wylie asked and on impulse invited him to lunch. He saw hesitation, reluctance, and guessed Pinky was thinking of those last unfriendly days at White Oak. Wylie didn't want to start anything anew but was curious about what the redhead had been doing with himself.

He took Pinky to the Press Room, a converted brick townhouse where a single teletype machine clattered away and news stories were framed on walls. Very few members of the working press could afford the club. Mostly it was used by business and professional men who joined because of food and the bar, especially the latter. The state allowed no liquor-by-the-drink establishments, yet some clubs were above the law.

The dining room was white, the draperies chartreuse, the walls hung with golden oval mirrors which created a deceiving spaciousness. Some of the city's best-dressed women lunched at the round linen-covered tables, a break from bouts of shopping.

"The way you live," Pinky, who'd never been to the Press Room before, said. "You sure the police won't raid this place?"

"Not if they want to hold their jobs," Wylie said. "And even though people here are well dressed, have money, and use good manners, don't hold it against them, okay?"

"I didn't realize the town had a joint like this. I can't help thinking about the coal miners. Right now while these painted-up ladies are daintily sipping their cocktails, hungry, desperate men are killing themselves down in a stinking wet blackness hacking coal. For what? To pay for decorous carousing?"

"Truce, Pinky. For a few minutes at least, let's try to be nice to each other."

"What to you does 'nice' mean exactly?"

"It means we're civilized, at least for the period of time it takes to eat our food. Now I want a drink, if my drinking won't offend you."

"I see, drinking is civilized. Well it won't. I'm learning most of the world is, or are, uh, sots."

"You just thought of Mr. Sip."

"That's right. He haunts me. That's part of the system I guess."

"What system?"

"Of being civilized."

"Have a small glass of wine."

"'Wine is a mocker, strong drink is raging, and he who is deceived thereby is not wise,'" Pinky said, his reddish brown eyes never still.

"The truth if I ever heard it," Wylie said and ordered a scotch. A waitress wearing a green dress with a white apron and cap brought it.

"I might as well tell you I feel uncomfortable in here," Pinky said.

"I can see that. You shouldn't resent people having a good time. How you like WVU?"

"I work all the time, but I love it. I'm crazy for the books."

"You look fit. You must be doing more than hit the books."

"I play baseball and swim. I try to swim fifteen minutes every day. I also been helping a brick mason during breaks. Carrying mud up a ladder keeps me in shape."

"What's your major?"

"I'm thinking of law school, though for a while I considered becoming a minister."

Wylie sipped his scotch without comment. He wondered whether that funny little church that Pinky belonged to had even a backwoods seminary.

"It's what my mother wanted," Pinky said. "I dropped lots of sweat making the decision."

"You'll be a fine lawyer, and I'll try to bring you some business," Wylie said, thinking a crumb here and there I'll bring you.

"I don't intend handling paternity suits."

Wylie laughed, considering the remark pretty risqué for Pinky. West Virginia University was definitely doing something for him.

"Wish I liked the books the way you do," Wylie said.

"You don't need books because you run on style. Me, I don't have that, so I'm forced to grub. What you majoring in?"

"History but I'm gravitating toward finance."

"Sure, that's the place for you. You're used to money, at home with it, and it buys what you want, which is pleasure. You know something? You smile when you sleep. I noticed it at White Oak. Most people look troubled when they're sleeping, but you're content with the life you have."

"Are you insulting me?"

"Simple statement of fact. The world's your own private grocery store where you just walk in and pull any stuff you want right off the shelf."

"You're certain you're not trying to insult me?"

"You'd know for sure if I was. Were."

A group of ladies at a nearby table laughed. Rings and other jewelry sparkled. Their teeth flashed. Pinky eyed them as if judging. His expression was condemnatory. Don't, Wylie thought, let him get serious and start preaching.

"You got a girl up in Morgantown?"

"I look at them but don't have time for more," Pinky said. "Last thing in the world I need at this minute is complications with a girl."

"I never thought of a girl as a complication."

"In your social circle they're not. They're something else on the shelf you pick up, take out, and toss in the can when you're finished. In my crowd when you go with a girl, you're supposed to be moral and have honorable intentions. You still sparking Bebe?"

Sparking—another of the old-fashioned words Pinky came up with. Nobody under sixty used sparking except him.

"She has a fellow from another college," Wylie said. "I go mostly with a girl from a place named MacGlauglin."

"The coal camp?"

"I'm surprised you've heard of it."

"They had big strikes there early in the century. My great-uncle was killed by scabs."

Wylie pictured the granite mansion, the stone wall, and a machine gun. Don't, he told himself, go further into it with Pinky.

London Airy came by the table. He wore a pale blue gabardine suit and white bucks. His golden hair was tangled in curls. He was so fair he dazzled.

He carried a stinger. He was the only person Wylie knew who drank stingers regularly. He sat to talk about White Oak. Pinky took part glumly, ordered a ham sandwich from the waitress, and chewed with lots of jaw motion. He still resented the alcohol in his orange juice and the girls from Bernice's.

"I've got an appointment," he said, wiping the napkin across his mouth.

"Have dessert," Wylie said.

"I don't eat desserts."

He left without offering to pay for his lunch or thanking Wylie. Wylie and London watched him weave away among the tables. Pinky might be impressed with the Press Room's glitter, yet he wasn't cowed. His stride dared anybody to stand in his way. A few women looked after him.

"Nobody will ever tame him," London said and sighed. "You can put a jacket and tie on him, but underneath he'll always remain a ridge runner."

"Agreed," Wylie said.

"He feels morally superior."

"Who isn't morally superior to you?"

"I'm decadent, true, but at least I'm polite and correct. I'm always kind to servants. He didn't even leave a tip for the darling waitress, though her thighs are rather fat. Do you suppose they chafe?"

27

After his senior year at Washington and Lee, Wylie and Trish skirted talk about marriage. She'd been to Europe twice, the last time for six months, and her accent had changed. Often she sounded British. She'd become more svelte and continental. She plucked her black

126

brows into a high thin Parisian line. She'd learned other things in France. He didn't inquire about her teacher.

Each weekend she was home, Wylie drove down to MacGlauglin. He needed to make no arrangements. Josh and the other servants knew him, and his room would be ready.

He and Trish cantered horses up through the wooded mountains beyond the coal camp where her father had ordered trails cut. Wylie could ride well enough—he'd had lessons—though not at her level. She was so competitive she tried to maneuver him into contests. She jumped the paddock fence, he used the gate. She charged downhill along a wet trail while he held his chestnut to a trot. She waited for him among ferns of the glen.

"You'll never be called dashing," she said.

"I'll never be called dead either."

The glen was three miles from the mansion, a shadowy cove between two high, scalped ridges. A fast but lifeless yellowish stream twined through pale wild grass. Water beat so hard against rocks of a bend that spray rose to form a faint spectrum. Blue and yellow wildflowers grew up the mountainside to raw red overburden bulldozers had shoved from a stripping operation.

As he and Trish lay deep in the rough spicy wild grass, a large muddy stone pounded down the mountain, the stone hitting trees and bounding higher and higher as it gathered speed. Trish rolled off him. They believed it was a natural rock fall till they heard laughter.

Trish reclasped her lacy brassiere and buttoned her ratcatcher while Wylie tucked at his clothes. Another stone smashed down the slope. Trish was furious. She ran for Demon, her midnight-black gelding. He shied and jerked at reins tied to a locust limb. She flipped the reins over his head as she stepped fast into the saddle. Using her leather bat, she whipped Demon up the mountain.

Wylie tried to mount his chestnut. Each time he lifted a boot to the stirrup, the horse wheeled. Finally, a leg over, he grabbed the mane and almost was flung off as he raced after Trish. She was shouting among trees of the slope. The footing became so steep and treacherous, he clutched his horse around its neck.

The stone rollers were two young boys who fled along a thornapple swath underneath a power line. Trish attacked them. She swung her bat so hard it whistled. The boys were no longer laughing but glanced back fearfully. One fell, a skinny urchin blackened by grime and cinders. He wore overalls too large for him with nothing underneath and no shoes.

Trish cut him off with Demon. Whichever direction the boy tried to escape, she blocked. Like a Cossack, she slashed him. The bat cracked loudly against his smutty skin. The boy cowered first and then squalled.

"God, no, Miss!" he hollered. He dropped to the ground and covered his head.

She slid from Demon and whipped the boy till he balled himself among thorn apples and screamed. He really wasn't hurt much, but the smack of the bat sounded so loud he believed he was being killed. Wylie jumped from the saddle, hurried behind Trish, and held her so she couldn't strike the boy further.

"Coal-camp trash!" she spat. "Tell anybody what you saw, and I'll come to your house with a knife and cut off your little peter!"

She broke free for one last slash at the boy as he lurched away to run screaming along the power line. She was so exhausted she held to Wylie and breathed hard against his chest. She pushed free and stood with her jodhpured legs spread, the bat dangling, she a slim, raging conquistador.

"He won't rat on us," she said. "He'll protect that precious little wop prick of his!"

Yet that night she appeared ladylike, even demure, when she descended the staircase wearing a cream gown and her jewelry. After dinner, she, her father, and Wylie sat on the terrace and looked down through gaps in the spiked iron gate to the coal camp, which gleamed unblemished in the cooling darkness. Windows of the simple white clapboard church were lit. On certain slight shifts of air, frenzied voices floated up:

> Wash me, wash me in the Blood!
> Yes!
> Clean the sin off me!
> Lord God!
> Put Your sword in my hand!
> Tell it!
> Cut old Satan to his knees!

"What'll you do?" Trish asked as she and Wylie toed the glider. Her father had gone inside to the phone. Each time the glider moved rearward, Trish's creamy high heels clicked against slate. They heard more wild revival hymn singing and her father's petulant voice. Wylie turned to her.

"I'm considering lifting your silks and placing my hand you know where."

"You can do that anytime. I mean now you've finished college."

"Toying with the idea of proposing to you, though I admit I've been relishing life as it is."

"We don't want to get married."

"We don't?" he asked and drew away to look at her.

"Oh hell, I don't know, everything becomes so formal. Life practically stops."

"That doesn't have to be."

"Nobody means for it to stop, but it always happens. Soon as people marry, they follow rules and learn so much about each other it destroys the excitement and mystery."

"You wouldn't care for a house and children?"

"I have a house, and as for children, when I let my body suffer that indignity, the game's over. I'll puff up, my skin tone will die, and my pretty ankles will settle and swell like a washerwoman's."

"Married I could reach for you whenever I want."

"You've never had to reach very far for me."

Her father walked out through the french door. He wore his tailored tuxedo and carried a pair of field glasses. He arranged the leather strap around his neck before lifting them to his eyes. He stood at the stone railing to peer down at the camp—like a general about to order a barrage. Miners and their families still sang at the glimmering church.

"You never know what they're up to," Mr. St. George said. "Union scum sneaking around in darkness."

"And snakes," Trish said. "They're probably using the snakes. Ugh!"

She raised her chin to air her throat. The breeze, smelling of laurel and coal, blew off the ridges. Mr. St. George kept his field glasses to his eyes. Trish's hand slid across Wylie's lap and squeezed.

"Ought to sell," Mr. St. George said. "Bethlehem's made an offer, a damn good one. Let them worry about vermin."

Grumbling, he lowered the glasses, said goodnight, and walked to his den, where he fixed a drink to carry upstairs. A light came on in his bedroom.

"He'll never sell," Trish said. "He loves the fight."

"Does he use those field glasses on us?"

"Of course, and he's had you investigated. I read the report, which states you're prompt in payment of your debts, suffer no physical defects, and have no criminal record. You're also not a Jew or nigger. In sum you are sanitary and fit to keep me company."

Wylie was annoyed at being looked into, but she laughed.

"He checks everybody out, even the cooks. Some other entries: no morals charges against you, that is, you're not a fruit. You're Episcopalian and Republican. Your father's estate is respectable, if not overwhelming."

"Anything else?"

"You are reputed to have a smashing backhand."

"Happy I passed the test."

"The important test you passed is with me."

"Fine, but if we don't get married, what do we do?"

"Besides shacking up and living a life of sin? I've been thinking of trying some acting, maybe apprenticing down at the Barter Theatre."

"I didn't know you'd ever been in a play."

"I haven't but always sensed I'd be good at acting."

"Then I guess I'll go to business school."

"Brilliant. When we at last combine, we're going to need some-body in the family who can count."

And her pretty fingers were inside his fly.

28

While she was at Barter in Abingdon, Wylie went to The Wharton School of Finance. His Washington and Lee grades were at best marginal in meeting Wharton's entrance requirements, but his father used kinsmen in Philadelphia as well as Elk Land and Lumber's coal and banking connections.

"They owe us a little something in Pennsylvania," Wylie's father said. "We've made enough of them rich."

Wylie respected Wharton, realized he could and should learn a lot, yet found himself gazing out windows, sleeping late, or idling around Bookbinders. He had a roommate, a Jewish youth named Sam Kansky from Cleveland.

"You ever work?" Sam asked, fretted by Wylie. Intense Sam seemed constantly in crisis and roamed their two rooms with dark longish hair awry, dark eyes alight, his arms flinging. He cared about everything, and when he read a newspaper, it was as if battling it.

"I may be working right now," Wylie said. "You can't tell from my facial expression." Wylie was lazing on his bed. "Great thoughts may be passing through my mind."

"They're causing something to push through your pants."

"Got a beef against the human female?"

"I like everything in its place."

"Me too. I don't go for it when it's not between the legs. I'm just not attracted to freaks."

Trish never wrote, so Wylie telephoned every second night. That too irritated Sam Kansky because Wylie had ordered a private phone installed and while Sam sat studying, books piled around him as if he were in a foxhole, Wylie lazed about talking love. Sam would begin twitching.

"I'm always tired," Trish said. "They rouse us from bed at six in the morning to paint and haul scenery. I don't feel clean."

"How's the acting?"

"Actually I'm not bad."

Whenever she appeared in a new play, he flew down to the Tri-City Airport and rented a car to drive to Abingdon for opening night. Like a stage-door Johnny, he carried bouquets. She was not surprised he showed up. She expected it of him. Though never the star of anything, she held herself as if she were of everything.

She disliked, and was disliked by, the other actors. They were, in her opinion, grubby. They could look so stylish and beautiful onstage, but afterwards they resembled damaged rubber toys somebody had let the air out of. They smelled, she said, as bad as coal miners.

She used theatrical mannerisms. She smoked her Chesterfields in a jade holder and cussed like a tough broad. She was lofty one moment, common the next. She had a way of standing with a hand on a lowered hip, the right foot set perpendicular to the left, her expression bored, like a great lady hearing the world's applause and being surfeited by it.

131

"I'm finding the real me," she said.

She became a better actress than Wylie expected, particularly light roles where no subtlety or innerness was necessary. She herself was a showpiece, a sleek, raven-haired beauty, and when she made entrances, there was a stir at recognition of her special presence. Her natural arrogance furnished her every step a royal bearing which demanded eyes.

She despised light roles. She aspired to serious drama, particularly Eugene O'Neill and Tennessee Williams, yet wasn't compounded for Anna Christie or Blanche Dubois. Trish was too certain of her life, its security, too lacking in a knowledge of suffering. Her acting stayed on the outside.

The truth was, Wylie realized, that neither he nor Trish wanted to work to the extent desperately ambitious people must. They wouldn't lay their lives on the line. Trish liked the hardship of an actress' life only as a part of the drama of herself, her picture of herself racing around clutching scripts, a free-wheeling bohemian, full of sacrifice for art and the theater, yet always contained, groomed, a white Jaguar waiting in the parking lot, a velvet-lined tiered box brimming with jewelry atop her dressing table.

During July of her second summer at Barter, she took a leave of absence. She wasn't sick, she said, just run down. She drove the Jaguar back to MacGlauglin and sunned herself around the rippling pool. She wanted to regain her tan. She bought a pile of novels— she wouldn't read paperbacks, they were too difficult to hold—and sprawled on a yellow chaise where she drank and smoked, still using the jade holder.

"Have to build myself up," she said, turning onto her stomach so Wylie could rub a sweet-smelling oil on her back and legs.

"Scotch and Chesterfields are a wonderful way to build yourself up," Wylie said.

"I don't drink or smoke that much." She raised her head to frown at him. "I swim a lot."

"A joke, kid."

"When you act, truly act, you burn spirit as fuel. Finally the tank empties, and you have to refill."

"So what we're doing is refilling our tank."

"You shit."

She talked about returning to Barter. She read plays and phoned directors to discuss parts. Yet days passed with her hardly lifting an arm or leg in the immaculate mountain sunshine. Wylie was easily able to convince her to join him for a sailing trip on the Chesapeake Bay.

Blue Bales chartered the forty-seven-foot schooner *Pilgrim,* and he, Sis Asters, Bebe Stanniker, London Airy, Trish, and Wylie let the humid, indolent summer air breathe them out over the torpid waters for a month's wandering from port to port. They ate steamed crabs, flounder, and drank gallons of iced golden beer. The girls stretched themselves on the deck and basted their flesh.

By the time Wylie and Trish, bleached and baked, stepped ashore at Gloucester Point for the drive back to West Virginia, she had stopped mentioning Barter.

29

Wylie wasn't bounced from Wharton. Rather he saw those numbers winding through textbooks and case histories, all those labyrinthine balance sheets which had not the feel of actual money beneath them. The figures didn't seem as important as keeping his backhand firm and sure.

After withdrawing and returning to his parents' house, he accepted a job with Thornhill & Co., local stock brokers whose cluttered offices were on the third floor rear of a bank building which had gone bust during the early 1930s. Wylie considered working for his father at Elk Land and Lumber, but there wasn't enough for two men and Miss Burdette to do.

Joseph "Thorny" Thornhill had talked to Wylie after a game of golf. They sat in the grill of the Pinnacle Rock Club. Thorny wore oxblood cordovans, a tan cotton suit, and his black-and-orange Princeton tie. Already his flaxen hair was creeping back from his shiny brow, though he was only twenty-five.

Thorny had a blimp inside him, not yet fully inflated, but expanding. Throughout his years he would become broader at the girth and tapered on the ends till he seemed centered in his stomach.

"Why me?" Wylie asked when Thorny offered the job.

"One, you're old family and automatically in," Thorny said. "Two, you're attractive and well liked. Three, you have access to capital. Four, you're a golfer, though not as accomplished as I am. Golf is important in this business. Enough for a start?"

"Can't see myself peddling securities."

"This is much more than peddling, Wylie. In time we could develop a major regional firm. It's my dream. Moreover, stocks are heating up, yet Harris, Upham's the only brokerage house in town with a national wire."

"Carpetbaggers."

"That's it. Why let the New York sharpies take our money when we have the brains down here?"

Wylie started work the first week in September. Thornhill & Co. had been in securities even before the Great Depression and stayed with them during the bad times of the 1930s, selling mostly government and municipal bonds. It was no grand business but did have a reputation for conservatism and integrity. The gold-leaf sign on the dark oaken doorway of the office had long ago tarnished and flaked.

Wylie discovered at Thornhill & Co. that he could make money and liked doing it. He more than liked it. He found he had a passion and fever for the game. He felt a hot excitement in his head and belly at the flowering of his money sense. His instincts for the high dollar were authentic.

After the period of training, licensing, and settling in, he no longer doubted he'd be a success. The phone on the desk of his beige cubicle began to ring so often that his calls had to be routed through a secretary. People believed in him, his name. Before six months were up, he exceeded his draw from the firm. Each week he totaled his commission slips and plotted them on a sheet of graph paper. He loved the ascending line. For the first time he understood he possessed an ability to become rich on his own.

During the spring he drove his new Mercury convertible up to New York to visit Trish. Right after Christmas she'd left Mac-Glauglin and rented an apartment on the East Side, two bedrooms and a narrow balcony with a view of a sunless patch of river.

"I'll make or break it in this town," she said, pacing in front of him, her heels rapping the parquet floor. She had on a white turtleneck sweater, charcoal slacks, and black pumps. She smoked and drank fast. Her thin face was combative, as if old James MacGlauglin were resurrecting himself in her lash-striped violet eyes to face down a riot of miners advancing on his mansion.

She did some modeling for Lord & Taylor's and finally got a part in a play, an Off-Broadway production called *The Sibyls,* an experimental drama in the round where she portrayed a shuffling crone who carried a wooden staff and a serpent which writhed at her rag-bound bosom. At one point, among wild dancing and drunken pandemonium, she rushed onstage and held the snake over her head as she cried, "The end is coming! Run to the caves!"

Trish believed *The Sibyls* would make it to Broadway. Wylie never admitted he didn't understand the drama's meaning. He suspected the flaw was in himself, not the play, since it was drawing an audience and had good reviews tacked to a cork bulletin board of the shabby green tongue-and-groove lobby. Still he wondered why his lovely Trish would be cast as a hag.

He learned the truth about *The Sibyls* the day he drove over the potholed road to MacGlauglin to sell Mr. St. George stock. Dark purplish clouds slid fast over the scalped ridges, and Wylie heard thunder, but rain never fell. Dust from cinders, lifted by wind, stung his eyes.

"Junk!" Mr. St. George said of the play. "Trish and that damn snake. What the hell were the actors talking about?" He crunched ice from his scotch. "All that moaning and jumping up and down. Goddamn piece of junk!"

"I want to see it again," Wylie said. "I'm sure I missed important lines."

"There are no important lines. It's just a piece of crap I bought her."

"You backed the production?"

"Might as well have thrown my money onto the goddamn fire!" His lip curled over the edge of his glass.

Trish hadn't mentioned her father's being behind the play. It explained how she got the part. *The Sybyls* ran through April, and she came home in the white Jaguar. She and Wylie had dinner with her father before driving across the state line to Kentucky and a garish motel.

Milky in faint light from the bathroom, she dropped her silk slip over a chair and crossed to the bed, her nakedness luminous, her

135

black hair a cowl. She liked her loving fancy, teetering on the perverse, and so did he. Continental she called it. Yet her thin body never quieted. Even after the best he could do for her, she restlessly prowled the room.

She'd drive from MacGlauglin to the capital on shopping trips and stride into Thornhill & Co., her arms full of packages, as if the firm were her property. She liked to sit by Wylie's desk, smoke, and make faces at him as he worked.

On July 4 he drove her to the Pinnacle Rock Club's cocktail party. The valley was smoky and abrasive, but sunlight gilded the top of the hill, and a breeze lifted oak leaves and strands of listless willows.

Ladies wore bright summer dresses and mingled on the lawn with men in colorful slacks and blazers. Candy-striped umbrellas opened above round white tables. A buffet was laid out—linen cloths, silver punch bowls, shrimp, melon balls, crab. Swift black waiters carried drinks on trays, and beside the green tennis courts a jazz quintet played.

"It died," Trish said of *The Sibyls* as she leaned to a platter of crab claws, causing the tiny gold cross around her neck to swing forward. She wore a pleated white skirt, a blue blouse, and ruby earrings shaped like horseshoes. "The last night we performed for less than twenty people. I let Horace go in the Jersey Meadows."

Horace was the snake, a North American puff adder with yellow eyes that had blackness at their center, though he was harmless, even affectionate. Wylie wondered whether Trish's father would pay her way into another production and guessed the father might not have to. Something about Trish had changed. She had a lingering quality, a sort of laying back. She could finally be ready for marriage.

"Have I told you how glad I am you're here?" Wylie asked. He nudged his thigh against hers, and she smiled and showed the red tip of her tongue as she returned the pressure.

It was then Wylie spotted Pinky. Unlike other men on the lawn, he wore a business suit, chalk gray, and brown shoes which had cloddish rubber soles. He stood apart from groups.

"Who is it?" Trish asked.

Wylie introduced Pinky to her. She gave him a fast, judging once-over as he lifted his hand to shake hers. Trish didn't like shaking hands, and it was bad form for the man to offer first, but she reluctantly raised hers and allowed Pinky a touch of fingers. He was startled by its briefness.

Curious how Pinky got an invite to the party, Wylie would've chatted awhile, but Trish appeared bored and shifted her weight from one brown-and-white pump to the other. She gazed toward the tennis courts where couples danced. She'd weighed Pinky and found him wanting.

Wylie danced with her. Later, while she was in the powder room, he searched for Pinky but couldn't find him. He asked London, who had on a salmon-colored jacket and lemon slacks.

"Sis again," London said, rolling his merry eyes. "Though she's ready to dump him for good. About time. He stood out like a crow in the snow."

When Wylie mentioned to his parents he'd seen Pinky at the Pinnacle Rock Club, both were interested.

"I don't suppose he's a member," Wylie's father said.

"No," Wylie said.

"You should encourage him," Wylie's mother said. "You know how hard it is for a young lawyer to get started. And you ought to keep up with your friends."

Friends we are not, Wylie thought, but smiled at his mother.

"Tell him I miss his coming by the office," Wylie's father said.

"Tell him he owes us a visit," the mother said.

The next Tuesday Wylie reluctantly but dutifully ran a finger down a page of the phone book to locate Pinky's name. It was in small print and followed by the abbreviation "atty." He called the number three times before getting an answer. He really didn't want an answer.

"I'll buy you lunch," Wylie said.

"Why should you buy me anything?" Pinky asked.

"Your graduation present."

"I didn't graduate. I took the bar exam early, passed, and quit school to go to work. Some of us do have to work."

"I wish I could say I missed your sarcasm."

"I charge for it now. Why not come by the office so I can send you a bill?"

After the market closed, Wylie walked past River Street to what had once been called Whisky Row but was now officially Coal Avenue. He passed auto-parts stores, pawn shops, second-run movie houses, and hotels you walked up a flight of steps to find the desk. Legless beggars displayed their stumps and banged tin cups against gritty pavement. A Salvation Army band played. The area smelled of popcorn, gasoline fumes, and the unwashed.

Pinky's office was over a bakery, one room, no reception desk, no secretary. The walls were a flaking green, the desk gray metal which appeared scratched and dented. Instead of file cabinets, he used cardboard boxes pushed into corners. Beside the door stood a wooden hat rack. In front of his desk he'd positioned two straight wooden chairs.

He worked in his shirtsleeves, his ratty maroon tie loosened. He'd had that tie at White Oak. The dirty window behind him was open, and street noises invaded the room. From a movie next door came sounds of shooting, cathedral bells, and screams. Bread odors rose from the bakery.

"I see you're impressed with the layout," he said.

"Actually it's what I expected, knowing your prejudice against comfort," Wylie said. Again he glanced at the crummy walls and green drabness. Pinky should've been a monk.

"If you're wondering how business is, I netted seventy-four dollars last month. Best money I ever made. You notice some money spends better than other?"

"I'm not certain I believe that."

"How would you know? You've always had money. To you it's like air."

"That's the old Pinky."

"You look slick as a banker."

"And you look like a hillbilly shyster who just nailed up his shingle."

"Brother, don't feel sorry for me. I've got prospects."

"And a great view."

"That's humanity out there. You wouldn't know anything about that. You deal in dollars."

"Never understood work could be such fun."

"For some it's that way. For others it's a lousy, unfair, stinking battle."

138

"For you?"

"Not for me. I told you I have prospects. I'll do all right, but you walk down Coal Avenue and see the poor bastards ground up by the system."

"You're on a crusade?"

"I realize it sounds stupid to you, but I believe everybody ought to have a fair chance."

"A noble sentiment."

"You still don't care about anything except yourself."

"Wrong, there are a number of people I care about, including my parents, my friends, my colleagues at Thornhill & Co., my customers, and a very pretty lady named Trish whom I hope to marry soon."

"She's pretty all right, a blueblood, and I smelled the money on her at fifty feet. It's the one good thing money can do, the one thing I really approve of, putting a high gloss on a pretty girl."

The frosted glass of his office door rattled, and a hunchback Negro sidled in dragging a stiff leg. To move his head, the man had to turn his entire body. His dark filmy eyes rolled upward.

"Be with you in a minute, Harmon, just have a seat," Pinky said.

The Negro scraped his way to the other straight chair and gave his body to it. He sat wheezing. He smelled of sweat, snuff, and coal dust.

Wylie and Pinky walked into the brown corridor, which needed sweeping and whose boards had grooves in them from years of feet.

"Funny thing is I'm going out to MacGlauglin," Pinky said. "Some of my clients are thinking of bringing an action against your future father-in-law."

"Maybe you'll see Trish."

"I have to take a couple of depositions from his miners, and then I'll sue his ass."

Wylie stopped on the steps to look back at Pinky. "That's the first time I ever heard you use profanity."

"Ass is profanity?"

"At one time you thought it was."

"It's the company I keep. Most people I know are corrupt— like you."

"Welcome to the human race."

He didn't like that and frowned. Maybe he was torturing himself with some spiritual rebuke, perhaps a jeremiad from the Chosen of God Tabernacle or his mad raving mother. He turned away, entered his office, and closed the door.

30

Trish let it out. She and Wylie lay on Joseph's towels spread over the warm concrete beside her father's swimming pool. She untied yellow straps of her two-piece bathing suit so that her whole back would tan. When she raised her body to talk, she held the halter over her breasts in order to keep them from hanging free. Not that she was modest. She had often hung them over his face in the night.

"He came to the house?" Wylie asked. They were speaking of Pinky.

"To the front door. I didn't remember him from the July Fourth party. He said you told him to drop by."

"He bent the truth considerably."

"He practically forced me to invite him inside. I introduced him to Daddy."

"Does your father understand Pinky's bringing a legal action against him?"

"What fun!"

"Doubt your father will agree."

"Daddy's ears might shoot steam, but he likes Pinky. He even remembered his name."

"Pinky's been here more than once?"

"He invited himself to join me for a dip. You ever see him swim? Fantastic the way he scuds through the water. And he has this most marvelous half gainer."

"I've seen his most marvelous half gainer," Wylie said and reached for a Chesterfield. Trish eyed him as she sipped iced tea through a red plastic straw. "How many times has he been here?"

"I don't keep count, but he did drive down again yesterday morning."

"You invited him?"

"Don't be funny. He's brassy and brash. I can't understand Daddy's taking to him. Well maybe I can. Pinky has a certain vigor. Daddy loves vigor."

"And I lack it?"

"Don't be defensive. Daddy likes you too."

"Anything besides vigor?"

"Pinky can be entertaining. He told a story about a deacon in his church who always dropped a dollar in the collection but took back fifty cents. One Sunday the ushers tricked him by not providing silver for change. The deacon hesitated, tore his dollar, and left half in the plate. The next Sunday he gave the other half. Pinky made faces and talked hillbilly as he told the story. Daddy laughed so hard he nearly choked on his tod."

"I think I may choke Pinky."

"Lover, you don't have to worry," she said and stroked her cool, deft fingers over Wylie's shoulder and down his back. They curved around his waist to his stomach where they tickled him. The index finger slipped beneath the front of his bathing trunks.

"What about your father and his binoculars?" Wylie asked.

"He's gone to Roanoke for a railroad meeting," she said.

And they did it in the pool.

31

Still Wylie telephoned Pinky the next morning. Pinky evaded an invitation to lunch at the Coal & Coke Club.

"I wouldn't feel at home there," he said.

Wylie usually ate at the Coal & Coke. He liked the heavy intractable linen napkins and the cut-glass water carafes placed on each table. The somber curtains and carpets were so thick, the darkly paneled walls so solid, that a gunshot would hardly have penetrated the padded silence of the rooms. He was the third generation of his family to hold membership.

A man's lunch was served at the Coal & Coke, no thin soups or delicate little salads but lamb chops, thick slices of beef and pork, baked beans, Brussels sprouts, and steaming whipped potatoes. Desserts were hot puddings and sugary pies. Some older members still tucked their napkins into their collars. Morgan the Elder would've felt comfortable at the Coal & Coke.

"You've been feeling at home other places," Wylie said.

"Listen, I owe you a meal and insist you join me at my club," Pinky said.

"You belong to a club?"

"Don't faint. Meet me in front of the post office at twelve-thirty."

The post office was a block from Thornhill & Co., the building pigeon-spattered gray stone with Doric pilasters. In front stood a fountain, though no water squirted through the gap-mouthed dolphin, an iron fish rampant. The clam-shaped bowl beneath caught only gum wrappers, rain, and cigarette butts.

Wylie was at the post office on time. As he waited near the fountain, he was curious about the club Pinky had joined. It couldn't be much.

Pinky came along in the crowd from Commerce Street with a tall, bearded young Negro better dressed than he. They shook hands and parted at the corner. Pinky appeared rumpled and bedeviled. His white shirt needed stuffing in, his maroon tie was off-center. He carried a brown leather briefcase which looked as if it'd been used for third base. His red hair was longer, particularly the sideburns. His worn brown shoes scuffed the hot pavement.

"So I'm late, sue me," he said.

When they walked toward Mountain State Bank, Wylie thought maybe Pinky was tricking him and had been accepted into the Coal & Coke Club, though no member would ever be allowed through the door without a jacket. Then they passed the bank's great bronze portals and turned toward the grime and din of River Steet. Pinky led him into an arcade.

The arcade had dirty frosted skylights, and pigeons pecked on the glass. At either side of the mosaic pavement steep metal steps and ramps led to balconies and offices. One office belonged to a chiropodist, a Dr. Petras, and his name was painted large on a wooden sign in the shape of an outsized foot.

Along ground level were a newsstand, a fruit market, and a café with open sides and a standup counter. Whorls of steam caused glass and mirrors to sweat. Mahomet's advertised in slashes of white soapy writing Syrian beans, stuffed grapes, and shishkabab.

"My club," Pinky said of the café.

"Let's go back to the Coal and Coke. I'll borrow you a jacket."

"Old boy, if you don't like my hospitality, clear out."

"It doesn't appear clean," Wylie said, staring at the speckled, imitation marble counter.

"I've eaten here for months and only twenty-two people have died of ptomaine."

The Syrians working behind the counter were all dark men who wore aprons. They appeared threatening but knew Pinky and called him by name. He recommended a lamb sandwich with pickles and horseradish. When the cold white plate was laid before Wylie, he was in no hurry to lift the weighty sandwich to his mouth.

"Wylie, honest to God, it won't kill you," Pinky said. "You need to find out how the other half lives."

"Why?"

"You wouldn't want to journey through life without being touched by it."

"I like to control who touches me and whom I touch."

"Starve then!" Pinky said and chomped into his sandwich.

Wylie nibbled at the thick dark bread. Fumes of horseradish spun into his nose and sinuses. His eyes watered. The slab meat was peppery, and dill scoured his mouth. The tough, chewy bread tasted of sesame. He took a larger bite.

"You see, the common people are not complete idiots," Pinky said, nodding. "What may seem vulgar to you can still be good."

"I admit I was wrong."

"We're making progress. In a couple more years you'll be able to walk into Woolworth's and buy a pair of socks without feeling shame."

"The hell I will."

They drank mugs of black chicory coffee and swallowed blueberry pie topped with scoops of vanilla ice cream. Wylie wiped his mouth on a paper napkin, lit a cigarette, and blew smoke toward the ceiling. Pinky paid the sullen Arab girl at the cash register.

"I won't tell anybody you been eating like an ordinary American," he said, stopping at the fruit market to buy a bag of oranges. The owner was also Syrian, and Pinky bargained with the excitable belly-heavy man till he got a dime off the price.

He and Wylie walked from the arcade toward Commerce Street. They waded through flocks of slovenly pigeons which, instead of flying, merely hobbled out of the way. Pinky had an appointment. He looked at his cheap watch, but Wylie drew him into the shade of a sickly maple the city had planted in an oval of soil surrounded by concrete.

"I need a word with you," Wylie said.

"I'm already late," Pinky said, winding the watch.

"You can give me a minute to sound like a Victorian father. What are your intentions regarding Trish?"

"She's a wonderful girl—that black hair, those violet eyes, she could play Cleopatra. Wait a second. How come you're looking at me so hard? You worried about us?"

"I'd like to know why you been sneaking around behind my back."

"All right, you got me. I'll confess. The truth is I'm searching for a rich father-in-law to further my legal career." He glanced about and lowered his voice as if revealing a secret which might be overheard. "Please don't tell anyone."

"Not funny," Wylie said.

"I admit I haven't been doing a lot of laughing."

"Meaning?"

"I'm smitten. I mean I'm really knocked out."

"I don't like the sound of this."

"I just wanted one more look at her. I knew she wouldn't remember me from the Fourth of July party. She'd eyed me as if I were a bug. Anyhow, I waited out there in the hallway till she came down those medieval steps. A cold ice princess she was. All the bone went out of me. I was smitten."

"Your definition of smitten?"

"I love her."

"You what?" Wylie rasped, tossing his cigarette into the gutter.

"I didn't want to," Pinky said and twisted his shoe on the cigarette. "I left her house but had to go back for another look. I believed I wouldn't react the same way a second time. It was worse. Sight of her puts me in pain."

"So you showed her your half gainer."

"Couldn't help myself."

"I'd like to know what you intend."

"She's hooked me. I can't stop seeing her."

"She and I are going to marry."

144

"I'd marry her too if I had the chance."

"Stay away from MacGlauglin."

"I doubt I can agree to that."

"She doesn't want you bothering her."

"She hasn't indicated that to me."

"I'll arrange that."

"You're free to do what you want and so am I."

"You bastard!"

"I'm being as fair with you as I can."

They stood covered by tattered shade, hot and uncomfortable, the dusty heat shimmering around them and rising between the begrimed buildings. Pigeons flew up sluggishly and circled. Pinky again looked at his watch and offered to shake before leaving. Wylie wouldn't take his hand.

32

Trish became interested in ceramics, and her father bought her an electric kiln, a large complicated professional model which required rewiring part of the mansion. The kiln was installed in a third-floor room which had a northern exposure.

When Wylie visited her, Trish often wore a straw-colored smock. She would have colorful dabs of paint on her. She produced tiles of Aztec design executed in red and black glaze. She was writing fashionable New York stores in hope of finding a sales outlet.

He hated mentioning Pinky, yet had the feeling they were meeting. To see her, Pinky would practically have to sneak into Mac-Glauglin, for Wylie was at the mansion three or four times a week, plus the whole of Saturdays and Sundays. Wylie asked too many questions.

"Why not come right out with it?" Trish said. She sat on a high wooden stool in her studio and wore the smock and sandals. She'd fixed her black hair in a twist bound by a red ribbon.

"Come out with what?" he asked.

"You've been trying to trap me. All these questions. Do I spend all day in the studio? Have I had any visitors? Don't I get lonely? Just come right out and ask me about him."

"All right, I'm asking," Wylie said.

"Haven't seen him since I don't know when." She scratched a knee of her black velvet slacks with a bulb-handled gouge.

"Glad to hear it."

"Not since day before yesterday." She laughed. "Joke."

"We better have a talk."

"Trish doesn't like talks." She bent to her workbench.

"Neither does Wylie but he doesn't see how we can avoid this one."

"You're going to fuss at Trish."

"I don't want to fuss at her or anybody."

"I'm just playing around a little before you put the shackles on me."

"It's making me nervous."

"Wouldn't think you'd let a creature like Pinky bother you so much."

"Why wouldn't I?"

"You don't believe he's as good as you are."

"Where you're concerned, that's right, I don't."

"Where we're concerned," she said and slid from her stool, strode with her full stride to the kiln, and squinted to read gauges. She appeared industrially chic. "He both admires and is envious of you."

"Any particular reason?"

"Why would he not be envious? You have Trish."

"I agree that's reason for envy, if indeed I have her."

"He believes you have superior breeding."

"Can't argue with that, though I'm surprised he cares much about breeding," Wylie said and pictured Pinky in his ill-fitting suits and broken shoes.

"He does, and he doesn't. He's torn. He wants your English face and aristocratic nose. He's ashamed of his rosy complexion. He's worried you're better than he is, not physically, at least not mostly physically, but in some qualitative way."

"You seem to know a whole lot about him."

"He didn't reveal himself all at once. I fit pieces together. He told me when he was a boy, your family served hamburger to your Irish setter."

"That's being envious of a dog."

"His father's a secret drinker. He remembers his mother crying because she had no nylons to wear to church. My guess is Pinky's always wanted to live in your house, sleep in your bed, and listen to operas on Saturday afternoons with your mother. He wants your parents."

"He must've really opened up to you."

"I know how to worm things out of people. In sum he considers you the original super-keen kid while at the same time resenting you."

She crossed back to her workbench and picked up a small pointed brush, which she dipped into a vermilion pot. She again bent to her tiles. She wore a gold bracelet and bright ceramic earrings shaped and colored like jungle parrots.

"What about a November wedding?" Wylie asked.

"What's in it for me?"

"I'm in it for you."

"I'd like just a few more life experiences before we lower the lid."

"You make marriage sound like a burial."

"Don't be surly. I'll let you know when the time's right."

An alarm sounded on her crackling kiln, the signal that it had reached critical heat. She hurried to it, the classiest artisan Wylie had ever seen. She pulled on huge asbestos gloves and lifted out a steaming tray of ceramic wafers—each a yellow eye with a black pupil on a scarlet background.

33

She wasn't finished with the theater world either. She explained to Wylie she'd received a call from a producer-director in New York named Claybough who wanted her to read for a play.

"I'm excited," she said. "I'll fly up and carry my ceramics to show the stores. I still have my apartment."

"I'm surprised your father let you keep that apartment all these months."

"The landlord's a prick with a firm lease, and I left a lot of stuff there. I didn't want to sublet and have strangers fingering my things."

"I'll go with you," Wylie said. He needed a holiday from Thornhill & Co.

"Love, I'm extremely serious about this play. I'll have to draw into myself and prepare my mind."

"You're telling me you don't want me."

"I'll want you very much when it's over, but this is like getting ready for war."

He drove her from MacGlauglin to the capital airport. She wore lemon-colored high heels, a lemon linen suit, and a pale pink scarf. Her luggage matched. She waved as she climbed steps to the plane, like a model in an airline ad, her smile and jewelry glinting in sunlight, her hair a black helmet, a breeze curling her skirt around tensed calves. People stared, thinking her a star, and Wylie felt proud of her beauty. She blew him a kiss.

That was Tuesday, and he phoned her Thursday while home proofing Thornhill & Co.'s monthly market letter. He and Thorny did the letter. He read Wylie's copy, Wylie his. They were putting a buy recommendation on Wheeling and Bethlehem steels.

"How's it going?" he asked Trish. He wore pajamas and was propped among pillows on his double bed.

"Nothing's definite yet. The script's complicated. If I could reach through this old phone and grab you, I would, but, lover, please don't bother me with calls till this is over. I need singleness of mind and purpose."

The following Saturday morning Wylie's mother gestured him into the music room and sat him beside her in his father's leather wing chair. Her phonograph played *Thaïs,* Amelita Galli-Curci's, and his mother gazed out the window toward the shadowed woods, waiting for the aria to end before speaking. To interrupt music, in her thinking, went beyond mere bad manners to sacrilege.

As if praying, her head was bowed, her eyes closed. After the music stopped, her fingers uncurled, her shoulders dropped. Troughs of her wavy brown hair were darker than the crests. She raised her long fair face and smiled.

"I believe it's time you have this," she said and from her lap lifted a black cube.

She handed him the cube, which was an ancient leather box with a golden hook clasp. Inside it held immaculate cotton, and under the cotton white velvet. A slit of velvet enclosed and protected a diamond ring, a major stone surrounded by satellites of lesser value. Age had smoothed the platinum band to delicacy, but the ring had recently been cleaned.

"It belonged to my grandmother. It's a blue diamond, almost three carats, and my grandfather brought it home from Africa to be cut and set."

"I'm in awe," Wylie said, holding the ring to the light.

"I had the mounting inspected and tightened. You'd be surprised what it's appraised for. I hope it fits Trish's finger."

Sunday morning Wylie woke to look at the ring on his bedside table. He turned to the window. The valley appeared clear of haze and vapors. A shower had freshened the greenery of the hills. The river lay like a copper snake in sunshine, and church bells rang.

He stood naked and felt the warm moist air graze his body. He ran fingers along his stomach and chest to his nipples. He wanted Trish. When she saw the ring, she'd forgive him any intrusion on her theatrical work.

He telephoned the airport. United had a flight at ten via Washington to New York. It was even possible Trish had finished her reading for the play and was ready for a celebration. The two of them would have a champagne orgy, romp in bed, and sometime during the night he's slide the ring onto her finger.

From LaGuardia he took a cab to Trish's apartment on East 86th Street. The uniformed doorman, an aging lumpy Irishman named Pete, recognized Wylie. Pete stood with his hands behind him, his legs spread, rocking heel to toe in the shade of a blue canopy. He touched the polished bill of his cap.

"Don't announce me," Wylie said and started into the foyer, where tropical plants grew from urns set along the carpeted corridor. Chandeliers lighted it. He felt pretty sure Trish would still be in bed.

"And who would I announce you to?" Pete asked, stepping after him.

"Miss Trish out already?" Wylie asked and checked his watch. It was not yet one-thirty.

"Well, sir, she's definitely not in."

"Will you let me go up and wait?"

"Such a wait might be long and lonely, as I haven't seen Miss Trish since Friday noon."

Wylie tried to order his thoughts. She would hardly be involved night and day in the reading. He waited till a bus passed and the air quieted before he spoke.

149

"Perhaps you missed her going out or coming in."

"Not likely, sir. I'm on duty so much that to me feet it's a shame. And when I go off, I always check with Johnny, the other doorman. I do believe she's not here unless she arrived by helicopter and entered by the roof, and we have no pad up there for landings."

"Would you take a look at her apartment? She has lots of baggage. You can't be sure whether she slipped in without you or Johnny noticing."

Pete rubbed his reddened porous chin and considered. Wylie reached for his wallet, yet Pete stayed his hand.

"Sir, I don't think we ought to do that. I know you're very close to Miss Trish, but then I don't have all the facts about your relationship, do I? Pretty ladies lead complicated lives."

"At least ring her for me."

"That I'll do gladly."

There was no answer from her apartment, and Pete turned questioningly from the house phone to Wylie. Wylie said he'd be back. He left the cool, hushed foyer and walked to Third Avenue, where he found a bar. It was nearly empty. He ordered a beer he didn't drink.

He attempted to remember the name of her producer-director. Claybough it was, Buck Claybough, who'd been involved in *The Sibyls*. Wylie stood to walk to the pay phone and look through the Manhattan book. He found Buck Claybough's name with an address on Patchin Place.

When Wylie dialed, a girl with a lisp answered. She called Buck to the phone. He sounded irritated and spiteful.

"The reading, who?" he asked.

Wylie again identified himself and said he was trying to find Trish St. George.

"You her father?"

"A close friend."

"Haven't seen her. Is this a trick?" He coughed long and loudly. "Her father's been trying to sue me."

"You didn't hear she's in New York?"

"All I've heard recently is closing doors," he said and from the background came laughter.

Wylie sat a moment fingering his beer. He returned to the phone, took out his change, and got more from the bartender. At the MacGlauglin mansion, Josh answered.

"Not coming till tonight, Mr. Wylie."

"Not coming from where?"

"She don't tell me," Josh said.

Wylie rode a cab to LaGuardia, where he was able to exchange his ticket for a late-afternoon flight. By seven he was home. He drove straight from the airport to MacGlauglin, which he reached a few minutes after nine.

From a garage that had one gasoline pump and a rain-rotted wooden marquee, he dialed the mansion. As he held the phone, he looked up through grimy panes to the hill and the glow of windows beyond the wall. Coal miners sitting on bottle crates watched him. Again Josh answered. Wylie asked whether Trish was back yet.

"Can't be," Josh said. "Too quiet around here."

Only one paved road coursed along the cindered valley. Wylie parked his Mercury on a weedy, rutted trail which led to an abandoned tipple. The tipple squatted like a great black spider in darkness. From the trail he was able to watch the road.

Suppose Trish didn't come at all? Something could be badly wrong. He thought of kidnapping and rape. Those didn't make sense. Whatever happened had done so on Friday. Word would've been heard by now. Or would it? His mind was going wild. He shook his head, smoked, and watched the deserted road. He would give her till twelve and then alert Mr. St. George.

At eleven forty-three the old Chevy rattled past, its radio playing. Two people inside were sitting as one. With headlights switched off, Wylie followed up the hill and through the opened iron gateway to the lighted courtyard. He braked, ran to the Chevy, and hit Pinky in the face just as he was stepping out.

Trish screamed. Wylie and Pinky closed, fell, and rolled over cobblestones and across damp grass to the fishpond. They tumbled into the pond and became tangled among water lilies, which were snaky and slimy. They fought their way upward, though Pinky wasn't hitting as much as he was attempting to protect himself.

"I couldn't help it, Wylie! Honest to God, I couldn't stop myself!"

Trish had run into the mansion, and her father hurried out wearing silky black-and-white pajamas and bedroom slippers. He fired one of his English shotguns into the air. The blast caused Wylie to hesitate just enough for Pinky to scramble away. Wylie would've pursued, but servants caught and pulled at him. They held his arms. Dalmatians barked and lunged. Wet, bruised, and bloody, Wylie heaved for air. Mr. St. George kicked at the dogs and shouted.

"Both of you, off my property!" he ordered. "I'll set the sheriff on you, and I own the sheriff in this county. You first, Cody. Jump in that heap of junk and roll it out of here!"

Dabbing at his nose, Pinky staggered to his car. He collapsed to the seat and had difficulty starting the engine. The weak battery turned it over just once each time he toed the starter. Finally the engine caught. Pinky wove the Chevy around the circle and sank down the hill past the spiked gate. His red taillights jiggled.

Josh and the gardener held Wylie. They too wore pajamas. Wylie feared he would vomit. Mr. St. George lowered his fowling piece and became affable.

"Care for a drink?"

"If I could wash up," Wylie said.

Which he did after following Mr. St. George into the mansion. Mr. St. George swabbed the Purdy's barrels with sheepskin patches and buffed the metal parts using an oiled flannel cloth before racking the shotgun behind glass. Wylie, in control of himself now, glanced at the baronial stairway.

"Don't bother her tonight," Mr. St. George said. "She's a willful girl who must be handled lightly."

Wylie drank his scotch straight. Josh brought Mr. St. George a white bathrobe. Mr. St. George was jolly. His left eyelid didn't flutter. He was entertained.

"That redheaded sonofabitch is bringing a legal action against me," Mr. St. George said. "He's eaten my bread and apparently used my daughter, but he's setting the law on me."

"You should've shot him."

"My finger itched on the trigger."

Wylie finished his drink, set the glass down, and looked at Mr. St. George. Mr. St. George raised his scotch and nodded his permission to leave.

On his way back to the city Wylie tried to catch Pinky. He hoped the old Chevy would give out and that he'd find Pinky exposed on

152

some lonely moonlit mountain road. Wylie still wanted to fight and drove those viperish roads with a daring fueled by fury.

By the time he reached his parents' home, he felt weak and again nauseated. He slipped into the house for a shower and first aid. When on Monday morning his mother exclaimed over his abrasions and swollen face, he told his parents he'd had a minor wreck. His father was confident insurance would cover the loss.

34

Trish played her last scene with Wylie eight days later. She telephoned Thornhill & Co. and asked him to drive down to Mac-Glauglin for lunch. His impulse was to hang up on her but realized this was something which needed to be got through—a ritual finish.

The summer neared an ending, the day rainy. Fog lay motionless above the glistening hollows. Cinders and slag had a gloss. As he drove up the hill to the mansion, fog blew away like a curtain being lifted. Then the fog slid back to take possession.

Trish wasn't at the house. Josh, in an apron and polishing silver, told Wylie she'd gone to the garden. He, under his umbrella, found her among bent dripping shrubs, bedraggled flowers, and wet marble statues. She wore her yellow slicker but no hat, causing her black hair to string out longer.

The Dalmatians ran beside her. They dashed about in hope of enticing her into a game, but she paused quietly at the ivy-twined sundial, pensive, her finger touching the pointer.

"Hope you're not the type who socks women," she said. She had on yellow rubber boots.

"I came for a good lunch."

"We'll have that." She seemed smaller. "I don't usually explain things to people, but I want to explain this."

He stood beside her, the umbrella sheltering them and the sundial, rain patting the black fabric.

"It's difficult for me," she said.

"Easiest thing in the world for me."

"Wylie, be kind."

As they strolled among soggy boxwood, she talked. A few lupines and chrysanthemums bloomed, mostly orange and rust colors, yet

153

drooped from the wetness. Trish moved with her arms straight and her face lowered as if repentant—or at least her idea of how repentance should be postured.

"I really didn't mean it to go that far," she said. "Even when involved, I couldn't believe it was me."

"How long were you with him?"

"Just the once, a one-night stand in a cheap motel. I did go to New York and lugged my ceramic samples around. I might have a sale at Tiffany's, the buyer's interested."

"But you and Pinky planned it out ahead of time."

"Oh sure. Now don't look so long-suffering. I've never been virginal, and you above all people should know that."

"Morality just doesn't count," he said, but even as he spoke he felt foolish.

"You and I, we're not moral people," she said and laughed. "And it's not your moral code that's hurt, it's your pride. You can't stand the thought of sharing me even once with Pinky."

Rather than answer, Wylie picked up a red-striped croquet ball and rolled it across the grass for the Dalmatians. They raced after it. The ball and the dogs' feet left bright tracks in the wetness.

"I want you to know I really didn't like him that much," she said. "It was a sort of curiosity, nothing more. He was never even for a second to me what you are."

"Trish, let's just go inside, eat, and say good-by."

"It's more important, what you and I had, than a silly roll in the hay."

"What we had already seems a long time ago."

"You're making it like that, not me," she said and stepped in front of him to hug him. She pressed her body against his in the rain. He was still affected by her touch, the strong softness. He could become aroused, yet he didn't kid himself that the old feeling was in any way remediable.

"He called me every day," she said of Pinky, drawing back. "He sent flowers, and he was so freakish and physical."

"Okay, you went for him."

"But I never really went for him. He fired me up is all, a temporary heat."

She took Wylie's hand, and they walked. He kept the umbrella over her.

"I didn't enjoy the lust so much either," she said. "All the time I told myself nothing really important was happening. He was no great lay, not nearly as artful a fuck as you."

It was the first time he'd heard a so-called nice girl use that word, and it was just like her to do it. She always had to be galloping at the head of the field. He would've withdrawn his hand, but she wouldn't let him.

They wandered into beads of fog till they reached the iron gate. Below, the sodden valley was dim and lifeless, the fog motionless over it. The working people were underground.

"You going to say anything?" she asked, glancing at Wylie's face.

"Where'd he meet you?"

"Huntington. He was at the airport with his crummy car to take me to the crummy motel which smelled of mildew. What made you suspicious?"

"I flew to New York for a celebration," he said and didn't mention his grandmother's ring.

"Well it's a mess, isn't it? Do you suppose there's anything we can do to make repairs? It isn't as if either of us were celibate."

They strolled along inside the wall and under the black legs of the iron water tank, the top of which was lost in the fog. Wylie no longer felt outrage but realized marriage would be stupid. He'd never be able to trust her. He couldn't live under the pressure of forever wondering what or who would tempt her next.

"I think we ought to give ourselves some time," he said, an evasion, and she knew it.

"Good idea there, sport," she said and stepped upward to kiss his mouth. "Now let's eat that lunch."

Josh served them tomato aspic salad, salmon, and a chilled bottle of Rhine wine. Lump coal burned in the dining room fireplace. Rain beat the windows. A muffled explosion caused the golden wine to ripple in the crystal goblets. The sound came not so much through Wylie's ears as from the floor through his legs. Distant thunder maybe, or perhaps something under the earth.

At parting, she stood on the wet cobblestones and waved when he drove between the spiked gates and down the hill. He felt as if he'd reached the end of a long run. He looked back once but spied only the wall, the rain, and the drifting fog.

35

He didn't see Trish again for more than a year. For all he knew she could be laying Pinky and half the world. Then in the Sunday *Gazette* he read of her engagement.

Her photograph was the largest on the society page, the picture not formal, not nuptial, she wearing a loose dark cardigan, a white collar, and a pair of her ceramic earrings shaped like lightning streaks. Her black hair was windblown, as if she were out walking the dogs. Anybody could look at the picture and judge her rich.

Her fiancé was the owner of a barge line which hauled coal down the Kanawha to the Ohio River. They would live on a horse farm near Point Pleasant, eleven hundred acres, the white plank fences as immaculate as church steeples, the grass as green as money.

Wylie pictured her dashing over jumps on her Kentucky thoroughbred, her slim body bent to the full gallop, her strong calves booted, her beauty given to the flow of speed. Maybe she'd have an affair with her trainer while her robust, profane husband was away on the rivers.

Hers was an April wedding, held not in the MacGlauglin mansion, but at The Greenbrier. There were two dance bands, champagne fountains, and private planes hired by Trish's father to land guests at the airport beside the polo field. Wylie sent a pair of silver candlesticks but didn't go to the ceremony or reception.

On the evening of the wedding day, he received a phone call from Pinky.

"You got to understand," Pinky said. "I tried to marry her. I wanted her to be my wife."

Wylie hung up, but Pinky called back.

"Please, let me come over and bring a bottle," he said.

"I don't like you," Wylie said.

"I feel like a kicked dog."

"The dog part I know to be true."

Pinky came anyway, carrying his bottle in a brown paper bag. Wylie had never known him to drink except the time at White Oak when they spiked his orange juice.

"Don't hate me," he said at the doorway. He kept a distance between them, his face held back as if fearful of being hit. He looked cheap, untrimmed, a door-to-door salesman peddling brushes or Bibles. He was already a little drunk.

Wylie wouldn't have let him in, but his parents were happy to see Pinky. They didn't know the reason for the breakup with Trish and made over him. They sat him in an armchair of the music room and questioned him about lawyering. They wanted to serve him cake and tea. Pinky handled himself carefully, not wishing them to know he'd been drinking. His brown paper bag had been left on the hall table just inside the door.

Later he and Wylie went down to the paneled game room and bar. Pinky again had his bottle, the cheapest bourbon sold in the state stores, a brand named Mountain Honey. Wylie wouldn't drink it, not ever.

"Maybe you could get me a little Coca-Cola for a mix," Pinky said.

"I'm getting you nothing," Wylie said, thinking it was just like Pinky not to know bourbon should be drunk only with branch water.

"Okay," Pinky said and unscrewed the cap from the Mountain Honey and drank straight from the bottle. He went into a coughing fit. "Lord, what people do to their bodies."

"When did you start doing it to yours?"

"I haven't started. I'm drinking because it's traditional. Supposed to do something desperate on the day the woman I love marries. Drinking is more sensible than jumping off a cliff."

"In your case I advise the latter."

"You got to be hurting too. We could share our grief."

"Pinky, go home."

"I won't forget her, I know that," Pinky said and crossed behind the pool table to one of the chintz sofas from the old house in the valley. He sat without being asked. Above him on the white wall hung an antique print of an American eagle. Wylie continued to stand near the door. "I'll never forget her."

"Oh come on."

"I mean it. She was in my blood. I woke every morning thinking of her. I went to bed every night wanting her."

"Apparently you got at least part of her."

"Wylie, I honest-to-God loved her."

"You'll find another girl to snake."

"That hurts," he said and tilted the bottle to drink. "How many times I have to tell you I'm sorry. I hated doing it to you. I felt awful. I feel awful now if it's any consolation."

"It isn't."

"See, you're suffering much as me."

"If I were, I wouldn't let others see it."

"Showing would be ungentlemanly."

"Something like that."

"Code of the class."

"Go home."

"Need another little drink," he said, again slurping from the bottle. A trickle of bourbon ran over his chin to his rumpled white shirt. He wiped at it. He was coughing and making a face.

"Not here, you don't."

"Another cut, insinuating I can't hold my liquor. Another class barrier. You don't realize how upset I am. How'm I supposed to keep my mind on the law? Course I don't have much of a practice. Even the cockroaches are fleeing my office. I'm considering taking a job with the IRS. I'll get my kicks by prosecuting bloated capitalists." He sighed and looked mournful. "God I loved her, and she's probably in bed with him right now."

"Pinky, one of the smartest ideas you ever had is not drinking. It doesn't suit you."

"Unlike you I didn't go to college to learn how. I went to study and make something of myself. I believe there are important aspects of life and many answers to be found. I could be a good lawyer if anybody would let me. Lawyering is a class occupation too. They do definitely have me pressed to the wall."

"I need to get to bed early," Wylie said.

"I have been disappointed in love," Pinky said. "All right, you don't want me here. You've never heard of forgiveness. I shall drive down the hill to my place in the valley. The valley is where I belong, not up here."

He gathered himself to stand, steadied himself on the pool table, and launched himself toward the doorway. Wylie let him out through the back entrance. Pinky, his pants cuffs dragging the ground, walked off into the darkness. He still held the bottle.

36

Through a trust arrangement with Mountain State Bank, Wylie's father gave him $125,000, which he invested as capital in Thornhill & Co. He was then voted a partnership and his name printed on the firm's crisp white stationery. The firm moved down to new ground-floor quarters on Commerce Street where Wylie had a secretary, his office a full window plus paneling deeply sheened, tawny carpeting, and impressionistic pastels of mountain streams, covered bridges, and blue valleys.

The market was strong. The higher the Dow-Jones, the more dollars customers carried through the polished oak doors. There were days when money seemed to fall from the sky.

Wylie and Thorny still wrote the market letter, and weekly their mailing list grew. The letter was in such demand they decided to start charging for it, seventy-five cents an issue or thirty dollars a year. They soon had subscriptions for three hundred copies.

They dreamed of making Thornhill & Co. so overpowering in the region no other firm would tread on their territory, but it wasn't that alone or the surging figures in Wylie's bank account which kept him working long hours. He was delighted, even enraptured, by finance. A man who'd never been in the game—poet, socialist, or divine—couldn't understand the exhilaration of counting what one's fiscal labors had created. The feeling bordered on the mystical and ecstatic. Money became music in his blood, a song in his genes.

He arranged lectures on stocks and the market before various city organizations—the East End Women's Club, several economics classes at Morris Harvey College, an employees' symposium at Union Carbide's plant beside the river. He always distributed free copies of the Thornhill & Co. market letter.

159

His was a soft sell, a genteel one, and he used a portable black-board to make simplified presentations. He showed audiences what compound growth could do in companies like IBM, Eastman Kodak, and Du Pont. He projected that growth ten years into the future and watched greed ignite eyes to shininess.

It was at Union Carbide's Recreation Center that a sedate blonde whose gray suit gave her a demure professional appearance raised her hand.

"Isn't it dangerous to attempt to predict the future of anything by its past?" she asked. "Every trend must reach a completion."

"In this case I don't believe it's dangerous because we have a country wonderfully blessed with natural resources and a dynamic citizenry. The creative energy arising from the interaction of the two is inexorable. Mathematics demand that stocks reflect it."

"Stocks do go down," the blonde persisted.

"Agreed. You protect yourself against drops by diversification. Say you invest in ten companies. Five should grow, three or four hold steady, one or two might falter. You should seek to be right more than wrong, not find perfection, which is as lacking in the market as everywhere else."

"I've heard that when elevator boys are talking stocks, it's time to beware," the blonde said.

"Where do you find them in this day of automatic elevators?" Wylie asked and got a laugh.

"I admit I haven't heard any actual elevator boys talking stocks, but I did hear a rug salesman say he was buying Sperry Rand on margin."

"He won't be a rug salesman long. He'll own the company."

The girl wasn't satisfied with Wylie's answers, but she sat down, politely skeptical, and primly smoothed her lap. She'd had an exact way of speaking, like an English teacher, or a foreigner who thinks in one language and talks in another.

He forgot her till the evening of a Kanawha Symphony concert. His mother was an organizer of the Civic Music Association, to which she gave large amounts of her time and money. At least twice a year she invited Aldo Pacelli, the argumentative, explosive conductor, to the house for dinner and flattery. She never spoke about it

160

with Wylie, but he knew she expected him to take his place in helping with the association's projects.

That cold December evening he and his father escorted her to the concert. They had aisle seats, and since all the people in their section bought season tickets, the performances were like old-home week. Friends called and waved. Jewelry flashed, furs rasped, and bracelets clinked. Wylie's mother carried her bound scores from her library.

First on the program was *Eine kleine Nachtmusik*. Wylie tried to remember his music appreciation course from Washington and Lee and worked at following the ins and outs of sonata form. As he watched the orchestra and concentrated, his eyes stopped on the cello section.

One of the cellists was the blond young woman from Union Carbide, or at least he believed her to be. Stage lighting made her skin pallid, her features flat. She wore a dove-gray Grecian gown and was very busy at her instrument, frowning, lifting her eyes swiftly from the music to glance at Maestro Pacelli, who used his long ivory baton as if it were both a saber and a languid willow branch.

"You really responded to the Mozart," Wylie's mother whispered, pleased with him.

During the second half of the program, the orchestra played selections from Gluck's *Orfeo ed Euridice*. When Pacelli had his musicians stand to accept applause, the girl curtsied gracefully. Hers was a classical presence, a merger of beauty and culture, of sweep and softness.

After the concert while his mother stopped backstage to offer congratulations, Wylie slipped away to the cluttered, rope-tangled area where players loosened their ties, smoked, and laid instruments in cases. The girl was zipping up the black cover over her cello.

"Carry your fiddle for you, lady?" he offered.

She tilted her head to look up at him. Her eyes were light brown and direct.

"The handsome young man who peddles financial dreams," she said.

"We're all peddling something—in your case Mozart and Gluck."

"Don't put music and securities in the same category, though I suppose you are respectable enough to tote Gertrude. Careful, she's an old maid."

He fitted Gertrude the cello into the back seat of her Plymouth. Wind blew around the concrete Civic Auditorium, rustling programs people had dropped, tumbling the paper into the night. She closed the collar of her plain dark coat and buttoned it under her chin.

"You knew me, but I don't know you," he said.

"You going to try to sell me shares of U.S. Baloney and Malarkey?"

"I hope to sell you myself."

"My name is Anne Abrams, and my phone number is 26-034."

With that she dipped into her Plymouth, pulled the door shut, started the engine, and, exhaust steaming, drove away across the parking lot.

He quickly wrote her number down on his program and walked back into the auditorium. His mother was searching for him in the lobby. Stately in her silver gown and glistening mink, she asked where he'd been.

"Chatting with musicians," he told her.

"It pleases me to have you take such an interest in the association," she said and hugged him.

37

Anne Abrams wasn't Jewish, and she drank only one pink lady before a meal. She worked in the Products Research Division of Union Carbide; the laboratory experimented with a new process for strengthening synthetic rubber. She came from St. Louis, where her father was a retired minister, and her speech had a black cadence. She'd gone two years to Mount Holyoke and earned her chemical engineering degree from the University of Missouri.

Her hands were small, her fingers short and practical. In repose she touched those fingers to her cheeks and allowed the heel of the hands to collapse under her chin. Her brown eyes looked at everything the way an engineer would, critically, seeking angles, weights, and stresses. She used her fork and knife like a person who hated excessive motion. He told her she was the first female engineer he'd ever taken to dinner.

"Like to know how many men have used that line on me? You all peer at me as if expecting me to produce an alembic and emit clouds of noxious vapors."

He needed to be careful with her. Trish had liked common talk, had been excited by the obscene, and this girl was not so much straitlaced as decent. Propriety was her banner.

Valentine's Day he drove her to the Pinnacle Rock Club dance and introduced her to friends. She wore a new gown, lavender, the shoulders bare, though the dress dropped modestly toward her breasts. She wasn't embarrassed by the attention she drew.

"How long you been keeping that sweet thing to yourself?" London asked in the locker room, where he combed his golden hair. His tailored tuxedo set off his fairness. He was the first of them to own a ruffled shirt. "Listen, does she dance close?"

"Not with degenerates like you she doesn't."

"All the biddies are nervous. They hope their daughters will catch the most eligible Wylie DuVal. Well I'm trying her."

"Watch yourself."

"I'll say please before laying a hand on a boob."

During the spring Wylie learned she played a serious, determined game of tennis. She was grim when she hit a ball badly or placed a shot stupidly. They made a good team for mixed doubles, and most weekends entered club tournaments. By then she knew him well enough to be critical.

"You never smash," she said. "You hit overheads as if the whole thing were boring."

"Waste of energy to kill a shot. Just poke it where they ain't."

"To show you cared would be bad form. You remind me of an English gentleman on the cricket green."

"Anne, that's the nicest thing you ever said to me."

"He means it!" she cried and raised her palms as if asking for help.

They dated two or three times a week, went to movies and concerts, parties and dances. At an art exhibition he saw Pinky trying to puzzle out an abstract oil. Wylie didn't introduce him to Anne.

They won the mixed-doubles cup awarded by the Pinnacle Rock Club in late August. After drinks on the terrace, Wylie drove Anne up to his parents' house instead of her apartment. They rose above haze to sunlight.

163

Wylie's mother had just come in from her little flower garden. Her wicker basket, which she carried over a forearm, was overflowing with waxy red and yellow blooms. She wore gloves, her coolie clothes, and white shoes. She held her snips.

She clicked those snips at sight of Anne. She went to Anne and presented her a hybrid marigold from the basket. Wylie's father came down the steps and spun his courtly charm around Anne. In minutes she was relaxed and laughing.

Wylie sensed they really liked her. It was more than just form. His parents had welcomed Trish, yet never been easy with her. They were wary of some MacGlauglin bizarreness springing out at them.

Anne's apartment in the valley was on the second floor of a Victorian frame house which had once belonged to a man who sold shoes, suits, and silk shirts to company stores in coal camps. On the stairway landing stood a bronze Cupid wired for light bulbs.

Anne had repainted her rooms and furnished them with pieces bought at auctions and flea markets, no antiques, but solid practical items. She'd scraped paint to finish chairs and a bed, using vinegar and boiled linseed oil to put a natural finish on the wood. Her walls were decorated with photographs snapped by her using her Nikon—a silver cracking tower, a steamboat passing under the old downtown bridge, mist rising over the river.

When he drove her home at night, he fixed himself a drink—not with her liquor, she never bought it, but from his own bottle set in her kitchen cabinet. Even alone with him she wouldn't drop her armor. He might draw her down to the green sofa, kiss her neck and mouth, even work fingers to the soft flesh above her nylons, but she'd permit it only a moment before pushing him aside and pulling her legs up between them.

"Let's not get carried away," she told him.

"Why not?"

"I don't like losing control of myself ever."

He didn't resent her holding herself back because he never burned for her as he had for Trish. He respected Anne's goodness. He was mature now, his days of lusting past—a man ready for marriage and a family. Thinking of his father and his father's father, he chose decency not to penalize himself or set upon his brow a crown of thorns but as a privilege. Decency, he believed, existed in his heritage and blood.

He carried his great-grandmother's blue diamond, the one meant for Trish, to Anne's apartment during a September Sunday afternoon. She wore a sweater, brown slacks, her walking shoes. She'd been practicing her cello and held the bow.

"It's the most vulgar gem I've ever seen!" she said, holding the diamond on her finger out at arm's length. "Unfortunately I can't accept it."

"Why?" he asked, stunned. He'd believed marriage was what she wanted.

"You haven't asked my father."

"You're serious?"

"I want my father's blessing."

"Can't we do it by telephone?"

"Definitely not."

They flew to St. Louis Friday afternoon and were met by no one, though the day was drizzling and windy. The taxi driver followed Anne's directions to a neighborhood of small homes in the western part of the city. Her parents' house was a one-story dwelling with a tiny yard and no furniture on the porch. Except for curtains, it hardly looked lived in.

Anne's mother was a plain, matronly woman who was pleasant enough but withdrawn. She spoke just above a whisper as if fearful of waking the world. She had on an apron and wore her gray hair in a bun. She'd fixed them meatloaf for supper.

The father had suffered a stroke which paralyzed the right side of his body, including his face, half of which sagged, even the eye. That eye seemed to be witnessing horrors. He was a lean man, slight and austere, his hair white, his voice slow and trembling but not defensive. He could feed himself, yet had to be helped from chair to bed.

Wylie had his talk with the father on Sunday before he and Anne left. They sat in the drab living room among furniture cast off by congregations. A black upright piano with a hymnal open on it stood against a wall. Chair arms had lace doilies on them. A bare wooden cross was fixed to a wall.

"Are you a Christian man?" the father asked Wylie.

165

"I strive to be, yes, sir."

"Will you repeat the Apostles' Creed with me?"

Luckily Wylie knew it from his confirmation classes at St. Stephen's and chapel at White Oak. Saying the words was like a ball rolling down the steps. He didn't challenge the words or think it necessary. He couldn't accept the resurrection of the body—that seemed an impossibility—but tradition confirmed the value of the creed and everything else about the church. One went along with it as he did with respect for elders and honoring parents. If Anne's father took the words literally, fine. Wylie would never intentionally upset him.

On the plane back, Anne quieted and turned her face to the window and lights passing beneath in the darkness below.

"Did I receive permission or not?" Wylie asked, because her father hadn't given him a definite answer.

"You're not taking the ring back," she said. "You passed, but just."

"Where'd I go wrong?"

"He thinks you're glib, which is true. Daddy likes serious people."

"You don't consider me serious?"

"Not in the way he means. Daddy struggles constantly with spiritual matters. I doubt you've done much of that. He also lives in hope and believes there's a chance for you and all men."

"Sporting of him," Wylie said.

38

They married at St. Mark's Calvary Church in St. Louis, a small wedding, the pews in the stone nave mostly empty. Anne's father attended, his wheelchair pushed to the altar rail. London and Blue ushered.

Now licensed, Anne still gave herself to no abandon. On their Bermuda honeymoon, her passion remained ladylike and correctly reined. She muted the few outcries of pleasure he was able to produce in her as if medicine to be swallowed. He expected little else and felt a tenderness for her, a sort of fatherly affection. There would be no burnout in this marriage because there was no fire. Good sense and respect would dominate.

Announcements were mailed, and gifts poured in, an avalanche of silver and cut glass. A package came from Pinky. Wylie's mother had sent him an announcement. Anne opened the box and spread tissue paper to uncover four rose-decorated finger bowls.

Wylie moved from his parents' house on the hill to Anne's apartment, where they'd live till able to decide on a residence of their own. The apartment had a narrow balcony at the rear, and during warm evenings after work, they drank wine, ate meals, and looked at the elms across the lawn of an overgrown Romanesque structure which had been a convent for the Sisters of the Sacred Heart. SALE signs were nailed to the doddering elms.

Anne showed Wylie Pinky's picture in the paper. He hadn't joined the IRS after all. The headline read, SUIT BROUGHT BY UNUSUAL PLAINTIFFS. Pinky stood among a gathering of disabled miners. The group was called Broken Men, Inc., and it had instigated legal action against a dozen coal companies, the state of West Virginia, and the United States of America.

"Can't he find anybody else to take on?" Anne asked.

In the newspaper Pinky was quoted:

"The problem is how to litigate on behalf of all the poor men from the mines who've been used up and discarded. Piece by piece doing so would take forever. It occurred to me to form a corporation of the broken. Have it duly registered with the secretary of state and issue stock. Any coal grubber who's been chewed up by the system and received unjust compensation can join by buying one share of stock for a dollar. We now have thirty-seven stockholders and are growing. We'll sue as a corporation, the same way GM or U.S. Steel does. Of course the coal-company lawyers will fight. They'll claim it's illegal, so Broken Men, Inc., will need to prevail in the appellate courts."

The name Broken Men, Inc., began to be seen frequently in the newspapers. Pinky brought a $5,000,000 suit on behalf of his stockholders. The amount seemed ludicrous and caused much laughter along Commerce Street. For a time the action couldn't go forward in the face of a countersuit by defendants that such litigation was patently unconstitutional. The circuit court of appeals upheld this opinion. Pinky bumped the case to the state supreme court, a three-man body which sat at the capital.

He argued the case before the court. The other side hired ex–lieutenant governor Asters, Sis's father, to present its arguments.

167

The justices took from May till November to decide and announce that the Broken Men suit could proceed. The vote was 2 to 1, and Pinky's pictures again appeared in papers.

The trial came up on the February docket when snow sheathed the ground and chunks of ice bobbed down the Kanawha. The suit had made the national wire of Associated Press and was the lead story on local radio and TV shows.

"Isn't it exciting?" Wylie's mother asked. "All those important attorneys being confounded by Amos."

Thorny slipped off from the office for an hour to watch Pinky at work in the courthouse. Thorny had taken to smoking cigars. He liked to hold a cigar clamped in the exact center of his mouth and talk without moving his teeth.

"He's slick as an eel in oil," Thorny said of Pinky. "You got to see him in action."

"I've seen enough of his actions," Wylie said.

"You're missing a great free show."

On an unbusy Wednesday afternoon Wylie's father called and asked whether they might walk the three blocks together to the sooty courthouse, which had a Chinese-type red-tile roof and the female stone figure of Justice armed and blindfolded.

Wylie and his father sat at the rear of the courtroom, where illumination from the globed bulbs was like gloaming. The benches were dull black pews as were the rails and paneling, the wood seeming to absorb most of the light.

Pinky sat alone at the plaintiff's table while across the aisle at defense a battery of attorneys were ranged, all mature men experienced in the labyrinthine corridors of their profession.

Pinky appeared isolated, ruddily vulnerable, much too young. Behind him in the spectators' seats were his miners, the stockholders of Broken Men, Inc. Some had their wives and children sitting beside them. The mountain people were scrubbed and stoic except when they stared at Pinky. Then they acted as if he were Joshua and they the children of Israel awaiting only the trumpet's call to attack the judge and jury.

Pinky had the clerk swear in Montgomery Gallison as a witness, Gallison president of the Yellow Eagle Coal Co. He was not imperial and haughty like Mr. St. George but gave off beams of power, a

168

heavy, square-jawed balding man who had a way of looking down his splayed nose as if taking aim.

"How often you go into your mines?" Pinky asked, not standing in front of the witness box or striding before the jury but sitting with elbows straddling his legal tablet on the plaintiff's table.

"Normally I don't go to the mines," Monty Gallison answered. "Don't have to. I pay mining engineers to do that work."

"If you don't go in, how do you know the conditions which exist?"

"I receive weekly reports on all Yellow Eagle's operations."

"You receive clean pieces of paper that you lay on a neat desk, and you think you know what's happening in your mines?"

"Your Honor, Mr. Gallison has no responsibility to enter his diggings or culpability arising therefrom," ex-lieutenant governor Asters said, standing, he chief counsel for the defense group. He had wavy white hair and a raptorial profile. Across the vest of his blue suit he wore a golden chain. Even motionless he seemed on the point of giving a peroration. "He's hired skilled, professional personnel to undertake and direct all operations."

Judge Sharpel sustained him. The judge was a backwoodsman who'd educated himself in the law by reading it. Aged, mottled, his gray hair bristly, he tongued a demure wad of tobacco cradled in his left cheek. From time to time he tilted sideways to drop mahogany globules from his stained mouth into the dead center of a brass spittoon. The spitton was kept polished by the bailiffs.

"Then you don't go into your mines ever?" Pinky asked Monty Gallison.

"Now and then of course."

"When's the last time?"

"Offhand I'm not certain."

"You can't remember?"

"Not to the minute and hour."

"During the last week did you enter a mine, any mine at all?"

"No."

"In the last month?"

"I don't believe so."

"In the last six weeks?"

"I don't keep a diary of when I go to the mines."

"In the last two months?"

"Your Honor, I believe Mr. Cody is at it again, which is taking us nowhere and wasting the time of this court," ex-lieutenant governor Asters said.

"In the last three months?" Pinky asked, ignoring the objection.

"Mr. Cody, you know where you're going?" Judge Sharpel asked.

"Hope so, Your Honor."

"So does the court," the judge said and spat.

"In the last six months?" Pinky asked.

"I don't remember!" Monty Gallison answered and looked as if he'd lunge from the witness box to choke and stomp Pinky.

Pinky called other coal operators to ask them the same questions he had Monty. Only one had recently been in his mines, and he just a few yards past the entry. The operators were furious at being made to appear unfeeling absentee landlords. Choleric Mr. St. George rumbled, sputtered, and twitched. His eyelid fluttered like a bee's wing. He wanted his machine gun.

"Enough of this," Judge Sharpel ordered Pinky.

In front of the jury shabbily-clothed Pinky acted injured, wronged. He exploited his youth by seeming harried, innocently confused, weary. That youth and rawness jarred against the ex-lieutenant governor and the other suave attorneys. Wylie saw the four women on the jury follow Pinky with the eyes of worried mothers. They and the male jurors didn't wish to see an underdog humiliated and cut to bits by worldly and elegant legal aristocrats. Pinky stood out like an uncouth fundamentalist preacher in a cathedral.

He called miners to the stand. The first was Bud Gasser—middle-aged and bent under an invisible burden. Bud wore no hat, but if he'd had one, he would've clutched it in his left hand. The right hand fitted into the jacket pocket of his coarse black Sunday suit.

"What happened?" Pinky asked.

"Went into the mine as usual on the hoot-owl mantrip," Bud answered.

"How is as usual?"

"We ride the belt in. Lie down on the belt, and the operator runs her in reverse."

"You lie down on the conveyor used to bring out coal?"

"Ride it to the work face."

"How far?"

"There's more than one belt, altogether with some walking about

170

two miles." He began coughing and covered his mouth with his palm. "We crawl some too."

"The belt rough?"

"Put bumps and bruises all over you. Knock you silly."

"What then?" Pinky asked, still sitting at the plaintiff's table.

"We come to the work face but didn't like the roof."

"Did you complain?"

"Sure."

"To who?"

"The super."

"The superintendent. Wasn't the roof bolted?"

"They wasn't using bolts in that mine. Timbers was cracking and popping. Splinters come up on posts like hair on a scared dog."

"The weight of the mountain on timbers caused them to buckle and splinter."

"Right."

"Anything else?"

"We heard that old mountain talking."

"A mountain can talk?"

"A mountain can whistle 'Dixie.' It was saying, 'Look out below.'"

"What'd you do?"

"Hollered for the super to come see. Wouldn't fool with no coal till he seen himself."

"What'd he tell you?"

"He told us we could get us a job with the ladies sewing quilts."

"He told you you were acting like women to shame you into working that coal."

"Sure did and some."

"Then what happened."

"We started bringing her out. We cut into the seam face with a joy—"

"A what?"

"A mining machine made by Joy Manufacturing. The drum has cutting teeth on it that chews right into the coal."

"What then?"

"The roof come down."

"You had no warning."

"It come like *whoosh*."

"How many of you?"

171

"Five."

"Trapped how long?"

"Four days."

"What'd you do during those four days?"

"Wasn't nothing you could do. Just laid there under the coal."

"You lay under that mountain without food, water, or sanitation four whole days?"

"Had to."

"Were you hurt?"

"My legs was broken, some ribs too. My hand was hurt."

"What happened to the other men?"

"Two was dead."

"What moneys did you receive for the pain and damage to your body and mind?"

"Counting Social Security, workers' compensation, and union retirement $230 a month."

"How much from Yellow Eagle Coal Co.?"

"They paid hospital and doctor bills."

"You were disabled and almost killed and that's all?"

"They sent me some flowers."

"You have a wife?"

"Yes, sir."

"Children?"

"Three boys and a girl."

"All of you live on $230 a month?"

"If you can call it living."

"You're unable to work?"

"Too busted up."

"Where are you still busted up?"

"Got one hand. Not much you can do with only one hand."

"Will you show us?"

"Sure," Bud Gasser said and twisted sideways in the witness chair to withdraw his right hand from his jacket pocket. The hand was a plastic-glassy prosthetic device shaped like fingers in repose.

"Don't work none," he said.

"May I see it?" Pinky asked.

"You want me to unhitch?"

"If it's no trouble."

Bud Gasser pulled back the sleeves of his jacket and shirt. The hand was attached to his stump by a system of darkened leather straps and a leather cuff. After unbuckling the straps, he lifted the hand to Pinky.

For the first time Pinky stood from the plaintiff's table. He crossed to the witness box, took the hand, and slowly turned it over to examine it. He walked toward the jurors, who gazed at the hand.

"Like to have a look at this?" he asked and offered the hand to the elderly white foreman.

The foreman shook his head rapidly and leaned back as if the hand might seize him. Pinky offered it to other jurors. They pushed away in their chairs.

"With the court's permission, I'll ask the clerk to place the hand in evidence as plaintiff's exhibit number one," Pinky said and carried the hand to the bench. Judge Sharpel came from the mountains and knew the sight of blood. He merely shifted his wad and nodded to the clerk.

The clerk, a sallow, bespectacled man who wore a polka-dot bowtie and provided the Bible for swearings in, took the hand, marked a tag with his pencil, tied the tag to the thumb, and set the hand on the table before the judge's bench.

Pinky crossed to the table, reexamined the hand, and placed it back on the table not softly, not carefully, but with a toss which caused a thump.

That thump was the first of many. Each miner Pinky called to the stand was mutilated. Prosthetic devices began to pile up—an artificial arm, a leg, another hand. Grunting, a miner removed a foot, his hightop shoe still on it, the black leather shined. It too thumped the table before the judge's bench, which started to resemble a shrine, like Lourdes, where exultant pilgrims discarded crutches, canes, and braces as testimony to the sufferings and afflictions they'd been delivered from.

Pinky requested men to remove clothing to display wounds and scars. A youth revealed lug brands across his back where he'd been run over by a crawler tractor. A black man's nose was missing. A miner popped out an agate eye. The jury stared as the eye clicked against the table.

A miner had to be helped to the witness box by Pinky. He was a loose-fleshed spastic whose spine curved him rearward. He could sit erect only after Pinky wedged him into the witness chair. His mouth jerked, his hands flapped.

"Your age?" Pinky asked.

"Thirty-five," the man answered, his voice a wavering rasp, high-pitched, feminine.

"What happened to you?"

"The machine come after me."

"Why did it come after you?"

"Defective."

"You complain to your section foreman?"

"Ten times anyhow."

"What'd he do?"

"Said he'd have it looked to."

"Did he?"

"Not that I saw."

"What then?"

"I was trying to move the machine to the face."

"Go on."

"I set the brake and was standing alongside feeding the power cable. A gear slipped, then whirling teeth spun and come after me."

"What are the teeth?"

"Steel spikes. Near ate me."

"How long were you in the hospital?"

"I'm still in the hospital."

"How many years?"

"Six."

"Are your hospital bills being paid?"

"At first but lately they say I used up all my entitlements."

"What did the machine do to you?"

"Broke about every bone in my body, including my teeth."

"How many operations you had?"

"Eleven."

"Eleven operations in six years. Anything else, Mr. Hawkins?"

"Yeah."

"Will you tell it?"

"Nah."

"Then will you answer this question: Are you still a man?"

"Nah, took that too."

174

Pinky helped Hawkins remove his jacket, shirt, and underwear. The miner's chest had been carved on so many times he appeared laced. Reddish, fist-sized lumps stuck from his loose gray body. Sutures strung along his flesh like gaily colored fringes.

Pinky's last witness couldn't make it to the courtroom.

"His name is Jess Ackers," Pinky explained to Judge Sharpel. "He's been burned so badly no hair will grow on him."

Ex-lieutenant governor Asters and two other defense attorneys rose quickly to object.

"Plaintiff's counsel is giving testimony," they said.

"Just trying to be descriptive," Pinky said, acting surprised and as if being treated unfairly. He was sweaty and disheveled.

"If your witness can't appear, you can submit a proper affidavit," the judge said, again shifting his chaw.

"I'm hoping for that affidavit any second," Pinky said.

"You expect the court to wait on your convenience?" the judge asked.

"If you could allow me a couple more minutes," Pinky said. "Jess Ackers intended to be here himself, yet had to be rushed to the hospital to undergo an emergency operation. Jess has not only been terribly burned by a series of firedamp, that is, methane explosions, but also one of his legs was crushed by a runaway mine car. Doctors have been trying to save that leg, cutting it off little by little, taking his toes first, then half his foot, then the ankle, just whittling away on him over the years as if he was a stick of wood—a living stick of wood."

"Your Honor!" the defense attorneys called.

"Mr. Cody, you surely know I'll not permit you to carry on this way in front of the jury," Judge Sharpel said. "If you have evidence, put it on. Otherwise sit down."

"Judge, I do believe I've got it here," Pinky said, turning from the bench to the dark double doors of the courtroom. Being detained by bailiffs was a tall, tan Negro wearing the white uniform and shoes of a hospital orderly. He was out of breath.

"Let him come forward," Pinky called to the bailiff. "Your Honor, here's my witness if the clerk will be good enough to swear him."

The young Negro carried a brown rectangular cardboard box, the kind a dress or suit of clothes might be packed in. It was tied with yellow twine. He offered the box to Pinky, but Pinky instructed him to take it on to the witness stand. Seated, the Negro held the box on his lap. His name was Richard Ennis.

"How long you worked at Valley General?" Pinky asked.

"Going on five years."

"Your job in a particular section of the hospital?"

"Surgical wing, the OR."

"The operating room."

"One of them. We got three."

"You work there today?"

"I just ran from the OR right to here."

"What was going on in the OR?"

"An operation. That's what we do there."

"Tell us the name of the patient."

"Jess Jacob Ackers of Cabin Creek, West by God Virginia."

"How do you know his name and address?"

"I read his medical tag before wheeling him to the table."

"Though you're not a doctor, Mr. Ennis, from your nearly five years of experience in the OR would you call what was being done to Mr. Ackers minor or major surgery."

"Major. They cut deep."

"With your own eyes you saw the surgeons cutting on Jess Ackers?"

"I was standing by with the pail."

"What part of his body was being cut on?"

"His right leg, what's left of it."

"They took most of his right leg."

"It's gone now."

"You have something with you in that box?"

Richard Ennis nodded and lifted the box slightly from his lap.

"You brought it from the hospital?" Pinky asked.

"From the OR."

Pinky paused to allow everybody time to eye the box. Even Judge Sharpel stilled his chaw and edged over to look. Richard held a hand at each end of the box to steady it.

"Open it for us," Pinky said.

Richard untied the yellow twine, coiled it around his fingers, and stuck it into a side pocket of his uniform. He shook the box while holding the top so the bottom would fall onto his lap.

The bumping around of whatever was inside sounded through the quietness of the courtroom. Bodies became motionless, faces

176

rigid. While Richard held the top, Pinky took the box's bottom and placed it on the table used for evidence. Inside lay a bundle wrapped with gauze. The jury, the defense attorneys, and Judge Sharpel stared and fidgeted.

"Mr. Cody, what you doing to us?" the judge asked.

"Your Honor, I have here an object I'd like to place in evidence after I show it to you," Pinky said and reached into the box to lift out the wrapped bundle. A tail end of gauze had fallen loose.

"I don't think I like the road you've taken," the judge said.

"Sir, what I have here is a special sort of affidavit from Jess Ackers, who can't be with us today because of his burns and his amputated leg."

"What you holding?" the judge asked.

"That's what I'm going to show you," Pinky said and began unwrapping the bundle. He did it slowly, methodically, allowing the gauze to trail down and gather on his shoes.

"Your Honor, plaintiff's counsel is attempting to sway the jurors through the presentation of ghoulish, sensational artifice!" ex-lieutenant governor Asters cried out.

"Stop it!" the judge ordered Pinky.

"Stop what?" Pinky asked, unwrapping the bundle.

"Whatever trick you're up to, I'm ordering you to stop," the judge said.

Pinky stilled his fingers, but the gauze had been peeled down to a brownish red stain. People gasped and turned away their faces. A woman juror raised her balled handkerchief to her mouth, closed her eyes, and bowed her head.

"I'm ordering you to put that thing back in the box!" Judge Sharpel said.

"Your Honor, what I'm holding here is evidence vital to the plaintiff's case."

"You're not turning my courtroom into a butcher shop!"

"Your Honor, with all respect, this is the people's courtroom, and I want this jury to see evidence which will aid it in making a reasoned judgment," Pinky said and unwound another gauzy loop, revealing a larger splotch of blood.

"Put it away or I'll have the bailiff take it from you!" the judge said.

"May I approach the bench?" Pinky asked.

"No, you can't approach this bench, and you're not going to succeed in what you're trying!" the judge said. Holding his gavel like a hatchet, he stood. Others rose—attorneys, jurors, spectators. Talking surged. Judge Sharpel beat both his gavel and hand against the bench.

Pinky stopped unwrapping but held the bloody bundle as if it were an offering. The judge banged and slapped the bench till he finally quieted the courtroom. He peered fiercely down at Pinky.

"I want that thing out of here!" he said.

"Exception, Your Honor, and I'd like it recorded you're denying the plaintiff's counsel the right to introduce evidence," Pinky said.

"It's not evidence, it's theater!"

"If you'd lost this, I think you'd likely consider it evidence."

"Put it away!"

"I will, sir, but, note my appeal."

Pinky turned to cross to the box on the table. As he approached it, he purposely stumbled on gauze trailing around his legs. To save himself from falling, he dropped the bundle, and it thudded on the floor. It rolled toward the jurors.

People whimpered, cried out, and a woman screamed. Eyes bugged in horror. The object wasn't completely revealed, but there was a shocking flash of bloody flesh and a stub of bone. A juror wept.

The judge shouted for his bailiffs, and uniforms closed around Pinky. No one wanted to touch the object. Pinky lifted it, rewrapped it, and set it gently inside the box. Judge Sharpel adjourned the terror in his court, and he himself escaped through the doorway behind his bench.

When three days later the jury took the case, the defense attorneys had thoroughly cross-examined all the Broken Men and showed to the jurors the releases the men had signed relieving the various coal companies of further responsibility for injury. Pinky rebutted, drawing testimony that most of the men had signed the releases while in the hospital under medication and without the benefit of advice from counsel.

During the closing arguments, the prosthetic devices were not on the table. The area where they had been placed was a stark, accusing emptiness.

The jury stayed out seven hours, not long considering the diversity and complexity of the injuries. The verdict awarded Pinky's Broken Men, Inc., the full $5,000,000. On appeal from ex-lieutenant governor Asters and the other defense attorneys, the West Virginia Supreme Court upheld the judgment, though the tribunal adjudicated a reduction in compensation to $2,900,000. That worked out to some $60,000 for each injured miner.

Pictures appeared in newspapers and magazines of Pinky, his Broken Men gathered around him, holding the check and fanning himself as if he were burning up.

39

He was hot, endlessly dogged by petitioners, constantly in court. When he walked along Commerce Street, people often moved beside him. He could've been a congressman with patronage to dispense.

He still dressed sloppily, though he did trade in the dilapidated Chevy for a white Oldsmobile. He must've been eating better too, for he no longer resembled the gaunt, big-eyed men he often represented.

Through Anne, Wylie learned Pinky was dating too, the girl Esther Chappel, the only daughter of a city merchant. Wylie had known and liked Esther from way back. She wasn't wild like Sis, Bebe, or Trish, but reserved, not so much prudish as possessed of a sort of gentle spirituality. Wylie had once escorted her to a Christmas tea dance, and at her door afterwards she would allow him to kiss her only on the cheek.

Yet she was athletic, one of the best female golfers in the valley. The den of her father's house glittered with silver trophies she'd won. Wylie thought her plain except her legs, which were nicely muscled. Her sandy hair she cut short as if not wanting to be bothered by it. Her face was a little too round.

She never dated much, mainly because she wouldn't permit herself to be casually used. Men asked her out occasionally, but none steadily, and no whispered stories were told about her in the Pinnacle Rock locker rooms. Most often she was seen on the fairway punching balls toward the practice green.

She competed so frequently she smelled of grass. Wylie drew her as a partner in a best-ball match and was startled to see how she curved her body into a stroke. That anyone as withdrawn could give herself so completely to a physical act didn't seem possible.

For months he wouldn't see her at all. Then the showboat *Gordon C. Greene* paddled up the Mississippi River to the Ohio, where it

179

played at Cincinnati before continuing along the Kanawha to the city. A calliope tooted across town, posters appeared bright on power poles, and torches flickered over the dark water.

The same Friday night Wylie drove Anne to a performance, Pinky arrived with Esther. He was on his manners, opening doors for her, helping her take off her blue silk wrap, and standing practically every time she moved a finger. His red hair had been trimmed, but his gray summer suit didn't fit well and needed pressing. His shirt did appear clean.

At intermission Anne insisted on speaking. They stood under lanterns strung along the foredeck. The women drew together, genuinely fond of one another. Wylie had to talk to Pinky. Esther's legs were as pretty as ever.

"Thought maybe you were in this production," Wylie said. "The way you act in the courtroom, you could certainly make it on the stage."

"Me, act? I have no idea what you mean."

"The performance with the leg was gruesome."

"It was still warm," Pinky said. "I felt the body heat through the gauze."

"Amos!" Esther said. Obviously she knew him well enough to fuss.

She and Anne walked to the ladies' room. Wylie and Pinky waited self-consciously at the railing and looked toward the lights and fires of Union Carbide. The cracking towers were silver columns in the night. The air carried a confusion of biting chemical odors, but the Kanawha, gliding quietly, had taken on the sibilant beauty of darkness.

"You're a lucky guy to be squiring a gal like Esther," Wylie said. He would attempt to be sociable.

"I knew you'd think that because she's one of you."

"One of what?"

"The crowd, the gang, the club, whatever it is you all are. She belongs. And her father doesn't like me."

"If I were you, I wouldn't take her father out."

"You've never known what it's like to be disapproved of by a girl's parents."

"I guess not."

"You don't have to tell me. Listen, Wylie, I like this girl. I'd appreciate it if you didn't go out of your way to make me look bad in front of her."

Anne and Esther came back, their faces tinted by the glow from lanterns. When the gong sounded for the second act of *Little Nell*, they spoke their good-bys. Pinky offered Esther his arm and led her back toward the theater.

"How'd they get together?" Wylie whispered.

"I can tell you," Anne said. "Ladies' room talk. She was working in her father's store. Pinky, at the shirt counter, had a nosebleed. She hurried him to a couch in the business office where he could lie down. She hadn't thought he even noticed her. That night he telephoned to ask her to a baseball game. She twice made excuses before going out with him the first time."

Pinky and Esther were at the Pinnacle Rock Thanksgiving dance. Esther had membership through her father, being an unmarried daughter, and was thus permitted to invite a guest. Pinky wore a tuxedo, the first Wylie had seen on him. Wylie would've bet it was rented, not bought.

At Anne's urging, Wylie danced with Esther. She was perfumed, had on a rose chiffon gown, and felt strong, yet supple in his arms.

"He's done so much for himself, worked his way through college and battled to be a lawyer," she said. "How many of our generation have achieved half that?"

"He's tough all right," Wylie agreed.

He went down the circular steps to get drinks for Anne and himself. Outside the broad windows and beyond the terrace the projection of stone called Pinnacle Rock was illuminated by a spotlight, like a ship's prow, worn away by wind and time, headed into the night.

Pinky stood at the red-leather bar shaking his head. Alexander, the red-jacketed black bartender, was in no hurry to serve him.

"The spades up here are the biggest snobs," Pinky said. "They know I don't belong. They sense it and snoot me."

"Maybe I can help," Wylie said and held up a finger. Alexander came at once.

"I don't care whether I drink or not," Pinky said. "Esther likes her tod. For a while I stuck to ginger ale, but deception is too complicated. Everybody treats me like a freak. So I'm learning to dally with scotch. I honestly don't understand how anybody can enjoy a liquid which tastes as if it's brewed in a toilet."

Anne invited Esther and Pinky to sit at her and Wylie's table near the band. Pinky danced adequately, though where he'd learned Wylie

181

had no idea. Maybe Esther had coached him behind closed doors. Pinky brought her a second highball from the bar but continued to fake his own drinking with a single glass of scotch and soda.

Wylie had spoken to Emerson Smythe, already a little tipsy yet elaborately genial because vinous geniality was his avocation. A few years older than Wylie, Emerson had been born into a second-generation coal family, and through the filter of time his money became sanitized and cultured, straining out memories of near starved immigrants who'd fled to this country from County Cork, human cattle in the dark pit of an iron ship.

Emerson kept glancing at the table. Wylie believed he was looking at Anne or Esther, for Emerson liked to think he loved the ladies, all ladies, including secretaries, salesgirls, and waitresses, whose smooth bottoms he passed his veined white hand over. He didn't bed them—he was too effete—but he valued loveliness in women as he would in a Greek amphora or an ivory figurine of the second Ming dynasty.

Wylie didn't realize Emerson was watching Pinky till Pinky went for Esther's fur wrap and his own brown overcoat. Above the dance music Wylie sensed more than heard or saw a stir at the cloakroom, a shifting and repositioning of bodies. Wylie stood, excused himself from Esther and Anne, and crossed out of the ballroom.

"Did you check your arms, legs, and eyeballs?" Emerson was asking Pinky. Emerson was thin as a stick, limber, and his black hair lay flat along his skull, hair trained to perfect obedience.

"I just want to get the coats and go home," Pinky said. "Now, Emerson, if you'll move—"

"Don't you call me Emerson. Only my friends can do that."

"Okay, Mr. Smythe, just get out of the way and I'm gone."

"What's happening here?" Heine Stahl asked, he the club manager, a small, chubby first-generation American who moved about as if marching at drill. He had a habit of clapping his hands for servants.

"I shouldn't think you'd want to take your pleasure at a place where you've bled so many of the membership," Emerson said to Pinky.

"Somebody's bleeding?" Heine asked.

Fingers touched Wylie's arm. It was Esther looking to him for help.

182

"He's a guest, Em," Wylie said and eased himself between Emerson and Pinky.

"He's a snake in the grass!" Emerson said. "That's what you've taken to your bosom, Wylie, a damned serpent!"

"He doesn't have a bosom," Pinky said to Emerson.

"Let's all remember our manners," Heine Stahl said.

"We'll just slip out," Esther said, taking hold of Pinky's arm.

"Really enjoyed the party," Pinky said as he and Esther sidled around Emerson, but Emerson wouldn't quit. He was holding a drink, and in a sort of limber glide he stepped to Pinky and tossed the scotch into his face.

Ice cubes bounced from Pinky to the golden carpet. Liquor dripped from him over his tuxedo, shirt, and shoes. Scotch had splashed onto Esther, causing wetness at her throat and spotting her rose chiffon gown. Helplessly she touched her neck.

Pinky's face flamed, and he snarled as he snatched Emerson's shoulder, jerked him around, and grabbed him by the collar and the seat of his skinny pants. Emerson shot up on his tiptoes.

Pinky rushed him into the ballroom. Dancers scattered. Faster and faster Pinky propelled him. Emerson was frightened first by his lack of grace and then by his increasing speed. He made a tiny, flutelike noise.

When Pinky hit full stride, he tossed Emerson skating and windmilling along the waxed amber floor. Emerson lost his footing. He shrieked as he fell and spun as if on ice, his white spindly legs kicking like an overturned insect.

He skidded into the glitter and flash of the band. Music racks, burnished instruments, and chairs toppled. Musicians leaped out of the way. The bass drum thumped. Sheet music settled around Emerson.

He lay aghast, a gilt trombone across his chest, his mouth open, and one delicately slippered foot probing feebly the skin of the drum. He still held tightly to his empty highball glass.

40

During early spring Pinky telephoned to ask Wylie to serve as a groomsman in his wedding. Wylie quickly made an excuse that he would be away from the city on the May weekend of the ceremony. He'd find some reason to leave town.

183

"I'll get Esther to change the date," Pinky said.

Wylie, both embarrassed and angry, told Pinky he'd come to see him that night. He resented Pinky's putting him into such an uncomfortable position. They weren't friends and really never had been. Moreover, among Wylie's customers at Thornhill & Co., there was lots of bad feeling about Pinky and his courtroom forays.

"But you have to do it," Anne said to Wylie the same evening as they ate dinner.

"Anne, I don't like the guy."

"He must've needed you badly or he wouldn't have called," she said. "And your parents would expect you to."

"They don't know Pinky the way I do."

"You're going to refuse?"

"As gently as I can."

Wylie drove through the warm darkness to Pinky's place, an efficiency in a five-story brick building built during the 1920s. The Brinkley Apartments were near the New York Central tracks and vibrated when trains passed.

His Wrong-Side address was not so much shabby as temporary. Everything gave the impression he'd never bothered to finish unpacking. Law books lay on the floor. Drawers had been left open. Clothes were strewed about. On a shaky card table he'd been repairing a portable typewriter. His Bible was half covered by a sheet of his unmade single bed. The only hint of decoration and humanity was a golfing photograph of Esther on top of the refrigerator.

"You've never forgotten I stole your watch and your girl," Pinky said after Wylie explained he wouldn't serve in the wedding no matter what the date. They sat on two straight wooden chairs facing each other across the card table. Above them shone a bright bare bulb in a tarnished flowery metal socket.

"I haven't dwelt on it," Wylie said.

"But you think about it whenever you see me. I wish you'd remember I did give the watch back and lost the girl too."

Wylie said nothing. He sat toward the front of the chair to let Pinky know he didn't intend to stay. Pinky nodded and ran his hand over his hair. His bare feet were stretched beneath the card table. He wore pants to his gray business suit and a white undershirt. He rubbed an arm. His body had more red curly hair on it than ever.

"Wylie, I'm going to make you a pitch. I hope you'll take it seriously. First I'd like to ask you to remember I didn't come from much and have a little patience with me. I'm not knocking my parents. They're the best they can be. I love them. A lot of what I've done is out of ignorance and lack of opportunity. I didn't start with your advantages, but I am getting the picture."

Pinky continued rubbing his arm and leaned back in his chair. From somewhere in the building came the sound of pounding.

"Esther means everything to me," he said. "I not only love, I respect her. Now a wedding belongs to a woman, not the man. He's just kind of a piece to be pushed around. I confess I'm having trouble finding respectable groomsmen."

"I don't like you, Pinky."

"Hear me out. I have people I can ask, but they wouldn't look proper standing before the altar at St. Stephen's Episcopal Church. Not that I myself care. I want things right for Esther, and I'm desperate. I'm so desperate I'll beg you if I have to. With you I'll have some gentility on my side of the aisle—for her sake, not mine. I know you're really fond of her, and it's for her I'm asking you to do this thing."

"You're manipulating me."

"Sure. I'm exploiting your decency."

He laughed, but Wylie stood to leave. In his bare feet Pinky padded to the door to open it.

"Old Trish," Pinky said. "Actually you shouldn't hold that against me any longer. She would've made either of us miserable."

"Probably."

"I saw her recently. I was in Washington on some legal business for the UMW. She came into the Statler restaurant. She wore a red dress, long black gloves, and black shoes. With her was a young army officer, a major. She didn't see me. She acted as if she owned the place. I tell you we're lucky men not to have won her."

41

The wedding was at seven in the evening. The polished ebony pews on the bride's side of the aisle filled with many of the city's most prominent families. Only a scattering, Wylie's parents among them, sat on Pinky's side. Some were his Broken Men, a few of them Negroes, all wearing those stiff, dark woolly suits. The other groomsman and best man was a redheaded cousin of Pinky's named Bartholomew who sold industrial pumps to the mines.

During the organ prelude, spotlights were switched on outside to ignite the stained-glass windows of the nave. Trouble with the pipe organ caused alarm and confusion. The sexton, while using a screwdriver to repair an electrical connection, knocked over a vase of white roses.

Pinky's mother and father arrived. They hadn't attended the rehearsal or the dinner following at the Pinnacle Rock Club. The mother wore a green dress which was clean and neat but no gown. Her wild black hair had been captured into braided coils. At any instant, Wylie felt, her clothes might drop away and her hair unbind itself to reveal the fanatic prophetess, but she sat fixed and stared at the stained-glass window of the apse, which portrayed a bleeding, agonized Christ between thieves on the cross. Wylie wondered whether she'd been drugged.

Pinky's father appeared unquiet. Though too unstable to serve as his son's best man, for once he wasn't drunk. Despite the air-conditioning, he continually wiped sweat from his face and neck with a striped handkerchief. He wore a rented tuxedo Pinky had gotten him into. It fitted poorly.

St. Stephen's was nothing like the Tabernacle of the Chosen of God, yet Pinky spoke his vows firmly and loudly. He knew his cues to kneel and rise. His hand trembled only slightly as he fitted the ring onto Esther's finger. He looked into her lace-shadowed face and smiled. Wylie glanced at Esther's father and saw the elderly gentleman trying very hard not to show his dismay.

Esther and Pinky drove to the Cloisters at Sea Island for their honeymoon. Wylie thought of Pinky under the live oaks and Spanish moss, riding in carriages along dappled lanes, sitting among silver and candlelight. He was careful not to let Anne hear him snort.

When Esther and Pinky came back, they bought a two-story Victorian house in the valley. The house was near the capitol, an area changing fast because the state government was bidding for private residences in order to raze and replace them with concrete statist mausoleums. Pinky considered the house not a residence but an investment. Someday the government would meet his price.

There was a porch around three sides. Esther dug up the small yard at the rear to replant it in flowers. They didn't have much furniture, though they'd received many fancy presents from her friends. Her father would've rained gifts on her, but she refused to allow him to push too deeply into her marriage. She protected Pinky's sensitivity.

He worked fleetingly on the house—painting, replacing a floorboard, repairing plaster—yet he was so tangled in legal squabbles he had little time for domesticity. His life was in the courtroom, where he'd become a legal brawler, always in the ring.

"He comes home nights so tired he's dazed," Anne said, she closer than ever to Esther.

Esther invited Anne and Wylie to her first dinner. Wylie balked at going. He sure as hell didn't intend to develop any reciprocal social ties with Pinky. Wylie felt he'd gone far beyond the call of duty by being in the wedding.

"All right, you'll have to call Esther and explain why we can't," Anne said. "I won't."

Anne knew he couldn't do that, so the four of them ate on a cheap maple table lighted by a silver candelabrum, which was a wedding present. The entire meal was an odd combination of the fine and bargain basement: pork chops on Wedgewood, A&P french dressing in an antique cruet, milk drunk from crystal goblets. Pinky, his head lowered over his plate, finished before the rest of them really got started.

"He wolfs his food," Esther said.

"I never learned to eat for entertainment," Pinky said. He wore an open shirt and a sweater, though Esther had on a blue party dress and jewelry.

"He doesn't even taste it," Esther said.

"Nolo contendere," Pinky said. "At Sea Island the waiters kept sniffing around me as if they smelled a dead mule. Their way of indicating they didn't consider me gentry. I felt like standing and stating I was aware I'm no gentleman and that the day I become one I'd gladly give up the ghost."

"He doesn't mean that," Esther said, her glance at Pinky an appeal for him to behave.

"I mean it all right. Being a gentleman's the same as being dead. No gentleman ever did anything worthwhile to help the human race."

He'd spoken too angrily and bitterly. Esther looked down at her plate so they wouldn't see the green wetness of her eyes. Anne frowned at Wylie.

"I'll get some hot rolls," Esther said, standing.

"I'll help," Anne said, and she rose to follow Esther through the swinging kitchen door.

Pinky sat tapping a finger against the linen tablecloth. He acted as if Wylie weren't sitting at the table.

"Pinky, let's get a breath of air," Wylie said and led him from the dining room to the front porch, where lumber and building materials were stacked.

"Some air," Pinky said. It smelled of chemicals, and the moon was barely visible through smog.

"You trying to break up your marriage?" Wylie asked.

"I'm up to my armpits in gentlemen," Pinky said and banged a hand against a porch post. "You peel a gentleman, you'll find a bastard who's grown fat and sleek on the sweat and blood of some poor underfed peon."

"This isn't a union meeting. We're just having dinner."

"I knew she'd take your side."

"We're not choosing sides. What's happening here is you're ruining your wife's first dinner party. Now I don't care about you, but I do about her. See if you can stop being a coal-camp hick long enough to remember some basic manners."

His fingers balled to fists, his mouth worked, his chin trembled. He turned away to look toward the river and the hills. He willed himself to coolness.

"You're right, but I want you to know you just came within a hair of a punch in your gentlemanly face!"

They walked back into the house and the dining room. The ladies were at the table, Anne angry, Esther defensive from hurt. Pinky made himself pleasant by telling the story of a trial before a deaf judge who mistook a witness for the defendant and ordered the witness taken to jail. Pinky drew out the story, using gestures and changing his voice to assume various parts. Anne first, and then Esther, finally gave in to laughter.

After vanilla ice cream served in silver dishes, Wylie played his

Eddy Duchin routine on the battered upright piano which had been left in the house. Pinky brought out his harmonica, the instrument wrapped in a clean white cloth. He played "San Antonio Rose," "Red River Valley," and "The Miner's Lament." He was still good and chugged No. 9 over the mountain to create the forlorn cry of a steam whistle. His performance impressed Anne, and Esther was again happy.

During the summer Esther came to see Wylie at Thornhill & Co. She wanted him to look over the portfolio of securities left to her by her mother. They were worth some $55,000 at current market, all railroad commons—Norfolk & Western, Chesapeake & Ohio, and the Pennsylvania.

"Your stocks don't require much handling," Wylie told her.

"You mean it wouldn't pay you?" she asked. She sat at the side of his desk, her exciting legs crossed, her nylon knees just covered by her lilac cotton skirt.

"It's not that. There's simply no reason to disturb your holdings," he said. He reached for his loose-leaf binder. "They're solid, safe, and provide good rent. I'll write them in my book, and if anything happens which affects them, I'll call."

She thanked him but didn't stand to leave. Apparently she wanted something more. He smiled and waited. She repositioned her purse on her lap.

"Amos works day and night," she said. Like Wylie's father and mother, she always called Pinky Amos. "In bed I feel him thinking instead of sleeping. He's wearing himself out."

"He should exercise more," Wylie said. "It'd help him sleep."

"My belief exactly. I bought him a tennis racket, but he's never used it. I believe he might play with you. He thinks the world of you. He wouldn't even consider golf. He considers all golfers to be decadent exploiters of mankind." She smiled.

"Maybe one day he and I'll get together for a game," Wylie said to be polite. He had no intention of squandering his tennis time with a hacker, especially one as unpleasant as Pinky.

Still Esther didn't leave. She recrossed her legs, adjusted her skirt, and brushed fingers along a thigh. Pinky hadn't given her much of a diamond.

189

"Where would you play?" she asked.

"Possibly the club," Wylie said, thinking, Never.

"Isn't there some limitation on that? He and I aren't members."

Of course Wylie knew they weren't. Her privileges granted through her father's membership had ceased at marriage.

"I'm afraid so," Wylie said, relieved she realized he wouldn't be able to invite Pinky to play on the club courts because Pinky lived within the city limits.

"I hoped you'd be able to meet on something like a regular basis," she said.

"We'll find another place," Wylie said. Like hell.

"Wylie, I know I keep asking too much of you, but would you help us get into the club? I miss my golf."

"I'll see you're mailed an application," he said, hoping she was requesting only an endorsement, which he'd gladly give. Because of her past membership and association, her name should go to the head of the waiting list. Still it would be tough, maybe impossible. There was the problem of Pinky's unpopularity with the membership as well as the difficulty between him and Emerson Smythe.

"Amos is a deserving man," Esther said. "He has a right to recreation. He's a rising attorney, and his achievement ought to be recognized. I want you to know he hasn't asked me to do this. It's entirely my idea. He'll probably think it's betrayal that I talked to you about joining."

"Betrayal of what?"

"It isn't logical. He feels he has an eternal obligation to the men he's helped, the miners and laboring people. They wouldn't need to know where he relaxes and enjoys himself."

She sighed and stood. Wylie accompanied her to the door. As he watched her walk away, he groaned inwardly from this burden whose name was Pinky.

It was that night they heard on the news that Sis Asters, who'd been studying art in California, was found murdered at her Los Angeles apartment, her naked body mutilated. The police held a wild-eyed, long-haired young man from Beaumont, Texas. He, rapturous on angel dust, claimed he was a mystic in the universal church of God's love and had been ordered by divine command to kill her because she was feeding and growing fat upon his soul.

42

Anne and Esther conspired against Wylie about the tennis. They kept telling Pinky Wylie would love to have a game with him. On a Saturday morning two weeks after Esther had come to Thornhill & Co., Pinky telephoned.

"You really want to play with me?" he asked.

"It's moot, Pinky, since we can't go to the club."

"We won't have to. I know another place. Listen, would you mind driving? My car's sick and in the garage."

Wylie was angry and started to call back and say he just remembered he had a game lined up, but Anne wouldn't let him. Think of Esther, she told him. Well he was getting damn tired of thinking of Esther.

At one o'clock Wylie drove by Pinky's house, where he was cutting grass using a push mower. He had on white shorts, but his shirt was brown with long sleeves and buttons up the front, probably the same he'd worn to his office. His shoes were sneakers, hightops, the kind for basketball. He did own a good racket, a Lee.

He rolled his lawn mower to his garage as Esther, appearing nervous, waved to Wylie from the porch. He and Pinky got into Wylie's new Austin-Healey. Pinky gave directions to drive westward along the valley and across the Elk River to the Wrong Side where smokestack shadows lay across windowless industrial buildings.

He ordered Wylie to stop the car at a public elementary school, which was enclosed by a chain-link fence. The school, built of brick and stone, had absorbed the grimy, besmeared complexion of the neighborhood. Behind it was a single tennis court, not clay or an all-weather surface, but pitted asphalt. The lines had faded, the net was ragged. Pinky tried the fence gate, and it was locked.

"We climb," he said, reaching for the fence.

"No we don't!"

"Come on, everybody does it."

"If they wanted people to use that court, the gate would be open."

"I'm a lawyer, and if we're arrested and convicted, I'll take the case all the way to the Supreme Court at no charge to you."

Pinky climbed the fence and stood waiting. Wylie hesitated, thought of Anne and Esther, and he too went up and over. He snagged a white sock on wire and jammed his right ankle slightly in jumping down to the cindered playground. He feared leaving his Austin-Healey parked at the curb of the scabby street. He disliked draping his clean towel over the blackened iron post that held one end of the tattered net. The new balls he'd brought were immediately smudged.

The game was bizarre. Pinky knew something of form but was stiffly mechanical, as if performing from a list of directions. When he hit balls, he used too much power. They arched over the fence. Patiently he climbed to retrieve them.

Often he missed balls altogether. Wylie placed shots to him in ideal position for returns, but Pinky's rigid swing was wrongly timed. Wylie thought of the good sets he could be having at the club with Blue Bales and some of the young doctors.

"Okay, Coach, tell me what I'm doing wrong," Pinky said after he climbed the fence for about the twentieth time. He leaned his racket to the iron post and wiped his face on his forearm. He hadn't brought a towel.

"Try a softer touch," Wylie said.

"I'm trying to take the ball on the rise."

"Taking the ball on the rise is an advanced technique unsuitable for your level of play."

"It's what Don Budge advises—always taking the ball on the rise."

"You talked to Don Budge?"

"I checked out his book from the library."

"Pinky, my advice is for you to splurge and buy yourself lessons."

"You think it's impossible to learn from a book?"

"I think you learn by good basic instruction and lots of practice."

"I don't have time for lots of practice."

They again hit balls, but Pinky didn't improve. Three unwashed black children, shirtless and shoeless, hooked fingers into the fence to watch.

When Pinky next knocked a ball over, one of the children clawed it off the street, and the three of them ran.

Pinky shouted, waved his racket, and sprinted to the fence. He climbed it and pounded after them. He hollered and swung his racket as if it were a war club. Dark, resentful faces gazed at him from doorways and windows of shantylike dwellings.

192

Wylie wished only to be away from the ratty neighborhood. He edged toward his Austin-Healey. Through diamond grids of the fence, he saw Pinky coming back—jogging, puffing, sweating, but holding the dirty ball. He climbed the fence and crossed the court.

"I've had enough," Wylie said.

"I realize you're uncomfortable having to play at such an unclassy location."

"For God's sake, Pinky, sure I'm uncomfortable, but maybe you ought not to be acting poorhouse either when you have a lovely wife who's used to more."

"She hasn't complained," he said and swung his Lee so viciously it hissed.

"Because she's too damn nice."

"You mean she was raised—excuse me, reared—to your refined way of life."

"I mean you're a working lawyer making good money and shouldn't have to play tennis in the slums."

"This particular slum is where I went to school."

"Well it's time you leave school behind."

Pinky kicked cinders and swung his racket as if chopping wood. Wylie crossed to the fence, climbed it, and walked to the Austin-Healey. Pinky came after him. Without speaking, they drove back through the Wrong Side. Brush and debris swirled in the high and muddy Elk River. Suddenly Pinky motioned Wylie to pull in at a drive-in where a giant hamburger revolved around a golden steeple. The steeple spewed bluish broiler fumes.

"You will drink a beer not served at the country club, won't you?" Pinky asked.

"You're a reverse snob. Everything has to be crummy for you to like it."

The drive-in, named the George Washington, had high-school girls as carhops. They wore red-white-and-blue caps, shirts, and shorts. Crushed paper cups with Washington's periwigged profile on them littered the concrete parking area.

"You might be surprised to learn I don't consider this place crummy," Pinky said. "Service is fast, and the beer is reasonably priced, two things not true of the Pinnacle Rock Club."

"Is that what we're talking about, the Pinnacle Rock Club?"

193

"Esther misses her golfing chums. Notice how I used the word 'chums.' I'm being sophisticated."

"Where does she play now?"

"It'll probably amaze you to discover that lots of fine and decent people use the municipal links."

"She doesn't belong there."

"Wylie, you have this idea that some people are born to privilege. We're in America, the old U.S. of A. where everybody's equal."

"You a lawyer or preacher?"

"I forgot morality makes you nervous."

"What makes me nervous is a man who won't consider his wife's feelings."

"What makes me nervous is an organization of snots who play at being English. This is West Virginia, remember? People can afford to live here because of the poor stinking grubbers who troop underground to hack out coal. Green lawns, white clubhouses, and turquoise pools don't change that. We exist up here in sunlight and plenty because poor bastard miners are working themselves into the hereafter down there."

He pointed beneath them as if men were loading coal right under the Austin-Healey. Talking to him was useless. Wylie was ready to leave and bumped the heel of a hand against the steering wheel. Pinky sat staring at the murky river and blowing into his bottle of Falls City. Wylie started the engine. Pinky reached across and switched it off.

"I have pressures on me," he said.

Wylie wasn't interested in pressures or problems. He could still make it to the club for a set of tennis if he got rid of Pinky.

"I've been offered a good case," Pinky said.

"That's pressure?"

"By a bank. Banks in the state are preparing to contest an act of the legislature which assesses for tax purposes certain trust assets. They're hiring a consortium of lawyers, and I've been invited to join."

"You're not happy about it?"

"Banks!" he said and kicked the Austin-Healey's black carpeting. "In league with insurance companies, corporations, and the rest of the sleek and rich."

"Let me see if I understand. You're saying a bank, corporation, or insurance company has no right to legal process. Simply by being, they're wrong."

"You're sticking it to me."

"You're acting stupid. Banks, corporations, and insurance companies are people too. Last I heard they had the same rights as the rest of us citizens."

"I've thought about that. Lord, have I. It's the only reason I'm considering the offer."

"So what's the problem?"

"I don't want anybody to believe I'm selling out. If banks didn't have what I think's a legitimate complaint, I wouldn't glance at the case."

"It never occurred to me you were selling out."

"The big guys always win by buying the best lawyers. How do I know they're not buying me?"

"You expect them to hire dumb lawyers?"

"I've always represented the working man."

"Seems to me you'd want to represent justice."

"My tempter," he said and lifted the bottle for a last swig of beer. "What?"

"You keep opening doors for me into places I don't want to go."

43

Anne decided they ought to do something about getting Esther back into the Pinnacle Rock Club no matter what Pinky thought. She made Wylie study the twelve-member list of the Board of Governors. He was a friend to most and, Anne argued, Esther deserved special membership consideration. Pinky might sneak in at her side.

The unscalable barrier was Emerson Smythe, who served as a governor. Whenever he met Pinky, Emerson glared as if he spied Judas risen. Tumbling constantly through Emerson's mind were explosive, mortifying images of his being spun on his back crashing into the bandstand during the Thanksgiving dance.

Anne lobbied for Esther in the course of her social engagements while Wylie did the same as he transacted business at Thornhill &

Co. He reminded governors of old times when Esther and her parents belonged to the crowd. He spoke of her trophies. He never mentioned Pinky's name.

"If only her husband was a little easier to get along with," Big Jon Maynard said. Jon had been an All-American tackle at Pitt and now owned two Chevrolet agencies. He was Chairman of the Board of Governors.

"You hear he's been invited to join the consortium representing the banks in the trust case?" Wylie asked over lunch they were eating at the Coal & Coke Club. Since Jon had brought up Pinky, it was the best defense Wylie could make.

"No and frankly I'm surprised."

"He's one hell of a lawyer, Jon, a comer. And it's my definite belief Esther will keep him under control."

"She's always bought her cars from us," Jon said.

During games of golf, locker-room chatter, and drinks at the bar, Wylie prepared the ground. Always he kept the emphasis on Esther and her family, particularly her father, whose gift had made the building of squash courts possible. The father had won the senior championship, and Wylie pointed out his name on the Game Room plaque. Wylie spoke to club manager Heine Stahl, who ordered a maid to polish the brass nameplate.

When he and Anne had done all they could, they turned their thinking to Emerson Smythe. They hoped Emerson's term on the board would expire at the annual election, but he was renominated for two more years.

"Why not go to him?" Anne asked. "You sell difficult men securities. You ought to be able to handle a marshmallow like Emerson."

"He's no marshmallow. Under that languid exterior is a bitchy wasp ready to sting."

Emerson played neither golf nor tennis. On the links Wylie could've dropped a hole or two to sweeten him into a generous mood. Emerson, however, arrived at his office in Mountain State Bank by ten every morning, stayed till three, and drove up to the Pinnacle Rock Club to begin his long evening of gentlemanly imbibing. He'd been married, but his wife, a society girl from Baltimore, had divorced him and returned to Maryland.

196

On Monday night when Wylie parked in the white gleam from the clubhouse, he hoped the magic mellowness of the bottle would be upon Emerson. Snow drifted in the wind, the flakes disappearing as soon as they touched the ground. He walked into the rosy warm foyer and hung his coat. The ballroom was dark and cold, though flaming poinsettias had been placed about. As he expected, few people were dining.

Emerson sat in a green lounge chair facing the plate-glass window. Lights of the valley flickered through the snow. Snow fell too on Pinnacle Rock itself, the bow of stone jutting into darkness. From Alexander at the bar, Wylie got a scotch and went to sit beside Emerson. Emerson's limberness stiffened, and his blackish eyes glinted over his highball glass as if it were a rampart.

"I hope it's not trouble at home," he said. "Not seen you here at night without Anne since you married."

"She's at orchestra practice."

"You should have her portrait done, wearing her Grecian gown, the lustrous wood of the cello complementing her classic beauty."

"I've been considering doing just that," Wylie said, thinking, Grease 'em up.

"Lucky man to have such a woman," Emerson said. He wore a suit and vest, the cloth black except for a faint blue pin stripe. The signet ring on the little finger of his left hand was a subdued ember under the lamplight. "Pat was such an absolute virago. Married me for my money and carted off a batch of it with her. Mercifully the courts left me a pittance."

He drank slowly but devotedly, his body again so limp it seemed boneless. Wylie couldn't imagine a woman loving him even for money.

"I don't know why I stay around this abysmal valley," he said. "I ought to sell out and move to Palm Beach."

It was his refrain, and meaningless. He always complained. Both wine and whine were at the heart of him. The state's economy might falter, but he sold his coal under long-term contract to U.S. Steel, and checks arrived at his office with the regularity of the moon's unalterable phases.

In Wylie's drinking he adopted Em's rhythms. They didn't need to instruct Alexander to keep bringing double scotches. Alexander had served Em so long that the bartender's black ears had become tuned to the song of Em's ice.

At eight-thirty Wylie and Emerson entered the hushed dining room for a meal of flounder stuffed with crab meat. They drank a bottle of Liebfraumilch and carried snifters of brandy to the Trophy Room, where they sat on a tiger-striped sofa before a log fire. Em provided the Cuban cigars.

"It's been pleasant, Wylie. If I didn't know you were without guile, I'd believe you were attempting to blindside me."

"I confess I'm guilty of trying."

"Well you've got me in the proper mood. Will my checkbook be required?"

"Won't cost you a cent."

"You're running for office?"

"I'm still of sound mind. What I need's a favor."

"I don't grant favors blindly. You're not asking for the loan of my mistress, are you?"

They laughed, Wylie wondering whether or not Em had a mistress. He doubted it. Alexander came to pour more brandy. Wylie waited till the barman left and Emerson was puffing contentedly on his cigar, his thin features composed, his skinny legs stretched toward the fire, the ankles crossed. He wore black silk socks.

"Em, I'm sure you believe with me we ought to stand by our old friends."

Emerson drew his slippered feet to the sofa, leaned to the chrome stand to bump the long ash from his cigar, and raised his dark refocused eyes to Wylie.

"I believe I know where you're taking me," he said.

"Esther's been one of us a long time."

"We're not talking about dear Esther but a sonofabitch I hate!"

"I'm talking about Esther."

"No you don't. You can't hide that coal-camp *arriviste* behind her. Frankly, Wylie, I'm disappointed in your taking up with such trash. He doesn't belong at Pinnacle Rock. Esther's a wonderful girl I'm very fond of, but one must draw the line."

"For Esther's sake I'm asking you to forget Pinky when I put her up for membership."

Emerson shook his head. Despite his languor, down in that prissy, willowy body was a cunning intelligence.

"You can't put her up alone. It would have to be a family membership. I tell you I not only intend to oppose Mr. Cody, I'll burn down the damn clubhouse if he's ever again allowed in the door."

"I wish you'd take some time and reconsider."

"The membership here's already become tainted. You know how I fought to keep out the chemical people."

"Chemical people" was his term for the engineers and executives who worked for Union Carbide and Du Pont.

"You have to agree they've brought vitality to the club," Wylie said. "They're bright, educated, enthusiastic."

"Oh I don't feel terribly unhappy with them, though I'm not a hundred percent comfortable either, not the way I am with the valley's old families—as, for example, I am with you."

He leaned forward, set his cigar in the metal groove of the ashstand, and sipped his brandy. Silently Alexander moved in with a refill.

"Let me define the problem more fully," he said. "I've always thought of us up here as the permanent families in the valley, heirs of the pioneers who tamed a wild land, the people, in short, who came to stay. Those folks in the chemical crowd are transferred in for a year or two and then assigned elsewhere. Most are attractive, agreed, and some of the women beautiful, but they don't really belong because the company owns them and will eventually take them away."

"Esther and her people belong to the valley."

"So does her husband—to a cabin up a hollow. We have large coal interests among our membership who resent him for arousing the miners. I myself personally detest him. He's a smart lawyer, granted, but he's no gentleman. My advice is that you tell Esther that a local group is forming a new country club, the membership to be made up of the disgruntled who can't get in here at Pinnacle Rock. I'm certain they'd accept Pinky Cody. As for Esther, I'm truly sorry, but perhaps one day her children will be welcomed through these doors."

"Em, you realize how pompous that sounds?"

"Don't overstep yourself. I've been a friend of your family for

199

years. You don't want to sacrifice me for a thing like Pinky Cody."

Wylie stood, said goodnight, and left the glowing clubhouse. He smelled smoke from the chimneys, and snow had begun to accumulate. He drove through it to his house, where he reported to Anne that Pinky and Esther had no chance in this world of gaining membership in Pinnacle Rock.

He turned out to be wrong for two reasons. First the consortium of attorneys representing the banks succeeded in nullifying the West Virginia statute taxing trust assets. It took eighteen months, and Pinky's discovery and research of an 1890 case involving a fiduciary ruling by an intermediate court was cited and considered to be weighty in the decision handed down. Among bankers he became acceptable.

The second reason was Emerson Smythe himself. He lived alone in his family's nineteenth-century mansion on the river, a place of high hedges, white columns, and drawn blinds. The city police and two frantic mothers, let in back through the kitchen by a fearful Negro housekeeper, discovered Em lying naked and drunk on an oriental rug, his bluish white body sparkling with sugary gumdrops, while around him laughed and skipped two six-year-old girls in pigtails and starched blue pinafores.

The arrest made no newspapers, and Em didn't go to jail, but people knew. He resigned by letter from the Pinnacle Rock Club's Board of Governors. Immediately Anne urged Esther to submit an application for membership. Thirty days Mr. and Mrs. Amos Cody's name was posted on the door of the business office. Wylie heard locker-room grumbling but no organized opposition.

"All you'll have to do now is mail in your check," Anne said over the telephone to Esther.

"I don't know whether Amos will let me. He still plays tennis behind that awful school."

"Do it for him."

"He might kill me," she said.

44

The first summer Esther and Pinky were members at Pinnacle Rock, she played lots of golf, but he hardly appeared. Then the city tore down the old school that had the court behind it. He had little choice if he wanted a game of tennis. There were no public courts. He had to come up the hill.

His tennis had improved. He'd practiced against a wall of the school and developed more of an eye and feel for the game. Maybe too he still read books from the public library, like the one Don Budge wrote in the early '40s.

Pinky had always been physically quick, a natural athlete, and his style of play was hard and charging. His aggressiveness intimidated more decorous people who preferred to stand at the baseline and assume graceful poses as they stroked the ball. After a match with Pinky, some left the court acting as if he'd won through rudeness. They were startled and galled by his unyielding attack.

By then Wylie had a son, Pinky a daughter. On sunny days Esther and Anne brought the babies to the club to splash in the children's pool. The ladies, wearing beach hats, sat in the dappled shallows, the water lapping at their matronly thighs. Wylie still didn't care to socialize with Pinky, but at day's end there were drinks on the terrace. They watched smog of the valley merge into twilight. Pinky no longer made a big thing of swallowing a scotch or two.

He was hauling in money. He bought a Buick for himself and a Chevy station wagon for Esther. He'd hired a secretary and moved to a suite of offices in the Kanawha Building. From his window the view was to the river and the new bridge.

He accompanied Esther to a club dance. She manipulated him into buying, instead of renting, a tuxedo. Pinky was nervous. Maybe he feared some of his Broken Men would peep through panes of the ballroom windows and see him among the glittering rich.

"Where'd he learn to dance so well?" Wylie asked Anne. Her breasts were larger now, her body softer, all angles gone. She had to watch her weight.

"Esther told me he has a book," she said and laughed.

"I should've guessed."

"He takes it a chapter at a time, studies the diagrams, and buys records. They roll up the living-room rug and practice. More than just practice, Esther says. They work at dancing."

Pinky too became concerned about his weight. He wasn't fat, not near it, but his flesh had loosened and become even rosier. To harden himself, he jogged in place while waiting for serves. Instead of walking, he ran after balls rolling into adjoining courts. At the end of a match, he jumped the net.

Esther now bought his clothes, which were conservatively tailored and fitted nicely. She inspected him before letting him out of the house. He wore suits downtown, and in cold weather not only a vest and an overcoat but also a hat. His new way of dressing embarrassed him.

"I wouldn't wear this suit out to the coal fields," he said, stroking the lapel of his gray flannel jacket. "When I do business with the insurance companies, I need to meet them on even ground. Everybody's judged by what he wears, including the judge. This suit allows me to pad my bill a good twenty percent."

He came by Thornhill & Co. on a wintry day when snow blew between the buildings on Commerce Street and filmed Wylie's office window. Besides himself and Thorny, the firm now worked four registered representatives, all from good families and colleges. Five girls were secretary-clerks. The beige carpeting was as thick and springy as any in town, and studded chairs were covered with genuine leather. Cherry wainscoting gave the place the reassuring patina of a trust department. Thornhill & Co. had a grandfather clock ticking solemnly in the reception area.

Snow melted on the shoulders of Pinky's bluish black overcoat. He carried an alligator attaché case which had a golden clasp. He dropped gray gloves into a gray hat.

"Want to invest some money for me?" he asked.

"I think you might be happier with somebody else advising you," Wylie said.

"The answer I figured I'd get," Pinky said and left Wylie's office to walk to Thorny's.

Later, after Pinky returned to work, Thorny came to Wylie. Thorny's strong teeth were clamped on a cigar. He wore no jacket, his sleeves were rolled up, and his striped college tie hung loose. His flaxen hair had retreated even farther from his forehead, and the blimp in him had taken on more gas.

"You didn't want his business?" Thorny asked, dropping into a chair and dangling one fat leg over its arm.

"I know him too well."

"You mean you think he's dishonest?"

"I mean I just don't want him too close around me."

"He gave me a good order but was uncomfortable in my office."

"I can explain that. It's the first time in his life he's had money to invest in stocks, and he's a little ashamed of himself for seeming to be a capitalist. I'd guess he considers extra money a betrayal of goodness, that you can't be rich and decent. It's his religious background, at least partly, splinters left in him from his days in the Chosen of God Tabernacle. He's afraid he's robbing the poor."

"I'll have to hold his hand," Thorny said.

"He has a coal-camp mentality. A miner becomes uncomfortable when he gets a little ahead. First thing he does is go on a spree or find a reason to wildcat strike so he can be relieved of his excess money."

Wylie had heard the last at a Coal & Coke Club convocation sponsored by the Southern Bituminous Operators. There was still too much coal and too little demand. Jobless men continued to leave the state for the industrial centers of Detroit, Cleveland, Chicago. West Virginians had become the Okies of this generation.

"You think I shouldn't have taken him on?" Thorny asked.

"It might work for you. I just don't want him all over me."

"I bought him 200 shares of Ma Bell. He asked whether AT&T was a monopoly. I told him yes and so is the American Bar Association. I explained he didn't have to pay for five business days, but he wanted to get that part over with—like a man waiting for the stab of a doctor's hypodermic. As he wrote his check, his fingers trembled. He lifted the hand and stared at it. 'Lord look what money's doing to me,' he said."

45

On a Wednesday afternoon in late February, Wylie's father drove up the hill, took his second shower of the day, and changed into wool slacks, a sleeveless sweater, and a tweed jacket before joining Wylie's mother in the music room for their evening drink. He sat in a wing chair half turned to the window so he could look from the log fire to the snow piling up on the sill.

"You might call Dr. Airy," he said to Wylie's mother.

She quickly crossed to him. He suffered pain in his chest and was sweating. She telephoned the Medical Arts Building, but Dr. Airy had left his office. She tracked him to the Pinnacle Rock Club, where he was preparing to play squash with Esther's father. Wearing his white shorts and polo shirt under his overcoat, Dr. Airy drove fast to the house.

Wylie's father still sat in his chair. He'd kept his head up and held to both leather arms. His feet were drawn together. Wylie's mother bent over him, her hand on his. As Dr. Airy reached the house, Wylie's father jerked, his mouth opened, and he groaned. He then slumped forward in ungraceful death.

Just prior to the funeral, Wylie lifted the gauze veil over the casket to remove the crested gold ring from his father's finger and put it on his own. For weeks the coldness of his father's flesh seemed to stay in the metal.

Wylie's mother never lost control. Like royalty she received mourners, her back straight, her somber eyes steady and focused. As Wylie held her arm under the flapping canopy at the cemetery, she stood firm except when Father Bonney intoned "the valley of the shadow of death," her body quivered. Wind fluttered pages of the priest's Bible.

Both before and after the funeral, Pinky was constantly at the house. He held Wylie's mother, talked to her soothingly, kissed her. He answered telephones and the door. He brought food. He offered to stay during the nights.

"He gives her no rest," Wylie said.

"He loved your father," Anne said.

"I'm the one who should be comforting my mother, not him."

A month after the funeral Pinky still came by the house four or five times a week. He'd sit with Wylie's mother in her bedroom and talk about God—the God he brought from the cinderblock tabernacle. He intended to give peace to her, but she was fretted.

"I'm going to speak to him," Wylie said.

"Not yet," Anne said. "There are times she wants him."

If Wylie's mother ever wept, she did it where he couldn't detect tears. As she recovered, she became clenched and brittle, not knowing what to do with herself. She roamed her house chasing memories. Wylie found her sitting passively with a suit of his father's clothes laid across her lap.

"I can't really believe he'll not walk in the door," she said. "I know he's gone but any minute I expect to hear his step. I think I'll see him around every corner."

Despite her courage, she wasn't able to adjust. She took too much medicine and started drinking earlier in the day. She didn't show her decline except by becoming more deliberate and removed, as if listening for a voice far out at sea. Wylie and Anne had to repeat themselves to her.

She wrecked the Chrysler, nothing terrible, but she hit the stone entranceway to the house with the car's right fender. Viola and Ed helped her inside to her bed. They called Wylie to come up from the valley. His mother was just shaken, yet he and Anne felt she could do no more driving. Wylie went to Dr. Airy, who, unlike London with his golden locks, had gray hair so sparse it splotched his scalp like lichen on a rock. He smoked a sporty pipe, and his white smock crackled.

"Can't you cut down on your medicine?" Wylie asked.

"I'm slowly weaning her," Dr. Airy said, puffing.

The more he shut off the medicine, the more she increased her drinking. Viola found bottles around the house, scotch under the bed, a fifth of vodka in a hatbox, bourbon behind the Verdi. Wylie left the liquor there. He wouldn't shame his mother by letting her know he'd caught her boozing.

He not only had to look after his mother, but also help settle his father's estate. His father had left affairs in order with a will drawn by former lieutenant governor Asters and codicils in his own hand concerning the disposition of moneys to church and charities as well as cash to Ed and Viola.

Miss Burdette closed Elk Land and Lumber's doors for a week. Wylie sat at the dark, heavy desk, and as he fingered papers he heard sounds from the kitchen. He crossed softly to the empty pantry and listened.

Miss Burdette was weeping. She stood in a shadowed corner of the bare kitchen and lowered her prudish face to her hands. Palms muffled her crying. When she realized Wylie had discovered her, she moaned, choked, and sagged. He helped walk her spinsterish, pear-shaped body to a chair where he removed her glasses, wet a wash-cloth at the sink, and wiped her face.

"Oh I miss him!" she said. "He was so kind!"

Wylie drove her to her apartment in the East End and left her shoeless on her Murphy bed. As he returned to his father's office he thought Miss Burdette had shown more grief than his mother.

He continued going through his father's desk. Business papers and articles were routine till he came across a green metal box at the rear of the bottom right-hand drawer. The box was locked, but he had his father's key ring. The smallest key fitted.

Inside were clean bundles of money, each bound by a thick rub-ber band. The amount came to $25,000. Also in the box were me-mentos—his SAE pin from Washington and Lee, his White Oak ring, an unloaded derringer, and snapshots, one of him and Wylie's mother wearing large straw hats and holding bicycles beside a ruined Spanish mission.

At the bottom of the box lay a sealed white envelope with Wylie's name on it. The letter carried the date January 1.

Wylie, for some time I haven't been feeling well. I didn't want to trouble you or your mother.

The money in the box I've kept around for emergencies, you know, revolu-tions and such. It should be reported as part of my estate. You don't want any battles with the revenue people, who always win.

In the past few months I've tried to sum up my beliefs. I hope you won't think I'm indulging myself with these remarks. I've not been a religious person, but I've always believed in decency and fairness to my fellow man. It seems to me those two values are as good as any to build a life upon.

If I should be snatched away, I want you first and foremost to care for your mother. As for Miss Burdette, she should receive $5,000 from Elk Land and Lumber as a bonus. She has served well, and I'm certain you would never cast her out.

When I leave this world, I will live on in you. Think well of me. I have loved you dearly.

As he sat in the lavish shade of his father's office, Wylie's eyes be-came hot and wet. More than anything else his father had cham-pioned the goodness in men, the quality which Wylie intended to make the center of his own life.

Saddened but inspired, he locked the office and drove up the hill to his mother's house. As he was taking off his coat, the doorbell chimed, and it was Pinky.

"I believe she's resting," Wylie said, though chances were his mother was sitting on the edge of her bed staring out the window toward the river.

"I brought her a book," Pinky said and handed it to Wylie. The title was *Death: The Entrance to the Glory of Immortal Life.*

"She shouldn't be reading this," Wylie said, thinking, Pinky and his how-to books—tennis, dancing, salvation. "She's morbid enough now."

"The message is inspirational and comforting."

"My mother's tired and drawn tight. She needs peace."

"You're stopping me from seeing her?"

"She ought to be left alone by well-meaning people who use up her strength."

"Sure," Pinky said and set his hat on his head as he started for the door. "You know I love her as I loved your father. I'm just trying to do the right thing." He opened the door. A corner of his mouth turned down. "My father died a few months ago."

"I hadn't heard," Wylie said, shocked.

"Esther wanted to tell you and everybody, but it wouldn't have meant anything since you never really knew him. Nobody knew him much. He was a drunk, a quiet, dedicated drunk. The only reason he kept his job down at the Assessor's Office was his veteran's status. We held a private graveside service in Arlington. He was a hero, an authentic, bemedaled hero, one of the men who captured Reichsmarschall Göring. Sergeant Cody commanded a tank and rolled that Pershing over the grass of a country estate where Göring sat at a table in the flower garden. Tea things had been set out and a Luger. Dad could've stirred Göring's tea with the nose of his 90-millimeter cannon. Know what he said to Göring? 'Buddy, you could lose some weight.'"

"Did he have a favorite charity?" Wylie asked. "I'd like to send a check."

"No charities or causes. He's better off gone. He was meant for war, nothing else. Everything afterwards bored him. He should've stayed in the army. Civilian life tormented him. What bothers me is he gave so much and we give so little. I'm missing all my country's wars—you and I are. How can a man be anything if he won't go to war for his country?"

"I'm sorry, Pinky."

"I found something in a drawer under some old shorts of his. A poem. A very short poem, and I never saw him read a book. I'll recite it for you:

> Young
> I hoped for things to come.
>
> Old and sore
> I pray Don't hurt me more.

I can't get over him writing that. He did it in pencil on the back of an electric bill."

"I'm so damn sorry."

"Not really. You want to be because that's the correct attitude, but you never knew my father and never cared to. He was repulsive to you, crude. He didn't have the grace and style you find as necessary as air. I'm not blaming you. I just remember that in all the years since White Oak, you've never once asked about him—whether he was dead or alive."

46

Wylie still had Miss Burdette to think about, and concern for her involved the problem of what to do with Elk Land and Lumber. Elk was not a stockholder corporation. The company had belonged altogether to Wylie's father, as it had belonged to his father, and it would now be Wylie's.

Wylie's father had left his estate other than Elk Land and Lumber in trust, with Wylie's mother being named primary beneficiary. Mountain State Bank and Wylie were to act as cotrustees.

He'd been employed long enough by his father to know there wasn't sufficient work at Elk to keep even one man overly busy. His father had made an art of using up his day. Long ago he could've turned the business loose by handing it over to the bank to administer, as Wylie might do now. Mountain State Bank would happily hire Miss Burdette in return for commissions collected on Elk's operations. Wylie, however, didn't want to see Miss Burdette swimming in a sea of secretaries. His father would've never been happy with that.

He hated thinking about giving up his partnership at Thornhill & Co. He made good money and had himself developed a sizable part of the business. Elk Land and Lumber was fine but inherited. Thornhill & Co. he'd helped build.

"While we wouldn't collapse if you left, it'd cause a mighty hole in our organization," Thorny said. He had everybody smoking cigars. The receptionist kept a humidor on her desk for customers.

"I'd never take my capital out as long as you need it," Wylie said.

"Capital's important, but not the most important item. You're worth ten times what you have in the firm."

Wylie and Anne talked it over, lying warm under a blanket in their bed on a night when wind swept off the ridges and swirled about their apartment, the sound like shrouds of a ship during a gale.

"Can't you do both?" she asked. "I don't want you working harder than you already are, but you could let up a little on stocks and bonds."

"Wouldn't be fair to Thornhill & Co."

"All right, you tell me Miss Burdette does most of the work anyway at Elk. Give her more authority and let her run the show."

"Miss Burdette never made an independent decision in her life. She carried everything to my father."

"How old is she?"

"Pushing sixty I guess. It's hard to figure because she's always looked like Miss Burdette to me—sort of clucking and pigeony."

"She's your best hope," Anne said.

He decided to discuss the idea with his mother. On Thursday he drove up the hill to see her after work. The road was icy, and sleet bounced off the car's hood and windshield. At this time of day she would normally have been in her music room, but since Wylie's father's death she hadn't used the piano except to tap a note with one finger. She'd closed the top over the Steinway's keys.

Now she often sat in the kitchen. There was a view of the woods, though trees were stripped, the earth barren, the clotted stream frozen. It wasn't the view which kept her in the kitchen, or the cooking, but the nearness of the refrigerator and ice cubes. No matter what time Wylie arrived, she would have a drink sitting before her on the round pine table.

She often didn't hear him when he talked. Frequently she hadn't dressed but wore a quilted white housecoat. Her thin graying hair might be unbrushed, yet she'd have on jewelry. She looked through the window toward the sleet and woods, her hands still, her face slack. Then she came hostilely out of herself.

"I don't want to hear about business," she said.

"Why are you so angry?"

"You're supposed to make the decisions, so do it." She again turned to the window, and one bony beringed hand crept to the highball glass.

"I don't want to do anything you'd disapprove of," he said.

"I don't care. There's plenty of money, isn't there?"

"Yes."

"I won't have to worry if I become sick, will I?"

"No."

"Do what you think's best."

When he did call in Miss Burdette, Wylie was sitting at his father's desk before the fire. The logs crackled behind him, and roses from the florist had been arranged by him in a long-neck vase at the beveled bay window. She had used to provide the flowers, and Wylie's father always made up for her expenses in the Christmas bonus.

She came carrying her dictation pad. Her short body had settled even lower into her hips and legs. Her hair was mostly white now, parted in the middle. No rings graced her fingers. She wore the same tortoise-shell glasses, the lenses immaculate. She sat at the side of the desk, and it occurred to him he'd never seen her cross her stubby legs. While taking dictation, she kept both low rubber heels bonded to the floor.

Wylie told her he wanted her to become executive vice-president of Elk Land and Lumber. She raised her face, pushed the eraser end of her pencil into her throat, and froze.

"Don't answer for a moment," Wylie said. "First let me explain. By accepting the position, you'd be pleasing my father. You know how much he not only depended on you but also trusted your judgment. Nobody understands the operation of this business better than you. Furthermore, by taking the job, you'd be of great help to me and my mother. Lastly, the promotion will be of considerable benefit because you'll receive a hefty increase in salary."

Slowly she closed the steno pad on her lap. She fitted the yellow pencil into the wire spirals of the binding. Nails of her short thick fingers were unpainted but filed to a perfect uniformity.

"I don't feel qualified," she said, her voice as timorous as a girl's.

"You definitely have the qualifications and ability."

"Did your father tell you that?"

"Not in so many words, but you know you were much more to him than just an employee."

She blushed and was again close to weeping. From the long sleeve of her plain brown dress she drew a handkerchief. She sniffled and dabbed at her rapidly blinking eyes.

"How can I handle such responsibility?"

"What we'll do is, you and I, meet every Monday and Friday. Each Monday we can set the course for the week's work, and on Friday tie up any loose ends. If a problem surfaces you feel you can't act on alone, I'm as close as the telephone. Any day we can talk over lunch."

"I've always brought my sandwich and eaten here."

"No longer. All executive vice-presidents should eat a good lunch. From now on, this desk is yours."

Wylie stood, stepped away from the high-backed leather chair, and gestured for her to sit in it. She wouldn't approach the chair.

"I might be able to get used to his desk but never his chair," she said. "I wouldn't feel right."

"I'll order you another then," he said. After finishing work that afternoon, he stopped by an office-supply store to have one sent over. The store agreed to keep the old chair for Wylie till the new house he and Anne were building on the hill was finished. There the father's chair would go into the den.

For a few days Miss Burdette sat tensely at the desk as if the police might break in and accuse her of fraud. Wylie gentled her into the job. Within a month she ran Elk Land and Lumber so well he wasn't needed except to show his approval. She guided the company far more efficiently than Wylie and his father had. They'd really only gotten in her way.

47

At the end of September Wylie, Anne, and their two sons moved into the new house on the hill. They'd not been able to buy property overlooking the river—none was left—but found an acre on a wooded knoll reputed to have once been an Indian burial mound. A stream trickled along the north side where mossy boulders upheaved from moist black earth. The house was Georgian, bricked in Flemish bond, three stories with a slate roof and dormers.

Pinky too intended to build. The state of West Virginia made a bid on his valley home, triple what he paid for it, and he had to move under threat of condemnation. Esther also wanted to live on the hill, believing it would offer a better life to her daughter. Pinky couldn't stand against her arguments. He might battle the valley's caste system, but for his daughter he desired nobility.

His problem was finding a lot. No amount of money could produce what didn't exist. He would be forced to buy half a mile or more back from a view of the river. At least that's what Wylie believed till Anne returned from a luncheon with Esther and told him Pinky had purchased a plot with a view not only across the river, but upstream and down as well.

"Impossible!" Wylie said. "I've been over every inch of that ground, and nothing suitable's for sale."

"Is there a place called Buzzards' Roost?" Anne asked.

Buzzards' Roost, the cliffside where Wylie and his generation had driven and parked to drink their first beer and study sex. That strip of rock was far too narrow and rugged for any kind of house.

"I only know what Esther told me," Anne said. "Pinky's hired an architect from Pittsburgh."

The architect's drawing set steel beams into the face of the rock and braced them down the cliffside. Workers would have to dangle over the edge to drill and bolt together the webbed system of support. The house was then to be cantilevered over the valley and suspended hundreds of feet above it.

From the city people watched the house grow. It was constructed of redwood, glass, and local stones colored a yellowish tan which had the radiance of mica. Sunshine made them spectral prisms which changed with every light, and they were able to capture even the subdued sheen of the moon. The redwood panels were octagonal surfaces interrupted by rectangles of glass bluish like insect eyes.

At completion, Anne and Wylie received an invitation for drinks and a tour. Pinky met them outside on the graveled ledge. From the rear the structure appeared small because only one flat story showed. Past the door the area opened to luminosity, giving the sensation of space and sky. Projected from the cliff, a person could indeed look up or down the river or out across the valley to the capitol's hazy dome and a range of hills, one speckled with white chips—the tombstones, Wylie realized, in the municipal cemetery.

There were three stories of decks. Glass doors slid open to them and the scary view. The feeling Wylie had was that he stood on a ship crossing through the sky, the wind furnishing motion and sound like a prow parting vast sunlit sea.

On decks were redwood chairs, chaises, and colored air mattresses for sunbathing. Bright umbrellas stuck from centers of metal tables. The base of each umbrella was rooted against the wind's force by fitting it into a concrete tub. Under eaves metal speakers of a hi-fi broadcast show tunes. The most spectacular detail was the small swimming pool, it too over space, the aluminum and fiberglass liner supported by a mesh of steel struts.

"Don't know how I'll ever pay for it," Pinky said. "The Mountain State Bank owns me body and soul."

"He went completely berserk in the planning," Esther said. "Ten times a day he called the architect to add things."

Pinky proudly showed off every item. He turned on scarlet faucets of the flesh-colored bathroom to demonstrate the miracle of water running from the sky. There were three bathrooms, each with scales. He flushed the johns as if providing music.

He flipped chrome toggles to open drapes and slide automatic doors. Lush violins from hi-fi speakers floated down like misty notes from the empyrean. TV babbled in practically every room. He stroked the walnut paneling of the halls as if the wood were a woman's skin.

He led them to the solarium, its glass panes opened out. Luxuriant waxy plants grew from clay pots painted red. Hanging baskets swung in a breeze and scented the air with a fragrance of multi-colored blooms. Wind chimes tinkled. In gilded cages four canaries sprang about.

"Watch this," Pinky said as they walked into another room. He knuckled a wall switch which started an artificial stream purling over small, beautifully clean white rocks. A miniature waterwheel spun and furnished the mechanical power to a music box, which played the West Virginia University fight song. On the stream's banks porcelain fishermen held tiny rods over the stream.

The bar was built of coal that had been cut into blocks, mortared, and lacquered so no one would be smudged. Stools were of saddle leather. Each bottle had a silver disc chained around its neck to identify the contents. Beyond a rainbow of glass was an aquarium wall where exotic fish gaped among excited seaweed.

"Since coal holds up this state, I thought I'd honor it in my drinking," Pinky said. He snapped his fingers. At the end of the bar stood a toy Ferris wheel, and riding in each seat were toy figures, some of them lovers. "What'll you have?"

When Anne asked for bourbon, Pinky twisted a dial and punched a button. The Ferris wheel turned jerkily. A music box played "How Dry I Am" till the wheel stopped. From under a red seat a spout appeared and filled a two-ounce silver jigger with bourbon.

"Bravo!" Anne called, and Pinky grinned.

His and Esther's bed was large enough for a mob, the coverlet chartreuse silk, the headboard white satin. In the headboard were switches for music, curtains, lights, and lamps. The bed had a vibrator, and Pinky made Anne and Wylie lie on it to be tranquilized.

He showed them his office, where law books covered two walls. On his modern blond desk were adding and dictating machines. Photographs of Esther and their daughter had been framed and hung. Among the law books Wylie spotted a thick scriptural commentary, a Sunday-school quarterly, and the Bible Pinky had used at White Oak.

The yellow kitchen's refrigerator was large enough to store a side of beef. At the center of the room stood a meat block Pinky had bought from a coal-camp grocery store in liquidation. Old blood-stained grooves left by the butcher's cleaver. In free moments Esther would work to sand the stains out.

Brass pots hung from hooks on the steel canopy over the electric stove. Air blew in from an opened glass door. The deck just off the kitchen had a screened area where Pinky and Esther ate breakfast, their view downriver to the steaming silver jungle of tanks, compressors, and towers at Union Carbide's Belle Island plant.

The living room was deeply carpeted in maroon, and the cathedral ceiling had groined beams. Lying across black andirons in the stone fireplace were specially cut, outsized sycamore logs. A lighted cabinet held many of Esther's golf trophies. On a paneled wall a coat of arms was displayed.

"A new high in vulgarity," Wylie said as he drove Anne home.

"He's like an orphan in a candy store," she said. "Did you ever see him laugh and clown so much?"

"I'm surprised Esther went along with it," Wylie said. "She has taste."

"She also has the good sense to let him have what he's been dreaming of," Anne said. "When he's happy, so's Esther."

"All those gadgets, the mechanical stream, the scarlet faucets in flesh-colored bathrooms, and he actually flushed the johns for us."

"Agreed, he's overdone it, gone a little wild, but notice he never told us what anything costs. He's learned not to mention exact amounts of money. The house is him, and he's had nerve enough to do it his way instead of going traditional like everybody else on the hill. Incidentally he wanted you to be pleased. It was as if he'd taken a test and was waiting for you to give him a grade."

"F for flagrant is what I give him."

Late in the month he and Anne had to go to a formal dinner at Pinky's. They drank and ate on the deck off the dining room. Dusk slipped in like smoke, and Esther lit tall white candles protected by hurricane lamps. She and Anne were lovely in the flames' glow, both mothers, both possessing the sureness of self and sex that generated the best in female poise and grace.

What Pinky lacked in poise and grace, he had in enthusiasm. He wore a white suit, a blue tie, and the silver cuff links Wylie's mother had given him for a Christmas present years ago. He'd hired a black maid named Maggie, who wore a gray serving uniform and brought in his daughter to be inspected and praised.

The child, Martha, would have Pinky's red hair and jaw, but Esther's genes had filtered the rawness of his coloring and bone from the little girl. He romped and spun with her. He kissed her knees, her feet, her belly, all the while making howling noises till the daughter was wild with glee. Fussily Esther made him release the child and herself took Martha to her bed.

Maggie carried in iced shrimp, Greek salad, and rack of lamb, but Pinky kept standing as he supervised the meal. The night grew darker, the sky cleared. The river was a blackness wound about embers of the city. The golden capitol dome outshone the moon. Coal barges slid silently as ghost boats across the shiny water. Navigation lights flashed.

Maggie set finger bowls before them. Smiling, Pinky winked at Wylie and suddenly stood to walk into the house. Esther looked after him, yet didn't follow. Ann excused herself for a trip to the powder room. When she came back, she gave Wylie a strange look. Pinky again joined them.

He lifted his glass of imported Bordeaux and rolled it between his palms. He'd lately been reading up on wines.

"Don't know when I've ever been happier," he said. "I want to thank my friends for coming and sharing my joy in this house and also to toast my wife, who's had to suffer through a whole lot these past months as a result of my wild and unpredictable conduct."

Esther, her low-cut gold lamé gown swishing, stood to hug him. He kissed her mouth. They would be using that absurd bed for more than mere sleep before the night was finished.

On the drive home, Wylie asked Anne what the look she'd given him at the table meant.

"I saw something coming back from the powder room," she said. "Pinky was in the nursery, his arms cradling Martha. I started to speak but realized he wasn't talking or singing a lullaby to the child. His eyes were closed and his head bowed as if praying."

"Well wasn't he? Not that I'm surprised."

"No, he was crying."

"You sure?"

"He was crying quietly and completely."

"Why?"

"I don't know, yet have a theory, which is he wasn't because of grief or despair but from joy."

"Joy about what?"

"The heights he's achieved, and the overflowing goodness of his life."

Book Three

48

In October while Wylie worked up a stock pension plan for a partnership of surgeons, he sensed a change of rhythm at Thornhill & Co. He believed some special news must be coming—a rise in AT&T's dividend or a split by GM. When he stood to look from his office doorway, he saw customers backing away from the tape.

"My temple is not a house of trade!"

It was a woman's voice shrill and disturbed, and it belonged to Pinky's mother. Her fingers were lifted above her head as if lightning would zigzag from the tips. She was disordered, her dark hair tangled, her skin splotched, her purple dress torn at the hem. She wore not stockings but rolled-down white socks and sandals. Her legs needed shaving. On her head was set a warped hat which had once been decorated with artificial flowers. Only stubble remained. Her white gloves were ripped at the fingers and soiled. Her wild smoky eyes seemed lidless.

"Repent!" she shouted. "Bend your knee to the Lord!"

Customers and employees stared at her as if she would slay them. Wylie turned to his desk, quickly dialed Pinky's office, and whispered to his secretary. She said Pinky had gone to court. Wylie told her to get word to him that his mother was at Thornhill & Co.

Wylie put down the phone, ran a hand over his hair, and left his office to walk toward Mrs. Cody. Her hands were still lifted, her voice verged on a scream.

"Drive the heathen out!" she commanded. "Whip them from the temple!"

Wylie made his face smile as he moved toward her.

"Hello, Mrs. Cody, how good to see you."

She wheeled to glare. Beads of spit hung from her pale, trembling mouth.

"You more than anyone!" she howled at him.

"Why not come and sit down," Wylie said. He saw Thorny on the phone—most probably calling the hospital or the police. Wylie attempted to step close enough to Mrs. Cody to touch and coax her into his office.

"Accursed one!" she said and flung her fingers at him as if they would part from the rest of her hand and strike him.

People were backed to walls and desks, their faces rigid. Wylie continued to make himself smile and talk softly.

"Mrs. Cody, I really think you ought to quiet yourself and come into my office."

"The Lord's despised!" she said, and spit sprayed from her mouth. She stood under the moving tape where numbers flew past because of the day's heavy volume. Thorny sidled to Wylie, and as he whispered he kept his eyes on Mrs. Cody.

"The police are coming with an ambulance."

"So's Pinky I hope," Wylie said.

The police arrived first, two stout, white officers who held their wooden nightsticks ready. Mrs. Cody wouldn't allow them near her. She hissed and flung her fingers, and those actions baffled them.

Pinky came rushing into the office. He was sweating and out of breath. His tie trailed over the shoulder of his gray suit. He paused to look at his mother and take in the situation. Blowing, he wiped his reddened face, fingered his collar, and moved toward her.

"Mom, for goodness sake, what you doing here?"

She lowered her hands and set those raging eyes on him.

"You are God's," she said.

"Mom, this isn't the place."

"What happened to your promise to the Lord?"

"Why didn't you tell me you wanted to come downtown? I'd have driven you."

"You promised to serve the living Lord."

"Which I mean to do," he said and tried to take hold of her, but she pulled free.

"To glorify His holy name!"

"I will, Mom, now come on. We'll take us a little walk."

He reached for her arm, but she bent away backwards. Crablike she dodged chairs and scuttled into Thorny's elegant office, where she caught up his silver letter opener. She pulled the stiletto from its leather sheath and held it like a dagger.

"We better get into this," the senior policeman, a corporal, said to Pinky.

"No!" Pinky ordered and looked to Wylie. "Bring me a basin of water, some soap, and a towel."

"Do what?" Wylie asked.

"Any container of water."

Doreen, Wylie's brunette secretary, helped. She cared for the office's plants and flowers, which were set into glazed ceramic pots. She ran lavatory water into one of the brightly ornate lotus bowls. Wylie picked up a bar of soap from the sink and tore off a long strip of paper towel.

"It's a ceremony of our church," Pinky said, taking the towel, soap, and bowl. He crossed toward his mother, who stood behind Thorny's desk. She hissed and lifted the letter opener. Pinky carried the bowl in both hands like an offering dedicated to her. She bared her teeth.

"You have to do it, Mom," Pinky said.

"You are besotted with sin!" she said.

"We'll hold the ceremony. You can't refuse the ceremony."

"You were to wield God's sword!"

"I intend to, but now you sit. To refuse the ceremony is a sin."

Slowly, as if her strength were seeping away, she lowered the letter opener. Pinky stepped forward and set the bowl on the carpet in front of her. When he rose, he placed a hand on each of her shoulders and gently pressed till she sat in Thorny's executive chair.

Pinky unlaced her shoes and drew them off. He peeled down her girlish white socks. Her feet were squatly misshapen, the horned nails long and cracked, tufts of black hair growing from the toes.

He lifted each foot, dipped it into the water, and lathered it. He rinsed and dried the feet, his fingers slow and loving against his mother's flesh.

Mrs. Cody softened, her breathing quieted, her eyes found lids. Under Pinky's touch, she became submissive and dreamy. He rolled the white socks over her feet, fitted on her shoes, and tied the laces. She began to cry, not wildly, no loss of control, but the patient weeping of a person who long had suffered pain. On her lap lay the silver stiletto. Pinky placed it atop Thorny's blue desk blotter.

He helped his mother stand. She slid her arms around him and wept into his shirt. Kindly he loosened himself to turn her toward the doorway.

As they left, Pinky looked around him. On his face was the old angry defiance. His mother's feet shuffled over the fine carpet. Her head lolled, her eyes were nearly shut, yet she also smiled as her ragged hands fastened around Pinky's guiding arm.

49

Pinky brought Thornhill & Co. more of his money to invest, though he didn't much care for Thorny's conservative advice on securities. Somehow among all his other work, Pinky found time to read books on the stock market. He formed his own ideas and rarely asked for an opinion. He used Thorny as a mere conduit to the Exchange.

"Populists are in the saddle," Pinky said to Thorny. "Maybe they should be, certainly I don't object, but old-line companies won't be allowed by unions, the antitrusters, and our legislators to pile up the big profits of yesteryear. Only a young company too small to be a target and producing a hot product is going to succeed big in today's world. Put your money on the racehorses, not the plow animals."

He'd come so far. Often Wylie felt he himself had been born fully formed, at least in his mind and attitudes. He'd never had to think out his position in life. Pinky on the other hand kept growing and changing.

He spotted economic trends before Thornhill & Co. and bought fledgling electronic firms whose exotic names and anemic balance sheets froze the hearts of bankers. His market savvy both pleased and irked Thorny. Pinky was the student surpassing the teacher.

He picked a security named High Fly Aviation and Technology, a manufacturer of civilian aircraft. The company's only factory was a converted furniture plant in Louisiana. The production schedule called for three planes a month.

"They can't make money with that output," Thorny argued. "Plus the fact I talked to a pilot, and he says the aircraft has performance problems."

"Buy me another 500 shares. And I want some warrants."

The stock was selling for $1.75. Warrants could be had for 20 cents.

"You undergoing a death wish?" Thorny asked. "The company's a dog."

"Friend, you don't understand. High Fly possesses glamour. Run the name over your tongue as if tasting wine. Savor the dream in it."

"A name created by a PR man."

"Granted, yet High Fly Aviation and Technology is commercial poetry. The company lacks cash, and the product is possibly not the best, but those things have little to do with price movement. Here's the situation. The market, despite minor setbacks, has been going up for almost a generation. Rising prices are all many people know, and they'll no longer be satisfied with annual gains of 10 or 15 percent. Greed enters the picture, and they'll expect 20 and 30 percent appreciation, at least the chance of it. Technology promises that, the brainy little companies with dream power. It's all psychology, like the movies. People will stampede to buy romance."

He was right about High Fly Aviation and Technology—so right, people around Thornhill & Co. shook their heads and bemoaned not following his lead. The stock began its climb during the summer by eighths and quarters of a point. Then during the fall it moved up $2.00 in a week. By winter the stock sold for $7.00 a share. Pinky had a paper profit of nearly $30,000.

"I'm admitting I was wrong," Thorny told him. "My advice is sell enough shares to recover your costs."

"Not sell time yet. Let's buy another 1,000."

"You better remember nothing grows to the sky."

"High Fly A&T lives in the sky."

"Follow the coward's rule by selling half and riding with the rest."

"All or nothing, Thorny, that's how I play the game."

"It's not a game, and people get hurt thinking it is."

"I appreciate your concern, but I see things differently. People have riches galloping through their skulls. They are high on money, and the finish line is not in sight."

Tottering, snappish old Mr. Thornhill continued to poke around where he wasn't wanted and got hold of Pinky's account sheets. He'd been an infantry captain during World War I and used to march with the American Legion on Armistice Day. Palsy shook him, and a partial paralysis caused him to hold his right arm across his chest like a man forever honoring the playing of "The Star-Spangled Banner."

"This is rank speculation," he said after summoning Thorny to stand before him. "We are not a casino!"

"He acts with full knowledge of the risks, and it's making us good money."

"There's no substitute for investment based on value. I believe your customer would be happier dealing with another firm."

"Dad, I've done all I could to talk him out of the stocks he chooses, and if I'd been successful, he'd be a lot poorer than he is right now. Nobody's been hurt, and Pinky Cody's a special kind of person who sees things more clearly than the rest of us."

"He's luckier than a two-headed silver dollar."

"Tell you the truth, Dad, I've never been able to figure out where luck stops and ability begins."

"You'll allow him to keep plunging?"

"I consider him an intelligent adult who can make his own decisions."

"Close the door on your way out."

After that conversation, Thorny really pulled for Pinky. He wanted his father to be wrong, to find out despite age and experience that this was a new era with new ways.

During early March High Fly A&T scared Thorny. It fell from $8.00 a share to $5.50, hung there two weeks, and then spurted to $10.00. At that price the warrants Pinky held reached parity and had real value. His profit now approached $57,000.

By May High Fly A&T was white hot, rising from $10.00 to $14.00. In the middle of the month it went up $3.50 during a single day's trading. Thorny telephoned Pershing & Co., the firm's New York correspondent.

"We don't know anything," said Bruce Cadwallader, the Princeton graduate who took Wylie and Thorny to dinner whenever they were in the city. "We've asked around, and there are rumors—a merger, a buy-out, a type of new engine—but nothing you can get a grip on."

"What do your instincts tell you?" Thorny inquired.

"Looks like a top to me. I'd bail out."

Thorny telephoned Pinky's office. The secretary said he'd flown to Wheeling to take depositions on a breach of contract suit against Mingo Collieries. She'd have him call first thing when he returned.

Three days passed before Thorny heard from Pinky. Meanwhile High Fly A&T was up another half dollar. Pinky's profit was now over $80,000.

"You looking for me?" Pinky asked when he called Thorny.

"You know what your stock's doing?"

"What stock?"

"Oh funny."

"I don't follow stocks. Too mundane."

"Come on over and let's talk."

"Too mundane at Thornhill & Co. Want lunch?"

Pinky no longer ate at the standup counter of Mahomet's Café but walked Commerce Street to the Daniel Boone Hotel. He wouldn't, Pinky said, talk seriously about anything except buying a new tennis racket. He asked Thorny's advice.

"Forget Dunlop and Spalding," Thorny told him "We need to discuss your next move on High Fly A&T."

"No business over bread," Pinky said.

"You're burning out my circuits," Thorny said.

"You have a nervous breakdown? Never happens to fat people. Can't you see I'm working at becoming genteel? No vulgar money talk."

Pinky ordered them coffee and cigars. He occasionally smoked the panatellas Thornhill & Co. gave away, not inhaling, but blowing the smoke in front of his face and watching it like a child bemused by soap bubbles.

"Please," Thorny said. "I can't sleep nights."

"All right, I've made up my mind," Pinky said.

"Sell?"

"Buy another 500 shares."

"I won't do it!" Thorny exclaimed, causing people at other tables to look.

"You have to," Pinky said, eyeing his smoke. "The customer is always right."

"I don't want your business on this thing."

"Whoa now, Thorny. I'm in control here. The dream index of the American public is still pointing upward. As long as people see what they want to happen rather than what is happening, the market will rise."

"What components make up your dream index?"

"You have to promise to keep it a secret. First I measure the amount of chrome on American cars. Next I stand at the counter and observe whether children buy the cheaper hard candy or the more expensive chocolate. Children reflect their parents' financial outlook. Lastly I spy on the pigeons in front of the YMCA. If the pigeons are being fed, our citizens are feeling pleased and prosperous, the perfect weather for an up market."

"Be serious."

"Never been more serious in my life."

Pinky got his additional 500 shares of High Fly A&T. Old Mr. Thornhill, who each day studied customers' sales and purchases, glowered and jammed his cane into the carpet.

Hourly Thorny went to the wire to track the price of High Fly A&T. The stock was now $19.00 a share bid. For the next six weeks it traded between $18.00 and $19.25. Then it moved up to $21.75. The same day a buy recommendation appeared in an over-the-counter market letter of a New York firm. High Fly A&T might, the letter stated, own valuable patents on an engine that held promise of significant fuel economy.

That was Friday, and Pinky called at two-thirty in the afternoon.

"Sell that turkey," he said.

"Stocks, warrants, everything?" Thorny asked.

"Quick as you can. No dickering. Just dump it."

Thorny feared Pinky's shares would depress the price, but it held. In less than twenty minutes, Pinky's holdings in High Fly A&T

were gone at an average of $20.75. His profit was $127,899.27. Old Mr. Thornhill left the office early.

Thorny carried the check up to the cliff house, where Pinky sat on a sunny deck, rolling a striped rubber ball to his delighted daughter.

"He never mentioned the investment to me," Esther said, the check quivering in her ladylike fingers.

"I'm really a modest fellow for someone so talented," Pinky said.

Wylie, Thorny, and the whole office kept watching High Fly A&T. For another month the price held, and on an interday basis rose to $21.75. Then the stock started eroding, nothing wild, just dollars seeping away, a slow leak, yet relentless. It rose a few points when the *Wall Street Journal* reported that Ford Motor was taking a look at the engine. Ford allowed its option to lapse, and High Fly A&T finally settled to $9.00 a share.

"How'd you know?" everybody asked Pinky. They suspected he'd had inside information.

"The dream index," Pinky said.

"What changed?" Thorny asked.

"Not chrome on cars, not candy, but pigeons. Pigeons were the clincher. They got greedy, arrogant, choosy about what they ate. I could no longer count their ribs. Sure sign of overconfidence."

"Wait a second, pigeons' ribs don't show, and you couldn't count them anyhow under all those feathers."

"I couldn't? Well then I guess I made one hell of a mistake."

Pinky left the office laughing, and the story circulated around the city for weeks.

50

Anne's father, the Presbyterian clergyman, came down with a blood infection. She, Wylie, and the children flew to St. Louis. Her father's white hair stayed disordered no matter how many times brushed. He wore pajamas, a plaid bathrobe, and slippers. The frame house was so small his cough sounded loudly through it. His jaundice caused him to appear slightly Oriental. Sick or not, he was a man who had to keep busy and worked at doing a new translation of Luke from the Greek.

He was as companionable to Wylie as he could be. Severe of na-

229

ture, he apparently believed God's service an eternal battle in which only the stanchest warriors would be saved. He attempted to be patient with Wylie's lack of interest in theological questions. After the Presbyterian fashion, he did respect thriftiness and asked advice where to make a tiny investment in the market.

"Safety above all," he said. "But I'd like to put my money into a company fair to its employees, competitors, and customers."

"I'm not able to judge the spiritual depths of a corporation," Wylie said. "I'm not certain one ought to try. In the business world the real sin is inefficiency, the wasting of capital, which is the residue of man's sweat."

"You're equating conscience and morality with efficiency?" Anne's father asked behind the handkerchief he'd been coughing into.

"Dad, I know you can run circles around me with your thinking and training, but, yes, I do believe inefficiency a corporate evil, particularly the careless use of money. If the most moral of companies goes bankrupt, it has committed an unpardonable financial transgression."

"Wylie, God doesn't run the world in the same fashion as the president of General Motors directs his Detroit factories."

"No theological snares, please. I just hope God's a gentleman."

Wylie intended it as a jest, yet for a moment Anne's father stared speechlessly. Wylie quickly changed the subject to electric utilities, which would provide safety and yield. He remembered, however, his father had used the same line about God being a gentleman. St. Stephen's had constantly been after Wylie's father to become more active in the church. He'd told the vicar that while he believed in being generous, in setting an example of weekly attendance, and in trying to adapt the Christian message to his life he still considered man's speaking of God with any certainty a presumption since the relationship of a person to the universe was in degree equal to that of an ant to Einstein. Man could and should hope for God, but to go much farther was likely to be foolish and even dangerous.

Anne's mother seemed to toil forever in her kitchen. She wanted Anne and the children to stay longer. Wylie's small sons were medicine to their grandparents, and Anne's father loved them almost as much as he did his Calvin.

Wylie flew back to West Virginia, where he settled in for some hard work. He intended to clear his desk so he and Anne could take a vacation trip to England during the spring. He cut down on his lunches and squash games. Doreen brought him sandwiches from the drugstore, and Sarah, Viola's niece and Anne's maid, fixed his dinner and left it in the oven. Nights he drove back to the office.

Wednesday late as he worked alone at his desk, the phone rang. He thought it might be Anne calling from St. Louis. It was London. His voice sounded different. Usually he was gleeful and always seemed to be at a party.

"I'm in jail," he said.

"Where you belong," Wylie said, playing what he thought to be a game.

"I'm not fooling. I'm in the city jail and need help. Please keep it quiet."

"What'd you do, put Spanish fly in the cheese dip?"

"Wylie, this is terribly serious."

Wylie drove through cold rain along shiny River Street to the Municipal Building, like the courthouse, granite with spires. On each landing of its concrete front steps empty flower urns had collected cigarette butts and pools of dark water, which reflected globed lights.

A newspaper lay spread over a table in the basement squad room. Metal chairs lacked arrangement. A radiator, painted tan like the rest of the room, steamed and banged. The air was nauseously hot. The unwatched teletype clicked away. An elderly man wearing prison denim pushed a broom across the floor. He pointed Wylie down the dimly lighted corridor.

The duty officer, a dark, muscled young man who'd loosened his black tie and unbuttoned the collar of his blue shirt, sat at a desk. He held a half-eaten bar of peanut brittle. He wore his floppy billed cap.

"You his attorney?" he asked and wiped the back of his hand across his full crumb-specked lips.

"His friend."

The officer grinned, and his broad fingers lifted the peanut brittle to his mouth. He leaned back in his chair. He thumped his stomach.

"He's had his one call, and we don't allow visitors this time of night."

"Don't tie me up in red tape, please."

"Why not?"

"Because I'll buy fifty dollars' worth of tickets to the next Policemen's Ball."

"We don't have a Policemen's Ball. We do sponsor a Brunswick stew and yard auction."

"I'll contribute a keg of beer."

"You just better remember."

He wrote down Wylie's name, patted his clothes, and led him into the dusky, urinous-smelling cellblock. Prisoners in cages rose from bunks to stare. When the officer stopped to unlock London's cell, some laughed, whistled, and slicked their eyebrows.

London was drawn up on a bare mattress of a bunk. His fair hands pulled against his chest as if he'd been wounded. He was naked except for silky white panties. He seemed more than naked—hairless like a shaved speed swimmer, though from his head his golden hair grew full and long. It had the shape and gloss of professional care. He appeared to be trying to hide within his small, shapely body.

"Can't I have some clothes?" he asked the officer.

"Want your dress, sweetie?" the officer said. Hoots from prisoners who'd left their bunks and stood gripping the tan bars.

London didn't answer. His legs were pulled to the side so that even in fear his body seemed femininely graceful. He closed his eyes, bowed his head, and moaned. His cherubic face was puffy, like a person who'd wept for hours. The officer locked Wylie inside the cell and walked off crunching peanut brittle.

"God, Wylie, don't look at me," London said, his eyes clenched.

"Where should I look?"

"Just turn your head and get me a lawyer."

"Can't get yourself one?"

"Not anybody I know. Hire somebody from Bluefield or Huntington." He turned his face side to side. "This'll kill my parents."

"What will?" Wylie asked, though he stared at London's finger- and toenails. They'd been painted scarlet.

"Don't question me."

"I have to know what to tell a lawyer."

London rubbed his temples with his pretty fingertips. In the steamy cell his fair skin had beaded a tiny sweat. Shadows above his aqua eyes were tinted. His blond lashes had become black and very long.

"They call it a vice charge," he said.

"I need details."

"It sounds so common put into words. A few of us were pretending and having a gay time."

He covered his face and began to cry. He still appeared graceful. He dropped his hands. Mascara was bizarrely shocking, streaking his cheeks' whiteness. Wylie thought of him as he used to be—the fair shimmering jester of White Oak School and the Christmas dances, his life scored to music and laughter.

"Be specific," Wylie said.

"Promise you won't make fun of me. If you do, I'll die."

"I promise."

"All right, God, I don't know how to say it—I belong to this group which meets at members' houses. We're kind of theatrical."

"You put on plays?"

"At first we just dressed and sat around. On a dare once when we were drinking we left the house and brought people back. We began doing that."

"What people?"

"Wylie, for God's sake, we dressed like women and went out to pick up men we could love."

Again whistles, laughing, and hoots from prisoners, as the word traveled along the cells. London fully covered his face and wept. Darkened tears slid from beneath his maidenly palms. He smelled of sweat and perfume.

"Tell me the rest," Wylie said.

"The police set us up. They had two young patrolmen wearing jeans and leather jackets strut their stuff along River Street. In front of the bus station I believed I'd arranged a date and took one of them home. Don't tell me how much you disapprove and, God, please don't laugh!"

He toppled forward to the mattress and pressed his face into it.

"I'm not laughing," Wylie said. "Are your parents in town?"

"Luckily they're at St. Croix for two weeks," London said into the mattress.

"All right, I'll do what I can."

Wylie called for the officer. He came unhurriedly and jangled his keys. They left London weeping. Prisoners prissed and flirted with Wylie as he passed their cells. He and the officer walked back to the

233

desk, on which sat a half empty mug of coffee. The officer glanced at the electric wall clock and wrote the time beside Wylie's name.

"Do the newspapers know about him?" Wylie asked.

"Not yet, but they'll be around early in the morning."

"I can tell you that anything you do to keep this private will be appreciated in high places."

"Buddy, keeping things private ain't part of my job."

Wylie left the building and walked to his car. He sat thinking. Rain tapped the roof. He didn't want to involve his own attorney, Pym Waxman, or the firm's, Bentley Parsons. He had to be careful whom he talked to. He thought of Pinky, drove back to Thornhill & Co., and dialed. Esther, wakened by the call, answered. She roused Pinky to the phone.

"How can a man, if London is a man, do things like that?" Pinky asked, his voice a growl.

"Will you help?" Wylie asked.

"No."

"Then give me the name of a good out-of-town lawyer."

"I want you to understand. I'll help most anybody down and out, but not a person who plays around with sexual perversion. London wasn't cornered, exploited, or forced into any of that. He chose it."

"Just give me the name."

"Let me think. I can give you a name, but if you want it hushed, I doubt that's the best way to go about things."

"How then?"

"A thought occurs to me. How well do you know Jacob Samuelson?"

Jacob Samuelson, a Kanawha County judge, an oblique power in much of local politics. Wylie's father had known him, though they'd never been close or met socially. He was a Democrat while Wylie's father, like Wylie himself, made an annual contribution to the Republican cause. In newspaper pictures of the mighty, the judge always seemed to be standing at the edge of the photo.

"Try knocking on his door," Pinky said. "You might mention you talked to me. We've had some dealings."

As Wylie drove toward the Samuelson house he wondered about the kind of dealings Pinky had with the judge. Pinky was mixing more in politics. He'd backed a colored attorney for city council, arguing that in order to prevent racial disorder like that taking place in other cities, a Negro should be awarded a seat of authority. The attorney, named Ashberry, had won by less than a hundred votes.

Judge Jacob Samuelson still lived in the valley, a stone house which had a silver flagpole in the yard and a wet hedge flanking the walk to the front door. Rain popped against blowing magnolia leaves. Wylie rang the bell three times, causing dogs to bark.

Downstairs lights switched on, and the judge's wife peeped through a mullioned window. She was a sturdy woman who wore a hairnet and a flowered dressing gown. She wouldn't open the door till Wylie loudly called his name and apologized for bothering her so late.

She opened the door a crack, peered at him, and invited him in out of the rain. Two English setters barked at him, and she shushed them. The judge, wearing a shirt, trousers, and bedroom slippers, came hurriedly down the steps. He carried a pearl-handled revolver.

"Always let me answer the door at night," he told Mrs. Samuelson.

"You were snoring away," she said, clutching her dressing gown tightly to her throat.

The judge recognized Wylie, shook his hand, and led him to a combination study and gun room. Metal gleamed like jewelry where he kept his collection of pistols under glass.

He was tall, fit, his baldness a tonsure. He used a white cloth to wipe the revolver he'd brought down the steps. He stroked the gun. From a cabinet drawer he lifted a can of oil. Wylie glimpsed cotton patches and jointed cleaning rods. The air became acrid with the odor of powder solvent.

The judge chatted easily. He asked a casual question about coal stocks. He unlocked a glass lid to show a pistol he'd received from Germany. The steel shone like a surgical instrument and was engraved with stags and hounds. Supposedly the gun had belonged to Kaiser Wilhelm II.

"I doubt its authenticity, though I do have a letter fully sworn to and executed by a reputable dealer in Cologne," the judge said. "Still it's a beautiful work even if I've been cheated." He laid the pistol back into its dark velvet nest, closed the glass lid, and locked it. "Well, Wylie, I can deduce from the hour somebody's in trouble. I hope it's not you."

Wylie told him about London. The judge watched with the steady eyes of a man used to seeing far into men. He seemed undisturbed.

"Why did you come to me?"

"Pinky Cody suggested you might be able to help."

"Did he suggest how?"

"No, sir, he didn't, but I guess he meant you could advise me. I'm sure you understand how badly London's parents will be hurt."

"How could the boy be so unthoughtful? Dressing like a woman and picking up men at the Greyhound station. If I had that sickness, I'd at least go to another city where I wouldn't shame my kin."

"So far the papers don't have the story."

"We're fortunate there. Excuse me while I make a call."

He left Wylie among the glitter of guns. Mrs. Samuelson came to the doorway to invite Wylie into the living room for coffee. Over the fireplace hung a new oil portrait of the judge wearing his judicial robes.

"Do you think it's too idealized?" she asked, fingering her double chin and worriedly eyeing the portrait. "He's handsome, but I don't want him to appear Jovian."

Wylie assured her he thought the picture fine. They drank coffee before a log fire revived with a long spearlike poker. When the judge returned, he indicated Wylie was to follow. Wylie thanked Mrs. Samuelson for the coffee.

He followed the judge back to the gun room. The judge closed the door and picked up the pearl-handled revolver he'd wiped. He sighted along the barrel toward a framed picture on the wall, a photograph of young men wearing military uniforms, campaign hats, puttees.

"We may be in luck," he said. "There's a possibility of police entrapment. Furthermore the regular duty officer's in the hospital, and booking won't be official till eight in the morning."

He lowered the revolver using fingertips of both hands the way a person might place a precious gem in a vault. As he spoke he looked not at Wylie but at the gun.

"We are charged in this state with corruption. The *Wall Street Journal* tells us we are third only to Massachusetts and Mississippi. I hate it. I am not a corrupt man."

He still stared at the revolver.

"I sit on the bench and see so much injustice. I watch men go to jail who shouldn't and others walk free who ought to be punished with the full severity of the law. As I grow older, the division be-

236

tween justice and reality increasingly distresses me. The law is often lame and blind."

He talked as if lecturing. Wylie kept quiet. He sensed the judge was treading fragile ground and didn't want to spook him.

"I've reached a point in my life where I'm weary of being a party to suffering. I don't care to inflict or witness it. I particularly don't relish being an agent of pain to good people like Dr. and Mrs. Airy. Melissa was a beautiful girl I once had a crush on, and Ed is the finest practitioner of medicine in this valley. I cringe at the thought of what their son's actions might do to them, a young man disgraced here in his hometown, possibly sent off to prison where God knows what the brutes might devise to torment such a slight and pretty boy. No judge of conscience would care to lay that grief upon another human being."

He laid the revolver on his desk and turned to Wylie.

"Now comes the distasteful part," he said. "You're bound to understand no wheels roll without oil. Technically, till eight o'clock in the morning, London's not been arrested. Moreover, the city's case is not without flaw."

Wylie nodded and heard a distant music. Mrs. Samuelson must've switched on a radio or TV.

"We're a political state. Everybody's in politics—the legislature, the police, the judges. It's a sticky stuff we can't peel from our society. There are men in the courthouse who need help in the coming election. Elections are their livelihood. These men don't like what they have to do. They would prefer to be as pure as preachers, but they must support families and send children to college. They are not bad. They are merely as defective as they have to be."

Lifting a foot, he sat on the edge of his desk and rubbed his hands as if washing them.

"London must leave town. He must leave this state. Can you obtain that promise from him?"

"Yes."

"Now about the oil. It will have to be in cash, nothing larger than twenties, no packets of consecutive numbers. The amount is $3,500. It must not be done carelessly."

"Do I bring you the money?"

"Good Lord, no. I want you to erase this visit from your mind. I'll

237

never see the money. I won't know what becomes of it. You'll be contacted. I can't tell you where or when. Have the cash ready."

He walked Wylie to the door. Mrs. Samuelson had gone upstairs, and the music was coming from there. To Wylie it sounded a little like Eddy Duchin.

He shook the judge's hand and walked through the cold wetness to his car. He drove to the police station, where the officer was dozing, his face sunk almost to the magazine opened on his desk. He sat up quickly. It was 2:27 A.M.

"Never heard of that particular citizen," he said when asked about London and didn't even wink.

Wylie drove to London's apartment, a new yellow brick building by the river. The apartment had white balconies and an antenna with a blinking red light on top. The elevator to the sixth floor was swift and silent. London didn't open his door till he peeped through the Judas hole.

He wore buckled black slippers, pearl slacks, and a wine turtleneck sweater. His rooms were furnished in Swedish modern. Metal sculptures stood about on wooden pedestals. Sunbursts and whorls of expressionistic paintings fired the walls. The carpets were tufted white. The place smelled of incense, and an elaborate hi-fi system set into a cabinet played a Debussy sonata.

Though pale and jittery, London was able to smile. He held a drink and offered Wylie one. Wylie shook his head, refused to sit, and told London he'd have to leave town immediately. London slumped. He pressed a palm against his forehead and groaned.

"For the Lord's sake, what I did wasn't that bad," he said. "Have I hurt anybody? No. All right, so I like to take it in the fanny once in a while. It goes on all over the world. I still think I have the best taste this side of Manhattan. Of course I don't even count Philadelphia. To be perfectly frank, I believe I'm beautiful."

"It's not you, it's your parents we're thinking of."

"Oh, Jesus, I know. They'll throw fits." He whimpered. "And I've rented space to start a boutique. I've got a name for it: Leather World."

"You can find another place more suited to your life-style."

"I can tell you I resent like hell being driven out."

"There's no other way," Wylie said and glanced from a window. The blinking light on the antenna tinted the darkness red. "And I'll need money, quite a bit, quickly, from you."

"How'm I supposed to get money? I never have money."

"I'll lend you $3,500, but I want it back."

"I'll pay, Wylie, honest to God I will." He hinged his wrist to his nose and looked about him. "What do I do with my things?"

"Hire a mover to pack and transfer your stuff. Sublet the apartment. Get away now and arrange details from out of state by telephone."

"Can't I have even three days?"

"Want to go back to jail?"

"Ugh!" London said and shivered. "All right, stop playing savior, will you? I'll leave as soon as I humanly can."

He was gone by nine that morning. During the afternoon, after the market closed, a clean, bright young man entered Wylie's office. He wore a banker's pin-striped suit, the vest hung with a gold chain and an ODK key. Because he had the look of a college senior, Wylie believed he might be searching for a job at Thornhill & Co.

"I'm collecting for the orphans," the young man said and smiled.

"What orphans?"

"Any orphans, anywhere, anyhow."

The young man held up his hands as if helpless and continued to smile. Wylie opened the bottom drawer of his desk, where the $3,500 was bundled in a brown paper sack. The young man didn't open the sack to count the money.

"Sir, the orphans will pray for you," he said.

51

On the terrace of the Pinnacle Rock Club Esther talked to Wylie about her new son. Pinky showered in the locker room, and Anne sat at the pool to watch the children. The summer afternoon was still and rawly hot, the sun red. She would have no other name for her baby but Amos.

"I want you to be the godfather," she said. "Anne's already agreed to serve as godmother."

Wylie couldn't buck his wife and Esther. Moreover, he owed Pinky for his helping London by way of Judge Samuelson. He was, however, surprised that the cinderblock Chosen of God Tabernacle would have anything as sophisticated as godparents.

"There's more," Anne said as they drove home from the club. She wore a loose blue dress and a straw sunhat. Children had brought her body a softness of line, a completion. "We're mounting a benign conspiracy against Pinky. Have you seen the Tabernacle lately? It's run-down and has a leaky roof. Esther says hardly twenty people come to services. Out of his own pocket Pinky is supporting it almost alone. Esther hopes to hold the ceremony somewhere else. She wants her children to grow up at St. Stephen's as you and she did."

"You're talking about Pinky changing churches?"

"He won't agree. They've talked it over again and again. If you and Father Bonney could speak to him."

"I don't like doing this."

"Nobody likes it but it's for the children's good."

Wylie made an appointment with Father Bonney the same week. The priest ran around the church gym coaching the basketball team. The team played in an interdenominational league and currently held second place. Father Bonney wore basketball shoes, a sweat suit, and a white brow band.

He was an energetic man of thirty-seven who had thin graying hair and a tuft of goatee. He spoke rapidly and moved quickly even in the pulpit as if urging people to get a move on spiritually. Dandruff sprinkled his shoulders.

"We miss your father," he said as he and Wylie walked from the gym to the church study, the room sweet from a breeze blowing over lilac blooms outside the open casements. "He was the vestry's mainstay. If we needed uniforms or had a shortage in the organ fund, money always appeared magically. I was rarely able to trace a good work to him, yet I sensed who was responsible."

"He liked giving."

"He did, and I hope you'll soon take your place on the vestry. Your name's been mentioned." He brushed at dandruff on a shoulder. "Nothing would make us happier."

"I'd be delighted to serve," Wylie said, thinking how pleased his mother would be.

"Of course you will. You're very much like your father. Sometimes I see him in you. Now as to Amos Cody, Esther's talked with me. I'm perfectly willing to give him instruction, but it's my understanding he isn't sure in his own mind."

"I thought we might double-team him."

"I'm not convinced that's such a good idea. Some people you can reach directly, others you wend your way to. Amos keeps staring at my clerical collar. I believe it makes him uncomfortable. Why don't you try it alone? Feel him out. If you need me, I'll come arunning." He fingered the referee's whistle hung around his neck. "Let's pray for him now, each of us."

"I'll leave that to you if you don't mind," Wylie said.

"You don't believe in prayer?" Father Bonney asked, leaning back and smiling.

"I believe in praying, I mean you doing it, but sometimes I think God would need a lot of ears," Wylie said, sorry he'd stumbled into this. Often Father Bonney took his office a little too seriously.

"Perhaps God does."

"It's never seemed quite logical to me."

"Logic is a man-made word. Possibly it doesn't exist in the hereafter."

"Nothing might exist in the hereafter," Wylie said and immediately regretted letting the thought escape. He was becoming too entangled.

"Oh, my!" Father Bonney said and lifted the whistle as if he might blow it. "Surely you consider yourself a Christian and don't believe we can live without a conviction of immortality, which is the true basis of morality."

"I believe in morality."

"In it, but not it."

"Father, don't press me, please. I serve the best I can."

"I'd simply like to know what your credo is."

"All right, I believe in being kind."

"That's your morality?"

"I think it's a lot."

"And God?"

"All good things we don't understand we equate with God."

"What about the bad things?"

241

"The opposite of God—which we give names to, or used to anyway, like Satan, the Devil, the Deceiver."

"Lord help us."

"Till he does we have to help each other."

"Perhaps it's not Mr. Cody I ought to be giving instructions to but you," Father Bonney said and actually blew the whistle.

Wylie left the church feeling heat in his face. He resented Father Bonney's cornering him like that. Wylie did serve the church generously. He performed the duties asked of him. He wasn't a professional religionist. That was the terrain of Father Bonney and other ministers, the way they earned their bread.

Still he had his talk with Pinky, three days later, the conversation beginning in the locker room of the Pinnacle Rock Club. Pinky wiped his ruddy body with a towel and complained about a lack of wind. He grabbed flesh at his stomach and shook it as if it would detach.

"Got to get rid of this thing," he said. "I'm starting to resemble a successful middle-class lawyer."

They walked from the locker room up the steps to the bar, where it was sunny. A warm rain had cleansed the valley of smoke. Traffic crossed the new silver bridge over the river whose water was tinted by a greenish film of fallen pollen. Cars slid above the water like brightly colored beetles.

"Can't leave him unbaptized," Pinky said, speaking of his son. "But at the Tabernacle we're temporarily without a preacher."

"Father Bonney at St. Stephen's will oblige."

"I know Esther's been at him. She's been at everybody. I can't do it. People around town will believe I'm social climbing. I'm not. It's just at the moment the Tabernacle is falling apart, both the congregation and the physical plant—chairs without legs, piano out of tune, dangerous wiring."

Pinky gnawed at ice cubes from his scotch.

"I realize Esther's not comfortable at the Tabernacle," he said. "My children won't be either. To Esther, faith's like a garden party with the Lord pouring tea."

"Not fair," Wylie objected, wishing he were on the links instead of having to listen to this.

"Sure, St. Stephen's a nice place, clean, the carpets soft, the air prettified by stained glass," Pinky said. "That setting fits the way Esther was brought up, but not me. I was taught God is all in all. I used to stretch out on the bare floor to humble myself before praying."

Wylie felt restless and even agitated that Anne and Esther had gotten him involved in this—all this God talk, this God excess of Pinky's. How could anyone really know anything for certain about God in the world?

"I'd feel I was betraying my church if I left," Pinky said. "There's less than fifty of us remaining. St. Stephen's would be nice I know. Put on your new Easter suit, stand on the steps, and tip your hat to the ladies. Sin doesn't count, or all the people being gutted."

"Decent people aware of sin and suffering go to St. Stephen's— loving, generous people who serve in their way. Don't make them criminals."

"But deep down it doesn't mean much to you. In your belly I'm talking about. You ever been terrified of God? Of course not. I have. I'm becoming the typical overpaid legal eagle with a fat bank account and pumpkin stomach, but I'm still afraid of God."

Wylie looked past him and the line of red barstools to the swept flagstone terrace and colored umbrellas. Music and laughter drifted through the open windows. A pretty young girl in a short tennis dress walked confidently toward the courts, a racket on her shoulder. He loved the way the dress lapped at her tan thighs.

"I'm afraid of something else too," Pinky said. "I got no right to throw stones. Fact is I'm ashamed."

Wylie simply waited. He wasn't allowing himself to be drawn further into Pinky's religious obsessions.

"Could kick my tail from here to Tennessee," Pinky said. His knuckle rapped the bar. "I shouldn't be telling you this, but I need advice." He lowered his voice and watched red-jacketed Alexander pass carrying a stack of glass ashtrays. "I never thought I'd do such a thing." He shook his head as if he couldn't believe it of himself. "I love Esther more than my life, yet—I guess you could call what I did cheating on her. At the bar convention I had a little too much to drink and there was this friendly woman lawyer."

His eyes shut, and he hunched like a person expecting a lash.

"Does Esther know?" Wylie asked, also keeping watch on Alexander.

"Not yet, but I'll have to tell her."

"You will not!"

"I've always been honest with her, and she with me."

"You're overreacting. Has anybody been hurt?"

"Can't you see how I'm hurting?"

"I'm talking about real damage. Nothing's broken. You feel guilty, but it'll pass. Esther never has to know. The main thing is not to cause her pain. Life goes on."

"You're so damn slick," Pinky said, raising his face to Wiley. "So easy, no paying, no judgment. Don't you realize if God doesn't care enough to punish us, He doesn't care at all?"

Wylie wouldn't step into that. Pinky was still snagged in the web of his youth's Pentecostal fanaticism. Decades might be required to free him.

"Let's have another quick drink and go home," Wylie said.

"You never let anything disturb you, do you?" Pinky asked, staring now, his eyes set. "You always been true to Anne, I guess. Never led astray."

"That's a subject I don't intend discussing with anyone," Wylie said, backing off the barstool.

"Hey wait, you mean maybe you have been?" Pinky asked and pointed at Wylie. Alexander glanced up from a table he was wiping.

"I'm leaving," Wylie said, signed his bar ticket, and drove home. He told Anne he hadn't had much luck playing the proselytizer.

"And don't ever ask me to do it again," he said.

She and Esther, however, didn't give up. Still it was a year before they convinced Pinky to enter a St. Stephen's confirmation class. At the christening of his baby son Amos, Wylie and Anne stood as godparents at the baptismal font beside Esther and Pinky in the roseate light of the vaulted nave.

The commotion came from the sacristy at the side of the marble altar. Wylie thought Pinky's mother might be entering to disrupt the service. It wasn't she but the sexton, who'd bumped a cabinet and knocked over a chalice.

Pinky looked toward the sound with the bloodless fright of a man who heard the angel of death's all-encompassing wings descending.

52

July 4, Esther and Pinky threw a seafood fiesta at the Pinnacle Rock Club. They provided clams, scallops, blue crabs, and speckled trout flown in from Norfolk. Pinky also hired an immense black chef from Goat's Wharf, Virginia, to supervise the bubbling caldrons set up on the lawn near the tennis courts.

A red-and-white nylon tent was erected, which, like Araby, swelled placidly with humid summer air. Strolling musicians played a violin, an accordion, and an alto saxophone. The musicians dressed like cutthroat pirates.

Though the fiesta started during the late afternoon, the invitation specified formal attire. Men grumbled about having to wear black tie and stand around holding drinks in the hot sunlight, but the ladies were smiling and fervent as they moved past wearing bright, swishing gowns.

Under the striped tent Alexander directed white-jacketed waiters to carry out trays of drinks, wines, and canapes. Trestle tables covered by linen cloths held dips and crystal bowls of salad. The grounds had been sprayed to prevent ants, flies, or insects from tainting the perfection of the party.

The chef from Goat's Wharf was an idol of black fat whose flesh gathered in rolls around his great body, sagging dollops, and all his creases were shiny with sweat. He wore Bermuda shorts, a broad white apron, and was barefooted. On his head he cocked a feathered hat, and from his neck dangled a string of bleached shark's teeth. His grin displayed teeth like casino dice, and in the steam from his caldrons he appeared a cannibal king.

Pinky and Esther greeted guests. Heine Stahl, the club manager, stood close to do their bidding. Jewels caught shafts of sunlight which fanned through musky leaves of drowsing oaks.

Servants set tables around the central tent, at each place a white folding chair and a party hat. An ice sculpture of Neptune riding an arching dolphin was a centerpiece among vases of freshly cut flowers.

245

The chef piled high on silver salvers the boiled shrimp from South Carolina.

Wylie watched Pinky step among the city's elite. At one time Pinky would never have dared use the first names of men whom he chatted and laughed with, but now he was not only at ease but also courted. An outsider would certainly have judged him well born.

When everyone was seated, he stood from his place at the head table and held a wine glass raised as he called out: "To this home of freedom and land of opportunity!" The strolling musicians played a thin, jivey "Star-Spangled Banner," causing guests to rise clutching napkins, forks and goblets.

During the meal a waiter approached Heine Stahl, who was having more liquor brought from the clubhouse. Heine frowned, looked toward the front gate, and moved off briskly across the grass.

At the head table with Pinky and Esther were her father and a number of powers from the valley—George Clendennin, banker; Luther Thomas, state supreme court judge; and Waldo Arbogast, the mayor. The most prominent guest was Senator Sam Straugh of Washington. Others listened and laughed. Esther looked lovingly at Pinky.

At the club's stone gateway, something was happening. Several waiters had joined Heine Stahl there. They blocked the entrance and closed the gate. Heine touched his cropped hair, adjusted his bowtie, and shot his cuffs. He ordered the waiters back to their stations. The strolling musicians moved among tables, and the cannibal king rowed his wooden oar into an iron pot of tumbling hush puppies frying in deep fat.

Wylie saw the man climb the ivy-covered wall. Two more followed. They drew up a stout woman and a small boy. The men had on dark woolly suits, white shirts, ties. The boy was in tennis shoes, shorts, and a T-shirt. The woman wore a shapeless brown dress, probably off the rack of a coal-camp store.

The men had to be miners from some dismal hollow. They jumped down backwards from the wall and helped the woman and the boy to the ground. Like Wylie, other guests watched as the group gathered and moved toward the tent. The men were unsure. The woman urged them on. The boy hung to the rear. They stopped, whispered, and stood waiting with the vegetal patience of hill people.

A waiter noticed. He stared, turned to the bar, and spoke to Heine, who was making notations on an account pad. Heine strode from the bar and approached the group. He talked to the men and was answered by the oldest. The flap which was his empty left coat sleeve had been pinned to his shoulder. The boy, age six or seven, stood as solemnly as the adults, his eyes lifted to Heine's precise, aspish mouth.

Heine was becoming aroused. His hands jerked up and down, and he gestured for waiters. Pinky still hadn't seen the group, though several guests at his table had turned their heads.

As Heine and the waiters attempted to herd the miners, the boy, and the woman toward the wall, she shouted.

"Mr. Cody, you forget about us? You ain't been talking to us much lately."

Because of the strolling musicians, Pinky still didn't hear. More guests, however, slid their eyes toward the confrontation. Pinky was telling a story. Esther interrupted it by laying a hand on his arm. At the same time the music stopped. He looked toward the lawn.

The group was backing off slowly as Heine and his waiters formed a half-moon about them. For a moment Pinky wasn't able to grasp what he saw. He then stood from the table. Esther would've gone with him, but he motioned her to stay.

Pinky crossed the grass toward the group. The woman began talking at him before he reached her. He shook the boy's and men's hands. Only the redness of his neck belied his cordiality. Heine was talking into one ear, the woman into the other.

Pinky listened and considered. All his guests were now watching. He nodded, turned to Heine, and the two of them walked back toward the tables. Heine was excited.

"Let me call the police!"

"It's my party," Pinky said.

"You're violating rules. Facilities would never have been rented to you for this."

"Set them a table and serve them," Pinky said.

"Impossible!" Heine said.

"Listen, you little Prussian, I'll tell you once more. Get a table and food for my guests. If you won't, I'll do it myself, and if you try to interfere, I'll not only knock you on your can, I'll haul you into court for slander and defamation. I'll hound you out of this club and any other job you find in this valley. Do you understand, Mein Herr?"

Furious and mottled, Heine understood. His fists quivered against his tuxedo trousers, sending shivers of anger all the way to his ankles. He turned to his waiters and spoke as if he'd risen from under water.

Waiters carried the table, covered it, and unfolded chairs. They set on it a partially melted ice Neptune and flowers. The miners sat in sunshine—rigid figures like stone statuary. They looked at the hot crabs on their plates as if the creatures might claw them. The boy was unsure what to do with his large linen napkin.

Pinky stayed beside them a while. Who were they? Some remnant, Wylie guessed, from the old Broken Men organization Pinky had represented. He showed them how to crack crabs and probe for meat. His hands on shoulders of two of the men, he chatted in the leisurely fashion of mountain people.

At a signal from Esther, the musicians began to play. Guests faced their food, but wonder and explanations swept rows of diners. They kept glancing toward Pinky, who still socialized with the group. The boy smiled, the men laughed, and instants of softness further rounded the woman's body.

Finally he walked them to the gate, where they talked. There was handshaking, and he waved. He crossed back toward the head table. Except for drowsy chirring locusts in wild cherry trees along the ridge, it was quiet. He went to his seat.

Senator Sam Straugh stood and started the applause. All the guests rose, and even the black waiters clapped out of sight of Heine. Esther kissed Pinky, who acted surprised. Applause sounded like a distant comber breaking over the twilight hills.

53

Wylie's mother continued her tippling, and on a summer afternoon as she sat at the kitchen table, she felt giddy. She tried to make it to her bed, but she was so dizzy, she reeled and collapsed. Viola found her crawling across the floor and telephoned Wylie at Thornhill & Co.

He drove her to the hospital, where besmocked Dr. Airy waited at the emergency entrance. Orderlies rolled Wylie's mother away down a fluorescent corridor.

She underwent a battery of tests. As long as she lay still, she felt the ground was steady beneath her, but when she moved about, the dizziness returned, and she grabbed for support. She said it was like being seasick and reminded her of a crossing she and Wylie's father made on the *Santa Rosa*.

At the end of four days all test results were in. His smock crackling, his pipe lit, Dr. Airy clipped up X rays on the display screen in his office. He used his pencil to point to a pea-sized shadow on the brain's right anterior lobe.

She went under the knife two days later. Her greatest distress was having to submit to the shaving of her head. In an operation which lasted all morning, the specialist, a Dr. Gorman, severed the growth, the lab checked it, and the grain of flesh was judged non-malignant.

Dr. Airy, expansive in relief, lit his pipe and told Wylie that London was living in New Orleans and had opened a boutique.

"Of course I wish I could've kept him here with us in the valley," he said. "He has roaming blood in his veins."

When the bandages were unwound and discarded, Wylie's mother wore colored kerchiefs over her head to hide the long scar. Anne and Wylie had been visiting her at the hospital once a day, and Pinky was with her again.

"I want him," Wylie's mother said.

Pinky brought her flowers and a small bedside radio so she could listen to the opera. He sat at her bedside evenings. Once when Wylie entered the room, Pinky was holding her hand.

After Wylie drove her home, she settled in and began to play her Steinway, a thing she hadn't done since his father's death. Wylie carried Gertrude, Anne's cello, up to the house, and his mother and wife performed. The mother appeared younger and happier than she had for months. She was no longer drinking.

"I get tipsy on music," she said.

During September while playing the andante in a Richard Strauss sonata, her left hand wouldn't obey, causing her brittle fingers to strike clinkers. She and Anne laughed and again started the piece, but the hand simply wouldn't function correctly. Wylie's mother sat looking at it as it if weren't connected to her.

She returned to the hospital for more tests. Dr. Airy slid the pencil from his smock to point at more X rays. The tip stopped at a pearl shape in her skull.

249

"It's not the same," he said. "You can see it's several inches from where we first cut. I see no alternative but to go in for another exploration."

A second time they shaved her head, and following the operation she stayed at the hospital till after Christmas. Before Wylie could, Pinky provided a tree and trimmings for her room. He hung a holly wreath on her door. He rushed a fancy turkey dinner down from the Pinnacle Rock Club.

Using a cane, Wylie's mother learned to walk, though once home she never returned to her piano. During the winter she sat sunning herself in the hot moistness of the solarium, her face lifted, her eyes closed. By spring she was fussing half-heartedly at old Ed for his clumsy fingers and awkward feet in her flower garden.

On an April Friday as Wylie was about to leave Thornhill & Co. to play golf, Anne called. Viola had telephoned her. Anne had hurried up the hill and found Wylie's mother in the basement trying on old gowns.

"I think maybe something's slipped," Anne said.

The next call from Viola came during the Pinnacle Rock Spring Formal. Anne wore a white evening dress, Wylie his tails as they left the club for his mother's house. There all the windows were lighted. His mother sat in the living room, on her head a gray, broad-brimmed hat that had a feather sticking from it. Under her fur coat was her nightgown, and her feet were pushed into golden slippers, though without hose.

"Your father's taking me to dinner," she said, smiling. She wore rings, bracelets, a diamond necklace. "The club's chef has notified us he's received a shipment of fresh lobster."

"I don't think Dad can make it tonight," Wylie said, glancing at Anne, who appeared distressed.

"Your father would never break a date for lobster."

They drove her to the hospital, but this time Dr. Airy didn't take out his pencil.

"Another operation would just be carving her away," he said.

"What do we do?"

"Allow her to die in the dignity of her home."

He gave written instructions about medication, the idea being to make her last days as painless as possible. Pinky continued bringing flowers. Her friends visited, and Father Bonney from St. Stephen's called every Sunday afternoon to carry her Communion. She liked cards, and Anne played by the hour with her, as did Viola, whom the mother had taught Russian bank. Viola, who smelled of laundry soap, drew Wylie into the pantry.

"She after me to do it for money," Viola said. Old herself now, worn, her every move was made of slow deliberation.

"It's okay, I'll stake you. Just keep an account."

"What ifs I win?" Viola asked. She wore her green uniform with a white collar, but her brown, bulging shoes had broken under her weight. She was so black her skin reflected light.

"Any winnings are yours," Wylie said.

His mother was still too quick for Viola and took her for five to ten dollars a week without telling him. She kept the money hidden in a drawer of her French lowboy, a secretive little hoard of revolt against infirmity.

Wylie had a stairway elevator installed, and his children loved the sliding seat. When they were at their grandmother's, the working whine of the motor sounded constantly. His elder son, Wylie III, hiked to the house with two schoolboy friends and charged them a penny a ride on the elevator.

"Your money-making instincts preserved," Wylie's mother said.

All at once she did strange things. She was listening to Boito's *Mefistofele* and to their amazement began singing—attempting "L'Altra Notte In Fondo Al Mare" as if Renata Tebaldi. His mother's small, sweet voice cracked on the high notes. They believed she was joking till she became silent and hurt.

She kept searching for her past. She'd remember a snapshot, a locket, or a pair of slippers and demand Viola dig them out from trunks and closets. An item found was just as quickly tossed aside. She would sigh long and send grumbling Viola to find a piece of costume jewelry, a scarf, or a shriveled daisy pressed beteeen pages of a libretto.

She became more irritable. She fussed at Viola for not wearing a hair net while serving meals and stopped wanting to hear music, any music. Yet she was always happy to see Pinky, who brought her religious books. She lay on her bed with one such book open across her chest and asked Wylie whether she was dying. He denied it.

"There's nothing out there for me," she asked.

"Out where?" he asked.

251

"I'm reading the testimonial of a woman who was pronounced dead after a boating accident and revived. She said she rose out of herself to a hill which was dark but covered with lights—that the lights were being carried by beautiful gliding spirits. I've never seen any lights."

"You shouldn't read those books," Wylie said, furious at Pinky. "They're written by unstable, highly emotional people."

"It would be nice to see lights on a dark hill."

For her sixty-fifth birthday, Anne and Wylie invited in his mother's oldest and dearest friends. She was smiling and gracious. She'd had her whitening hair done. She wore her primrose gown and jewelry. Like a queen she sat in a brocaded high-backed chair to receive guests. The only bad moment came when she stood to blow out the candles on her cake. She was so thin that rings dropped from her fingers.

Suddenly she refused to leave her bed. She gave no reason but demanded that her four-poster be moved closer to the window so she could lie looking out at the river. All her meals were carried up by Viola.

"Go along with it," Dr. Airy advised.

On the night of a rioting fall storm which uprooted trees, spiked thunderbolts into the valley, and rent the darkness, she again talked of Wylie's father.

"I won't see him, will I?" she asked. "Not that he's in Hell or anyplace like that. To be bad, a person must have some sense of what badness is. Your father was good, but he lacked depth. He was polite, generous, and kind, yet could never love anything ugly. The things he loved were always easy, including an easy God."

"I don't want you reading any more of Pinky's books."

"You're your father's son—handsome, charming, at times breathtaking, but you too lack that sense of badness. In fact I don't think one can have charm and a deeper depth. They're incompatible."

"We're halting this conversation, and I'm dealing you a hand of cards."

During the following weeks, she became weaker and smaller, though her darkening eyes grew enormous. She refused food, cards, even Father Bonney. Wylie had already cut Pinky's visits. She grew morose, angry. As Wylie sat by her bed and attempted to feed her, he

252

mentioned that Miss Burdette sent her best wishes. Wylie's mother's face snapped around on her pillow.

"They slept together for years," she said.

"Mom!"

"They used the daybed upstairs at the office."

"But you had her here to the house," Wylie said, remembering the threadbare daybed in the musty back room used to store papers, tax forms, old ledgers. He thought of Miss Burdette's copious weeping after his father's death. Was it possible?

"Oh we're beautifully civilized," she said. "We forgive everything and have nothing to hold to."

"We have each other."

"It's not enough," she said and glanced at the night sky before turning her face again toward the wall. "It's what the Devil does to us—he overcivilizes us, and we lose everything."

The Devil! She'd never used the word seriously before. Damn Pinky!

That Saturday night she died. Wylie was with her. She raised her taut, trembling head from her pillow, gazed at him as if she wanted to be certain of his identity, and reached out. He gripped her skeletal fingers. She then let her head fall back and stared at the ceiling.

"I see no lights," she said. "Nothing."

He felt the life go out of her, kissed her hand, and wept.

54

Pinky was making significant money from his law practice and investments, and he carried a small clip-on slide rule so he could quickly calculate profit and loss in various arbitrage positions. His trades no longer unnerved Thorny. When in the late 1960s the market, as Pinky put it, headed south faster than a bullbat bucking birdshot, he piled up dollars on the short side. Many days his was the only serene face watching the tape at Thornhill & DuVal.

He scorned cash. What he wanted, he bought quick, no hesitation. He was still investing in valley real estate, much of it depressed. He and lawyer friends formed a partnership to purchase peeling, broken Victorian houses, which the partnership remodeled and transformed into modern offices for doctors, dentists, and other professionals.

Wylie's name was at last part of his firm. Old Mr. Thornhill had slumped forward from the bench while feeding pigeons in the Pioneers Cemetery. He now lay paralyzed in an upstairs bedroom of his stone house. Thorny became free at last to work his will at the office.

The afternoon DuVal was added to the gold leaf on the door, the firm served champagne as well as the usual cigars. He and Thorny were putting into motion plans for expansion—first a branch office in Kanawha City, later in Huntington, Bluefield, and Parkersburg. The expansion caused a shortage of customer men, and Wylie recruited for Thornhill & DuVal by visiting colleges, mostly in Virginia.

He now had the inheritance from his mother as well as his father. His income through the firm was rising 15 to 20 percent a year. To get high on the figures was easy, to soar on projections of mathematical progressions, to envision himself at middle age not just rich, but very rich, in the same league with Philadelphia and Boston fortunes. When he looked at his children, he began to think of dynasty.

Rather than sell his mother's house, he and Anne decided to get rid of their own smaller place and move in. Anne took charge of an immediate, extensive redecoraton, needed, he guessed, to put her stamp on things and to drive out ghosts. There was so much to throw away. Among trunks in the basement Wylie found the crated stained-glass window from his parents' old mansion on the river. He donated it to the Salvation Army for use in a chapel and received a tax deduction.

Thorny persuaded Wylie to attend a meeting Pinky called at the Coal & Coke Club, where he was at last a member. Pinky rented a conference room and served liquor. His guests were the upper stratum of doctors, lawyers, and coal operators. No women present because none was allowed in the club's solemn chambers. When Pinky had everybody feeling happy he told the waiters to arrange chairs facing a blackboard he'd supervised setting up.

"Keep on enjoying yourself while I talk," Pinky called out. He wore a tailored light blue suit, a vest, and a black tie. "Just hold up your hands, and the waiters will refill your glasses."

"Do we hold up our hands if we have to weewee?" Thorny asked.

"One finger will get you Cutty Sark and soda," Pinky answered amid the laughter.

He switched from the genial host to his serious, courtroom presence. His voice deepened, his face became maturely set, his gaze leveled. Despite the merriment, the guests quieted under the sweep of his reddish brown eyes.

"I've invited you here for several reasons," he said. "One, I consider you my friends. Secondly, and more important, I know each of you is fat at the bank."

Boos and heckling. "He's fixing to fleece us!" Billy Kidd, his drink raised, shouted. Billy was an eye-ear-throat man at Valley General.

"It'll be a golden fleece," Pinky said. "Any of you have objections to making money? Those who've been converted from making money may now leave and forever hold their peace."

"Hair will grow on your palms!" Blue Bales called.

Like an auctioneer waiting for a bid, Pinky looked into the laughing faces. They razzed and smart-talked him, but he wouldn't allow himself to be moved from his central seriousness. He made them know that horsing around and drinking were edges of the gathering, not the core.

"Truth is we should all be ashamed," he said. "Everybody in this room takes money out of this town. We take, take, take, but what do we give? Look at our valley. Walk up Commerce and down River Street. This city's ratty. The valley's dismal. Anybody driving through the capital of this state has got to believe we're one of the dirtiest, smelliest, most slovenly communities in the country. All the money's moved up to the hills, where it can't be seen. We've left a wasteland down here and owe the city better."

"Lay it on, brother," Buford Hogge called. Buford owned taxis, movie theaters, and a scrap-iron business.

"It's not too late," Pinky said. "We can redeem this valley."

"How much is this going to cost us?" Big Jon Maynard, the All-American from Pitt and owner of two Chevy agencies, asked.

"It's not going to cost but will make you money," Pinky said. "Better than that. Social considerations are involved. All the citizens of the valley will benefit."

"He's going to open a whorehouse," Wesley Leek said. Wesley, who'd inherited nearly 5 percent of the stock, was a director of Mountain State Bank.

"That might be a good investment for your trust department," Pinky said when laughter stopped. "And it might benefit you particularly, Wesley, you look so much like a frog. No pretty gal would get within ten feet of you even standing upwind. But whorehousing isn't what I have in mind."

Pinky then began a presentation of a real-estate venture, a project wherein a new corporation would buy up two central blocks of the city, a downtown tract of expiring houses and huddled, decrepit stores.

He explained that the houses and stores would be sold for salvage, the tract razed, and a complex of apartment towers constructed. At a signal from him a waiter carried a four-by-four-foot portfolio of architect's sketches to the blackboard and then set them in the chalk tray.

The balconied towers were white concrete and looked more like Miami or Los Angeles than West Virginia. They formed an enclave, the ground floor of which contained shops surrounding a recreation area of parks, fountains, and playgrounds. There would be a cafeteria, a medical center, an auditorium, and a tree-lined promenade with benches.

"The two blocks we're talking about are now a sore on the community," Pinky said. "We can transform them into a white gem which will dazzle everybody who visits the valley. The city will become bright and vibrant. Moreover, we can structure tenancy to include elderly people and the underprivileged. The social dividends will be tremendous."

"Social dividends are fine, but what about real money?" Hayes Grimm asked. Hayes was a tax attorney, and figures forever flowed in his mind.

"Don't worry, Hayes boy, you'll get yours," Pinky said. "You all know how difficult it is to find desirable space in the valley. Even when you're able to locate rental property, it's cramped, shabby, often vermin infested. Robbery and crime are problems. Development of the two blocks would slice away the city's rot and bring

256

light and a whole new tempo to the area. The valley will appear energetic and progressive."

When Pinky paused, his audience started talking, and questions were called to him. He held up his hands to quiet the room.

"First you want to know how it's done," he said. "Answer: we make a public offering of stock. I'm assuming it will go mostly into local hands. We get clearance from the Securities and Exchange Commission, issue a prospectus, and find us an underwriter. By use of various depreciation schedules, we'll have a cash flow largely tax-sheltered for years."

He signaled waiters to move among the chairs and hand out brochures. The jet black block printing was on glossy white paper—a description of the project, estimated costs and returns, and more architect's sketches. The name of the corporation to be, proclaimed in shimmering white letters on black: HILL CITY, INC.

"Now the figures you're looking at are all rough and nothing you should hold me to," Pinky said. "We had to start someplace to give you a general idea of this thing's shape. True, we'll need to borrow heavily, but that isn't all bad. If successful, it will leverage our earnings sharply higher."

Pages rustled, pencils scratched, and men rose with questions. Wylie turned pages. The brochure had a sweet odor as if the ink had been perfumed.

"There's a beautiful kicker in the deal," Pinky said. "You'll find that on page seven. Government money. A good chance, if not a sure thing, we can secure Urban Renewal funds, maybe not directly through the corporation, but through a co-effort with the city. It is in fact possible to get our hands on more public money than we have to put up ourselves. The ratio goes as high as four of Uncle Sam's dollars to one of our own. A loaf to us is mere crumbs from his table."

"What's the management setup?" Alf Craig asked. Alf's firm sold bulldozers and other heavy equipment to strip miners.

"During the formative years, I'll be president," Pinky said. "I'll propose a slate of directors for the stockholders to approve. I'll want a salary and stock options, but I'll be working full time to make the rest of you a barrel of money."

257

He took more questions. Brooks Farley, whose business was the design and manufacture of coal tipples, wondered how the corporation was certain it could buy up two entire city blocks.

"For some time agents have been purchasing options on property," Pinky said. "More than thirty owners have signed. With dickering I'm convinced we can get the rest. I'll sell those options to the corporation at cost plus five percent."

He'd come prepared and had all the answers. Waiters again passed out drinks. Guests milled about and leafed through brochures. They gathered at the blackboard to examine the sketches. Pinky had provided a calculator so the numbers could be checked out, and the numbers looked good.

As people left, Pinky stood at the door and shook hands. He winked at Wylie, who walked out beside Thorny.

"How'd I do?" Pinky asked.

"Merely sensational," Thorny said.

"Wylie?"

"They liked what they heard," Wylie said.

He and Thorny returned to Thornhill & DuVal, closed the door of Wylie's office, and sat. Thorny lit a cigar and blew smoke toward the ceiling.

"What'd you really think?" he asked Wylie.

"He was impressive."

"Sure, but what about the idea?"

"Biggest thing to hit town in my day."

"He's damn smart. He's been carrying the idea in his head for a couple of years but just got down to sharp-penciling it the past six months. Tell you the truth, I was a little surprised he hadn't mentioned it to me. He kept it secret from everybody but his architect and his accountant because he didn't want that property to rise to the moon and make the purchase of options prohibitive. Now I've got a little delight I want to share with you. Thornhill & DuVal can underwrite the offering."

"It's too wild for us."

"Hold it, friend. I disagree and strongly. I see this as our opportunity to put this firm on the map nationally. Hell, it could be the start of an expansion not only throughout the state but also into Virginia, Kentucky, even Pennsylvania. I see our name on a tombstone in the *Journal,* up there with Kuhn Loeb, Goldman Sachs, and Rothschild."

"Too many loose ends. Is he certain of the city's cooperation?"

"He's solid with the city. Has his man on the council."

"Government money's that easy to get?"

"Pinky's been wooing them in Washington. He's on a first-name basis with congressmen, particularly Senator Sam Straugh."

"It's nothing we ought to rush into," Wylie said.

Thorny removed the cigar from his mouth and pushed at his thin flaxen hair. His palm crossing his brow buffed it. He drummed fingers against his stomach.

"Pal of mine, you're not too crazy about Pinky, are you?"

"I'm not convinced he's big enough for this."

"I believe he is."

"Well it's not a question of personalities but business. Agreed, we might make a fortune. We could also get killed."

"I've felt you holding back before where he's concerned. I'd like to go on record here and now and say he's about the smartest, most able man I know. I have absolute confidence in his judgment."

"Apparently most people do."

"Allow me to lay it out for you. He's asked me to be on the board of Hill City, and Thornhill & DuVal will be both underwriters for the stock offering and financial advisors to the corporation. Wylie, the public will go for this, and the project will be the most stupendous event to hit around here since coal was discovered in them hills. It'll make us vulgar amounts of money and resurrect a city."

"Am I allowed to sleep on it?" Wylie asked.

"Just not too long," Thorny said.

55

Thornhill & DuVal would form a syndicate and be lead underwriter for the initial issue of Hill City, Inc.'s common stock. Thorny worked with the firm's New York correspondent and its Wall Street attorneys to gather information and figures for the SEC and a preliminary prospectus. He flew to New York at least once a week.

The syndicate, in consultation with Pinky, decided the offering should be 500,000 shares priced at $10.00 a share. As lead underwriter, Thornhill & DuVal would attempt to sell the greatest part of the stock. Thorny estimated the firm's gross profit would come to something over $180,000.00.

Ownership was to be held as much as possible within the valley first, the county second, and the state third. Such a distribution of shares would help defuse bureaucratic problems, zoning red tape, and carpetbagger charges often brought by backwoods politicians against absentee owners. Hill City must appear to be a local, public-spirited enterprise.

Pinky hired a publicity man from Indianapolis, a bouncy, grinning youth named Gordon, who spread his arms while talking as if about to break into song. The media carried planted stories about the project, and Pinky himself appeared on the city's TV station with charts, sketches, and a pointer he stabbed about like a foil.

At the beginning Wylie worried they kept too much stock for Thornhill & DuVal to distribute and that the firm might have to eat part of the offering. Then weeks before the official release of shares, tentatively set for the seventh of December, he and Thorny made the happy projection they might be oversubscribed. They discussed rationing of Hill City, Inc., to customers.

"It's heating up and could be hotter than hell's furnaces," Thorny said, shirtsleeved, tie loose, a cigar in his teeth. "I suspect we'll be hounded."

"I'm being romanced by a bank that's never dealt with us before," Wylie said.

"It's the small fry wanting in that's mucking the deal. We could refuse to sell anything less than two hundred shares."

"Can't go along with that. If we ration, we ought to do it pro rata."

"Not fair maybe, but more profitable."

"Only on the face of it. We want the broadest public support, particularly when it comes to negotiating with governmental authorities. We need to be allied with motherhood and the flag."

"So my thinking is we ought to up the number of shares offered. Till that time we take no more orders. From this minute on, anyone who calls will have to risk buying at market. People whose orders we've already received will maintain their relative percentages if they wish."

Word that Thornhill & DuVal would accept no further buy orders on the Hill City offering made the newspapers and TV. Demand for shares became intense. Wylie and Thorny telephoned other underwriters in the syndicate to ask them to release part of their allotment back to Thornhill & DuVal. None did because Hill City was hot everywhere.

Wylie had disgruntled customers. One was Blue Bales, who'd procrastinated giving his order.

"You mean you're not letting me in on this?" Blue asked.

"You were in from the beginning and should've called last week."

"How long have I been a customer?"

"There's no more stock."

"I thought we were friends."

"I can't sell something the firm doesn't have."

"How many shares you drawing down for yourself?"

"Not as many as you might think."

"Sell me a hundred of what you're in for."

"You're asking me to give my money to you."

"Damn right. Do it, and I'll be grateful. You know Bebe's mother died?"

Blue had married Bebe Stanniker, and her mother, a divorcée, had lived on Jekyll Island supported by alimony and generous dividends from her coal stocks.

"I read it in the paper," Wylie said. "Anne sent a contribution to the Cancer Fund."

"When the estate's settled, I expect the portfolio Bebe will inherit ought to undergo a complete review."

"I can't resist the pressure and am putting you down for one hundred shares."

"Thought you might see the light."

Wylie received two unusual calls, the first from Mr. St. George, Trish's father, who fumed over the telephone from his walled fortress in MacGlauglin. He claimed he'd always been fond of Wylie and that Wylie was displaying ingratitude for past favors by not awarding him a mere 1,000 shares. The fact that Wylie hadn't seen or heard from him in years Mr. St. George considered immaterial. He signed off cursing steadily.

The second call was Emerson Smythe's, the languid aesthete Pinky had heaved spinning into the Pinnacle Rock bandstand during the Thanksgiving dance so many seasons ago—precious, rarefied Emerson, who'd nearly gone to prison for child molestation. These days he never left his house but sent a servant to do the shopping and buy the liquor. Emerson pleaded for shares in Hill City.

"You're letting newcomers buy," he said. "You owe something to the old families."

"Em, class warfare is not part of the offering, and besides I'm surprised you'd have anything to do with Pinky Cody."

"I've forgiven him. That trash knew not what he did."

"You'll have to forgive me too 'cause at the moment there's no stock I can allot you."

During the two days before the sale, interest in Hill City became frenzied and hysterical. Thornhill & DuVal's phones rang even at night. Wylie received calls at home. The firm had inquiries from brokers as far away as Atlanta and Denver. *Barron's* wired for a copy of the prospectus.

A final meeting between Pinky and syndicate members raised the number of shares from 500,000 to 650,000. The additional stock was gone in less than two hours. Though it'd been believed $10.00 a share was all the market would bear, the price floated upward first to $12.50 and then to $14.00.

"Why not sixteen dollars?" Pinky asked as he sat at the head of the table in the boardroom of the Mountain State Bank Trust Department on December 6.

Thursday, December 7, 1970, the underwriters went to market with 650,000 shares of Hill City, Inc., at $17.75 a share. During the first hour of trading, the stock rose to $19.25. There were cheers at Thornhill & DuVal. Pinky himself came to watch the tape. People congratulated and made way for him. They wanted to lay hands on him, to absorb his magic.

He'd already piled up a lot of money. If he both exercised his options for Hill City shares and sold out, he would net $1,000,000 in a day. He never considered it. He was an excited and happy man who'd constructed reality on a dream.

"Can't get over it," he said. "One day an idea's nothing but marks on paper, and the next the paper changes hands and becomes money to build with. The whole process is glorious and crazy."

The offering was so successful it was written up in the *Journal*, nothing big, just half a column on page 34, but the story mentioned Pinky as well as Thornhill & DuVal. The firm ran a tombstone listing the underwriters, with Thornhill & DuVal's name at the top. The shares, which had leveled at $19.90, rose a point.

Thornhill & DuVal netted a quarter million for its participation. In addition, Thorny had 1,000 shares for himself, and Wylie had 400 after what he'd given up to Blue Bales.

"The best day of my life," Pinky said and did a jig before the tape. Immediately he became serious. "God keep me humble."

56

In early January, Thornhill & DuVal gave a party at the Coal & Coke Club. Rules were bent so that Esther, Anne, and other wives could enter the forbidden rooms. A band played, the drums rolled, and guests gathered to see Thorny present the certified check for $10,887,500.00 to Pinky, who held it above his head like a trophy.

He intended depositing the check with a newer bank in the valley, United Merchants and Miners, but Thorny advised against it.

"You want the old money to stay with you on this," Thorny said.

"I'll be invited to become a director at United Merchants and Miners."

"In time you'll be a director at Mountain State, and it'll mean much more."

"Proof I've arrived, huh?"

"A directorship at Mountain State is like knighthood."

"Okay, into Mountain State it goes. Lord, what's happening to me?"

"Some damn fine things."

The band played, and people called to him. He was drinking scotch, hugging Esther, and shaking hands. He became tipsy and bumped the speaker's table. Esther had to guide him out—Pinky laughing, waving, hearing applause even after it stopped.

From his office window Wylie watched Pinky hurry along Commerce Street on business for Hill City, Inc. He became so occupied he hired two young attorneys to tend his law practice. Only ripe cases drew Pinky into court. Moving down the street, he was a person people wanted to speak to and be recognized by. His hand seemed perpetually raised in greeting.

Thorny was elected to Hill City's board of directors. Pinky presided at meetings held in the revered chambers of Mountain State Bank. Twelve prominent men from the valley sat at the burnished table. Each place was set with a water carafe, a sanitized glass, a memo pad, and two sharpened yellow pencils. Gazing down from oil portraits were the righteous, unswerving eyes of the bank's past presidents.

As Pinky promised, he surrendered to Hill City, Inc., all land options he'd acquired. The main order of business at those first meetings was the purchase of the remaining real estate in the two-block area. Twenty-one owners of the seventy-three lots and structures involved still held out.

"Bandits wanting to rob us," Jay Tilson, senior vice-president of Mountain State, said.

"Can't blame them," Pinky said. "Most are in the money business. We don't dare lose momentum. I suggest we appoint a Buy Committee, influential men who go as a delegation to the holdouts and apply pressure, nice pressure, but pressure nevertheless."

The Buy Committee consisted of six men. When asked by Thorny, Wylie felt an obligation to serve. The committee visited landlords and sweet-talked them. Lofty words were spoken about the public good. Members used intricate lines of influence which finance creates in a multitude of strands.

Hill City, Inc., succeeded in acquiring all commercial property. Those who wouldn't accept checks were people who owned houses, mostly older couples fearful of disturbing dust that had settled around them. Their neighborhood lay moldering and they lived among decay, yet they refused to see it because they'd lost life's impetus.

The Buy Committee went to homes, the members sitting in dilapidated living rooms which had buckled linoleum on floors and pots of water hanging over smelly gas heaters to moisten dry air which seemed exhausted.

Red Jed Pauley lived in a brown frame two-story house that wasn't plumb. He was a retired locomotive engineer for the C&O, a steam man who'd once sat at the throttle of the Fast Flying Virginian as it sped spitting fire through the blackness of mountain nights. He and his wife kept cats, she frumpy and partly crippled. The place stank of feline urine. Red Jed had a woodworking shop in his garage where he built garden furniture.

"It's not the money," Red Jed told them, shifting his placid weight on a creaking straight chair. "We got nowheres else."

"We'll find you a location," Jay Tilson said. "You can erect a house that's modern and convenient with a shop in the basement."

"But we been living here so long," Mrs. Pauley said. She smoked cigarettes and held to her crutch. Springs of a stuffed chair twanged under her. "We've taken care of the house, and it's taken care of us." She sighed hopelessly. "Need a month of Sundays just to clean out the closets."

"Suppose you don't have to lose your house," Pinky said. "Suppose we buy a nice lot, pick up the house, and move it. You could leave everything in the drawers. Your eggs can stay in the refrigerator."

Wylie and others on the Buy Committee exchanged glances. Pinky hadn't been authorized to make that offer. Moving the house would cost many times its value.

"I just don't know," Red Jed said. "What you think, Mary?"

"It's got my head to spinning," Mrs. Pauley said. She turned her head side to side. "I figured I was in my dying place." She stroked a yellow cat, a tom with a haughtily vicious face. "Reckon they'd be happy somewheres else?"

"Not only a new lot and house moved to it, but we'll award you an additional five thousand dollars for the inconvenience," Pinky said.

They couldn't hold out against Pinky. He found property on high ground at the north end of the city near the B&O tracks. Red Jed liked the idea of being able to watch trains slide by below his front porch. Mrs. Pauley was to receive several cases of canned food for her cats. The Buy Committee also had to agree to move the garage. Gordon, Pinky's publicity man, transformed the expensive operation into an advertisement by seeing that pictures of the house and garage carried on flatbed trucks made all the media.

Earl Axon, a Marine veteran, was another holdout. He'd been a hunter, and his board-and-batten cottage held dusty trophies of deer, bear, and elk. He'd stuffed a squirrel and a fox. Cedar limbs were nailed up as perches for mounted birds, varieties common in the valley, including mourning doves, a robin, a red-tailed hawk. Only reluctantly did Earl allow the Buy Committee to enter his door.

"You're trying to screw me!" he said, a bald, angry man unshaved and unwashed. For a left hand he had a stainless steel mechanical claw. He'd built a ceiling-high pyramid of empty beer bottles in his living room.

"All we want is to make you a generous offer," Pinky said. "If you compare what property sold for in your neighborhood just six months ago against what Hill City will pay now, you'll see you're not being taken advantage of."

"If you're willing to pay so much, it must be worth more," Earl argued, his face squinted in cunning, his claw clicking like pruning shears.

"You wouldn't try to stick it to us, would you, Earl?" Big Jon Maynard asked.

"You don't know me well enough to call me Earl, and you're damn right I would because people in this country got to learn some things can't be bought."

Earl wouldn't deal. He wanted to be left alone to live out his life among animals he'd shot and mounted, each aglitter with dolls' eyes. The Buy Committee was forced to use connections within the city government. The cottage needed painting, the chimney had dropped bricks, and steps were rotted away. The Fire Marshal placed the property on his hazard list. Earl was presented with a court order stating he'd have to meet building-code specifications or his cottage would be condemned.

He still wouldn't sell or leave. When the police drove up to evict him, Earl poked a Browning out a window and rattled No. 8 bird-shot off the flashing squad car. Police radioed for backup support, and two officers had to bash in the rear door and take him with a rush that caused Earl to blast a hole through his ceiling. The beer bottles toppled.

"We hated doing it," Pinky told a reporter. "But that fellow's going to have more money than ever he saw before in his life, and 'fore long he'll thank us for what we did."

The last difficult transaction was a steepleless church where pigeons roosted and cooed, the African Baptist. Though tar-papered and nearly defunct, it still remained technically a place of worship. A legal quorum of the befuddled congregation had to be persuaded to sell, and the money would go to the church's national headquarters in Louisville.

Members assembled, mostly old Negroes tottering, bent, and dragging. They settled in bare, bone-smooth pews, which had taken on the hue of their skin's blackness. Torn and broken hymnbooks lay about, and racks held colorful Jesus fans supplied by a funeral home.

Pinky stood in the dark pulpit and explained Hill City's offer to the uplifted faces. He told them new churches were to be built around the Hill City complex where everybody would receive a welcome. An ancient matriarchal woman named Aunt Cornelia, who rocked while she sat like a traveler keeping balance on an errant earth, called out in full singing tones:

"What happens to the spirits of people who was borned and died here?"

"I share your concern," Pinky told her, his voice deep and pastoral. "Generations of your ancestors have worshipped in these pews. But God is not a building. Stones and a roof can't confine Him. The true church is in the human heart."

He convinced them, but just barely, the motion to sell passing by only three votes. Members of the Buy Committee quickly collected signatures from the congregation. Aunt Cornelia never signed. She sat humming a hymn and rocking before the empty altar.

Pinky ordered a plywood model of Hill City built and put on display in the marble lobby of Mountain State Bank. The scale model was enclosed by glass, each unit of the complex coded and described on an illuminated black-and-white map fastened to a wall. A sign announced that pre-construction leasing would be accepted through Magic Valley Development Corp., a Hill City subsidiary.

The Monday morning following Easter the bank watchman discovered the model had been vandalized. Smashed glass spread across the lobby floor, and the plywood buildings appeared to have been beaten with a hammer or club. Towers lay shattered, and red spray paint across the map proclaimed: SAVE THE PEOPLE!

A new Hill City model was constructed and this time covered by safety glass. A uniformed bank guard watched over the display. No offenders were arrested, though the police suspected a gang of black youths who called themselves Allah's Prophets.

When Hill City had its property, arcing wrecking balls started swinging, and yellow bulldozers clanked in to feed on debris. As the razing of the two blocks progressed, constant dust spun upward. People new to the city noticed and asked about it. All through the night heavy equipment rattled and ground away, the destruction brightened by diesel-tinted floodlights. Buildings were dynamited and fell, tremors reaching into cabinets and causing crystal to quake. Even high on the hill chandeliers swung and tinkled.

As first construction began, there was a dedication and celebration. Mayor Arbogast, the city council, Governor Winslow, Bishop Glass, and Senator Straugh climbed onto the bunting-draped platform. Judge Samuelson had a chair at the edge. Two high-school bands provided sparkling majorettes and marches. Hostesses in short skirts gave away key chains, served hot barbecue from aluminum tubs, and released balloons, which drifted upward into the disturbed summer air.

Pinky sat at the center of events. He appeared distinguished and in no manner unworthy of the praise heaped upon him. One had only to see the spread of pictures in the *Gazette* and the *Daily Mail* to know he felt he deserved it all.

57

Anne's father was stricken with severe angina pectoris, and she flew to St. Louis, though all planes had begun to frighten her. Wylie saw she carried Dramamine, a pillow, and magazines. He'd contributed money to the campaign of the state's new governor, the first Republican since 1934, and at Wylie's request the governor's office put through a VIP tag on Anne so she'd be babied by the airlines.

She stayed longer than expected. Despite the fact he called her every other night, she wrote him letters, a way of working off her tension. Her father was lucid one moment, badly confused the next. He claimed to see an angel perched at the foot of his bed.

I want to be home but am afraid of leaving Mother. She has more to do than she can count over. This morning Daddy asked me to read him the King James version of the Book of Job. It's his favorite literature and theology. Mother and I agree he's thinking of dying. The angel is gone, at least temporarily. Tonight I'll play Bach for him on a borrowed cello. I miss you.

Wylie continued long, profitable hours at the office. Arthritic Sarah fixed his meals but had Wednesday nights off. He thought of eating at the Coal & Coke Club and then decided to drive on up to

Pinnacle Rock to see whether he might find a squash game. He wasn't flabby, yet felt it. In the coolness of the high, resounding courts, Blue Bales challenged him to a match.

Blue was doing fine at his family's industrial supply house, he a vice-president in charge of pipe, casing, and drilling equipment leased and sold to prospectors for oil and gas. He'd also formed a corporation which developed and marketed cemetery plots. Blue's salesmen pushed tendrils through all parts of the state as well as into Kentucky and Ohio. He piloted a company plane to The Greenbrier on weekends to shoot golf.

He still moved as if oiled, but his hair was no longer bleached, and when money was involved, the foxiness of his face became transformed to wolf. They played to win, and Wylie felt good giving himself over to muscle and instinct, allowing his body to take charge and make its own decisions. Blood and bone sang in him. A few spectators in the glassed gallery applauded as he won the last game with a low perfectly placed bank shot to the backhand corner, which spun Blue into the wall.

Wylie'd worked up a dripping sweat, stood under hot needles of a shower, and sat wrapped in only a towel at the round oak table used for poker in the locker room. Blue furnished the scotch.

"I have difficulty believing it's real," Blue said. He relaxed and reared his bare shiny feet to the table. "You and I, Thorny, people like us, we're running things around here."

"We are?"

"Think about it. My father spends three months a year in Florida, yours is gone, and any day now one of us will be elected to Mountain State Bank's board of directors. Even London, the little fag, owns a successfully precious little boutique down New Orleans way. All the queers and dears love it. You're a financial wizard. Me, I play golf with Sam Snead. The world's in our hands."

"Terrifying thought."

"Hell, you love it, and so do I. Girls call me 'sir' now, waitresses and salespeople, and I hold my line walking down a street against the crowd. I intimidate the snottiest waiters."

He poured himself more scotch and reached for a cigarette. His toenails were beautifully trimmed. A pedicure? Wylie wondered. Or maybe Bebe did it for him.

"And Pinky," Blue said. "Whoever thought that coal-camp ridge runner from the Wrong Side would be wowing the valley. For a long time I believed he was the dumbest guy I ever met. What a surprise he turned out to be."

"I just thought of Sis Asters," Wylie said.

"Sure, I think of her now and then. Terrible. What a loving girl she was. That's the way I try to remember her, not with blood over her and all. Say, you recall old Lois May, the cousin of Bebe's from Wheeling you and I did the bang-bang with up on Buzzards' Roost? That hot little darling's become a nun. I swear 'fore God. Bebe found it out. Lois May's in a convent up in Pennsylvania. Sister Cecelia she is now. But generally speaking, the world's in our hands."

"Grand shape too."

"No sarcasm, please. Admitted, that's a damn mess in Vietnam, but we should be out of there soon. Look on the bright side—the market's hitting new highs, business has never been better, you have a nice family, children, so do I. This coming Saturday morning at ten I got a date to play a foursome and old Sam's my partner. How can you beat that?"

Anne returned that Saturday. Her father's condition had stabilized, and she'd been able to hire a practical nurse to help her mother care for him during the daylight hours. Still Anne was nervous, her body rigid with anxiety. The children easily angered her, and one evening Wylie came upon her crying before her dressing table mirror.

Thus he agreed when Esther invited them to fly with her and Pinky down to Jekyll Island. Anything to cheer Anne. Pinky arranged for the plane, the same Apache chartered on Hill City business, rather than drive the state's narrow twisting roads.

During the flight to Georgia, they nibbled salty hors d'oeuvres and sipped chilled white wine. Pinky had leased a beachfront house, the broad plate-glass doors and windows of the bedrooms seeming at high tide to fill with sea. Palm trees rattled fronds. At the rear flowering hedges gave privacy to a lighted pool. Finches, wrens, and robins flocked around a stone birdbath. Pelicans glided by the deck.

They had tennis privileges at the Neptune Club. Pinky's game was stronger. He no longer read books but took lessons from Beau Terry at Pinnacle Rock. Typically Pinky was able to win no more than a dozen points off Wylie during a set. Lately, however, his scores had been creeping upward.

The green court dazzled under the island sun, and Pinky bore down. Before Wylie felt he'd settled to their match, he was behind 5–3. In the past Pinky believed the net offered the most advantageous tactical position, and Wylie with his unhurried shots had been able to lob or pass him. This time Pinky changed his pattern of play and hit baseline to baseline—long, steady stroking while each waited for the other to falter.

Esther and Anne came to watch. They'd been walking on the beach and wore broad straw hats and striped robes over their bathing suits. They sat in the shade of an umbrella at the side of the court.

Wylie tightened his concentration. It was his serve, and he rarely gave Pinky his best, which was an American twist that hopped high to the backhand. Pinky couldn't handle it and would nearly always return a cripple easy to come in on and punch for a winner.

Instead of flopping his racket after Wylie's serve, Pinky chopped the ball low to Wylie's backhand. Since Wylie was moving toward the net, the shot was almost past him before he could react. He lunged, and the ball looped away long.

Wylie again gave Pinky the high top-spin serve. Pinky answered with a sliced return which curved cross court. Wylie tried to volley, but there was so much spin, the ball wobbled off his racket into the net.

Okay, Pinky had learned some new stuff from Beau Terry. No more twists. Wylie would hook the ball into Pinky's body, jam him so all he could do would be to wrist his racket and push off.

When Wylie served, Pinky stepped quickly to his left. He was thus able to take the ball on his forehand. He rolled a smoker down the line. Wylie wasn't within ten feet of the return. He looked after the ball and at Pinky. Esther and Anne applauded, as did a few tourists who'd stopped to watch.

"Something wrong?" Pinky asked. He was grinning and tapped the heel of his hand against the strings. Red hair on his stout legs gleamed.

It was set point. Wylie intended to use power. Being taller than Pinky, he'd hit a flat hard serve which would skid off the court. He tossed the ball before he realized Pinky was moving back. Pinky had read him. Wylie didn't stop the serve. He still believed he could brute the ball past Pinky. As Wylie's body leaned into it, he opened the racket face, and his arm came over with a whip in the wrist.

The serve was a screamer. Wylie didn't follow it to the net. He

271

assumed even if Pinky were lucky enough to make a return, the pace of the ball off his racket would carry it deep.

Pinky stood flatfooted and sliced. The ball kissed the tape and angled toward the backhand court. Wylie reached after it, but the ball bounced low. He was able to touch it with only the rim of his racket.

Pinky tossed his racket over his head, caught it, and did a shuffling cakewalk. He crossed to the net.

"You realize how many years it's taken me to beat you?"

"I didn't know it meant that much."

"Don't get mad on me, though I know you never in your life thought you'd lose a set of tennis to me."

"I'm happy for you. Ready for another?"

"I guess it's just the sunburn around the neck and ears that makes you look so sore. Well I got a confession. Beau and I plotted this out. We mapped tactics and strategy on paper. He also helped me develop a couple of new shots, which I've kept hidden till the optimum moment. One whole morning all he did was pound American twists at me."

"Your serve."

"Mind if I don't hurry? I want to savor this historic instant."

Just as they started the second set, a shower blew in off the ocean. Screaming gulls fled it. Wylie and Pinky hurried to the umbrella where Esther and Anne stood clutching their beach robes. Wylie caught the victory smile Esther gave Pinky. They ran for the house.

"I assume you didn't take a dive," Anne said as they changed clothes in their bedroom. The gray ocean, roughened by wind and rain, crashed white against the sand.

"He jumped me before I had it all together."

"I've never seen him more elated."

"I'll take him tomorrow."

"I had a strange feeling while I was watching," she said. "The sun's glare on the court made you flat and blurred. It was like seeing shadows play, and once I had this sensation he was you."

Wylie turned from the mirror where he was brushing his hair. He wore it longer these days, after the fashion. Anne had lifted her arms to allow a lavender gown to slide over her matronly body.

"It was the sun," she said. "For a second I forgot who was who. I know you don't resemble each other, but while you were stroking

272

from the baseline he looked like you. I glanced at Esther to see if she noticed. Apparently she didn't, but for a minute it was as if you were playing yourself."

"He doesn't have my form."

"He tries to."

"That'll be the day."

"I think it's a kind of worship."

"What?" Wylie asked, lowering his brush.

"I realize he treats you like everybody else, yet in the way he acts, dresses, and sometimes talks I have the definite feeling he's imitating you. I call that worship."

"I call it sunstroke."

They drove to the Heron's Nest for dinner. The storm was past, though palm trees thrashed and sailboats tacked fast across a moon stripe on the dark water. Sea birds wheeled and dived. A giant magnolia stood like a sentry guarding the sea, the leaves of clacking black armor capturing the slight glow of night.

They had drinks before their broiled dolphin. Wylie was thinking of what Anne had said in the bedroom. Pinky wore not seersucker like Wylie but a white suit, the uniform of the southern planter. His tie was wine colored, Wylie's a pale blue patterned by faint fleurs-de-lis. On the little finger of his left hand Pinky, like Wylie, did wear a ring, not a coat-of-arms signet, but one inscribed with his initials in English script.

Pinky was expansive and held up his martini, the glass reflecting candlelight.

"If I felt any better, I'd be translated into Heaven," he said. He leaned to Esther to kiss her cheek.

"You're drunk on my blood," Wylie said.

"I admit humbling you on the court was tasty," Pinky said, smiling. "But the best thing is I'm here with my wife and friends, drinking good liquor, and knowing life's going my way. I tell you it's grand."

Anne's eyes drifted to Wylie's. *Grand* was one of his words.

"I called home," Pinky said. "Construction is on schedule, and Hill City shares are now selling for twenty-one dollars. We have investors from fifteen states and one foreign country—a bank in Lebanon which made a significant investment on behalf of a client. Word does get around."

273

"The good word anyway," Anne said. She appeared coolly patrician wearing Wylie's mother's jewelry.

"We're almost seventy percent occupied before the first tower's completed," Pinky said. "Far ahead of what we hoped for. We're dickering with half a dozen retail organizations who want space. We're also having a reporter from *Architecture USA* down to look us over."

"He's bound to use words like 'original' and 'daring,'" Esther said, lovely in rose organdy and gems. "That is if he's got eyes."

"Everything useful and profitable is original and daring," Pinky said. "Easy things axiomatically are neither inventive nor of any great value. Think of electricity, the airplane, Gothic cathedrals."

"Gothic cathedrals profitable?" Anne asked as she feigned choking.

"They were for the Catholics. They inspired the faithful to drop their coins into the collection plate. More than that, they were profitable in the awe they created, the reverence. The spiritual return was high."

Shrilling sea birds circled the water, shadows in the night. Pinky stared at the sea.

"Course when I'm living fat like this I worry what the poor folks are doing," he said, the old religious guilt gathering in him.

"The miracle is he doesn't get ulcers, he's into so much," Anne said. She understood how moody he could be and was attempting to stop him from sinking farther.

"Wouldn't allow myself to have ulcers," Pinky said. "Simply mind over matter. I refuse to admit the possibility, just as I never entertain the notion I won't complete the Hill City project and go on to something bigger and better."

"He already has an idea in mind," Esther said.

"Many ideas in mind. One involves a monorail system over the valley to provide transportation. Paint it gold and think of the publicity for backward West Virginia. And we can sell water."

They all looked at him.

"There'll be a national shortage soon," Pinky said. "I read an article in *Scientific American*. We could build gigantic reservoirs in our mountains and use aqueducts to deliver it, letting gravity supply the power. One day our streams and rivers will become more valuable than coal or oil."

They heard loud voices, a disturbance inside the Heron's Nest. A drunken soldier stood at the coral bar and went *chu-chu-chu-chu-chu* as if he held an automatic weapon and was mowing people down. Waiters hustled him out. "Gimme peace!" he shouted.

"Trouble is, so little time," Pinky said, turning his eyes back to the table. He had a luster on him, not alone from the candles, but a sort of effluence, as if the flame were inside. "Ideas compound like money in the bank. Just when a man starts hitting his stride, he glances 'round to see the ugly face of old age leering at him."

"Dear one, you're hardly more than a babe in arms," Esther said and tickled him under his chin.

"I'd like to be going hard at eighty. Instead of taking Social Security and retiring to Florida, people ought to fire up. Maybe I'll establish some kind of industry that uses only senior citizens."

"Manufacture hearing aids and false teeth," Anne said.

"Or a gadget which captures moonbeams and bottles them," Pinky said. "Jekyll Island moonbeams ought to sell a million bottles a day. I guess if anybody has it licked, it's us sitting here. If the world has a top, we're on it."

He lifted his glass, causing them to do the same.

"I don't know about the rest of you, but he's making me feel good," Esther said.

They drove back to the beach house, and while the ladies went to primp, Wylie and Pinky stood on the deck and looked toward the changing phosphorescence of an ebbing ocean.

"I'd like you to come on the Hill City board, which I'm enlarging," Pinky said. "Sure, Thorny's already holding down a chair and ably, but you got good instincts for the dollar as well as connections we can use. Besides, the fortunes of Thornhill & DuVal and Hill City are closely linked."

"I guess I ought to say I'm honored," Wylie said, hesitant, attempting to think through the implications.

"You need to guess about it?" Pinky asked. As he lit a cigar he looked over the flame, his face yellowed by it.

"I didn't mean it the way it sounded."

"No, let's pursue this a second. You meant it. You're not really certain you're honored. Even after all these years you've never accepted me."

275

"Not true."

"It's true all right. Let me ask a question. At your mother's funeral, did you even consider me for a pallbearer?"

"I chose her oldest and closest friends."

"I was close to your mother, Wylie. We had deep talks. She desired spiritual food, a hunger which I tried to feed. But the point is did you even for one split second think of me? Don't bother to answer. Okay, I wait patiently. I haven't given up. I still hope one day you'll relent and accept me as a friend."

"You're embarrassing me."

"Accept me inside yourself, instinctively, without having to consult your built-in book of etiquette. Someday I'd like you to touch me—naturally, without forethought, a gesture of honest-to-God fondness."

"It would appear ridiculous at this moment, wouldn't it?" Wylie asked. He wished the ladies would hurry back.

"Yes it would, though there is one great truth I'd like to leave you with: there are worse things than appearing ridiculous."

Anne and Esther stepped from the orangy glow of the beach house. Wylie quietly exhaled. Pinky clapped his hands. He had a surprise to unveil. Inside was a spinet piano, and when he sat at it, he began to play *Clair de Lune*. Wylie's eyes again met Anne's. They thought it must be faked, that a phonograph had been switched on or the piano contained a revolving roll. No, he was really playing and doing it fairly well. He had to have been secretly taking lessons.

As he finished the piece, he allowed his short, practical fingers to remain on the keys. The notes lingered till overwhelmed by the rustling palms and the unhurried combers. Anne, Esther, and even Wylie were held in the magic aura Pinky had created. He freed them by drawing his hands from the piano and raising his happy face.

"Grand," he said. "Just simply grand!"

58

During the winter, Anne again had to fly to St. Louis because of her father. He lay in a coma at the hospital. Each night she called to speak to the children and give Wylie a report.

"He's so thin now," Anne said. "I could lift him in my arms."

Sarah looked after the children, and Wylie's habit was to work late and drive up to Pinnacle Rock for his drinks and dinner. On a Monday night he hoped for a squash game or a rubber of bridge, but the club's rooms were empty. Only Alexander waited at the bar.

Wylie hit a few balls, showered, and returned to the bar. He stopped short. Trish St. George sat on a stool. She wore a yellow knit dress bound around her waist by a wide black belt. Her black hair hung long and straight to her hips.

She was not matronly, her body not settled. She appeared slim and sleek. The old haughtiness still sharpened her face. Her crimson mouth twisted into a cynical smile. Her silken legs were crossed, and she jigged a yellow slipper which sported a tiny black bow.

She presented her cheek for him to kiss. He smelled the old perfume. She was drinking martinis and used a red plastic toothpick to lay a speared olive on her tongue. She moved but did not cover her knees for him to sit beside her.

She talked, mugged, and gestured with a cigarette. Her jigging foot caused him to think of the play of muscles in her inner thighs. Her body advertised sexual wisdom. She was a world traveler, a veteran of campaigns.

They reminisced, laughed, and bent toward each other as they drank. Her violet eyes were hooded by blue lids. He asked whether she'd eaten.

"I put myself on display here in the hope some friendly face would appear," she said.

They ate by a window in the blue-and-white dining room. A fog moved over the valley, masking the river and the city lights. The air was dusky, the electric candles unable to penetrate it far. A group of chemists and their wives had watched as Wylie held a chair for Trish—it white with a maroon cushion.

"Afraid you'll be talked about?" she asked. She had carried her drink to the table.

"You're worth the risk."

"You always knew exactly what to say," she said. "And you look so distinguished. You could pass for nobility."

"You're spreading it on too thick."

"You do look great. As for me, I've been visiting Pappy, who's outraged at the latest coal agreement. Of course his natural state is outrage. I've just been sitting around that old castle which smells of mildew and rugs that need beating. No matter how many lights you switch on, you can't read a book without a headache. Thus I upped and drove to the city to live a little."

"Lucky for me," Wylie said. He meant it. He was excited by her heated, perfumed presence. He thought of Anne at the bedside of her father. He'd not through their married years been able to exorcise completely her Calvinistic idea of sex. She never gave herself over entirely to her body.

"Pappy's about to drive me crazy," Trish said. "He was upset by my divorce. He's upset by everything. He believed my husband was a great little guy, but I'll tell you what John was. He was the kind of rich, pleasant, handsome man who has difficulty deciding between a trip to Pinehurst with the boys and a trip to the moon with me."

Wylie nodded, held up his hand for the waiter, and they ordered. He'd been reasonably faithful to Anne, straying only when out of town on business, mostly in New York with a stylish black investment analyst from Solomon Freres, who stripped of her gray career woman's suit could have been a gymnast. He would never be indiscreet to the point of hurting Anne, yet he now wanted Trish.

"We were both dumb," she said. "Our divorce was friendly, though we had a small argument over the silver. Occasionally he writes me notes. As the years pass I think we'll like each other more and more— and God are they passing."

She reached into her black-trimmed yellow handbag for another cigarette. A small plastic tube fell out, it containing red capsules with even redder bands around the centers. Was she sick? She winked and dropped them back into the bag. The capsules weren't for any illness.

"For a while John got religion," she said. "We were living in Florida, and he drove his Chris Craft to church every Sunday, some nutty chapel by the sea. People arrived on water skis and surfboards. He gave up drinking and prayed a lot. In fact he believed he prayed himself a blue marlin in the tournament."

Looking into her violet eyes was like meeting a lascivious challenge, a challenge and promise she would go as far as any man

278

dared. She'd never be the one to say stop. She would rise triumphant from every man's body. He stared at the pink tip of her tongue as she pinched a grain of tobacco from it and thought of it licking him.

Recklessly he wanted her. He was hot like a boy aroused by his first woman flesh. The rush and force of it made him slightly nauseated, but God he felt he had to have her. If never anything else, he had to have Trish.

Under the linen cloth he moved his hand to her lap. He pushed fingers beneath her dress and slip and up along her nylon thighs. She allowed the hand to rest between those warm thighs a moment, all the while smiling, her head cocked, one plucked black brow raised. Then casually, as if removing a teacup from a table, she lifted his hand and placed it back over the hardness of his own lap.

"On the town tonight?" she asked. "What would prim little Anne think?"

"Anne never has to know."

"I'm complimented, I mean honestly, but it's not for us, Sport. The sad truth is you no longer light my fire."

"Please," he said and again reached for her under the cloth, but her knees were pressed together, and she intercepted the hand.

"Don't beg," she said. "You're really not good at begging."

"That's a hell of a thing to say to me," he said. He was trembling, the bites of breaded veal he'd swallowed lodged high in his chest.

"I didn't intend to be ugly, but I know you wouldn't like me to lie. That'd be terrible at this stage of our relationship. I have nice thoughts about you, and we don't want to change that."

Angry, choked, humiliated, he couldn't finish his meal and ordered another drink. She sighed and ate, even taking dessert. She touched the napkin to her lips before standing and kissing his cheek. She left the table and him the bill. He stared at her crumpled napkin, which had a smudge of lipstick on it.

He hurried upstairs for his hat and coat. He waited outside by the empty unlighted pool. He heard the tap of her heels on the front steps of the clubhouse. He followed her to the parking lot, keeping a hedge between them. Her tan Mercedes backed quickly and sped out the gate.

He drove after her. She descended into the cold, foggy valley.

279

Traffic lights reflected from the wet dark pavement. She turned left onto River Street to Commerce, then left again. She turned right into the asphalt expanse of the Civic Auditorium lot, whose glinting blackness was chevroned with yellow parking stripes. He circled the auditorium and stopped before a flower shop, where a cat lazed in the display window.

Trish waited, her engine running, steam twirling from the exhaust. She lit a cigarette. It began to drizzle. The auditorium was dark. A white-walled black Cadillac passed, returned, drove into the lot and pulled alongside her Mercedes. The Cadillac left, and she followed.

They drove over the Elk River bridge to the Wrong Side and a motel on the slope of a hill, the cinderblock painted flamingo pink. Misty yellow lights burned between red doorways. In front a neon mountaineer tipped his demijohn.

Wylie moved his car closer to peer and see who was in the Cadillac. The man, who wore a hat and overcoat, had already arranged for a room, as he didn't go to the office but to an end unit. He unlocked the door and waited for Trish. She stepped around puddles. The man's face crossed under a yellow bulb. For an instant Wylie believed him to be Oriental.

Pinky!

Wylie couldn't move. Then his hands dropped from the steering wheel. The sonofabitch Pinky! He thought of them in a whorish room. Pinky was able to light her fire, but not Wylie. He wanted to leave the car and bang on the door. He slammed a fist into the seat beside him.

Fuming, he drove home. He couldn't sleep and began drinking. He lay naked on his bed and did a thing not done since he'd been a schoolboy. Jacking off, they'd called it, Wylie, Blue, and London in a circle jerk at White Oak. It gave no relief, and he sat on the bed's edge looking out at the window toward the darkness of the rainy woods.

When the phone rang, it was Anne calling from St. Louis. Her father had died, and she wept quietly.

"Beautiful in a way," she said. "He was happy and rose from the bed. He reached upward and cried out."

"To you?" Wylie asked.

"Not to me," she said. "He kept repeating it."

"Repeating what?"

"'Golden fire,'" she said. "That's what he kept saying. 'Golden fire.'"

59

Though Wylie had accepted a seat on Hill City, Inc.'s board, he avoided Pinky. He made excuses when he and Anne were invited up to Buzzards' Roost. He didn't tell Anne about Pinky and Trish. She was puzzled.

"I think we see too much of them," Wylie said.

"They're our friends, at least Esther and Pinky are mine."

"Sometimes you can put too much weight on a friendship. We'll appreciate it more later if we cool it awhile now."

"I just hope they understand," Anne said. "And Esther and I are having lunch."

Esther came to Wylie's office the last week in February. He'd been fearing that. She wore a fur jacket, a plaid skirt, and her walking shoes. She sat beside his desk and pulled at her rings.

"I've been thinking of selling my holdings and buying Hill City shares," she said. She pushed at her short sandy hair. Her lovely legs had grown heavier over the years. Because of her children, she was rarely now on the links.

"I'll of course do whatever you want, but I think you're well represented in Hill City through your husband's interests."

"When did you start calling him 'my husband'?"

"Just acting professionally."

"We haven't seen much of you lately."

"It's been a busy season here at the firm."

"You're not angry at us?"

"I could never be angry at you, Esther."

"But could you be at Amos?"

"He doesn't stay in the same place long enough for anybody to work up a case of anger against him."

"It's true. I hardly see him. When he's home he's usually sleeping, though he doesn't sleep well either. He slips out of bed three or four times at night to work at his desk."

"He's always had more push than the rest of us."

"Wylie, will you tell me the absolute truth about something and never reveal I asked?"

"I'll do my best," he said and knew what was coming.

She had difficulty fitting her mouth to the words. She lowered her eyes and gripped her fingers.

"Does Amos have a—a girl?"

Quickly she looked at Wylie, who was thinking fast.

"What makes you ask a question like that?" he said and forced a smile.

"Don't evade."

"I'm certain he loves you and would never be that unintelligent."

"Thanks," Esther said and nodded. Her face brightened. "Suspicious female. I know it's just his work. He gives himself completely to everything he does."

She walked from Thornhill & DuVal reassured, but on the first warm day of spring Anne called Wylie at the office. She was upset.

"Esther's left him," she said. "She's taken the children to her father's."

"You're sure?"

"I've been trying to catch up with her for days, but she's staying away from everybody. I ran into her at Kroger's. We sat in her car, and she broke down. Wylie, you've got to do something."

"What can I do?"

"Go to him. Go to him right now."

"Sorry, I can't work that into my day."

"You'll be sorrier if you don't. I won't give you any peace. I will in fact raise hell around this house from morn till night."

"He won't listen to me."

"Try!"

Wylie fretted about it through lunch and finally reached to the phone to call Hill City, Inc., at Mountain State Bank. Pinky was out of the office, but Wylie made an appointment through the secretary for three-thirty that afternoon.

Hill City, Inc., now had a corner suite on the seventh floor where enlarged architect's sketches and construction photographs were displayed on walls. The carpets, the desks, the chairs were a bronze color. Wylie had to go past two secretaries to reach Pinky's office.

His marble-grained desk was round except for a slot where his

282

chair fitted. On the desk lay stacks of financial papers, an electric calculator, and a complex communication system, which flashed a changing pattern of lights through plastic keys.

Pinky sat in the slot, his tie loose, the French cuffs of his blue-and-white-striped shirt rolled up. He wore black horn-rimmed glasses to do close work, and they'd slipped down his nose. He pulled them off, dropped them on the desk, and stood to greet Wylie.

"I wasn't sure you were still in the land of the living," he said and would've held out his hand except the communication console beeped. He motioned Wylie to a chair, punched a button, and held an ivory phone to his ear.

"Sure, Andy, I realize the kilns have to be overhauled now and again," Pinky said. "If somebody in this city goes without cement, it ought not to be Hill City after the business we been giving you."

He talked concrete, one moment tough, the next the good fellow. By the end of the conversation, he'd turned Andy Barron around and received a promise of increased delivery. Pinky laughed and rubbed his hands. The console lighted immediately with more calls.

"Can we talk without interruption?" Wylie asked. He hadn't sat.

Pinky punched a button, spoke to a secretary, and leaned back. He rubbed his palms to smooth his frazzled red hair.

"You been missing directors' meetings," he said.

"I'm resigning."

"What do you mean you're resigning?" Pinky asked and swung forward. "What the hell for?"

"I lied for you to your wife. I don't intend to be caught in that again."

Pinky slowly flattened his palms against his desk. He studied Wylie, his face calculating.

"I'll get her back," he said. "It's been a fever."

"You're giving up Trish?"

"Will you sit down, for God's sake! You're acting like a prosecutor. I'll work it out. How'd you know it was Trish?"

"What's the difference?"

"None I guess. Like an explanation?"

"What I'd like is not to be involved in any of this."

"I love Esther, honor and respect her, but I never got over Trish.

I know how an addict feels. Can't help myself. But it's nothing like what I feel for Esther." He lifted his hands, and they left moist palm prints on his desk. "I'll come up with something."

"Try coming up with the zipper on your fly."

"Wylie, you don't understand desperation. You never wanted anything so badly you believed you'd die without it. Look at my hands." He held them level in front of his face, and the fingers quaked. "That's what Trish does to me. She's not half the lady Esther is, but she's hot in my blood. Now stop looking at me as if I'm slime. I'm hurting. I'm in pain, and I need my friends to see me through this moment of weakness."

"Just scratch me off your friend list," Wylie said and turned to leave.

"Wait a damn minute," Pinky said. He stood and hurried around his desk. "Don't get moral with me. We're being just a little hypocritical here, aren't we? Trish told me that while you were feeding her, you were also feeling her up. Tell me you wouldn't have dipped into that if she'd let you."

"You'll receive my resignation in the mail, dated as of today."

"You fucking prig. What you looking at me for—cause I used the word *fucking*? It's a word you have to use these days, the best of people, a cult word which shows you're with it. What are you if you don't use that word?"

"I don't," Wylie said at the door.

"No, you're too pristine. You're so clean there's nothing inside you, a blank page that's never been written on."

Wylie pulled open the door, but Pinky stepped to it quickly and pushed it shut. His face was florid, his eyes wild.

"Know what's really bothering you?" Pinky asked. "You can't stand the idea Trish would want me rather than you—Amos Cody from the Wrong Side instead of the well-born Wylie DuVal. I'll tell you something. She came after me, right here to the office a night I was working late and within ten minutes was on her silken knees sucking me off."

Wylie swung, but Pinky blocked the blow and assumed his boxer's stance. Wylie thought of himself walking torn and bleeding back to Thornhill & DuVal. Swallowing fury, he opened the door.

"Go on, get out," Pinky said, his fists still raised. "God, Wylie, it must be wonderful to feel so uncomplicatedly and beautifully righteous."

60

Though Wylie wrote out and had Doreen type up his resignation from the Hill City board, Thorny persuaded him not to submit it just then.

"You don't want to hurt the project," Thorny said. "It's bigger than any of us personally. Loyalty to investors and the firm is involved here. My suggestion is wait till the annual meeting and quietly request your name not be put up for election."

The news was out about Pinky and Trish. Telephone lines sizzled. Esther and the children still stayed at her father's. Trish had flown to Paris. Pinky lived in his Buzzards' Roost aerie alone.

Blue Bales stopped by Wylie's office. He'd developed a habit of jerking his chin toward a shoulder as he talked. He twitched the shoulder. Pores of his face seemed larger and darker.

"This thing with Pinky going to affect Hill City?" he asked.

"No reason it should. He's still on the job."

"What's the stock selling for?"

"Thirty-two big ones."

"You actually sold shares today for thirty-two dollars?" His chin jerked toward his shoulder.

"Not me personally, but the last bid was thirty-two."

"I'm thinking of selling mine."

"Thornhill & DuVal will buy yours at thirty-two."

"I don't know," Blue said and fidgeted.

"You thinking of selling because of Pinky?"

"He's racing around and spending a lot of money. Might as well move into The Greenbrier, all the parties he gives." Twitch of the shoulder. "I hear Hill City's been experiencing construction delays."

"Normal in a project of this size."

"Delays could be bleeding the company."

"Hill City's balance sheet is clean, its lines of credit intact."

"Okay, just testing the waters. You know how I am about money."

"I remember the time a dollar didn't stay in your hand long enough for the eagle to set its wings."

"It's the game I'm in, the business. I've gotten so it bothers me to think there are people in this town who make more money than I do. Like doctors. All the doctors are getting rich and moving higher on the hill. I'm just as smart as any body mechanic. I want to live on the very top of the hill. You, too, you want it."

"It's burning no hole in me."

"You're too smooth to burn, and anyway you're almost there. Jesus, what's happened to us? We used to have fun—you, London, Bebe, Sis. All the girls, they're gone. I stare at myself in the mirror and wonder who the stranger is. You know what, Wylie, you look as if you'd been Simonized. You're so slick, you're shiny. I'm not accusing you of anything. I'm just telling you it's all changed."

"The last time you and I talked you told me we had the world in our hands."

"I must've been drunk or high on just making a pile of money." Both a jerk of the chin and twitch of the shoulder. "I guess I might as well tell you or you'll hear it somewhere else. Bebe and I are probably on the rocks. We're talking divorce. Don't act so surprised. She's always bitching. Claims I don't fulfill her. I fulfilled her with a new house, a fat bank account, and three bambini. What more does she expect? God, I hate to think how much this is going to cost me."

"Sorry, Blue."

"Sure, you're sorry, everybody's sorry, the whole world is crying for me. I should've guessed earlier. Came in late one night, and she was smoking grass. Lying on our bed smoking grass. Said she found it liberating. Then she began taking dancing. At her age. Wasn't spending much time around the house, and when I wanted a little loving I practically had to fight for it. I had her followed, hired a private investigator, and, Jesus, I can't believe it yet. She's been screwing her dancing teacher, a fruity fucking spade who wears beads and ballet slippers. A fucking jig!"

Wylie believed Blue might break down, but Blue rubbed his nose with the back of his hand and stood. He turned to finger the corners of his eyes.

"A living death it's been for me lately," he said. "How can so much change so quick? I didn't fulfill her, for God's sake!"

286

When Blue was gone, Wylie walked into Thorny's office and closed the door. Thorny had a scale model of his forty-foot ketch on his desk. He was trying to lose weight, but no matter how many times he adjusted his belt, his stomach sagged over it. Wylie told him a customer had made inquiries about the soundness of Hill City, Inc.

"Want to mention names?" Thorny asked.

"Blue."

"Blue's usually upset about something. I hear he's got personal problems, and anyway he doesn't own that much stock."

"We wouldn't want any bad talk about Hill City to spread."

"Look, I go to all the board meetings whether you do or not. Everything's jake."

"Still it might be good for you to talk personally to Pinky. Off the record. He's always performing at board meetings."

"Why don't you talk with him?"

"I'd rather not."

"Okay, I'll call him, and you can listen in on the extension."

When Thorny finally got Pinky, he waved to Wylie, who lifted his phone and covered the mouthpiece.

"The construction delays are the unions' fault, not Hill City's," Pinky said. "Just as we get rolling, there's another jurisdictional dispute. The bastards have put us behind schedule, but we're not that far behind, and our reserves are adequate to match contingencies. Moreover, we receive another shot of Uncle Sam's sugar on or around Ash Wednesday."

Thorny insisted Wylie attend the next board meeting. Wylie didn't shake Pinky's hand or sit near the head of the table, where he presided. Pinky appeared harried but on top of things. He brought in Hill City's treasurer, a thin, laconic accountant named Powers, who'd formerly worked for Ernst & Ernst. Powers was convincing in his projection of costs and funding.

The stock market had a bad month, but Thornhill & DuVal remained busy underwriting another issue, this one a mining equipment firm which had patents on a new process for air-cleaning coal at the tipple. Even bucking a limping economy, shares found demand.

When Wylie phoned customers to offer them Clean Coal, Inc.,

several questioned him about Hill City. He attempted to find the causes of investor restlessness.

"What's bothering you?" he asked Billy Kidd, the eye-ear-throat man at Valley General.

"The stock's been a dog recently," Billy said.

"You practically doubled your money. The shares are entitled to a rest."

"I'm used to ascent, not rest."

"In light of the Dow being off a hundred points, I'd say Hill City's price firmness is consoling."

"Reasonable tout, Wylie, old buddy, but I want it to go up, up, up so I can buy a new Porsche."

During late May, Hill City stock fell two points. Again Wylie attended a board meeting. No director had sold his holdings or knew anybody who'd shed his. Checking the stock book helped not at all because so many shares were held in street names.

"It's hot money from the New York sharpies," Pinky said. "That money wants action."

By Memorial Day the Dow-Jones had stabilized, and Hill City gained back its two points. Members of the board assumed speculators had been flushed out and that the stock now reposed in strong hands.

Still problems compounded. A group, mostly blacks, once residents of the area where towers were being raised, had formed a citizens' association to bring a lawsuit. These weren't people who'd sold property but renters that'd lived in blighted housing or upstairs over shoddy, deteriorating stores. A radical, contentious young lawyer named Pitts advised the group. His brief claimed his clients had been unable to find new domiciles they could afford. The association asked $1,000,000 in compensatory damages.

"My opinion is they can't prevail in the courts, but they can lift our legal costs," Pinky said. "Pitts is an ambulance chaser who'll take anything on contingency. So we defend ourselves and keep going. What hurts is that a few people will believe we're exploiting the poor. Hill City's resurrection of the area will help the needy more than anything that's happened in this valley, ever."

When Wylie worried about the pressure on Pinky or Hill City's progress, he'd leave Thornhill & DuVal and stroll to the building sites. After looking through spiraling dust raised by perpetually

288

rooting bulldozers and watching mantis-like cranes swing buckets of concrete to scaffolding where the pale towers pushed above dust to sunlight, he again became confident about the project. Sweating men were purposeful and calming. Jackhammers pounded, trucks lumbered, and at night the blue whiteness of welders' torches invaded far shadows. Out of chaos arose order.

More trouble with unions, this time a feud between elevator installers and electricians. Pickets stopped all work for ten days. The column of dust subsided. Pinky wined and dined union officials to bring them to agreement.

He called a special board meeting. Powers, the treasurer, handed around mimeographed figures on expenses, lines of credit, and a new estimated date of completion for segments of the complex. Hill City had run down its reserves, mainly because a third payment from the Department of Housing and Urban Development was late arriving.

"Do we know definitely the money's coming?" Wesley Leek asked.

"We've received their letter of intent," Powers answered.

"Any explanation of the delay from HUD?" Thorny asked.

"You know Washington," Pinky said. "Those birdbrain bureaucrats can't pour water from a shoe without a manual. I'll build a fire under them."

Thorny, who'd planned a surprise trip to Athens for his wife Ginger, asked Wylie to take his place and accompany Pinky on a flight to Washington. The chartered Apache set them down at the capital's National Airport. They rushed into the city to see Senator Sam Straugh, who asked them to lunch with him at the Continental, though Pinky would pick up the check.

The senator was hardly five feet six, but he had wavy, billowing white hair, which seemed to give him size. On the hustings he wore dark preacher suits and kept to countryfied manners, but in the Continental he was suave, knowing perfectly how to pronounce the French dishes the menu offered.

"I've had no satisfaction," he told Pinky and Wylie. "I've written and phoned, but everybody at HUD seems to be on vacation."

"We were led to believe we'd have the money by now," Pinky said.

"Nothing in this city is ever done on time," the senator said. He appeared courtly and at ease with life, yet the swiftness of his aquamarine eyes never slackened.

289

"Could anything be wrong?" Wylie asked.

"Wrong?" The senator lowered his wine glass.

"What could be wrong?" Pinky asked, looking hard at Wylie.

"I meant could there be some minor technical problem," Wylie said.

"I know of none," the senator said, and his fork slid expertly into an asparagus tip, which he immersed in a dish of hollandaise. "I shall, of course, continue to inquire."

Wylie and Pinky had hardly spoken, but as they flew home, Pinky turned, his expression peevish.

"Never suggest anything could be wrong," he said. "You plant the idea. Especially don't suggest it to a politician. They hate risk worse than a lady does lice."

"I didn't mean wrong in the sense of unlawful," Wylie said, not defensive, and definitely not apologetic. "I thought perhaps some procedural step had been neglected."

"Just allow me to handle Washington," Pinky said and stood to step forward into the co-pilot's seat. They were flying over the blue haze of wooded mountains, and he took the wheel. He'd had lessons. Sudden updrafts buffeted the Apache like hands beating the fuselage.

Each day members of the Hill City board wondered about the money from Washington. Thorny was back and wanted to call and ask but didn't like to seem to be pressing. He thought up excuses to phone, hoping Pinky would volunteer the news if he'd received the money. Wylie listened to a conversation, using the instrument in his office.

"It's nice of you to take such an interest," Pinky said to Thorny. "Let's see, in three days you've asked me to play golf, go boating, and get together for a poker game. You wouldn't have anything else on your mind, would you?"

"What else could I have on my mind?" Thorny asked.

"The great fish-eating bald eagle clutching a U.S. Treasury check in its talons."

"I admit my mind will be relieved when the money arrives."

"It's not coming."

"What?" Thorny shouted.

"It came this morning."

"You got it there right now?"

"Not exactly."

"Goddamn it, Pinky!"

"I mean not the actual money, though I have this rectangular green check with holes in it for $650,000. I'm grasping it in my sweaty little paw. I refuse to let go till I turn it over to the bank. You think these little holes will make a difference?"

"You sonofabitch, let's celebrate!"

"O ye of little faith," Pinky said.

61

During the dog days of summer, smog rasped the throat, and fire hung in the valley. Wylie bought a new thirty-foot Hatteras, which he moored at the boat club. He, Anne, and the children motored up the river in search of coolness. The water was hot and sluggish, and coal washings fouled the white hull.

He sent Anne and the children to Rehoboth Beach, where he now owned a cottage he rented when he didn't want the use of it for family and friends. While they were away, he became restless. Late at night, despite the house's air-conditioning, he'd feel as if he were choking. Uncommonly he had a nightmare, dreamed he was pursued by a relentlessly searing white light which caused him to scream and shrivel. He woke to find himself tangled in a sheet, his head covered by his cowering arms.

On the morning of Monday, August 24, two federal men arrived at Thornhill & DuVal. One was young and had a brown beard trimmed to a point. The other wore thick heavy glasses which he kept resetting on his narrow, moist nose. Each carried an identical black government-issue briefcase. They showed Wylie credentials and a court order granting them authority to examine Pinky's brokerage accounts.

"Why?" Wylie asked.

"We don't divulge that," the bearded one said. He did the talking. The bespectacled agent simply stared about as if weighing the value of all his eyes fell upon.

"You won't give any explanation?" Wylie asked.

"No."

The agent requested an office, a desk, a calculator, and Pinky's statements. Wylie put them in the conference room, where they closed the doors. He went immediately to Thorny.

"I don't know," Thorny said, whispering, though the agents couldn't possibly hear. "Let's alert Pinky."

Thorny closed his office door to call, but Pinky wasn't at Hill City. He wasn't, his maid said, at home either. He'd left no information about where he could be reached or when he'd be back.

The two federal men snooped all day and punched figures into the calculator. They wrote numbers on ledger sheets. They asked for more records and kept the doors of the conference room shut.

Wylie and Thorny would've left the office at four-thirty had the agents not still been working. Wylie reviewed customer holdings while Thorny smoked and paced. They both glanced repeatedly at the closed doors. It was almost six before the men came out carrying their briefcases.

"We'll want the use of the room tomorrow," the bearded one said. "Can it be locked?"

Wylie and Thorny watched them leave. Thorny made a fist, hooked it upward, and cursed.

"The bloodsuckers couldn't get an honest job," he said. "The government's the only one who'd hire them, and suddenly they find they possess almightiness. They take vengeance on anybody who's made a success of life."

"I want to know what's happening."

"The government giveth, and the government taketh away: blessed be the name of the government."

Thorny was about to light a cigar, but it never caught the flame. His expression became dreamy, far away, as if he heard a distant call. He grunted and sat heavily. His cigar dropped on the carpet.

"What is it?" Wylie asked, stooping for the cigar.

"Maybe I better see the doctor," Thorny said.

Wylie helped him lie on the floor and called Valley General. The hospital sent an ambulance. Wylie waited on a bench in the corridor. The pain Thorny felt wasn't a coronary as the doctors first suspected but a spasm of the heart muscle. For observation they put him in a private room.

That left it up to Wylie to locate Pinky. First he notified Thorny's wife, Ginger, who had her children at Virginia Beach. Then he called all the places Pinky might be—his house, the Pinnacle Rock Club, the Coal & Coke, the stable where he'd taken riding lessons.

Wylie tried the airport. Hill City had chartered no plane. He talked to the pilot, a World War II veteran named Gabe. Gabe hadn't flown Pinky out of the city in more than a week.

As a last resort, Wylie called Esther at her father's house. Her voice was cool and controlled.

"I don't know where he is," she said. "I don't want to."

On Tuesday at nine the federal men came back to Thornhill & DuVal. They stayed two more days, and during each Wylie attempted to contact Pinky. Not even the maid was at his house. Wylie called MacGlauglin in search of Trish. Old Josh, who sounded feeble, said she was still in Europe. He had no address or telephone number.

Wylie kept calling Hill City's office. He talked to Powers, whose voice was a dry monotone. He spoke as if each word were a coin being spent.

"Nobody puts a time clock on Mr. Cody," he said.

"Have government people been over there?"

"No. Everything's functioning normally and well. We've gained a day and a half on our construction schedule."

Wylie felt better after talking to Powers. Maybe the agents were simply making an audit of Pinky as an individual. Hill City didn't have to be involved. Pinky was a lawyer and could handle it. Certainly by the beginning of the week he'd be back.

Early Monday, Wylie again dialed Pinky's house. No answer. At nine Wylie called Hill City. The secretary reported Pinky hadn't come in. Wylie asked for Powers. He'd been to the office but left.

Throughout the morning Wylie tried both Pinky's house and Hill City. The secretary became defensive.

"Mr. DuVal, I told you I'd have Mr. Cody get in touch with you."

"He never has."

"I do the best I can."

"Has Mr. Powers returned?"

"No, sir."

"Who else is in the office?"

"Just Estelle and me—that's the other girl."

At two o'clock that afternoon Russ James, a Thornhill & DuVal

293

registered representative, came to Wylie's desk. Beau had received an order to sell 500 shares of Hill City, Inc. Thornhill & DuVal were the leading market maker in the stock. Hill City hadn't sold off, yet no bids waited on the wire. Wylie felt the firm had an obligation to buy and gave Russ authority to lower the price from $32.00 to $31.25.

"Who's the customer?" Wylie asked.

"A retired colonel who raises sheep down in Greenbrier County."

"I hoped it might be an estate," Wylie said. "Let's keep it quiet."

At a few minutes before three Wylie left Thornhill & DuVal and drove up the hill to Pinky's cliff house. Feebly stirring air failed to move the shroud of smoke hanging over the valley. The river had fallen, fouling the banks with a baked darkish mud.

He parked behind Pinky's black Cadillac on the white drive, crossed to the entrance, and rang the chimes. Nobody answered. The screen door wasn't latched. He opened it and tried the inner door. It gave to his hand.

Knocking and pushing inside, he called Pinky's name. Wylie walked through the vestibule to the cathedral living room, where light tinted blue from no-glare windows slanted over the piano to the framed coat of arms. A recent portrait of Esther sat on the floor and tilted to the wall—she wearing a dove-gray gown and sitting in a white iron lawn chair, her golden children standing on either side of her gracefully draped knees.

The artificial stream had been switched off, the waterwheel no longer turned. A gutted cigarette hung suspended in motionless water. He moved to the kitchen, where dirty plates, glasses, and cups were stacked on the butcher's block and in stainless steel sinks.

He walked corridors to the master bedroom. Clothes lay flung about on the chartreuse carpet. The great bed with its white satin headboard looked as if it hadn't been made or changed for days. Water dripped into the sunken tub of the flesh-toned bathroom. Canary cages were empty.

Wylie considered calling the police, yet saw no evidence of struggle or robbery, just mess. As he was leaving, he passed the coal bar, turned back, and watched a thin wisp of smoke spiral slowly upward from an amber glass ashtray shaped like the state of West Virginia.

He hurried through rooms and again called Pinky's name. He looked around corners into shadows. When he slid open the louvered

294

closet door of the son's room, Pinky was standing inside among the boy's clothes and toys. He held a highball glass.

"What the hell you doing in there?" Wylie asked, backing off.

"It's my closet, I paid for it, and by God if I want to stand here and enjoy a little privacy, it's my constitutional right."

Pinky shut the door.

"Come out!" Wylie said and opened the door.

Pinky had on madras shorts and green pajama tops. He'd not shaved. His stubble was curly, his red hair tangled. He wore no shoes.

"I like it here," he said and closed the door.

"This is important!" Wylie said through louvers.

"Thought you weren't associating with me."

"Open the door."

"This is a private accommodation."

"I'm not kidding."

"You're a snot. If you were my friend, you'd come in for a visit, but you're a snot from way back."

Across the hall Wylie glimpsed the rosy marble surface of Esther's white dressing table. Face powder had spilled over it. Fingers had left prints.

"Trish been here?" Wylie asked and thought of her naked and brushing that hip-length black hair before the mirror. On the dressing table also were silver-framed photographs of Pinky's daughter Martha and his son Amos. Powder filmed them too.

"That's a personal question. That's an intimate family matter, and you have no right."

Wylie forced the door. Pinky inclined among balls, rackets, a bugle, an erector set, and clothes on hangers. He smacked his lips before listing forward and curving through the living room to the coal bar, where he clicked the switch on the Ferris wheel. It spun, activating the music box. The silver bucket filled with two ounces of scotch. Pinky emptied the bucket into his glass but added no water or ice.

Tropical fish in the aquarium behind the bar swam or hovered among murky, bubbling artificial seaweed. A black-and-white one had died and floated belly up. Pinky leaned to the glass to peer at the fish.

"Poor guy," he said. "His name was George."

"Pinky, you in trouble with the Feds?"

"Do I look like a man in trouble? I'm chomping high hog. Never been better. Everything's just grand."

He sucked air and flexed an arm to show off biceps, which couldn't be seen because his pajama sleeve covered the arm.

Telephones rang. He'd had them installed all over the house, including some in red waterproof boxes on the decks. He scowled, yanked the phone loose from under the bar counter, and slam-dunked it into a wastebasket.

"Two points, you sonsabitches!" he shouted at the ceiling. The other phones stopped ringing.

"Where's the maid?" Wylie asked.

"She's found a new situation."

"And Trish?"

"My gal Trish has a Kraut now. She's down at Cannes fucking her Kraut on his yacht. He gave her a leopard, an honest-to-God leopard with a jeweled collar."

"Tell me what's happening."

"In short she and I've had a little spat."

"Not between you and Trish but Hill City. What's happening at Hill City?"

"Hardly worth mentioning. A little money more or less. Nothing to become excited about."

He pushed his nose against the aquarium glass to gaze at George.

"I'll miss you," he said to the dead fish. Among bottles behind the bar lay a photograph of his children. They sat in front and back of him on a chestnut horse. He lifted the picture and kissed it. "Love my kids."

"Talk to me!" Wylie said.

"Only if you relax and have a drink." He set the photo down and patted it.

"I don't want a drink."

"How come you don't? You always wanted them. It was me who didn't."

"I don't have the need at this particular moment."

"Won't accept such a crummy excuse."

"Pinky, stop fooling around."

"Damn it, stop calling me Pinky! Always hated that name. Think I'm a shrimp scooped out the Gulp of Mexico? I'm a goddamn good

296

man, and my Christian name's Amos. Now I want you to drink with me, and if you won't, I'm asking you to leave and allow me to return to the privacy of my closet."

He held his glass in his left hand and, using his right, shoved away from the bar. He punched air around him as if fighting off attackers. The jabs unbalanced him slightly, and he steadied himself by reaching to the wall.

"All right," Wylie said. "Give me a drink."

The Ferris wheel spun, the music box played. Pinky served Wylie scotch without ice or water and drifted to the wall where he fingered switches that controlled the hi-fi. Operatic music seeped into the house. Wylie recognized a theme from *Thaïs*. He followed Pinky onto the deck. Pinky blinked into the sunshine and breathed deeply. Music played from the metal speakers under the eaves. He thumped his chest.

He set his drink on the railing and from the pocket of his pajama tops drew a pack of Chesterfields. He began to light them. He'd puff once or twice, make a face, and flip the cigarette over the railing to watch it fall, fall, fall through the hot haze of the valley toward the C&O tracks. Rails resembled stitching across cinders.

On the other side of the river the white stumps of Hill City towers were almost hidden by industrial smoke. Even this high, construction noises from the project could usually be heard, the heavy machinery, or earth tremors sensed, but now there rose no sound, and the deck felt quiet under Wylie's feet. God, not another labor dispute.

"I'm drinking," he said and faked it.

"Like a constipated old maid. Want a teacup?"

"What I want is you to explain the meaning of what's happening."

"The meaning of what's happening? You're questioning the significance of life? Well I've given it plenty of thought. My conclusion is life is muck and thorns. Prepares us for the glory to come. If we remain faithful and've been through enough, God reaches down and takes us up to Him in one of His many ways. Now some people love muck and never encounter thorns, like you. You got a hundred years ahead 'cause you've not even been scratched, whereas me, I been torn lots."

Phones rang. Pinky wheeled to a red box and snatched the instrument out.

"Mr. Cody's not here," he said. "Who am I? I'm his spiritual advisor, and I've advised him to get his spiritual ass in gear. You too, brother!"

Pinky ripped the phone from the box and two-handed it like a basketball into the shallow end of the pool. It sank among bubbles.

"Swisho, you sonsabitches!" Pinky shouted and turned back to the railing and his drink.

"Pinky, why are the Feds here?" Wylie asked.

"There you go, calling me Pinky."

"Sorry. I'll try to do better. Amos."

"A grand prophet Amos. Warned the Israelites they'd better lead moral lives or God would forsake them. God told them they'd better straighten up and fly right or He'd destroy them utterly. Think of being destroyed utterly."

"I'm calling you Amos and asking you please to fill me in on what's happening."

"Call me Cody. Buffalo Bill Cody. I'm supposedly kin to him. My father liked to believe we were kin to Buffalo Bill. Bunch of stuff probably. My father never knew who his people were. He was a hero though. A genuine bloody World War II hero. He would've liked to be Buffalo Bill."

"The government men," Wylie said.

"Of no importance. Bureaucratic flacks."

"They have a court order."

"Court order's mere bits of paper." He flipped another cigarette over the railing. Watching it fall away and slant inward toward the tracks made Wylie dizzy. Even more than he had as a boy he hated the edges of high places.

"What are they after?" he asked.

"Too trivial to worry about. Has no lasting importance. If you want to worry, do it about something significant—like your spiritual content, or lack of it."

"Don't start one of your sermons!"

"I was going to be a preaching man, not a Whiskey-palian, no licked member of St. Stephen's, but a working minister among smelly laboring people—truck drivers, coal grubbers, grocery clerks, hod carriers—the pack mules of this earth, so dumb they worry about salvation. They worry about eternity. What a stupid thing to do. Here's the world full of goodies—fine hooch, obliging ladies, grand houses on hills—and those idiots are concerned about the hereafter. Breaks me up and lays me out. Am I glad I'm superior to that."

Contrarieties of emotion contorted his face, a man trying to laugh and cry at the same time. He flipped another cigarette off the deck.

"The Feds," Wylie said.

"Haven't finished our discussion about spiritual content yet. You do have a soul? Surely along with everything else good, the Creator gave you a soul. Hold it. A thought occurs to me. When the Lord put you together, He provided you the best arms, legs, the best eyes, yet left out a moral sense. I think you slipped by the inspection station without it being discovered. Angel inspectors were looking the other way when you came down the line."

"Have the decency to stop sermonizing and—"

"Don't come at me with that decency crap again!" Pinky said, turning angrily. "Decency has nothing to do with salvation. The damned at least possess a conception of deity. What do you fucking decent godless men have to take before Judgment—toothpaste, clean underwear, a graceful backhand?"

He was so furious he breathed as if running hard. He faced back to the railing, lit a cigarette, his fingers trembling, and flipped it into the valley.

"Please," Wylie said.

"Please what?"

"Talk to me about the government men."

"They can't hurt me. They can inflict some little harm, agreed, but over the course of eternity, what can they do?"

"Why should they want to do anything?"

"They take a narrow view. Like military men, they go by the book. Losing a war is better than violating the book. And it's the wrong book."

"What violations?"

"I'm full of imperfections, unlike you. I'm consumed by them."

"Stay on the subject."

"That is the subject, and that's the trouble, I got off the track. Oh it's been one big glorious party, a real skyrocket, but it didn't mean anything, and I can't seem to find the rails again. Would you believe I'm afraid, me, Amos Cody?"

"Of the government?"

"You listening to me? The government's nothing. The government's gnats. I'm talking about my spiritual content, and I don't mean liquor."

"Let's get you a shower and some coffee."

"You can't believe, Wylie, that's what's been left out of you."

"I believe you must be in bad trouble and want to help, but I have to understand what the problem is."

Swaying, Pinky turned from the railing to look at Wylie, a long look showing neither anger nor disgust, but a sort of curiosity, as if he'd been away for years and needed to reacquaint himself with Wylie's face.

"You're a wonder," Pinky said and reached for his drink. "More than anyone you influenced me. I wanted to be like you, smooth and stylish. I wanted not only to act like you, I wanted to be inside, to feel through your fingers and see through your eyes."

"I'll make the coffee."

"Coffee he offers to give me. Oh you nourished me, Wylie, but all you ever gave was bread."

"Your liquor's talking."

"You owed me more than bread. You might've put a vision before me, and I could've shot for the peaks."

"Let's walk to the shower."

"You made me what I am today—you, my ideal, and the result is I'm not very much."

"Enough," Wylie said and tried to take hold of him, but Pinky shook free.

"I placed my feet on the wrong path," he said.

"What are the Feds doing here?"

"Oh them, those darlings, they're here because of long noses. The blood they live on is suspicion, which they suck up through the nose."

"Involving Hill City?"

"They have small minds. Open up their skulls and you discover they have brains the size of cocktail onions—cocktail onions full of figures from the valley of dry bones."

"Tell me about the figures."

"To do business with Uncle Sugar you have to submit ten thousand forms in triplicate. How can anybody submit ten thousand forms in triplicate without mistakes?"

"Be specific."

"Uncle Sugar contends our numbers relating to rents and lease projections are flawed, and he questions what we been counting as reserves. Good old uncle can turn nasty on occasions. In fact ugly."

"The government thinks we gave them bad figures?" Wylie asked and felt a surge of fear.

"Don't go cross-eyed on me. Nobody's lost money yet."

"Are we talking about suspicion of fraud?"

"Me, involved in fraud? You never knew a more honest man. Now if there's a little creative accounting, it was all done for the cause of transforming this scarred, tortured valley into a garden spot. If everybody keeps cool, nobody drops a dime."

He tossed the empty crumpled Chesterfield pack over the railing and watched it fall. He finished his drink, stared at its emptiness, and set the glass on a round redwood table. At the pool's edge a white underinflated rubber seahorse—a child's float—had blown over. He righted and petted it. He kissed it.

From the table he lifted black, outsized sunglasses to cover eyes which had suddenly become wet. He coursed into the house. At the bar he switched on the Ferris wheel twice—two silver buckets, four ounces, dumped into a pewter mug. He opened the refrigerator, but the trays held no ice. He slammed the door and drank scotch straight.

"Call your lawyer," Wylie said, attempting to regain control over a rioting of thoughts.

"What you mean, call my lawyer? I'm my lawyer, the best."

"What does Powers think?"

"It was Mr. Powers' suggestion and sleight of hand that caused trouble in the first place. A very artistic accountant. Case you've not noticed, Mr. Powers is no longer around. I do believe he may have left on an extended vacation."

"Listen, we got to sober you up and sort things out!"

"Relax. I can think straighter bombed than most people leaving church." He swayed and almost fell stooping to pet the white rubber seahorse. "My son rides this animal," he said. "Real thoroughbred name of Charley. Charley Horse we call him."

Wylie tried to think of somebody, anybody, to phone. Pinky wobbled away from the seahorse. He stood weaving in the deck's

301

sunlight, his legs stiff, his body pushed forward as if bucking a gale. He set his mug on the railing and lighted matches. He dropped them into the valley.

"Pinky—"

"Amos! Don't disturb me. I'm testing gravity and universal laws."

When he finished striking all the matches, he threw the empty book over the railing. Humming, he banked around the glimmering blue pool to a redwood chaise, which had wooden wheels. He settled heavily among yellow canvas pillows, his fleshy legs on either side of the chaise, his knees falling outward and tipping his feet to reveal smudged soles.

"We need to do something here!" Wylie pleaded. He felt sweat ooze from and soil his body.

"Don't hardly think you or members of Hill City's board are in big trouble," Pinky said. "The Feds may sniff around, but there's no way they can prove you knew anything."

"You're telling me they suspect we had something to do with the faulty figures?"

"Just play dumb. Ought to be easy for you. You always been dumb. If I'd had your opportunities, I'd be king of the mountain."

"I'm not letting you and Powers make me responsible for figures you cooked up!"

"I'm advising you to act dumb, which means be yourself, though I admit you're a gentleman dummy. Liked you even when I hated you. A long time ago, the hate and envy. Loved you too, as I do now, really, hollow as you are. I was better in everything but could never achieve your elegance. That I couldn't learn or buy. But you were dumb, Wylie, and still are. You never made any distinction between style and substance. It's kept you impervious."

"Give me a breakdown on the figures," Wylie said, dismissing the foolish talk. Fright struggled to plunge through him.

"Very simple figures. Little marks on little pieces of paper. Add them up, they come out. Nobody can convict you or the rest of our distinguished board members. An idiot lawyer could win for you. I confess I never intended to cause trouble. Hate trouble, though I made a good living off it. Not so good in another sense. Jumped the track somewhere. Hard to wade through all the money. Smother in money they throw at you. Regret any slight inconvenience, my fault.

No more envy in me. I honestly do love you, though you owed me more than bread. Not your fault. Nothing inside you. All outside— style, no substance. Elegant sawdust. Slice you open, out it'd pour."

"You're admitting that down the road we may be facing prosecution, even prison?" Wylie asked and wiped his face.

"You dumb ass, I'm not worried about prison—you can get over prison. What I'm worried about is Judgment."

He began to cry, just for an instant, and then thumbed corners of his eyes and reset his dark glasses. He stared at the seahorse near the edge of the sun-pierced pool.

"Was good once," he said. "I had great spirituality, something you're unmarred by, which gives you a kind of invincible beauty. Like the pagans, those white marble statues in museums. Now you seem pure and innocent and I so bad. Lost my family and everything. How'd things get reversed?"

He tried to stand, but his feet found no purchase on the plank decking. He had to heave his body from the chaise and steady himself using the redwood table. The table and its umbrella quivered. He turned into the house.

"It's necessary we get a hold on this thing!" Wylie said, moving after him.

Pinky raised a hand to gesture for quiet. He stood wobbling and listening. Wylie heard then—through strains of operatic music repeated like a broken record—a crunching of tires on gravel from the drive in back. Car doors slammed.

Pinky padded quickly away on bare feet. His fuzzy legs spraddled to balance him. Wylie followed through the living room to the vestibule. Pinky entered the lavatory, where he stood on tiptoes to part red-and-white curtains decorated with prancing horses pulling carriages. He peeped out the high small window.

"Those sonsabitches been haunting me!" he said, snapping the curtains closed. He tripped over bathroom scales as he hurried to lock the front door.

"Who?" Wylie asked and looked himself. Two husky, purposeful men crossed the glaring white drive toward the house. They wore rumpled metallic summer suits and heavy thick-soled shoes. One had on a bone-colored hat, the kind westerners favor. The men's strides were long.

"Best guess is they're bringing me an invite," Pinky whispered. "Probably want me to have tea and cookies in the office of the United States attorney. Don't much care for that kind of party."

"What'll you do?" Wylie asked as Pinky bumped past him.

"Need a little time. Can make everybody well. Now got to work the magic act and disappear."

He hurried to his son's room, where he stepped into the closet and drew the louvered door shut.

"You're acting crazy!" Wylie said through the louvers.

"Find a hiding place!" Pinky said back.

"I'm not hiding and this won't work!"

Telephones started ringing, and door chimes sounded, three rising tones. Pinky muttered to himself in there. Phones kept ringing, and the chimes gonged. He jerked open the closet door and backed out, a foot tangled in the erector set. He kicked free and circled.

Phones rang, and the chimes became insistent. Pinky ran to his bedroom. He stumbled to his hands and knees and tried to wiggle under the pleated chartreuse counterpane. The bed was too low. He shoved up, leaned toward the bathroom, reversed, and rushed to the spiral staircase which descended to the lowest of the house's three levels.

Wylie followed to the shadowed deck where Pinky gripped the railing, swayed, and gasped for air. He lifted a leg over the railing.

"No!" Wylie said and grabbed at him.

"Sh-h-h, they can't find me down under here. Done it before. Lots of beams and braces. Swing up when the sharks are gone. You tell them I'm not here."

"Watch it! Listen, come back—Pinky!"

"The name's Amos."

It was a slip, had to be just a slip. A foot went out, a knee slid off the ledge, and his fingers clawed at wire mesh he'd ordered put up to protect his children. Then he was gone.

As Wylie full of horror grasped the railing and looked over, Pinky fell away. He still wore the outsized sunglasses, yet Wylie saw the fear on him, terrible fear, and something else—a stab at the old swagger, the body splendor, and for a moment while Pinky dropped he tried to take control, to transform his fall into flight, or maybe a dive, a half gainer, one of those beautiful, lingering half gainers he performed off the high board at the Pinnacle Rock Club.

Gravity was too much, the acceleration, the irresistible pinwheeling. They flung him till he relinquished his body's grace.

62

The sickening sums of money lost—government money, the public's, Wylie's own. In days following Pinky's death, Hill City, Inc.'s stock sold off to $2.75 a share. Threats and charges flew about as if the valley were at war.

An impulse to run seized Wylie—to flee to Mexico or wherever men fled to elude disgrace. Then he felt shame he even considered not facing adversity as his father would have. He held his head up. He would be honorable.

At the office he and Thorny had to shear the firm's branches and finally close Thornhill & DuVal. They used all their capital in an attempt to stop the hemorrhaging. Gold leaf came off the windows, the brass plate beside the doors was unbolted and removed.

That ultimately Hill City, Inc., would be able to reorganize under Chapter 11 of the Federal Bankruptcy Act revived a meager hope. A few towers might be completed. Washington and city officials conferred.

Lawsuits would linger for years. Government attorneys and auditors demanded figures, a grand jury convened, and a true bill was handed down for the indictment of Powers, believed to be in Port-au-Prince, Haiti. Prosecutors were still undecided whether or not to bring action against Hill City's board of directors.

Ex-customers of Thornhill & DuVal remained bitter. They phoned or wrote abuse. They stopped by Wylie's table in the Coal & Coke Club dining room. He suffered a clumsy physical assault during the Pinnacle Rock Christmas dance when Billy Kidd, the eye-ear-throat specialist at Valley General, swung on him in the bar.

Wylie considered giving up his membership but rejected the idea. No, for Anne and his children's sake, he would not. He'd endure hostility and remain gentle in the face of it. As time passed he believed he could again win people to his side, most of them anyway. History taught that furors died. This one surely would.

Thorny, after a bout of drunkenness, found a job selling text-books. Miss Burdette admitted she was of an age to be eligible for Social Security and in addition retired from Elk Land and Lumber due a small pension. Thank God for Elk Land and Lumber. Without it, Wylie would've been overwhelmed.

Esther and her children continued to live at her father's. Her money was gone as was most of the father's because Pinky had borrowed from both. Auctioneers knocked down the house on Buzzards' Roost to a man of Syrian descent who manufactured lawn mowers and garden equipment. Mountain State Bank took the proceeds.

After the funeral, Esther—wildly sorrowing and disheveled—came to Wylie holding a bundle of stock certificates found in Pinky's desk. They represented shares of the old Broken Men, Inc., and Wylie had to explain to her they were worthless.

Trish remained untouched, though her father lost money on Hill City and made a profane phone call to Wylie. She married again, this time a Californian who owned vineyards. She flew her private Beechcraft.

Wylie liquidated stocks and property to satisfy debts and judgments. Lost were his Hatteras and the cottage at Rehoboth Beach. He had to accept distress prices because the market dropped in a free fall, the economy and country yielding to the humiliation of reversals in Vietnam.

Anne, shocked and bewildered by events, said Wylie should've done something to help save Pinky. What could he have done? When he became low, he reminded himself his health was good, his children were growing and obedient, and he still owned his house and Elk Land and Lumber. Anne would settle in and stick by him. Struggling he was, yet meeting his obligations and should be able to send his son to White Oak School.

He often remembered the hot August afternoon of Pinky's funeral. Wylie had been asked by Esther to serve as a pallbearer. Fewer than twenty people attended the hillside ceremony where Father Bonney's words were submerged by a sea of locusts chirring under the relentless sun. Pinky's mother wasn't told about his death. She first lived in a private hospital near Fairmont but transferred to a state institution south of Huntington. No family members stood at the grave.

Wylie was drawn to Pinky's plot on a windy Saturday morning in October. Swift white clouds with gray undersides tumbled into each other, and their blade-like shadows swept across pale grass and new tombstones, among which sparrows and a few last robins pecked. The sloping cemetery lay on the opposite side of the river from Pinky's house, but Wylie couldn't see the house through the valley's yellowish haze.

Pinky's earth was humped. Wylie stood looking at the unsown soil and thought of Pinky under it. As a chill wind blew against him, he felt a rush of resentment. It came with a force which surprised— like discovering powerful vestiges of anti-Semitism resided in him, or a hatred of blacks. Yet what had Pinky ever been to him except grief?

Still Pinky ghosted around Wylie, always returning to hover and provoke unquiet. During the dead of night Wylie sat up from his four-poster and spoke Pinky's name. He told Anne he'd been dreaming.

He did what he could for Esther and her children. He loaned her money till she got a job with Trojan Steel's billing department, a few thousand which she attempted to pay back twenty-five or thirty dollars at a time. He talked to Mr. Bruton, the new headmaster at White Oak, in the hope a scholarship might be contrived for Pinky's son when of age. Esther shook her head to that. She was thin, her face drained.

"He'll go to public schools," she said. "He shouldn't grow up thinking he's rich." She didn't quite cry. "You've been good to us, as I knew you would. Amos always loved you."

Wylie thought often about that. He stood at his bedroom window, staring into darkness after Anne was asleep, and wondered. Pinky had said terribly unjust things to him that last day. Was that part of love? Well, all needed to be put behind him. He had his life to rebuild. He looked across the valley to the hill where Pinnacle Rock like a ship's prow glowed through the night. One day again, perhaps in the spring, he would return to the courts and links.

During a gnawing, snowy February night he worked late preparing tax returns in the shadowed, cavernous office at Elk Land and Lumber. A hot fire crackled at his back. When he finished, the fire had burned down, and he reached for his scarf, overcoat, and hat to drive home. The streetlights blinked out, and people trudged through falling snow like burdened figures sunk deep into the earth.

Tires of his car hissed softly across heaping snow. Under the pall the asphalt was iced. Little other traffic moved. He passed an edge of the Hill City project, a skeletal dark tower jutting into snow and darkness.

Lights came on, the break in power repaired. Snow blew aslant them, coating surfaces and diffusing beams. The lights became ineffective against the blackness blooming from the valley.

He stopped at a signal near the old downtown bridge with its spidery iron superstructure. Redness tinted snow. Windows of a sporting goods store displayed skis, skates, and sleds. Golf balls had been taped onto wires to simulate a blizzard.

While he waited, he realized the building beyond was the former Chosen of God Tabernacle. Cinderblocks had been painted blue and white, and a plate-glass window installed. Over the doorway hung a round, tossing illuminated sign—the noble head of Chief Pontiac.

Through the darkening snow Wylie believed he spied a figure wandering in the building's shadow, a person haggard, robed, with black hair entangled, eyes fiercely lustrous, a raving woman whose hands were lifted in violent imprecation. Was the figure Pinky's mother hurling curses at him across the snow?

He quickened his windshield wipers and rubbed knuckles of his leather gloves against the steamed glass. She was gone. Surely she'd never been there. What he'd seen was hallucination, a specter in his confused and troubled mind. The snow stretched barren except for a glint of chrome from the fenced auto lot and a rim of light holding back the dark.

He drove too hurriedly through slush on the deserted bridge and up the icy hill. His tires skidded, the Mercury tipping into a spin, which stopped when a fender banged hard against the serpentine stone wall that served as a guard rail. Below the ledge his city sprawled—the black river, red signals along the snow-covered railroad tracks, blinking navigation lights, fires from the chemical plants, those flames licking skyward into snow.

He backed his car, his tires spinning, and steered with grave care around ascending curves and through the chaotic storm toward the sheltering warmth of his home and hearth.